GW00985736

1542

THE PURGE

ROBERT WILLIAM JONES

Table of Contents

Robert William Jones

1: FIVE SOVEREIGNS

Silas glanced down and along the wavy white mane that
folded around his dear horse's head. How does she do it?
He thought. She's getting so old now but serves me like a
she's a foal. This was Annie, once the only love of his life
and now second only to the woman than possessed his
heart, Wynnfrith. He sighed, dwelling on the events of the
past year and how much his life had changed. Once
ridiculed as a complete idiot, he was now respected, had
friends and was an accepted member of the Secret Agents
of the Word thanks, in part, to the King. How grand he
now looked. Shaking off his life-long reputation as the fool
of York, he wore a gown trimmed with furs and was trying
so hard to live up to his newly acquired appearance.
However, he was, on this crisp winter's day, incredibly cold.
    Silas didn't cope well with cold and this, combined with
his natural propensity to be nervous, often undermined his
new position when he was on a mission. A shaky
demeanour would not betoken authority. This was the
January of 1542 and the snows had frozen hard into the soil
making the ride challenging for both horse and rider. He
promised himself that he would try not to shiver when
delivering the message on his arrival. Eirik wouldn't shiver,
he thought, Thomas Farrier would stand in his sleeves

unmoved. I will be as they are, he decided. But then, shuddered at the thought.

As he walked Annie slowly toward Knapton, he gawped, daydreamed and pondered and gave thanks for the Grace so recently bestowed upon him. Knapton was only three miles outside of York but, curiously, was still within the diocese of Holy Trinity church where the Agents had, so often, met. He supposed he was on a mission this very day but, not for the first time, hadn't a clue what it was. Silas was to meet a man called Aelfraed who would be in the marketplace at Knapton and clearly evident as he only had one leg. Perhaps I should have asked which leg, thought Silas and then considered that bearing in mind the meagre population of Knapton, it probably wouldn't matter. He was certainly anxious about his cargo, Silas had never, ever seen five pounds before.

Silas's relationship with the Mayor of York, Robert Hall, had somewhat consolidated since they, and the Agents, had successfully halted the Cataclysm of 1541. However, Robert still didn't share much information with him although Silas was very aware that being alone on a road, carrying five pounds, was dangerous stuff. Silas had still not managed to shed that lifelong delusion of being a Lord. He now owned the best of clothes, even adopting those, most modern, of accessories, pantaloons, but nothing ever seemed to fit properly. It simply seemed that Silas had been put on this earth to be lampooned, although as he passed traders and pilgrims along the road he greeted each one as a superior would and, as was always the case, he attracted all sorts of curious and uncanny looks. He didn't care, this is what he did, and the mission was to be completed.

The only difference between the open road and the entrance to any village was, literally, that there were a few buildings there. No two structures the same and, sometimes, they were no more than an interruption to the endless, and frozen, mud. It was clear, however, that he was

2

entering Knapton. He walked Annie right up to where there were stalls and traders. These truly were hardy people, some wandering around in jerkins and hose as if it was a summer's day and the weather seemingly having no effect on the daily trade.

'I am on a secret mission to find a one-legged man!' he shouted not in the least aware of how stupid, inappropriate and rude this sounded. He attracted some very angry looks but, all the same, no one answered so, being Silas, he said it again and, this time, he was rewarded with a reply.

'Perhaps try the rope maker' said a woman very loudly, 'he's a big lad, got three legs!' Almost everyone laughed. Silas thought on this, still not really familiar with rude humour, and decided to reply,

'No. No, you misunderstand. Just one leg would do.'

More raucous laughter followed. He now had everyone's attention but the laughter was not to last. A very large and very tall man hobbled out from behind a stall where money was being exchanged and, as he came to the fore, the crowd parted and silenced.

'This do lad?' He asked showing Silas the wooded stump that took up half of his left leg. Alarmingly, Silas thought to ask if this counted as one leg as he could actually detect one and a half but, thankfully, for once, the Gods intervened and he just muttered an acknowledgement.

'I have a message from The Mayor of York my good man.' Said Silas.

'I know'. Replied Aelfraed, his patience already waning, 'but you were meant to deliver it discreetly.' Silas didn't really do anything discretely no matter how many times he was asked but did always feel stupid when he put his foot in it, which was often. He couldn't make sense of Aelfraed's accent and couldn't take his eyes off his ornate leg. It was a work of art, highly decorated, depicting a dramatic naval scene that circumvented the whole stump. Ships firing cannons, soldiers thrown overboard, giant fish and violent

3

seas. Silas was in the moment. That was, until, he heard laughing. When Silas heard laughing it almost always meant he'd done something wrong. He realised that, audibly, he'd been childishly re-enacting a war at sea. Completely lost in this fantasy, people looked on in amazement as the infant dressed as a Duke yet again made a tit of himself.

'Ahem… just collecting my thoughts good people. Yes…fine…er…log…er stump. Leg!' the laughter stopped and he realised that people were now looking at him as if he was a specimen. Aelfraed took hold of Annie's reins and gently guided her and Silas around the back of a small building where there was a single stable with fresh straw.

'Think I'd feel better dealing with you if you came down of your high horse lad' said Aelfraed. Silas immediately capitulated and then fully realised the actual size of this man. He was huge.

'You want to ask don't you?' growled Aelfraed 'no harm in that lad, bet you've not seen one of these before?' He added, glancing down at his stump. 'Fought at the battle of St Matthew I did, barely a lad myself. Cannons blazing, the Mary Rose rolling starboard to larboard, men in pieces all around me but beat the French Bretons we did. Taught them a lesson that day!'

'You were on the Mary Rose!?' asked Silas astonished, as everyone knew the names of King Henry's ships almost as if legend.

'Aye that I was, but lost this you see, so landlocked now lad.'

Silas had almost forgotten about the five pounds and simply wanted to sit near a warm fire and hear more of Aelfraed's stories but he was already aware that Aelfraed was ready and waiting for the transaction.

'Oh! Yes' said Silas, and removed a small and relatively insignificant purse from under his cloak. Aelfraed took it, checked the five sovereign coins then grunted approval.

However, he was astonished as Silas was now staring at him expectantly.

'Business is complete lad, you can be on your way' he said. Silas thought for a moment, presumably trying to work out how to phrase what he was bursting to say but then gave up and just said it,

'What's the money for then?' As Silas heard his own question ride on the frosty air, he thought it quite innocuous although, to practically anyone else, it was, admittedly, rude. He watched that very familiar sight of a face, known or otherwise, turning to beetroot, and waited for what followed. Aelfraed decided to keep the lid on his temper this day realising, as all do, that this young man had a bean or two missing.

'If I told you. Your friend, the Mayor, would be very upset. Let's just say this will keep me quiet for a while.'

Silas did have enough sense to realise that he had overstepped the mark but hadn't got a clue as to why Aelfraed would want to stop talking, even for money. Surely he wouldn't be able to run his stall if he didn't speak? Silas managed a few polite and authentic farewells and decided to leave. As he heard murmurs and chuckles from the villagers and he made his way out, he was reminded of his shortcomings and how he would have to work so much harder to become the Agent that others expected him to be.

He rode away and, as images of battle, death, rolling hulks and bronze cannons almost too heavy to bear filled his fluffy head, he became totally emerged in the untold tales of Aelfraed. So much so, he imagined a fellow seaman shouting out a warning of a broadside blast.

'Ho, pilgrim!' came the voice and it repeated. Silas often struggled to break out from his daydreams so it was only when he saw a stranger alongside him that he realised that he was almost asleep. Sometimes, on the road, people would greet one another. Sometimes they would ignore each another and then, there were times when they could be

5

downright bloody rude. A wandering rabble made up of traders, pilgrims, visitors, beggars and Knights of the realm, you would expect to pass people between hamlets and villages not least because, the tracks that masqueraded as poor excuses for roads, almost always went through populated areas. Someone had caught him up and was now alongside Silas seemingly just wanting to be friendly and share company on the road into York. They were now the only two people visible for miles.

'Been far?' asked the stranger.

'Oh…er…just as far as Knapton' Silas nervously replied.

'Lord Anthony Bask' added the gentleman. Now and again Silas made the sensible decision to think. When he thought he tended to make fewer mistakes. Well, usually. He had initially thought to answer by saying "no I'm called Lord Silas" and then realised that this wasn't what his new travelling companion meant. He told him that he was pleased to meet him and refrained from issuing the usual "Lord Silas" deception. They talked mostly about their horses. Sir Anthony was also on a white mare but taller and much younger than Annie and he himself modelled some very impressive winter furs.

'I love a maiden in York!' announced Silas and then wondered why the hell he had. Sir Anthony was a little embarrassed by this declaration but then realised that however politely you wanted to say it, Silas was not quite like others so he simply congratulated him. Sir Anthony also tried not to notice that Silas had become incredibly animated in his saddle. At first, it seemed as though he was just adjusting his position for comfort but as he, increasingly, started to slowly grind his groin into the saddle it became uncomfortably embarrassing for them both. He pushed his hips from side to side and then would thrust his codpiece into the leather as well as, intermittently, lifting his weight off the horse and sighing and moaning. Sir Anthony was losing patience so, as politely as he could, bade Silas farewell telling him that he had lost track of the time of day. As the distance slowly grew between the two horses, Silas dismounted and guided Annie beyond a coppice and behind some trees. His relief was audible as he took the longest pee he had probably ever had. But then it occurred to him that his loud sigh sounded most peculiar so, although he carried on relieving himself, he decided to keep quiet. It was then that he realised that it wasn't him making all the noise. He could hear a horse galloping at some speed from the village and, as he peeked between the trees and at the road, he saw someone, fully cloaked, ride up behind Sir Anthony and then bludgeon him so hard that he toppled from his steed. Once down, the hooded stranger dismounted and beat him about the head proclaiming,

'There's a message from Somerset you bastard!' and, as quickly, sped away back toward the direction of Knapton.

Silas was incredibly shocked and scared. Why on earth would someone attack this kind and inoffensive man and why would he come all the way from Somerset? He thought to intervene and even managed to wrestle with his natural propensity for cowardice but realised that, by the time he'd tied his hose and mounted Annie, the thug would be gone anyway. He now sought to help this poor man. He lay there with blood pouring from his scalp, groaning but barely conscious. Silas was repeatedly muttering to himself,

'Mustn't panic. Think. Think. What would Eirik do? what would Wynn do?' But he was panicking. He took off his own cloak and wrapped it around the head of Sir Anthony and decided that he would attempt to get this weighty body onto the horse. This became an impossible task for Silas so, in realising that Annie was several hands shorter, he tried again but with his own horse. Annie knelt to assist and then stood upright with Sir Anthony draped across her back. Everything else was relatively easy except Silas was still completely beside himself.

7

There was no hope of getting to York in haste. The roads were hard and this was a real test for Annie as Silas, now on the Knight's horse, pulled her along. He could see his own gown changing colour as it was now wrapped around the victim and some of the blood managed to drip onto the saddle and then along the road staining the icy ruts and drawing a crimson, zigzag line as they headed toward the city.

The easiest route was through Micklegate Bar and, by the time they reached it, Silas wasn't sure whether Sir Anthony was alive or not. At the Barbican, Silas reminded the guards that he was on Mayor's business although, naturally, his baggage attracted suspicious looks so they decided to alert the sheriff. All the same, Silas pleaded with the guards to let them enter the city. He told them that he had friends nearby that could help. The first part was true, the second probably not. Reluctantly, they said they would let him pass as long as he was clear about where he was going. Unfortunately, Silas was taking the horses and the victim to Godwin's workshop which was just inside the wall, in fact, the third lean-to along. Although he would find some comfort and support there, he would get little practical help and he had also led officials directly to me.

'Godwin! Mouse! Help!' cried Silas. I peeped through my shutter alarmed at what I could see. Godwin rushed out, picked up Sir Anthony and threw him onto his bench.

'Send for Elspeth!' Demanded Godwin. Silas dithered and halted. He left and returned again immediately. He shivered and started to weep and I was also completely useless as guards were now approaching the workshop so, sensibly, I hid and kept quiet. Eventually, Silas ran off to get Elspeth who was at the other side of York, at Bootham Bar. Godwin unwrapped the, now sodden, cloak of Silas's and, from where I hid, I could see the damage that had been done. Blood was still pouring out from the wound but he was unrecognisable due to the dirt and dried blood in his hair and on his face.

'Dead' Godwin declared and the guard reiterated that the sheriff would have to be alerted. Godwin agreed to cover the body and keep him in the workshop until an investigation had begun. In no time at all, Silas had returned with Elspeth and the Mayor, Robert Hall. Although he had since been pardoned, Silas had been in bother the previous year so now desperately needed the support of his employer if he was to face the law. He was anxiously about to explain what had happened when the sheriff arrived.

'God's teeth!! Not you people again!' he glared at Silas who was only reprieved the previous year because of the King's intervention. The sheriff knew that when two or more of this bunch got together, trouble followed.

'There's no getting away with it this time, lad. What on earth did you do to this poor traveller?'

Instead of simply telling him the story, Silas did what he always did and that was to panic, ramble and look guilty.

'Ok just slow down' said the sheriff 'tell me it as it happened.'

So, Silas did the best he could to relate the strange events of the past few hours. Robert appeared uncomfortable but, initially, said nothing. Once his story was told, it was probably fair to say that there was only Silas and the sheriff who hadn't been able to work out what had really taken place that morning. Arrangements were made to have the body removed and Silas agreed to further questioning. Surprisingly, the sheriff left.

I was so grateful that young Edward hadn't witnessed all this, I asked Elspeth to put me on a ledge where I could address Silas,

'Can't you see what has happened?' I asked him.

'Yes, I was having a pee, this steed came thundering…'

'No. No.' I said 'look at him Silas, his clothes, height, white horse.'

'Yes,' he replied pretending to understand what I was hinting at, but didn't.

'He's been mistaken for you' I added calmly.

It was always a joy watching Silas's face as his brain struggled to engage with new information and then, as expected, he flipped.

'You mean he wanted to kill me?! Me?! Why?! Are you sure Mouse?!'

Robert, the Mayor, told him that this was obvious and, if it wasn't for his peanut-sized bladder, he would now be decorating Godwin's bench instead of the most unfortunate Bask. Silas became very upset and, naturally, confused. We had no answers for him but, to be sure, this sent a chill down the spine of everyone present. This was a planned assassination and it surely meant that the entire Agents of the Word were also a target.

'Are you sure he said he was from Devon?' I asked him.

'Yes, yes….something like that.'

'Silas!' I growled. 'Like it, won't do! What did he say?!' It was then I realised that I needed to give him time to calm. After ten minutes he sat with his head in his hands and muttered,

'That's a present from Somerset.'

We went cold. This, surely, must have meant Edward Seymour, Duke of Somerset and our nemesis as we worked to thwart the Cataclysm in the previous year. Silas only made the connection when we made it for him. The rest of us exchanged sombre glances. Was this now retribution for stopping the Cataclysm? Are we to be picked off one by one? I could see the blood draw away from my friend's faces one by one.

'Look, it would be stupid to panic, because as yet, we know very little and, until we do, all we can do is remain circumspect and watch out for one another. Be particularly suspicious of strangers.'

A few minutes passed while I explained the meaning of circumspect to Silas and I advised him to stay within the walls for the time being.

'I gave Aelfraed the money to keep quiet. Can't imagine what went wrong!' He blurted.

Elspeth, Godwin and myself were all wise enough to know that this message should have been delivered to Robert and, Robert only and, when I turned to look at him, I could see the crimson fusion of anger and complete embarrassment written all over his chubby face. A deathly glare was the only reply received by Silas at this time.

'Silas, I understand why you brought this man here, but you have exposed us, exposed me. Our oath to the King stipulates that we should keep ourselves hidden, in low profile.' I said.

It wasn't my intention to make him feel even worse but, if there was more trouble to rain down on The Royal Secret Agents of the Word, we definitely needed to be more discrete.

'Come along with me Silas, spend the afternoon in the company of Wynnfrith, you can tell her of your adventure' said Elspeth.

His spirits lifted immediately and, just as they left, two constables came to remove the body. Godwin cleaned up the mess and got back to work.

Within the hour it was almost as if things had returned to normal. I had a workshop project of my own and desperately needed to make progress with it. I required as much "normal" as I could get after everything that had transpired in 1541. I had only been back in York for a few weeks having unexpectedly spent an early winter in the company of the King. Yes, once again I had become the focus of amusement at Court.

2: AS LOW AS ONE CAN GET

The days that immediately followed the Cataclysm of York were intense. Many were put to death and the fate of my Agents was in question. King Henry, in realising our depth of integrity and honesty, gave Royal assent to this humble body but had us swear an oath not to reveal ourselves unless he commanded it.

Previously, I had found myself in the King's company, ironically, as a spy and, although without my relationship with the King I would never have uncovered the Cataclysm plot, I had also unwittingly become his toy, a source of amusement. Overjoyed at his decision to leave the Agents be, I had every intention of returning to my former life, only to be summoned just one day after. Henry gave me an ultimatum, he would return to London with either the fool or the beast. This is how I was to be referred to now? A beast? The fool, of course, was Silas. I knew he wouldn't last five minutes in the capital so I volunteered, and Silas was none the wiser. Fortunately, the King agreed that I could be transported to London separately as I had no desire for the long and winding progress southward that he would take. In fact, I was there waiting for him when he eventually returned. For a hundred reasons, this was scary, inconvenient and unappealing not least as I knew that information regarding the Queen's dalliance with Thomas Culpeper, along with her earlier sexual adventures, would soon land on the King's desk.

I should have been grateful that he was, genuinely, pleased to see me.

'Little King Harry!!' He shouted across the Great Hall at Hampton Court 'How is my little King this day?'

Already I'm in a difficult position, I thought. He knows I can talk, but had told me not to unless I was in his privy chambers and alone. So I remained silent, now wearing the most ridiculous and ostentatious clothes imaginable, including a gown with real ermine. I had become an oddity for people to examine as they passed my cage and I knew that, sooner or later, I'd be expected to perform.

'Look, look!' he said to the gathered courtiers 'he rules in my stead!' Laughter, some genuine, the rest sycophantic. His huge head loomed large in front of the cage so that only I could hear,

'I have the most magnificent employ for you alone. It will be a delight.'

Oh God, no, I thought. As if I hadn't been through enough. One minute I'm his advisor, the next an Agent and now I was back to being the lead actor in the Royal freak show. I felt lost, lonely and completely losing my sense of purpose. Added to that, was an uncanny feeling of déjà vu as maids cleaned me and dressed me in ever more elaborate costumes of the period as they had done in Lincoln. I now had a new home in York and I was desperately missing it. This gave me some idea of how difficult people's lives were under his dictatorship, being torn from one's family at any given moment, not knowing if you were to see them again. So, in some senses, although I was looked after, I was now a slave with no control over my day to day actions and activities. Under different circumstances, I think I would have been happy to accede to all the King's desires as there was a part of me that had come to learn just how isolated this man was.

Before I knew it, the winter night had drawn in on us all, my cage curtains were closed and all the candles were out.

Creaking. Endless creaking and cracking. All the boards in this place were wooden and, despite Hampton Court having the best of everything, Henry's interior designers had left much of the upstairs furniture top-heavy. Huge four-poster beds, chests, wardrobes and drawers filled the rooms and every movement could be heard. Added to this was the contraction of all the beams as the roaring fires were extinguished and interior temperatures dropped in sympathy with the exterior. The building spoke a language of its own, telling tales of the many, many deaths, natural or not, that had befallen so many of its residents and visitors. It was hard to distinguish which sound was coming from where and I imagined at times that I was on the Great Harry or Mary Rose out at sea and was later to marvel that Silas had projected the same fantasy. When I didn't run this adventurous scenario, everything became incredibly daunting, eerie and sinister and I convinced myself that, one or more of the enemies I had made this very year, would creep in to cut me up in the night. I didn't sleep at all and welcomed the sounds of dawn. A change of outfit again, now dressed in the official livery of the Court leaving me further bemused and nervous. It was so difficult to work out who was who, the Court swarming with servants, nobles, Renaissance yuppies and those at the very top of this slimy pole. One man I did recognise for he was always with Henry and I had met him briefly in Lincoln. When all others had left the King's privy chamber there was always one man left, Thomas Heneage. Why not add another Tom into the mix? thought I. My thoughts, however, were interrupted as he made a direct line for my cage and, rather than my cage being carried, I was removed from it and picked up by Thomas Heneage. We retired into a small room, an ante-chamber where we were alone and he sat and then, put me down carefully on his lap.

'If only you knew the strange, wonderful and bloody unexpected things I have had to adapt to as Groom of the Stool. I see all, know all, and sometimes, do all!' He kindly chuckled 'and now I have a talking mouse as an apprentice!' and laughed kindly.

I do confess that, at this point, I panicked. Not so much because he knew my secret but because of his role. I was to be the King's arse wipe? I had literally hit rock bottom. Of all the appointments possible within the Court, this had to be the worst. I then realised that I had become fidgety, turning in circles on his lap. This amused him, I looked up to see a kind face that was seemingly enjoying watching me have an anxiety attack, although I'm convinced that he thought I was performing. And then, just as he was about to speak again, it dawned on me that his was, in fact, a most significant, prominent and senior position. Not only did the Groom of the Stool have access to almost every private conversation Henry had, he was also his confidante and was aware, in real-time, of his state of mind and physical health. That Tudor obsession with the gut and, particularly, bowel movement, wasn't altogether misplaced. It really was one of the few useful indicators of "regularity" and rude health. He spoke, snapping me out of my thoughts.

'The King has told me all. About the Agents and your unique gifts. Well done iron balls!' He laughed 'the King has the highest opinion of you, Mouse, and has chosen to keep you close-by and in his confidence.'

I was feeling better already, this man was not my enemy and, perhaps, I would be made available as an advisor? Then it dawned on me that, at best, I would probably still have to watch the King attending his toilet. How on earth did I get myself in these situations?

'You are to have a small room made, shall we say something a little more grand than your cage but still portable? No time to dally, my dear Micklegate, the King will have risen already.'

Before I could say a word, he gently put me in the palm of his right hand and we hurried in the direction of Henry's inner sanctum. We may have well have slipped into another dimension as, what I was about to confront, was so bizarre.

'God's teeth Thomas! I am already, almost mid-purge! Would you have me shit alone?!!' This really did take my breath away. There's a sentence you don't hear every day, I thought. Yes, very much I would like you to shit alone! Henry was, of course, exaggerating, he was only just out of his bed, aided by two strong but incredibly stressed servants. They manoeuvred this curmudgeonly hunk in the direction of his stool, lifted his sleeping gown and he dropped onto the seat which groaned under the behemoth.

'Ah Thomas I seeeee' He was already starting to strain and his conversation became punctuated with wheezes, grunts and groans 'you ha....uh...uhh...UH!...oo..have brought the moooooSEE! Ahhhhh. Oh Good God's arsehole! It burns! Iron booooolls...Ahh. Bastards! Don't just sit there...' and on it went. Everyone present now terrified as they had no clue as to how they would assist him in having a crap.

'I'm birthing bastard bricks hereeeee!...get the cook. I'll haaaa...have his bloody head!'

Hellfire, I thought. These people have to put up with this at least once a day? I was desperately hoping this wasn't a permanent job. There were always unanswered questions about whether the Groom actually did wipe the King's arse for him but, not only were we very close to getting an answer, it was clear that Thomas was very involved in the whole performance. He was now gently massaging the

King's lower back. The stench was unbearable. Someone really should be talking to the King about his diet, I thought. I looked around. Stoic to the last, there was no notable change in expression on the faces of anyone in the room. Except for me. I realised that I was whining and squirming, the performance and the smells beyond the tolerance of a mouse.

'The Ma....Mary Rose!' Shouted the King.

'The Mary Rose, Your Grace?' asked Thomas, seemingly bewildered.

'Stu...stu....stu...stuck up my arse!! The Mary Rose is stuck up the royal passage!'

One of the valets chuckled and Henry spotted it. As if he wasn't furious enough. Thomas, like an expert poker player, intervened promptly dismissing the valet before the King in his anger passed sentence, as well as the Mary Rose. Having your head removed for chuckling at a poo joke would, even for Henry, have seemed somewhat extreme. And then he stood. This truly was an ordeal possibly worse than the Tower. As the thin cloth of his night attire clung to his hairy ginger belly, the remnants of those over-used genitals dangled low looking as if they no longer had a place in this world. The lives that had been lost because of this now little and insignificant member. Wars fought, religions changed and ideologies imposed. Don't get me wrong, my eyes did not linger long on the Crown Jewels although it was very difficult to ignore the pathetic dangle and wobble that sympathised with the wiping of his backside. And, although most men would naturally have one nut hanging that bit lower than the other, it would be fair to say that these two hadn't kept company with one another for some considerable time. Thomas Heneage still didn't flinch. A picture of dignity, he wiped and cleansed the King and then cleaned his own hands and had the rags taken away. There's living history for you, I thought. Don't see that on Downton Abbey.

Seemingly relieved, the King talked to me incessantly. This truly was the most bizarre relationship and there was no doubt that he saw me as a friend and confidante. He started to speak of Queen Catherine,

'What a jewel she is Ironballs? What good company on that endless trudge to the dark north?'

He then shouted to one of his aides.

'Send for the Queen, we shall ride, this crisp morning. Get some air in our lungs!'

My first thoughts were selfish ones, hoping that I would get some peace if the King went out for the morning and, possibly, even break his neck. Unfair. I reprimanded myself. He'll die soon enough and, then, even more problems will ensue. And then I thought of Catherine. She was a time bomb. He would be told of her infidelities any day soon and I didn't want to still be in London when this happened. It was then that I realised that this was All Saints eve knowing full well what November 1st would bring.

Happily, I spent the rest of the morning in Thomas Heneage's quarters where I was warm and fed and amongst kind souls. Word soon came back that the King, with considerable assistance, and the Queen had ridden out and his entourage had actually managed to hunt a hart. All was well for now and he was happy as he returned and we could all hear his presence once again consume all before him. It was then that I saw, for the very first time, Thomas Cranmer, The Archbishop of Canterbury and co-conspirator in the Cataclysm plot. He talked quietly to the King, his face kind and his attitude benign and benevolent. It was hard to imagine that he could have been part of such a sinister plan. Perhaps, against his better judgement, he believed the scheme the best option for Henry, Prince Edward and the new faith but, at best, his judgement was surely impaired. They conversed in hushed tones which, for Henry, was some achievement and this told me that, despite recent events, their relationship was sound. As Cranmer left he walked past me, or at least that's what I thought until he stopped, bowed his head and said,

'Good day Sir Mouse, May God bless you.'

And then he walked by, leaving my head spinning with new questions and new fears. What had he been told? Does he know of the Agents? Does he know I can speak? I didn't feel threatened by him but no matter how disappointed I was that there were seemingly no consequences for his part in the Cataclysm, it was even more unnerving that he was calm and regaining the King's confidence. Of course, I thought, he is paused to play his ace card and usurp Queen Catherine.

I would not recommend any scenario where we know the future. This, if anything, was a handicap. I dreaded the first day of November and hoped that I could be as far away from Henry as possible.

As it turned out, I started November by, yet again, observing the King's genitals freely swinging from his nightgown and acknowledging that, at least at the start of the day, he was in good spirits. He announced his intention to go to the chapel and pray and those very words sent shivers down my spine.

'Come Mouse! We'll give thanks together this fine morning!'

Thankfully at this point, I was left alone with Thomas Heneage and the King so I felt comfortable responding,

'Surely Your Grace would benefit from a little rest following yesterday's activity?'

It sounded so lame. What was I doing? I was going to change history with a swift change of venue? Not likely.

'Bollocks Mouse! I'm in fine fettle this morning and desire to make good with my God!'

I bowed which appealed to his vanity and, seemingly, I wasn't going to get out of accompanying him.

I was carried by Thomas Heneage to the Chapel Royal, for a while forgetting what would confront me. This was a processional route, coming into its own whenever there were special days such as Holy days of obligation and, on those occasions, many courtiers and court staff would line the route just to see, and pay homage to, the King. I was, somewhat disappointed as there were only a few of the lower servants present this day. This alone should have informed me that something was afoot. My breathing paused as I entered the Chapel Royal. This had, possibly, one of the most beautiful ceilings of its day, only recently having been installed by Henry. Gold stars speckled amidst the azure firmament, interlaced with the most dynamic gold vaulting. Henry never failed to surprise me. This room alone spoke volumes about this man's faith, there was glory in every inch of its design. All of this was upstaged only by the peaceful and pious atmosphere which was as tangible as any of its attendees. I had understood that, quite often, Henry would worship alone, sometimes taking advantage of his own balcony within the Chapel, so I pondered as to why he had sought to fill it on this morning. Thomas Heneage sat and folded me comfortably into his gown so that I couldn't be seen but also giving me a clear view of everything. Today, unusually, Henry took centre stage and knelt to pray. All was quiet but not all was as expected. He had clearly invited over twenty officials and courtiers to join him this day and, initially, I presumed this was to see him at prayer. However, all eyes, although giving the pretence of prayer, were blinking open and shut at the King suggesting some expectation. No Queen. This was shocking in itself particularly as the King was, now, not at prayer alone. Why on earth would the Queen not be present at such a public Mass unless she was unwell? I so wanted to quiz Thomas Heneage but dared not.

I saw Thomas Cranmer enter. No surprise there, he was Minister to the Crown after all but I could tell by his pace and dramatic demeanour that he was not about to give Mass. Henry gave himself away somewhat as he took a brief backward glance over his shoulder, presumably checking that Cranmer had arrived on cue. He approached the King, fell to his knees and begged the King's mercy for "interrupting His Grace at prayer and would not have dared to do so if it were not to dispatch such dire news."

I saw through this melodrama straight away. This was completely staged and was possibly what these two had been whispering about the day before. Henry had been handed a letter which he opened and feigned disgust,

'Am I to be plagued forever by treacherous women?! Wives that are anything but pure?!'

In a single sentence, he had pronounced Queen Catherine guilty to a live audience. No doubt this performance would expedite the trial and demise of the Queen. I had no doubts whatsoever that, if this was his first hearing of the news, he would not react in this way. A veritable trail of destruction, no less would have ensued. Yet again I was confused. Did he really ride out with the Queen yesterday? What was said, if anything, if he did? However, I was certain of one thing, the events of the morning were arranged to guarantee optimum impact. Who would think that this Godly King would have to bear such tragic news whilst at prayer? And, even if the courtiers saw through this charade, the message was clear. This Queen must go. The atmosphere was electric, gossip would ensue, whispers would travel faster than wild horses and the Queen would have little or no support. I found a pocket in the gown of the benevolent Thomas Heneage and hid as I wanted no part in this. Soon, I was in the chamber of Thomas Heneage for the first time, an oasis amidst the perpetual madness that was the Court. He fed me, put me on his lap and then chose to confide in me.

'What a troubled soul His Grace is, and has been these many years. For all his failings he has been cuckolded, betrayed and humiliated.'

I was getting the feeling that Thomas wanted to open up to me, knowing that I had developed a unique and trustworthy relationship with Henry. This man surely knew more than anyone so, against character, I decided to keep quiet and let him talk.

'Oh! to see him so Mouse! Only days ago I found him on the floor of his privy chamber crying and howling as a child would when chastised by his mother. Tears, anger, prayers and beseeching God to give him the gift to understand the tragedies in his life. I had to console His Grace for over half an hour.'

This was more like it. The drama in the Chapel was just that, a performance. It was so hard to feel sorry for this tyrant knowing he had completely disregarded the numerous petitions from his many victims housed in the Tower over the years but there was something, perhaps reassuring, knowing that he was, after all, vulnerable. And then I remembered. When I was in the King's chamber, post-bowel purge, he had asked me about Catherine. Thank the Lord I was distracted. He clearly wanted to know if I was party to the Culpeper affair. On this occasion, I was passionately grateful for my stupidity.

'He's sending her away.'

Of course, he was and I confess that I was somewhat blinded by my admiration for Catherine having spent time in her company. Information regarding Henry Mannox, a lutanist and teacher who had been carelessly over-familiar with Catherine in her youth, had come to light. Then, information regarding a young Francis Dereham, gentleman pensioner in the Duke of Norfolk's livery, who had known Catherine intimately. Although all this was before her marriage to Henry there was an unspoken expectation by the King that his Queens should be chaste. Dereham's defence was in his assertion that the two of them were once betrothed and it is likely that Henry may have accepted this except for the irony that Catherine continued to deny it.

The Culpeper affair now added weight to all this and, it turns out, I wasn't the only one he had told about filling the King's shoes after his death. If this wasn't enough, the very idea that a maidservant, namely Lady Rochford, was complicit in this intrigue would push Henry over the edge. So, Catherine would be restricted to Hampton Court for a while and then sent to Syon House on November 14th, an indication in itself that the King was still in two minds, but she would eventually find herself in the Tower and executed in February. I thought myself a coward. I cared for Catherine and yet yearned to be back in York and away from the darkness of Hampton Court.

Thomas Heneage rambled on some more and I dozed. He was a kind and interesting man and I could see why he was chosen to be the one that was closest to Henry. Then, to my surprise, he dropped off too. This in itself may seem of no importance but from my point of view, there was a sudden realisation that I was free. Well, that is if you didn't count being surrounded by guards within the confines of a monarch's palace. However, I could not suppress my inclination to wander. I knew I could successfully negotiate the furniture, the corridors, and even people, unseen, but was nervously aware of the variety of fellow creatures, both wanted and unwanted, that lived within the walls.

I scurried out beyond Thomas's chambers and along the panelled corridor clueless as to what I was doing. I stopped as footsteps approached, congratulated myself on remaining hidden but then realised I hadn't a bloody clue where I was going. Free! Free from what dickhead? Now stuck in an ever-increasingly busy thoroughfare I didn't know why I had started this adventure but then, almost as if it was providence, I saw Cranmer again. He shuffled into an ante-chamber, unaccompanied, but now clasping a folded document. To this day I have no idea why I thought this may have been of any interest but I instinctively followed him. Looking up, I could see him poring over this parchment. The old fool started to mumble to himself but I hadn't a clue what he was saying until he said, quite clearly,

'Oh Lord, give me the wits to remember my duties!'

And then he wandered out again, seemingly having forgotten something. I bolted after him, stopped and then thought about the document. Realistically, I thought that it was probably of no interest whatsoever but, the previous year had been punctuated by diabolical plans, ancient texts and coded messages so I couldn't resist. I scratched my way up the table leg and, as I rested on its top, I beheld a panoramic view of the lawns and could see courtiers preparing to take part in the day's hunt. This was a colourful and awe-inspiring sight and successfully distracted me for a moment. That was, until I adjusted my codpiece that had been dragging along behind me and slowing my progress, in addition to it now slowly disappearing up my backside. Beneath the said, offending, codpiece was Cranmer's document and, as I took a few steps back to comprehend what was on it, I froze, dumbfounded. Now, as you wonder what this is I'm looking at, I have to say that I had no bloody idea but the title alone sent chills down my tail. "The Purge" it said. And, like so many words of this time, it could have meant a number of things. Henry emptying his bowels was described as purge but I was sure it was not referring to the rather large and inconsistent Royal arse, as this had all the semblance of a dire and secret plot. Where I became unstuck was when I realised that I could not make head or tail of it and can only tell you that it resembled a large spider's web and that where the web intersected there were symbols that meant nothing to me. Now panicking, I told myself that I must remember what I had seen although, every time I shut my eyes, the details just disappeared again. I decided to make some sort of mental order to this, trying as best as I could to assign similar letters or signs that I already knew and might remember. And then, I thanked the Lord for Cranmer's mumbling and shuffling as it alerted me to his sudden return. I leapt off the table with little regard for my safety, or where I would land, although I soon realised the close proximity of the fire. Now, to be clear, when I say fire, I'm not talking about one or two logs crackling away in the corner, this was huge! The fireplace was easily twelve feet across, stacked four feet high with six-foot logs and was roaring, Cranmer's table strategically placed so that, whilst he worked, his Holy arse was almost touching the flames. On the fire surround was a carving of the exodus from Egypt and my pantaloons had decided to hang themselves on the staff of Moses, no less. I suppose if had wanted a miracle I was, at least, in the right company. This wasn't good. As the fabric stretched, my most privy parts were pulled ever further skyward as the rest of me slowly lowered. I could hear a wheezing sound that was getting gradually louder and then realised it was me trying to negotiate the pain. As if this wasn't giving me away already, my highly coloured royal costume was almost as bright as the fire. I found myself trying to recreate the sound of the fire to hide my agony. Bloody ridiculous. My nuts wrapped around my neck, I was now doing burning log impressions. Amazingly, he didn't seem to notice so I tried very hard to be quiet but then, without warning, he spun around to warm his hands and screamed when he saw what was before him. He instantly knew what he had and he also knew he was just a moment away from getting rid of the King's favoured pet that always seemed to be somewhere he shouldn't be. Cranmer didn't hesitate, he lunged to grab me and managed to secure me by the tail. Unwittingly, he had offered me some relief although this relief was only to last a second or two. He swung me toward him in order to propel me back into the fire.

'Ah! Your Grace! I see you've uncovered my little jape!'

It was Thomas Heneage. Thank God. Thank God, I thought. Cranmer hesitated and glared. It was clear that he was unsure as to how he should proceed.

'Haha! I was so hoping that our little rodent here would make you jump Your Grace, how His Majesty loves to surprise people with his favourite pet.'

It was those last two words that halted Cranmer in his tracks. Burning this nuisance mouse undetected would have been some coup for the Archbishop but having someone witness the execution could well have had consequences. I was still dangling by the tail with my head now medium rare and the rest of me speedily catching up. His expression changed. You would best describe what his face was doing as gurning. This was his attempt at pretending he was party to the jest after all.

'But of course, Master Heneage, having fallen foul of your little joke, I was just taking time to admire the fineries adorning our little mouse.'

Those fineries now accommodating my entire rectum, I should add. He then attempted a chuckle which also had us both wondering if he was simply suffering from wind. Thomas moved to pull me away from the fire and Cranmer's hand and, as we parted company, both of them feigned laughter. Hurriedly, Heneage took me back to his chamber and put me down on his table. For a moment I thought he would bestow endless sympathies on me but I couldn't have been further from the truth.

'What is wrong with you Mouse?!' This wasn't rhetorical by the way 'you are constantly in the favour of the King, well dressed, fed, your secrets kept?'

He was furious and concerned and put his face very close to mine.

'You didn't speak in the presence of the Archbishop did you?'

'No, no. Absolutely not!'

'You sure Mouse?'

'Well…er…perhaps just a squeak' I admitted timidly.
'Are…you…sure?!'

This was the first time that I had ever heard or seen Thomas Heneage threaten. It dawned on me that both he and the King had gone to great pains to protect my secret and that my adventure really could have had serious consequences. It was clear that the perpetrators of the 1541 Cataclysm had their suspicions about this mouse that coincidently seemed to appear every time their plans were thwarted.

'My good friend Thomas, I swear. All I did was squeal as I was being burned.'

This sounded very reasonable as far as I was concerned and he seemed to accept it. His door was still open and there was some bustling outside. I could always tell it was the King approaching even when he hadn't spoken. There was a dramatic commotion that surrounded his transport now that he needed assistance getting around parts of the Palace. It was easy to pick out the sycophantic ramblings of those around him particularly those of status who were constantly badgering him about, what they regarded as, matters of great import. He stopped and deliberately looked in knowing nothing of my fireplace drama.

'Today Thomas If you please.'

'Of course, Your Grace.'

Came the reply, Thomas fully understanding of what this brief instruction meant and then the King shuffled away again.

'You're to return to York' he said very calmly 'arrangements will be made today. You will speak nothing of your time at Court, the King will summon you and the Agents if, and when, needed.'

For once I really was speechless and, even though this was a very sudden turn of events, within minutes I was prepared for my return home. By the time the week was out, I was out of London and very soon was happily back in my workshop bewildered at the pace of my exit. I could only wonder as to why the King wanted me gone but presumed that I may have reminded him too much of that hot summer's evening when Catherine tended to his ailments and when the King and I had first met. In a sensitive moment, I wondered if I'd offended him which told me that, whether I liked it or not, I had built a relationship, of some sort, with one of history's most tyrannical despots.

The welcome by those most dear to me in the astounding city of York certainly helped to dispel my, often dark, pondering but I just could not forget about the Archbishop's spider-like diagram and the dear young Queen who would soon face death. On my first evening back at Bootham Bar, I found myself reflecting on the life of this larger than life King.

3: THE SNICKLEWAYS

22 Years earlier...

Knowing Henry as I did, it was hard to imagine a time
when he was still King but, in almost all other respects, was
a completely different person. In 1520 he had been King
for just over ten years and was admired for his intellect,
knowledge of theology, athleticism, mastery of languages
and even music. You would only just detect the very first
rumblings of Protestantism in Europe, not really enough to
worry the body faithful. Within a year the Pope would
declare Henry "Defender of the Faith" and, although he
had no son yet, Princess Mary was four years old. England
was relatively stable and it is probably as well Henry had no
inkling of what the future held for him and for our beloved
England.

At this juncture in his reign, he was presenting
altogether different problems. Come 1519, he was enjoying
life with the lads of the Court, so much so that he was
neglecting his responsibilities. He surrounded himself with
what, at the time, would have been regarded as peers but,
put simply, were his mates. He jousted regularly with Sir
Nicholas Carew and Sir Edward Neville and when they
weren't jousting, they played dice, tennis, jested and merrily

drank into the night. It didn't help that, at this time, Henry and King Francis of France, not only saw themselves as allies, but fostered a friendly rivalry. On a recent visit, their French counterparts were seen to throw stones and eggs at the common people for fun which only served to inspire the English Court hooligans. Added to this, they were constantly mocking senior officials at Court. The habitual tomfoolery by these "young minions" as they were known, went too far and Henry's advisors put a stop to it, Henry himself recognising the damage it was doing to the regulation of affairs. Their dismissal from Court also became known as "The Purge" and it was made clear at home and abroad that change was afoot.

So, in June 1520, Francis and Henry met on the, now famous, field of cloth of gold which was not only an extraordinary exercise in diplomacy and propaganda but a blueprint for how you moved the Court and the army long distances.

Few people in York knew anything about the cloth of gold event. Many still existed in their own little worlds, ignorant of affairs beyond the walls unless, of course, those affairs directly affected them. If you were to wander away from Coppergate in a northerly fashion, you would enter the deepest and thickest part of the snickleways. Some buildings were literally leaning on one another and, for those who lived with all sorts of junk and litter surrounding them, you'd be hard pushed to see where the original foundations were. Hardly any of these had brick foundations, walls, or support. Some were of wattle and daub construction but some, even older buildings, were no more than a rickety pile of wood and had little to keep in the warm or keep out the cold. The snickleways, here, were so narrow that only one or two people abreast could navigate them. Some people kept animals which did little for the general hygiene of the place and there was an ever-present and unpleasant odour. This wasn't the worst of it for this, unintentionally intimate accommodation, also kept out much of the light.

It was very rare that you would see people at leisure in the snickleways, partly because any form of laziness (and certainly beggary) was frowned upon by Tudor society. Also, put simply, most people had to work if they were to survive. This also applied to children. For some, as soon as they could walk, they were put to use but that didn't mean there wasn't the odd hour where they would have to find their own amusement.

One, very short alley was known to locals simply as "dead." A most foreboding and unwelcoming pseudonym but one, at least, that did have an understandable origin. There was only one way into dead alley, unless you fancied fighting your way through branches, roots and stone, that is. At the end of it wasn't a wall but a church and, as this wasn't an accepted entrance to the church, no one went further than this end of dead alley. The church was, and still is, All Saints Pavement and a number of the poor of the snickleways would worship there. In complete contrast it was sometimes used as a 'butt' street on Sunday afternoons as its one-way disposition made it ideal for the archery practice. Odd as it sounds, refining archery skills was compulsory for all males aged between six and sixty as a way of the Crown ensuring that its citizens were always battle ready. Well, that, at least, was the theory. Therefore, those in nearby snickleways, who could be bothered to observe this rule, sometimes congregated in dead alley on Sundays to shoot, and then retrieve, arrows.

One very hot and sunny July day in 1520, a child played in the overshadowed and dark, dead alley. To him it was neither dark, dead or foreboding. In fact, it would be unimaginable to him that people thought of his home in that way. Few people passed because, as implied, it wasn't a thoroughfare. He sat comfortably amongst the filth completely ignoring the stench and grateful that the constant stream of urine had dried somewhat due to the warmth of the day. He was happily playing with his toys. This was a pair of sticks, well, two branches I suppose. In the hour he had to himself, the branches became the cross Jesus Christ died on, the sword of Henry V, the towers of York Minster and the tools used by builders on local churches. His attire was so scant and so dirty that if you stood at the accessible end of dead alley, looking into it, you probably wouldn't see him at all and, at six years old, there was still hardly anything of him and that included his self-esteem. He was skinny, unkempt but had the most noticeable fire-red hair. Apart from his mother's love he had had few experiences that gave him any self-worth and, most days, he was frightened of his own shadow. He had been given no education and his world was incredibly small but at least his father had filled his head with a few fantasies that now fuelled his imaginative playtime. He was, by and large, a lonely child and found himself often ridiculed by his peers sometimes because of his crimson locks, sometimes because he was so scrawny (although most kids were scrawny) and because of where he lived. The latter was particularly unfair as his mother kept the home spotless and doted on young Silas. However, by the age of six, Silas was certain that he was inferior to almost everyone.

But, he was, for the time-being, totally content, his mother just a moment away in a nearby house. Well, a shack. He was also puffed up with pride as his father, yes, his father, was with the King in France making swords and suits of armour. He had proudly mentioned this to some of the other local children but they scoffed and relentlessly made fun of him. However, Silas knew that, one day, Clifford the Smith, or Clifford Smith as he was sometimes called would return and he would carry little Silas around York on his shoulders. Happy in this thought, he pushed his long red hair out of his eyes and stood to admire the two lances he had made from the sticks. Not that he had done anything to them, they were now lances and that was that. He would step into the small slither of blazing light that pushed through this narrow alley as a reminder that it was summer, and would step back into the dark as if he was passing from one world to another. And then his happy day turned sour. He saw a shadow at the end of the alley. Jaxon. That was the name of the ten year old that stood at the entrance to Silas's world. Silas didn't recognise the other two boys but he knew that he was bound to get hurt if Jaxon was there. On this day, Jaxon and his accomplices had decided that if they collected enough stones they could pelt little Silas and there would be nowhere for him to run to. They were right. They laughed, particularly when the stones hit home and shouted "silly-arse" in mockery of his name. The third rock thrown hit the small boy directly on the forehead and blood poured out of it. He was dizzy and couldn't stand. He looked at his legs that were turning red with blood and then slumped into the waste of dead alley. He was aware of everything dimming before him and, in losing consciousness, he glanced at Jaxon who was not much bigger than him but was forever set apart from the other children by a cut on his neck that went almost from one ear to the other. The last sound Silas heard was a woman angrily chastising Jaxon and his ruffian accomplices who, rather than mock or challenge, decided to take flight.

The woman was Mary Smith. When Mary had bad days she pondered on the fact that in her relatively unremarkable life she also lived with an unremarkable name. She had peeped out to check on young Silas only to find him, yet again, the victim. She shouted and threatened as she chased these miscreants but gave up as she wanted to tend to her child. He was now crying so Mary placed him on her knee and mopped away the blood. It was a nasty cut but it would heal. She hugged him, reassuring him that he was the centre of her world, how things would change and talked about the grown-up Silas.

'One day you'll be a Mayor, or a squire. A Knight of the realm! Yes! A Knight. A Lord even! Lord Silas!'

Silas started to chuckle and his day was, in an instant, much brighter. He jumped off Mary's knee and took to his, completely imaginary, horse cantering around the incredibly small place in which they lived.

'I will fight for thee, fair maiden!' He announced and Mary giggled too. Little Silas continued to play indoors, having almost forgotten the traumas of the morning, while Mary carried on with her work.

Her work was quite unusual but did provide a few coins, or sometimes exchanged goods, though it would never make her rich. Although it was a modest craft, Silas loved to watch his mother make quills and was possibly partly why he later became infatuated with documents, crests, and people of rank. She was a perfectionist and it was this singular reason why she had secured some trade with the Minster and the many churches in York. Actually that's not entirely correct, it would be fair to say that Mary's pretty face helped her to get some initial interest from Hugh although she had never used her looks, or flirted with men, to gain trade. In the scheme of things Hugh was of little importance, he just lived nearby and Mary knew that he worked as a labourer at the Minster. To be fair to him, he had to be quite persuasive to even get the most junior clerks and clerics to take some samples so that he could promote Mary's craft. In time, all her clients came to know that she ran this little industry with integrity, as far as anyone knew she had never taken a feather from a bird that was owned by someone, always waiting for them to fall naturally. She was smart enough to know where to look but this was still no easy task as quills had to be made from large feathers, preferably from geese, swans and turkeys but she could just as easily fashion an owl or crow feather if the need arose. She had evolved a time-consuming, but effective, method of hardening and then shaping the quill which not only meant that these were great writers but also lasted. Clerics in the city spent all their days scribing so were grateful of a well-cut quill that was durable and effective without too much regular sharpening. Mary also insisted on scenting each one and, although, at first, this may have seen a little strange, it did become popular and was, presumably, her unique selling point. Ironically, Mary couldn't write but knew, almost for certain, that she would be bringing up Silas alone so this meagre income helped.

This all started as fun, a hobby if anything, but word soon travelled around the nearby snickleways that this woman was making quality quills. Hugh, possibly in the hope of impressing Mary, suggested the idea of giving a few to the lowest ranking scribes and, in short, this became a success. Hugh took on the role of an intermediary and without any arrangement being made with Mary, also decided to take a cut for himself.

Earlier that summer there had been an unusual death within the snickleways. Death wasn't unusual in itself. Mortality, particularly in children was high but on this occasion, a young woman had been found in one of the alleys with a mortal wound. There was little fuss but there were, noticeably, a class of individuals present that normally wouldn't be seen in the area. A young legal notary from the Minster, on seeing dead alley, instantly recognised the name but was, nevertheless, shocked by its appearance despite the notoriety that preceded it. Unaccompanied by Hugh the labourer, he decided to call in on Mary Smith, the now semi-famous woman that created those scented quills.

He knocked on the door and Mary's little face appeared. Shocked at the sight of a young gentleman appearing at her house, she trembled but politely asked,

'Good day, Sir. Is all well? What brings you here?'

Strangely, she presumed that there must have been something wrong if such a person had made his way off the respectable path and to her abode.

'All is well. Mrs Smith? I do have the right house?'

'Yes' she answered still very apprehensive.

'My name is William Fawkes, I work at the Minster.' Mary's whole demeanour changed in an instant as she now presumed this had something to do with the quills and hoped, desperately, that he hadn't come to complain.

'I was in the area on business and thought it prudent to give thanks to the lady that provided us regularly with fine quills!'

She softened and asked him to go inside. His clothes were so fine, plain but of some quality and it didn't escape Mary's attention that William was also quite handsome.

'How may I help you Sir.' She asked offering him a stool.

'May I be blunt?' He asked.

'Why of course.'

'It has come to our attention my dear lady that, whereas we used to acquire thirty quills for a farthing we now only get twenty for that amount.'

Mary instantly started to protest but William stopped her.

'And…I have already presumed that you are not seeing this profit?'

Mary was quite unsettled by this and started to cry.

'Oh no sir! As God is my witness I pass them on at forty a farthing and always have done. I assure you…'

'Now, now, please don't concern yourself. As you have probably already worked out, it is your friend Hugh who has been stealing from us both.'

'He's no friend of mine!' Said Mary now visibly quite angry.

'Of course, of course. Please do not ruffle yourself.'

Unfortunately it was too late and William's feather joke had fallen on stony ground. Mary barely managed to make ends meet as it was and now, she presumed, her good reputation was ruined. One can only imagine just how long it must have taken Mary to acquire, honestly, forty good feathers let alone the work. She cried and rambled as William patiently listened, inwardly chastising himself for handling this business so poorly. He was young and inexperienced and this, certainly, would be a lesson for him. Mary had a strange habit of scurrying, tidying and rearranging objects when she became anxious which, almost always, unsettled everyone else so William made an effort to calm her.

'You have my word that we will still require your magnificent quills, with an intermediary of my choice, but perhaps…'

He was now staring at the boy who was sitting silently in the corner.

'The boy, does he work?'

'He does little jobs for me sir but he's quite timid. I like to keep him close.'

'I understand but…what would you say if he ran one or two errands for me now and again? I would, of course, pay.'

For Mary, this was totally unexpected. The offer of any money at any time was nothing less than miraculous but Silas, dear little Silas, he was her world. How would he cope with such responsibly? She momentarily slumped into a melancholy state having been confronted with this conundrum. The silence was soon broken,

'I am…at your very service…sir….Lord Silas…messenger to the King!'

Mary and William both laughed leaving Silas wondering what the joke was. William smiled and looked at Mary's face full of pride and then turned to the boy.

'Then I am a very lucky man!' He said to Silas and then addressed Mary,

'I assure you, Mrs Smith that this will only be once every so often and I promise you that they will only be essential church or Minster errands'.

Mary smiled and even agreed to let William Fawkes take Silas on a walk so that he would be better acquainted with the district. Silas was so happy, he liked William, he was kind and he was easy to talk to, mostly because William tolerated the nonsense that Silas talked. Before he had left, William had been fully briefed by this doting mother. She told William Fawkes that her son was given to flights and ideas of fantasy, often said quite inappropriate things (without meaning any harm of course) and was, sadly, incurably clumsy but, she would add at the end,

'The sweetest child any mother could wish for.'

William's offer was honest and without strings. He could be forgiven for being struck by both Mary's beauty and her demure and honest disposition but he was, despite his youth, above such indiscretions, taking note of her social and marital status. Neither was this an act of altruism, this poor woman was easily competing with other suppliers, even allowing for Hugh's embezzlement. William was sharp and he would be sure that Hugh had his reckoning. The boy? Perhaps William Fawkes just took a liking to him or Silas was in the right place at the right time. The two never really had a relationship. Silas would be sent word to turn up at the Minster's Liberty gates and would then be given instructions regarding his tasks. On his first few errands he was accompanied by an older boy called David. David was really good at showing Silas routes around York but was to have no other discourse with him. He thought Silas an imbecile and had no patience with his ramblings. David also made sure that he took time to inform others that this boy was an idiot.

Within a week, Silas was able to pick up and deliver messages but couldn't get the hang of not speaking so, sadly, he was reprimanded often. On one occasion a Lady told him she would not receive the message until he had gone home, had a wash and come back clean-faced. He did just that except, unfortunately, by the time he had arrived home, he'd completely forgotten why he had returned so got the same reprimand twice. You can be assured that, even as a young child, Silas would manage to make a mess of things but, thankfully, this was an ideal first job as, generally speaking, he couldn't go far wrong in picking up a message from one person and then handing it to another.

Six months passed. Mary still making her quills and Silas hot-footing it around York. One snowy day in November, Silas's little boots newly patched up, he braved the elements to go for the very first time to an inn. Fortunately, this was very close to his home and he was already familiar with, ye golden fleece, along the Pavement and the indecipherable cacophony that emanated from it. Once there, he was to find the owner and simply hand over a message. Not for the first time, on arrival, he was given a clout around the ear and sent off but he had learned to stay and insist and then, usually on presentation of an authentic seal, attitudes toward him would change. Little Silas was then brought into this hub of drunken activity, some smiled at how small he was, others grimaced and this, in itself, almost frightened the life out of the child. He tried to keep himself to himself but, fascinated, decided to look around the room. One man, noticeable by his brashness and the passion with which he told his tall tales, almost instantly attracted Silas's attention. Silas could only see his back but it was the voice. What was it about the voice that felt familiar? Almost like home? Silas being Silas decided to take a few steps nearer until he was in touching distance. Another man, sitting at the same table, alerted the boastful drunk to the boy and he responded by whipping around to face him. There was a momentary silence and then Silas exploded with emotion,

'Pater! Oh Pater you're back from France!'

And he moved to embrace the man. Almost everyone laughed. The idea that Clifford Smith had actually heard of France would have been a stretch, let alone getting there and back.

'Why are they laughing Pater! Are you unharmed? Is all well with the King?'

More incredulous laughter but, as yet, Clifford had said nothing. His face was blush-red betraying both his shame and rising anger. By now Silas's little arms were touching his father.

'Get away with you! Don't know what you're talking about boy' and he turned to his drinking companions. Silas threw his arms around this large, cold frame but was thrown to the floor. Even this didn't stop him. Why would it? His father had returned. Why wouldn't he speak to him? Clifford realised that he was now in a very awkward position. His drinking companions were well aware of what was going on so, like it or not, he had to make a life changing decision. Life changing for Silas at least. He stood, grabbed the child and lifted him so his little face was aligned with his.

'Now listen here urchin, I don't know what you think it is that you know. I've never met you, never seen you before and I don't...have...any...children! And you can tell that to your soft mother too!'

As if it wasn't already obvious to everyone what his game was, he had now slipped up. The owner then physically removed Silas from Clifford's grip and threatened the man. He insisted that he sat down and said that if there were any further upsets he would also be removed. The inn owner then took Silas outside and gently put him down on the pavement. Silas was now shaking and crying uncontrollably so the landlord made some effort to console him.

'Do you understood what's happened here boy?'

But, at first, the only response was more tears. Little Silas was heartbroken and he was trying hard to make sense of this encounter.

'That's my father but he's pretending he doesn't want me. I don't understand!'

And then the bawling continued.

'Look lad, it's nothing to do with me but I suggest you forget him. Now get yourself home, It's getting dark and there's more snow coming'.

Silas very slowly made his way home feeling as though the Minster itself had collapsed on top of him. Although this seemed like the longest journey home possible, when he arrived there he remembered none of it. He was dirty, wet and shivering with cold and yet, he wasn't feeling any of it. He needed comfort, someone to tell him that this was a joke or a nightmare and the only person who could do that was his mother. Considered a simpleton by many, and incurably naïve, Silas did have enough sense to work out that his father had done a very bad thing and it was then that, for the first time, he wondered if his mother already knew. He so much wanted the sympathy only Mary could offer but considered that she had been living with this pain for some time. Momentarily he was angry with his mother, as in a child's mind this had the odour of a conspiracy, the sort only parents can concoct but then thought that, if she did know, she was keeping it secret to protect him so decided on a strategy, which in itself was a minor miracle for little Silas.

'Oh my dear boy! What a mess! Look at you, you're freezing to death. Come by the fire.'

Silas tried hard to hide his tears and, now completely naked and facing the fire, he decided to ask.

'Mater, how long will father be in France?'

There was a silence and he could hear his mother nervously scurrying about and tidying up which is what she did when she became anxious.

'Oh…er…well, let me see. I suppose that's up to the King…and er…the weather and how many ships he has… now let me feed you! There'll be nothing left of you to feed if I don't.'

It was the last part, the hurry to get away from the question that told Silas they she already knew. For a moment he was again angry at his mother. However, as he turned, he could see the strain that this one simple question had put on her.

'Well, it's of no importance' he said in a noticeably shaky voice. 'Eh Mater? We're managing fine just the two of us!'

Although Mary welcomed this noble sentiment from her only child, she looked at him now trying to work out if he knew something but then decided that it was imperative to respond.

'Yes my dove' now embracing him 'yes what an industrious and successful pair we are!'

This was Silas at his best, he had accessed his most admirable attribute, one that he would draw upon throughout his life and one that would often go unnoticed by others. Where his brain would regularly let him down, his heart took over and Silas's heart always knew best. As the next few weeks passed, the truth about his father weighed heavily upon him. Some would have become stronger but not Silas. This period in his life was when he first decided that there were two certainties of natural existence. Things had always gone wrong and, things will continue to go wrong.

However, his work was a distraction. Although he didn't see William Fawkes anymore, he had a pick-up point near the Minster where some junior clerk would give him instructions. So, interestingly, Silas had found his vocation early in life. He had little contact with other people and could cope easily with finding places and, most of the time, there were no complaints.

As the spring of 1521 breathed a new and bright palette of colour over the city, he found himself whistling as he carried home his week's pay to his beloved mother. His encounter with Clifford had been a singular one and he was never to see him again, no surprise happenings or revelations later in life like in stories, he was gone for good. Silas would often daydream, wondering why his father had lied but, more importantly, he would have loved to know whether or not he was ever in France and with the King. At such a young age it made no sense whatsoever but, as time passed, he managed to accept his fate. It would be fair to say that, besides the cat-calling from other children, and particularly the assaults from Jaxon, he was now genuinely content with his lot.

On this spring day, he approached the entrance to dead alley which, on most days, was sparsely populated but today, there were a number of gentlemen hovering about. Silas had in his hand four quills as he had, in addition to his own errands, successfully executed a delivery for Mary but still had yet to issue this final batch. He immediately hid them thinking that someone may be, yet again, asking questions about his mother's trade. One man was Roger Geggs the new sheriff of the city. Silas was impressed, it was extremely rare that dignitaries came to dead alley so he took a moment to admire the fine apparel donned by these important fellows. As he neared home it was clear that they were, in fact, congregating around his house. Still puzzled, he walked through this small crowd as if they weren't there. That was, until he felt a firm grip on his arm.

'Can't go in there young Silas. Just stay close to me.'

It was William Fawkes and, although this provided the child with some initial comfort, Silas though it very curious that he was there. He could now see that the door was ajar and there were others inside. A neighbour, Mrs Tumble, could be seen and she was talking to his mother but on closer inspection, Silas noticed that she was also crying.

'Nasty business this' said the sheriff puffed with self-importance 'fourth one in a year, nip this in the bud we will.'

In every sense of the word Silas was slow but not so slow that he couldn't decipher this already blunt message.

He knew there had been three previous murders and, in an instant, he broke down completely. He howled and shouted, cried and cursed, wrestled and wriggled but, eventually, succumbed to Mrs Tumble's embrace as she had come running out of the house. The little that was left of this child's world had been taken away in an instant and nothing would ever be the same again.

He slept on the floor of Mrs Tumble's abode that night but was not, at any point, allowed to see his mother. Mrs Tumble also accompanied him to the pauper's funeral but that is where their relationship ended.

At barely eight years old Silas was completely on his own.

The familiar shack that had been his family home was taken back by the landlord and he found himself, just one day after the funeral, standing in dead alley not able to either grasp what had happened or what he was to do next. However, he did have the gumption to turn up for work and this, at least, did carry on as normal. That was, until people learned that he had no fixed abode. Word got back to Fawkes who, as he had recently made acquaintance with a successful glass merchant, Robert Hall, suggested that he might use the boy for errands as the church simply could not employ such a child a day longer. Hall reluctantly agreed but subsequently counted his blessings as the boy would do, literally, any delivery asked of him at practically no cost. Having no options, no relatives, nothing and nobody, Silas, almost as if by clockwork, decided to simply carry on. He was later to reflect that these were months where he felt completely numb and without direction.

After some twelve months in his employ, one of Robert's associates at the guild asked about the boy and where he lived. Astonishingly, Robert had to admit that he had never asked, nor did he ever bother to ask and it would also be fair to add that he wasn't bothered. Initially, Silas had slept anywhere he could that was out of sight. The law was no respecter of age when it came to vagabonds so he was careful to slip into the narrowest recesses and to be quiet, ensuring also that he never missed a minute's work. Eventually, and quite cleverly, he had decided to do what no other had done and that was to attempt to access dead alley via the church yard. I say cleverly, others may say downright stupid for it was thick with bracken and roots that had tightened their iron grip on medieval gravestones. However, he was determined to push, squeeze and scrape his way through it. Although his clothes and flesh were much worse for wear because of this adventure, he did make it through, eventually reaching his intended destination. If anyone was to walk down dead alley by the normal route they may just have detected what could only be described as a dilapidated shed, so little of it still visible that you just wouldn't know what it was. Silas knew what it was, and where it was, mostly because it had always been the source of folklore and ghost stories but there was simply no way you could get at it. Most would regard it as worthless. Even before he made the journey, he knew that this would now be home. He followed the line of a thick root that had broken well into the small hut and squeezed his torn frame along it into the interior. Even with his minuscule presence, there was practically no room left to even stand up but he knew that, in time, he could clear it. He had some money and now he had somewhere to keep it. He decided there and then that his first purchase would be a knife, Silas had never stolen anything and he would, throughout his life, never once take anything that wasn't his. Besides the clothes on his back, his total assets amounted to four fine quills and a few coins. He would earn his way and would see this settlement as a fresh start. Within a matter of months he had a home and, even better, no one knew that he was there; the contrast between the harmony of his little abode and the world outside almost immeasurable as he was increasingly becoming an oddity and a figure of fun in

York. Although it's fair to say that Robert Hall never took much time to care about Silas's predicament, Silas would always be grateful of his patronage, recognising that, most probably, it saved his life.

Over the years little changed except that the errands eventually became missions and that Silas was considered even more strange but, he never forgot his mother's promise that one day he would become a Knight of the realm.

4: THE URCHIN

May 1541

Brother Bernard's journey from Limehostes was plagued by delays. His physical condition alone was starting to take its toll and, although he now was on a God-given quest to thwart the impending Cataclysm, his heart was heavy for the loss of his Brother and newly-won companion, Bede who had plummeted into the moat surrounding the Tower of London. He was also missing Eirik for, in Eirik, was security, confidence and that constant certainty that accompanied him, almost promising success. Somewhere around Bishops Stortford, Bernard with no strength remaining, lost hope and subsequently collapsed into a ditch that ran for miles along the, sometimes almost indistinguishable, road. He lay there and prayed. He prayed for Bede, for Eirik, for Elspeth but mostly for strength, both spiritually and physically, so that he could complete his task. His water had run out, he was filthy and every part of his physical frame ached. His legs, in particular, were now starting to give up on him. He could feel the cold of the mud seeping into his bedraggled cassock and, belligerently, he refused to move. He thought he heard some movement but it was just the rustling of the leaves on the large elm under which he now found himself sheltered but, it did reluctantly make him turn his head to the right. He became aware of a light, a random glint that was there and then gone, there again, gone again. It was the only thing that held his attention for the next ten minutes, still refusing to move and almost willing the Lord to pick him up or just let him go. Ten minutes passed and Bernard then found himself intrigued. For now, at least, God had done his job. Brother Bernard sat up and realised that only yards away, there was water. Flowing water. Although he wasn't to know it, this was the river Stort and, to Bernard, it appeared warm, even Heavenly. Of course, it wasn't warm but it was inviting enough for him to drag his carcass willingly out of the filth and investigate further. He didn't walk, his disposition was still such that he was now still half indulgent in human self-pity but he was now also expectant. He dragged himself the few yards, across a grass verge and onto the river embankment and, rather surprisingly, threw himself in. I say rather surprisingly because, initially, this wasn't his intention, he was simply drawn to the Heavenly sunlight reflected on the water. The shock to his system very rapidly reanimated him again and, in his panic, he couldn't work out if this was an intended route to end all or he simply felt that he needed a wash. Those thoughts lasted but a few seconds as, now, he was fighting to access the bank. His days at the monastery, on the island of Lindisfarne, flashed before him as did everything that had happened since but, predominantly, he was reminded of the devious Cataclysm plot devised by Cranmer, Wriothesley and Somerset and found himself upright on the grass verge feeling stronger and reinvigorated, his sense of purpose restored. And then, uncannily, he walked. He just carried on walking into the town dripping and sloshing as he limped. You would have thought this to be a completely different unkempt monk as, now, he was inspired once again.

On reflection, it would have been wise for Bernard to have ditched his monk's habit long ago as it was continuing to have a profound effect on how he was both perceived and received. Monks were now the enemy. No one would turn a blind eye at a priest walking down the high street but a monk? Surely they were all pensioned off or put to death if they had become rebels? People would be right in thinking this way and it would have been dangerous for anyone to consider hiding a monk or nun. However, there were sympathisers and Bernard could be assured of the odd piece of bread and some water or wine as long as he gave an assurance that he would continue on his way after receiving such charity. In Bishop Stortford he found refuge temporarily in a barn and, on his discovery, also found an understanding tenant farmer, but more importantly, he now managed to get his bearings. Again, deflated by the seemingly endless journey ahead of him, he did now, at least, understand what lay between him and Bury St Edmunds. The farmer even kindly put him five miles nearer as he had business north of the town. All of this was more than enough to restore Bernard's faith and, in turn, his general health and sense of purpose.

He was so delighted to arrive in Bury St Edmunds that you'd have thought that he had reached journey's end. He had learned, by now, to head for the nearest inn when arriving in any town, village or hamlet. When locals were drinking they were often at their most reasonable and he found, usually, that he could also strike up a conversation. Initially, he thought it wise to settle himself by the door whilst he was clearly so conspicuous. He immediately attracted attention and gossip but, unusually, it was the landlord who approached him first.

'What's your business here then monk?'

'I don't seek trouble' said Bernard 'I have an acquaintance locally and if you could help me find him I will leave you and your good patrons in peace.'

'You realise how dangerous it is travelling wearing that thing?' Said the landlord pointing aggressively at his habit.

'I do. But I won't remove it. It will come off when I'm dead and I no longer have any need for it. For now, it remains a devout part of my quest' replied Bernard.

'Quest is it? You sound like trouble. Are you mad? You must know that you'll get yourself killed with that cocky attitude?'

Bernard was now, uncharacteristically, losing patience.

'I have already been so close to death my friend, many times, even recently in the Tower...'

'The Tower?! The Tower of London! God's teeth man, half of Harry's army will be after you!'

He was now becoming both loud and very agitated so Bernard sought to calm him.

'My friend...apologies. I mean no harm. And no, I am of no real importance, nobody follows me. I simply need to connect with a local man now known simply as Samuel. If you could point me in the correct direction I will be gone before the day is out.'

It went quiet. This clearly meant something to the landlord. He stepped back and, as he pondered on this, the populace of the pub started to chatter again.

'Come with me but don't say a word' he said and Bernard immediately complied. Within seconds they were outside of the rear entrance to the inn. They then walked along a course that could not even be described as a path so Bernard deduced that this was used very rarely. In part, they were clearing the route as they went through it, pushing aside weeds, bracken and branches and Bernard was aware that they were travelling behind the buildings, unseen. They then arrived at a small opening, a patch of rough grass and, beyond, was the entrance to an extremely modest building.

'There! And I don't want to see you again!' Said the landlord abruptly and, as Bernard turned to thank him, he was already four strides back in the direction of the inn. With some trepidation, Brother Bernard knocked on this old and neglected door. As the ageing timber flaked and fell down into the weeds, he didn't even take time to consider that this could have been a trap, or even a jest, he just did it. In fact, he did it four times before he heard some movement from within. Then, slowly, the door was unbolted and, eventually, opened. The door shed more of its dead flakes and the leaves and branches crunched as the door broke them. There, looking back at him, was a man who could have been his brother albeit much cleaner and wearing layman's clothes. The most startling difference, however, was that he had a cut that ran vertically from above his right eye and then through it, blinding him. The wound finished at his cheek. Remembering what Eirik had told him, Bernard was instantly assured that this must be Brother Benedict, now known as Samuel. Like Bernard, he had scruffy grey hair and, ironically, a bald patch developing where once they would both have shaved a tonsure leaving a ring of hair resembling Christ's crown of thorns. Both their faces spoke of premature ageing and pain and their beards now hid their once clean-shaven monastic identities. However, the reception was not the one that Brother Bernard had envisioned. As soon as the door was ajar, Samuel tried to shut it again. Clearly, in a state of alarm, his voice was raised,

'Who sent you here?! You must leave at once! I accept no visitors. None! None!! Do you hear?'

And amidst this commotion, the door was being awkwardly pushed back against the undergrowth. Bernard was dumbfounded. He'd come all this way for this? Could I be mistaken? He thought. No. No, he was clearly once a monk, this must be the person I was sent to meet. Confused, Bernard considered walking away but then looked around. There was no one nearby who could hear Samuel's cries so he decided to push the issue.

'Brother. Dear Brother, I have travelled far, from London. From the Tower!' The pushing continued 'a mortal saviour, Eirik, sent me to find you in the hope that you may help me on my way back to the north.'

The door stopped moving instantly and, somewhat comically, Samuel's nose peeped through the half-inch gap that remained.

'Describe him.' He said calmly. Bernard did just that. Few people looked like Eirik, he wore his Viking heritage almost as a garment so Samuel was left in no doubt that, at the very least, the two had met. He conceded another half-inch, his bushy eyebrows now encroaching this narrow aperture.

'Why would he send you here?' Asked Samuel somewhat placated.

Bernard put his face close to the man on the other side of the door and promised him that he was now on a quest of the greatest importance and, that he would impart all if he would just let him inside. However, it was only when Bernard started to describe his extensive ailments and injuries that Samuel took pity on him. Now the door was opened in a kind and considerate manner but, as soon as Bernard was inside and the door was shut, Samuel was, yet again, agitated, and lunged for the wall to his right. Here, there were panels that were a little skewed and worn but, otherwise, could be regarded as inconspicuous. However, Bernard then noticed that there was a small, hidden, grab-handle and as Samuel took hold of it, the panel slid behind the one adjacent to it. Before he knew it, Bernard was hurried down some narrow and incredibly steep stone stairs, grazing his left arm on the stone wall as he descended. Besides being alarmed, Bernard was instantaneously bewildered as to how this modest building seemed to be an extension of a much older stone construction. At the foot of the stairs was a stone ante-chamber reminiscent of some of the smaller cells that Bernard had seen at the Tower of London and, if it wasn't for the fact that Samuel had brought a single, lit, candle, they would have been completely in the dark.

'Right my friend, I will offer you the hospitality you desire but only after you tell me all.' Said Samuel assertively. Bernard agreed but told him that first, he had a question,

'This room – it is here for the likes of me and you. Am I right?'

Samuel wasn't giving anything away. Not yet, at least. Bernard was completely accurate in his assumption, more than once this cellar had been used to hide monks and nuns, sometimes for months. This thought alone sent chills down Brother Bernard's spine. Bernard talked and talked and Samuel listened. More than an hour later, Bernard took a moment to put his face near to a small opening in the wall. Whoever had engineered this pit had, at least, the foresight to add in some meagre ventilation. He also noticed the inclusion of a small drain in the centre of the room. Having snatched what oxygen he could, he loosened his cassock as, now, he was incredibly hot as was Samuel. Bernard had told Samuel everything, including details of the impending Cataclysm. Then Samuel spoke.

'Forgive me, Brother, for I have been, and still am, in some danger. I was once just like you, determined to reverse the Reformation and support those who may have brought the King back to his senses but all was in vain. I was also captured, tortured and then escaped but, at that point, vowed never to return to that life. That's partly why I am so cautious. Brother Benedict is dead and I'd thank you to accept that. I only wish for constant solitude and a peaceful existence now where I can pray in private.'

Although Bernard resisted the temptation to recruit Samuel, he did tell him of his plans to return to Lindisfarne and re-establish the Abbey, facilitate renewed opposition to Henry and alert all to the Cataclysm plot. Samuel laughed. He laughed heartily which in itself seemed curious to Bernard as he hadn't as much as seen a smile from him so far. Then Samuel sighed and said, 'my dear Brother. Has your sight suffered! What did you see of Bury St Edmunds? The Abbey now in ruins. Gone. Do you really think that it will be any different in your homeland?'

Bernard's theory was that the revolution was still strong in the north, that they wouldn't give way as easily and then he realised he may have offended Samuel with this sentiment. Samuel waved his hand in disbelief and then leaned forward over the dying flame and looked directly into Bernard's eyes

'Do as I have done, Brother, you have served God well.'

Bernard was so tired, and this oppositional plan was so inviting that he almost gave up there and then. In fact, Bernard may well have said anything that would get him out of that man-made stone coffin but chose to say nothing, so Samuel stood and led the way back upstairs. Once the panel was put back, Bernard looked around. Samuel had certainly created a unique, comfortable domicile completely devoid of any reference to his past. At the front was a very small window with four panes of glass, each no more than two inches square. Bernard squinted to see what was beyond and could see the road but it was some distance away. It was highly unlikely that anyone would notice Samuel or consider visiting him. The conversation was now much lighter and Samuel fed his visitor but, every time Bernard spoke of his faith or God himself, the talk stopped. Samuel had absolutely drawn a line between himself and his former life. Therefore, it didn't take long before Bernard deduced that, despite what Eirik had said, Samuel was nothing like himself. His faith and his determination gone, the two monks would now walk completely different paths. It would be fair to say that things started to become awkward as it was clear that they had little in common and Bernard started to worry that he may have shared too much with this extremely curious hermit. Contented, and sipping some wine, Bernard sat back and decided to enjoy this temporary oasis before he took to the road again.

There were only two rooms in this abode, that is, if you discounted the hidden cellar, and, for the first time, Samuel disappeared. Bernard started to doze, his eyes heavy and drawing shut and then opening again, this repeating until he felt completely relaxed. His mind gently swirled, the wine warmed him and he drifted away. Scratch scratch. Scratch scratch scratch! His eyes were now wide again. What is that? Scratch scratch! Alarmed, he prepared himself to tackle whatever predator was causing the commotion but, as he looked to his right, noticing a modest table, he cleared his eyes to ensure that what he thought was there really was there.

'Urchin' He said quietly to himself. He was right. There was, of all things, a hedgehog on the table but, unusually scratching away at a piece of cloth. Then, Bernard considered for a moment why the cloth would make such a sound. He pushed his aching bones up out of the chair and hobbled toward the table. The creature was scratching at the cloth as if to remove it for, underneath, there was a tired piece of sackcloth now part revealed. Bernard instinctively pulled the upper cloth up to look at the sackcloth and on it was drawn the like of which he had never seen before. He limped around the other side, to see if it made any sense the other way up, not even realising that he was completely ignoring the intruder upon it. Still, it was nonsense to him. He made to sit down again but felt a sudden and other-worldly desire to return. Something was telling him to remember these images although he knew not why, as they meant absolutely nothing to him. As he heard Samuel returning, he sat down again wondering where the little hedgehog had gone. Bernard was neither alarmed or suspicious so told Samuel of the entire event and, as his emphasis was on the canny hog, Samuel remained relatively unconcerned about his painted sackcloth although he did go over and make sure it was completely covered. Added to this confusion was the bizarre appetite that Samuel seemed to have for birds. He had stuffed pheasants, pigeons and blackbirds on display and Bernard could see all sorts of wild-fowl in various stages of preparation, presumably to eat, although there was definitely too much there for one person.

So, back to business. Bernard was there to solicit help and direction on his way to the coast. Samuel obliged, packing bread and water and ably drawing a map which the monk could follow. Samuel had Bernard swear an oath that he would not reveal his whereabouts or identity and Bernard happily agreed. As night fell, Brother Bernard headed west toward Yarmouth.

5: JOURNEY'S END
November 1541...

This was possibly the biggest regret of Peter's life. What started as a noble quest to seek out Brother Bernard's connections in York, had now turned into a dark nightmare. Only a week on the road, he had found himself starving, not even sure if he was travelling in the right direction and acknowledging how damaging to the mind, solitude could be. The fishing boats of Bamburgh seemed so far away.

Eventually, a few miles outside of Newcastle, he spotted a tradesman who had pulled his cart to one side in order to rest and water his horse. Peter approached him and then, uncontrollably, broke down.

'Dear Sir, I plead for your help. I am surely lost and am completely without any hope of either finding employment or even any sense of completing my journey!' and he sobbed. Broken, he collapsed into the soft soil in front of this stranger. Peter had deliberately stopped short of asking for food as that was the most abominable characteristic, beggars were hated by all and often severely punished. It would be fair to say that, for many, murder made more sense than begging. King Henry had been very fond of passing lengthy, often difficult to decipher and, very strict, new laws. One such edict was entitled, "Act for the continue of statutes for beggars and vagabond small; against the conveyance of horse's and mares out of this realm; against Welshmen making affrays on the counties of Hereford, Gloucester and Salop; and against the vice of buggery."

Lawyers, ever since, have been trying to uncover the connection between each of these offences, if any. God help any gay Welsh beggar trying to sell horses, abroad, during his reign.

'My, my, young lad. What a state you're in!' replied the traveller.

Thank God, Peter whispered to himself, he speaks English, presuming that he must have, by now, ventured into a foreign land. Minding his own back, the man had to ask,

'Not a beggar are you lad?'

'No Sir, I come from a proud fishing family in Bamburgh and travelling to meet a friend in York.'

Peter winced as he knew that, if questioned about his friend, he wouldn't have an available or believable answer.

'York! Haha. Well, there's ambition. You can't just walk such a distance without provisions or a plan' said the man.

'I seek work so that I can commence the next stage of my journey' lied Peter, pretending that he did, in fact, have a plan.

'Well, you'll not go far wrong in Newcastle, just mind your manners, they won't take any lip there.'

He looked Peter up and down. His clothes were filthy and it was clear, from the way that they hung about him, that he had lost weight.

'Come sit on the back of my cart and I'll put you right.'

Peter didn't even feel an inkling of suspicion or caution, he just wanted to connect with another human. Any human, so did as he was told.

Surprisingly Elias, for that was the name he shared with Peter, shared his food instantly but was soon regretting it as

Peter, unwittingly, gave his best impression of a hog at a trough. He was desperately hungry.

'Right lad' He said assertively 'I'll give you my counsel for free but, after that, I'm on my way!'

Peter smiled, now warm inside, consoled and hanging onto this man's every word.

'See through those trees?' Peter nodded. 'That's Newcastle.'

Peter stood and moved forward so he could see properly beyond the clearing. He gasped, he had never seen a place populated so. He'd seen ships before but not so many and he had never witnessed a settlement so very large and groaning with numbers of people. He looked back at Elias apologetically, as he had already interrupted his speech.

'If you're to get to York on foot, you need to get yourself fit and well, you have far to go. Seek employment and lodgings there, in Newcastle, save a little money if you can and, if not, stock up on some grain and water for the next part of your journey. Don't steal a horse no matter how you are tempted! That would be the end of you. A good plan is Elias's plan. Free too. What do you say to that boy?'

Peter thanked him and thanked him again. And yes, this would seem like common sense to most but was seemingly beyond both Peter's commonality and all his senses. Renewed with a freely gifted purpose, he told Elias that he would head straight for the town but Elias stalled him as he had one more thing to add.

'When you get there ask for Pilgrim street and a woman called Rosina and mention me, Elias. I think she might give a few day's work and even a place to put your head down.'

Peter remembered his manners and thought about how his step-father would want him to behave,

'Sir, your benevolence, goodwill and valued counsel will not be forgotten. You have my life-long gratitude in return.'

'Haha. Well, I'll take that, young feller. You take care now and I wish you God speed!'

And before he knew it Elias and his cart were but a dot on the horizon. Full and optimistic, before the day was out, Peter, as promised, found himself lifting sacks in return for food and board, his board being straw in a dry out-house. God, these sacks are heavy! He thought to himself and, being both young and from an entirely different pace, he was almost totally unfamiliar with coal. Sadly, he soon became very familiar with this most valuable but filthy rock that resulted in him, and all that got near to it, becoming blackened from head to toe and leaving workmen coughing incessantly. How he yearned for the sunsets and beautiful beaches of Bamburgh. What on earth was he thinking of? Who do I know in York?! He could feel panic set in as he, yet again, realised the madness of his predicament.

Coal was being farmed and mined as early as the Middle Ages in parts of the north-west and north-east and it was particularly accessible in Newcastle as it was so near the surface along the River Tyne. The economic landscape of England was changing at a pace in the sixteenth century but few places as rapidly as here. As the name suggests, Newcastle was still a fortified town as the uneasy relationship with Scotland persisted, but the many nunneries and priories were disappearing. New industries were emerging and monopolies, particularly in coal, were established. Peter, whether he liked it or not, was rapidly entering the modern world and he didn't care for it very much. This was a very early glimpse of the future and the British industrial revolution where every day folk, although grateful for regular work, would give up all their days to the masters of mills, coal mines and factories. Individuality slowly disappearing as the juggernaut monopolies expanded and many cared only for progress and profit. He had never worked so hard before and, for the first few days, he ached everywhere. However, he did have pay, food and a bed which gave him a genuine sense of perspective. He now missed his family, the dramatic coast of the north-east and the fishing boat. His greatest dilemma was whether to head home or to persist in his daft and obsessive quest to York. He was, however, certain of one thing, he would not stay in Newcastle! Rosina and his gaffer were both reasonable people and bothered him little as long as the work was done but he had decided that, definitely, this was no life for him. He awoke one morning to realise that he had been there over three weeks and thought it wise to leave, having decided that the dying message of this Brother Bernard must be delivered to the city of York. He hadn't got a bloody clue as to who he would deliver this to but, his determination had returned and there was, again, no stopping him. Farewells were polite and business-like now leaving Peter with an assurance that he could look after himself for the rest of the journey. Bizarrely, he was given a singular piece of coal to take with him, leaving him proud of this, gift, prize, or souvenir depending on your stance. Almost everyone he encountered advised him to either stay there or, to go home but he would have none of it. He had also picked up some tips of how to collect wild berries and fruits and, they said, unless he knew better, he should avoid all mushrooms.

Peter's confidence was ten times what it was when he had left Bamburgh and, although he had far to go, he now had an idea of the distance and how he would break that up into achievable lengths.

Come deep winter, Peter found himself sitting on a grassy knoll looking down at York. The walls, the Minster, the churches, the people! Although Newcastle had been large and busy, he had never witnessed anything like this. It was a glorious winter's day, birds were exchanging points of view all around him and he revelled in the sight of people entering and leaving the city. To him, it appeared as though it was actually alive, breathing, talking and moving and he, having temporarily forgotten his goal, just wanted to be part of it. Joyous, he ran down to Walmgate. Giddy, he ran up to the guards. Winded, he was stopped! One of them had punched his stomach as he had tried, naively, to run past. In an instant, his world collapsed as did his body.

'What's your game laddie?'

Somewhat recovered, Peter was relieved that, although this man had the strangest accent, he could easily understand him.

'I have journeyed from Bamburgh to deliver the most important message.'

'Let's see then.'

Peter held up his minuscule scrap and the guard snatched it from him. There appeared on it a few, faded, Latin letters on one side and a strange mark on the other. He showed it to another guard and, not surprisingly, they laughed and enjoyed a few minutes respite from their inane duties whilst they mocked the boy. He was smart enough to avoid argument and grateful to have the parchment returned but chose to rapidly retreat, giving the impression that he was about to leave town. He lay low for over an hour, observing all movement. It was probably his age that made him stand out, he deduced, plenty of traders were wandering in and out without question. To his left, he saw three men arguing as they pushed a hand-cart through the gate. It was stacked high with an untidy and rickety collection of basket-ware with little of its itinerary secure. They would stop to pick something up, place it hap-hazard fashion on top then stop again as another one fell. Then, they would curse one another for their blatant inefficiencies. He could see the guards moving aside as they just wanted these idiots out of the way. Peter ran down. At first, he hid behind one of the men and, although they knew he was there, they were still over-occupied with the poorly organised cart. He then offered to pick up objects for them and hold them in place but was buzzing about so much no one quite knew what he was up to. Satisfied that he wasn't stealing, and still totally engaged in verbally abusing one another, they just let him pitch in. And, it worked. By the time he had run around the cart a fifth time, they were inside and, as a very large oval-shaped basked fell clumsily to the floor yet again, he ran as fast as he could, heading toward the building in front of him that seemed to occupy both land and sky.

Peter simply could not understand how such a beautiful colossus could exist. If it wasn't for the fact that, apart from its dimensions, it resembled a church, he would have thought this a supernatural apparition. On this day the Minster was decorated in white. A giant cake. Snow was plentiful around York but, for some reason, here, it simply looked as though it had been placed artistically upon the buttresses, towers, the gargoyles and grotesques, perfect in its presentation. He found himself somewhere between St Michael le Belfry and the south transept and his attention moved momentarily to the strangest of characters who was packing a cart, seemingly as if he had just finished performing a show. What a place this is? He said to himself. A city full of wonders! He basked in this entirely unique atmosphere and bathed in its beauty then chose to lean on one of the St Michael's buttresses possibly to see if it was real. He rested awhile, happily observing the movements of its citizens and visitors and then thought he should start his quest to find an ally of Brother Bernard. He had previously thought no further than this point, realising that, until he had arrived, he presumed everywhere to be the same; that being that, like Bamburgh, there would be a character like Gilly who knew all (or at least pretended that they did). Where was Gilly amongst this lot? He mused. A plan. Must have a plan. Come on Peter! But, whichever way you looked at it, he simply did not have a plan. So, he wandered into the square and stopped people completely at random.

'I have with me a message written by Brother Bernard.'

In his head this was adequate. Say it to enough people and I'll find the right one, he told himself. In his innocence, he was both irritating the population of York and possibly putting them in danger. So innocent was he, that he was astonished at how rude people were until, for the first time, someone told him in very certain terms that it was dangerous to talk of monks. It didn't stop him, so on he went, repeating his line. It was late afternoon before he even took a break. However, Peter, possibly being the first Renaissance lad to discover that advertising actually worked, decided that, even if he had to ask every person in York, he would. After all, he had given up so much to get there.

By about four o clock, and feeling decidedly cold and hungry, he felt that perhaps he had made a mistake. Perhaps Gilly was wrong and this monk had never been to York or, perhaps there's another York? However, he told himself that he would persist until dusk and would then seek employment the following day. Relentlessly, but politely, he continued to intercept everyone he saw now accepting the incessant rebuffs.

'I seek anyone who knows a monk called Brother Bernard'.

And, as he did, he instantly readied himself to apologise before trudging away to find his next victim. However, he realised that, on this occasion, this particular woman was, surprisingly, still talking to him. His mouth open, he turned his head to concentrate. She was saying the same things he had heard dozens of times about being dangerous, not mentioning monks, nuns and so forth but this woman was taking time to elaborate.

'So how would you know this man?' She asked.

'He was brutally murdered by the King's guards and so I helped to bury him. God bless his soul.'

'And where would that be?' She persisted.

'On the mainland, across from the Holy Isle.'

She could tell from his accent and these few facts that, possibly, he was being truthful.

'Walk with me lad, but don't speak' she instructed.

'Do you know him?!' Peter said excitedly.

'Not a word until we're indoors. Just walk with me.'

Counting his blessings, Peter did just that. In moments this woman was met by a young man, seemingly around twenty years old, who Peter presumed was her son. The woman said a few words, telling her son that she would explain who this stranger was, once indoors. They walked around the liberty wall that surrounded the huge exterior of the Minster and then toward St. Peter's school. Peter looked on in awe as the prestigious schoolboys left for the day. Unbeknownst to Peter, this was one of the best, and oldest, schools in the country and would be available only to the sons of those families of some significant standing. One boy approached them, greeted his brother and mother, listened to his mother's instruction and then walked south in silence. Within ten minutes they had entered a fine and very warm residence and, by this time, Peter was visibly nervous. The lady sat him down, sent the eldest, Thomas, upstairs, leaving just the three of them in the living quarters. She offered him some bread and then, finally spoke.

'I want you to tell my youngest here what you said but, to be clear, I want no part of it. He's smart enough now to know what to do. I'll be out in the kitchen if you need me.'

The two boys stared at each other, Peter being, at fifteen, a good six years older than the schoolboy, Edward Fawkes. Peter reiterated, in some detail, his mantra about Bernard. Unlike the ever-cautious adult population of York, Edward reacted unhesitatingly.

'What?!' Said Edward leaping to his feet, so Peter happily repeated the story but, this time, he was feeling more comfortable about also revealing the slither of parchment. Edward was truly astonished. He needed no persuading, the strange accent alone convinced him that this young man had come from the north-east. He stood glaring at this small, filthy and practically insignificant scrap. There was no doubting the marks. This was made by Brother Bernard and was, undeniably, the same as had been acquired, discovered and won during the previous year.

'I may be able to help you' said Edward 'but, first, you must tell me all.'

Peter did just that, revelling in how engaged the boy was with his tale.

'It is hard to know what to say, Peter. What you have is part of a much a larger message, one dear Brother Bernard managed to get away by pigeon …'

'Yes, yes!' said Peter interrupting 'that was just before he died, I saw the pigeon spiralling skyward'.

'Well, I can assure you if its importance but I dare not say anymore until I seek counsel.'

Edward's mother fed Peter and her sons yet again and Edward asked if he could venture out. Following some precise boundaries set out by his mother, Edward thanked and embraced her.

Before he knew it, Peter was whisked away down alleyways, across the river, past a partly demolished priory and right up to the gate at Micklegate Bar where Peter opened up Godwin's workshop frightening the bloody life out of me. I heard him tell Peter to sleep in the workshop and that he would return as soon as the sun was up and, of course, before the owner's arrival. Peter happily agreed and Edward took note to keep me hidden and I, sensibly, kept quiet. Peter snored as much as Godwin would have and had me awake all night but, true to his word, Edward returned with the very first beam of sunlight.

'Come with me, friend.'

He then chose to pop me in my box and take me with him.

Peter found himself back in the vicinity of the Minister and close by another Barbican, hoping that he wouldn't have to leave the city, as it was so damned hard getting back in. They arrived at a washhouse, knocked on the, now familiar, rickety door and a woman's voice invited them in. Peter met Elspeth and Wynnfrith for the first time. To Edward, Elspeth in particular seemed to have softened somewhat but still insisted on moving the barrel that hid the trap door and then taking them down into the cellar before there was any further discussion. Peter was made to repeat everything he had previously said to Edward, but in further detail and, when he had finished, he watched Wynnfrith and Elspeth carefully digest the story. Of all the agents, only Eirik would be able to recognise this boy as he had told them that, from afar, he had witnessed the death of Bernard and the burial carried out by fishermen. However, Eirik was temporarily out of York. So, Elspeth deduced that, again, given Peter's strong Northumberland accent, his dramatic journey, his ownership of the scrap and his detailed description of both Bernard and his demise, he simply must be trusted. She leaned forward and softly said,

'Well to start young un, I have to give you some bad news. This scrap of yours is…was…of great importance and was a clue to a great and demonic plot carried out by powerful people…'

'I knew it!' He blurted excitedly 'in my heart I knew it, the old monk wouldn't have gone to all that trouble…well, given his life for nothing! Who were they? What happened?!'

'I must disappoint you' said Wynn 'I cannot tell. The King himself has sworn us to secrecy.'

'The King?! The King!! You've met the King?' Peter spluttered, now on his feet.

Edward intervened, doing his best to appease the teenager. It was, unquestionably, too much for him to digest.

'Well, yes' said Elspeth 'which means you were right and, you have my admiration for pursuing this danger.' She paused, clearly making a choice, 'give me a minute, I can show you something that will hopefully raise your spirits again.'

She looked over at Wynnfrith and then at Edward, then to me, clearly for approval. We knew her intent so then there were calm and restrained nods of affirmation. Peter was sure that he saw the mouse nod and almost comment but was too wrapped up in the drama. Elspeth disappeared for moments and then returned. All the other scraps that had been acquired in the previous year were now stuck together onto a board using gum and looking like a half-farthing jigsaw puzzle. She politely asked Peter for his piece, that noticeably had very little on it and put it in its place. Complete, it now read:

Satan's in law hath spawned a plan
most evil. By Eadfriths' hand and
God's command, the Word must be saved
Once on an isle to the north of Stratford on
the avon. In lucifer's hands doth now resides
and in the minster to be placed
Here the cataclysm is assured

In truth, the only part they hadn't seen before was the reference to Satan's in-law. Instantly Edward said that this was clearly referencing the King's familial relationship to Edward Seymour, Duke of Somerset, one of the designers of the Cataclysm of 1541. There was no doubt that Peter's piece belonged to the original manuscript. Peter gazed in awe at this remarkable intrigue. He looked up at Elspeth, mouth wide open and then down at the board again and continued to do this with everyone in the room. It soon became clear that he hadn't a bloody clue what he was looking at.

'He can't flaming read! What's up with you all!' I blurted.

'Ohhh. Ooo, oh my. Help!' Said Peter in a frenzy and reached for the ladder upwards.

Oh God, here we go again, I thought.

'You just can't help yourself, can you? You're like a rose-thorn stuck under my nail, can't you just find a field to play in or preferably a road!' ranted Elspeth.

I had slipped up again, upset Elspeth and, not for the first time. Peter's posture was most curious as he was now half out of his seat and half in it, ready to run but making all sorts of groaning and gasping sounds.'

'God's teeth lad. Just sit down! The mouse speaks! That's it. News to you, but really old-hat to everyone else here!'

I seemingly just simply couldn't control this and I would even go as far as saying that, since my arrival, in summer 1541, I had worsened. Elspeth was now out of her seat and furious.

'Peter, please accept my apologies, for this is something you will have to get used to and I should remind our unhygienic rodent friend here that he is meant to be kept secret and, therefore, should keep his stinky mouth shut!'

There comes a point when I know I've crossed the line and I could now actually feel myself coming down from the frenzy. I turned and lay down in the corner of my box. Poor Peter, he was horrified and wishing he was back in his fishing boat. Edward intervened as if nothing had happened and drew his stool closer to Peter's.

'It took some time to get these scraps of parchment together, but they told of a diabolical plan that would affect all people of England for all time. Thanks to Brother Bernard the plan was successfully thwarted but, we can tell you no more' said Edward quite assertively.

Peter was, understandably, downhearted. His dreams of adventure were as smoke up a chimney and he now wondered what would become of him. Then, it occurred to him that no one had mentioned the obverse side of the parchment. Was that secret too? He asked himself and prevaricated for many minutes, almost choosing to say nothing.

'What about the other side?' He eventually said.

No one had any clue as to what he meant, presuming initially that "other side" referred to their opponents.

'What do you mean?' Asked Wynnfrith.

'There are also marks on the other side.'

This was followed by a very awkward pause as each present, including myself, was absolutely sure that the parchment was completely blank on the back.

'See!' He said with glee and there, absolutely, on the reverse side were strange marks clearly made by human hand. This was passed around in silence for all to see except for the mouse who was still in disgrace. I pretended not to be interested but was squirming to know what was there.

'Astonishing' said Elspeth 'this clearly isn't written with lemon, like all our other messages, it must have been there all along'.

'No' said Peter 'it wasn't there at all, and then, it was!'

Ed giggled.

'What do you mean?'

'I had it for weeks and weeks, the side you saw first was exposed over a candle flame but nothing at all on the other. That was, until one day I stood on the cliffs and held it up and, there, as if by magic, these marks appeared!'

'Was it sunny?' I asked still receiving a cold reception. Peter looked at Edward and asked,

'Should I talk to it?'

'Yes, yes' laughed Edward 'he's harmless, just really rude!'

'It was a beautiful sunny day' started Peter.

'Algae!' I said proud of myself.

'Wha?' Came the chorus.

'It grows in water!' It was at times like this that even I wished I could disappear back to where I had come from.

'Seaweed?' Quizzed Peter, being the only one in the room who had ever seen it, let alone heard of it.

'Yes' I, reluctantly, said presuming this made it easier for everyone to understand.'

I looked at everyone present.

'These are things that grow in the sea. You can use algae to write with and, even on paper or parchment, when it is exposed to sunlight, it starts to grow revealing the marks. It is unlikely that it appeared instantly but would have developed over a day or so.'

'Well I never' gasped Wynn.

'You making this up?' Said Ed very suspiciously.

'No, I'm bloody not! You want my counsel or not?!'

'Makes sense' added Peter. Who'd have thought it?'

'You know what this means?' I said knowing full well they didn't. I waited. And waited.

'We now have all the parts of the puzzle!' Said Edward proud of himself.

'No, no' I was now, at least, trying to be polite 'all the other scraps of parchment will have something written on the obverse side too.'

Their reaction to this, very clever, and, let's be frank, astonishing revelation was to stare at the board. Nothing. Literally, they did nothing. No wonder I'm so bloody impatient I told myself.

'Ladies, boil some water.'

Thankfully they obeyed. As I had been the one to teach them how to make a water-based gum in order to stick the pieces to the board, I knew that they could be removed easily with a little steam. Half an hour later, we all sat staring at blank parchment.

'It'll need some sun then' offered Peter.

'That it will, my bright young fisherman!'

'But it's freezing outside' said Wynn.

'Although it is a winter's day, Wynnfrith, there's still some warmth to the sun but, we cannot do is this in plain sight'.

'Holy Trinity church garden!' Said Edward.

'Absolutely!' I concurred and I was grateful that Edward was part of this. In just a year he had grown in many ways and could be trusted with anything. I was also counting our blessings that he was not in school the following day, he would be the ideal agent to send word to Father Matthew of our discovery and our plan.

So, the day after, at midday, we found ourselves in the walled garden of Holy Trinity church where we had met so many times before. Bede was there. Yes, Bede was still alive and, though it would be fair to say that his mental capacity had improved little, he had forged relationships with all Royal Secret Agents of the Word and enjoyed the affection poured upon him by all. It was on this very issue that Father Matthew led.

'Friends, I must remind you that we are instructed by King Henry himself not to congregate without his direction and, that such intrigue as you bring forth today, could put us all in danger.'

'Bollocks! Let's just get on with it!' I said.

'Is there a special hell for rodents Father?' asked Elspeth incisively.

He smiled acknowledging both her frustration and my rudeness.

'I get your drift Micklegate Mouse' he said and immediately carried out a small, wobbly table. The very one that had, so recently, reminded Mayor Robert of his obligations to his allies and to God himself.

Elspeth carefully turned the pieces so that they were arranged as before but revealing the other side. And there it was left for the whole afternoon. During that time we discussed the, presumed, attempt on Silas's life explaining in full what had happened on the road from Knapton that very week. It was interesting that Peter instantly thought the perpetrator to be a Scot. If nothing else, it gave us an idea of the brewing Scottish and English tensions in the far north, with ourselves acknowledging King Henry's displeasure that King James had not met him in York the previous year. Surprisingly, Peter was encouraged by the bad news, after all, he had travelled far for adventure. I personally told him that we would have to think very carefully before including him in any plans but also assuring him that he would neither be completely left out or sent back to Bamburgh.

Shortly before we lost the light completely, we returned to see what had happened. The rough transport over hundreds of miles, ill weather, constant man-handling and the application of gum had slightly damaged the algae itself but, as expected, there was some visible information that now covered the entire document. Edward held me in his hands so I could see the entirety of it as others looked on disappointed and struggling to make sense of it. Hairs stood up along my spine as I was the only one for whom it had any meaning. I refused to discuss it further and begged Edward to take me home and suggested Peter accompany us. Edward, seemingly wiser by the day said nought as we meandered home along Micklegate leaving everyone else dejected, confused and concerned.

6: THE KIDNAP

As we approached the workshop along Micklegate Bar, I was surprisingly comforted by the nearing farts, coughs and belches that told me, and half the population of York, that Godwin was present. His mood had lifted a little since the death of his little girl, Lizzy, but he would never be the same. Despite my affectionate jibes, Godwin was clearly worse for wear in terms of his general health and had developed a noticeable stoop due, not least, I was sure, to the fact that he worked such long hours. Out of earshot, I asked Edward why he was so poor and not a member of one of the prestigious and well-known York guilds. Edward whispered,

'Very sensitive subject that Mouse. Won't talk about it. Rumour has it that there was an incident years ago and he was expelled from the guild. He never complains about it, just carries on working hard. Shame though, he's probably the best carpenter in this part of Yorkshire.'

I was intrigued. I had found Godwin to be a man of unparalleled integrity and one that was ordinarily consumed only by his work and his family. What on earth could have happened to see him ostracised in such a way? I thought. Godwin turned his head and offered a friendly grunt as Edward whistled and then smiled at his boss. I say, boss, Edward only called in now because of his affection for old Godwin and, even though he didn't show it much, the carpenter was very glad of his company. The mouse, however, he could do without.

I then had one of those moments. Déjà vu I suppose. The day I arrived, meeting Ed and Godwin for the first time. How they hurriedly fitted out my workshop. It seemed so long ago. So much had happened, so many lives lost.

'What's up with him?!' Grunted Godwin.

He was staring at me thinking that my temporary trance was a bout of catalepsy.

'Nothing gaffer, he's just a bit gormless sometimes.'

Seemingly that adage about earning respect was true after all. Gormless? I chose to say nothing.

'Never known the little bugger to be so quiet, perhaps his time has come.' Added Godwin.

'I am here, you know!'

They both laughed and we could hear Peter chuckle outside. It seemed that, now, everyone knew how to push my buttons. Served me right, I suppose. Edward invited Peter in and introduced him, as a friend, to Godwin.

'Edward, I thank you for bringing me here but I feel compelled to speak further on this morning's discoveries. Please return me to the church and gather all the agents you can while I wait with Father Matthew' I said.

I saw on Peter's face the same excited expression that was so evident on young Edward's face when he encountered drama. Yes, I thought to myself, young people think they are invincible. Perhaps it is for the best.

'Back so soon Micklegate Mouse?' Said Father Matthew not in the least surprised as we arrived at the church. I told him that I felt it essential to gather as many agents as we could and, in response, he, yet again, reminded me of our contract with the King. In return, I assured him of the value of our meeting. We introduced Peter and went to some lengths to confirm that Father Matthew could be trusted.

'Father, I have every intention of supporting our King in his hour of need but, I believe we are in danger and believe it essential that we meet.'

'Well, I suppose' he said calmly 'it is highly unlikely anyone will know of our meetings but, I do urge caution, my friend.'

'Understood.'

Within half an hour, Elspeth and Wynnfrith were there and, soon after that, Robert Hall, the Mayor, made his grandiose entrance. We waited in silence knowing that the next appearance would be anything but grandiose.

Bang! The church door flew open, leaving three of Father Matthew's finest candle holders flying across the nave. In an attempt to catch one, Silas found himself prostrate in the centre of the aisle.

'Would you like a blessing my son?' asked Father Matthew as Wynnfrith stifled her laughter.

Silas did next what he had always done and that was to carry on as if nothing had happened, dusting off his hose and attempting the most fashionable type of bow where one leg was placed in front of the other. This turned out to be another mistake as every fibre of his being started to tremble. Wynnfrith was already out of her seat and had hold of his hand. This had the dual result of making him extremely happy and also stabilising him. As they all sat, Brother Bede hobbled out to join them. Peter was introduced yet again and the complete story was told of the last piece of parchment.

'My good friends I thank you for meeting at such short notice. I believe we are in danger but, as yet, I know not why.'

'Bloody obvious iron balls!' Blustered Robert 'it's retribution for thwarting the damn Cataclysm!'

'I think it's fair to assume just that' I said 'but, curiously, I can't help thinking that there's more. There's definitely something in the air that has, so far, evaded us all.'

'They will catch up with us one by one until the debt is settled!' Contributed Silas, nervously.

'But who?!' Asked Elspeth 'is it really credible that, having kept their heads, Cranmer, Wriothesley and Somerset would be bothered about the likes of us?'

She had a point. Cranmer would, on this very day, be finalising plans to have Catherine Howard and Lady Rochford arrested, his indispensability becoming greater by the day. Somerset would be consumed by the numerous potential conflicts of the day, not least the tension brewing between the English and the Scots. I pondered on this but could find no other solution for the time being.

'What's all this about another message?!' Asked Robert impatiently, clearly not having listened to my introduction.

I looked at everyone. My allies. My friends. To all outward appearances, a bunch of hopeless misfits but, even in the eyes of the King, they were people of the greatest integrity and had proven themselves to be stoic and dependable in the worst of situations.

'Dear Agents. It pains me to tell you that I cannot decipher the marks on the back of Brother Bernard's document. However, I have seen them, or certainly something similar, before.'

Elspeth, in particular, looked upon me with suspicion. Clearly, she thought that I had been keeping secrets so I instantly sought to reassure her.

'You may remember that, before my return from Hampton Court, I was almost burned alive by Cranmer himself. Whilst I was in his study I came across the most puzzling and cryptic diagram and took pains to remember what I saw but, sadly, I have no clue as to what those marks meant. There is no doubt, that what you see on Bernard's parchment, is of the same design!'

I could hear them gasp which was surprising as I hadn't really told them much, they just presumed that some drama and intrigue would surely exist behind this drawing.

'Until we know more, it is essential that we proceed with the greatest care and secrecy.'

'It is possible…' started Silas only to be interrupted by the loudest of bangs on the church door. I looked around, everyone, with the exception of Elspeth was panicking. The mere idea of threat had them dispensing with that stoicism I was currently bestowing upon them.

Thud! Thud! Thud! I think it was possibly the way it was done, authoritatively and sounding like the metal end of a staff, that was so alarming. Silas grabbed Wynn by the hand and disappeared into the room where the newly formed vestry team met, not realising that once inside they would be completely in the dark. I told Peter not to speak at all, as his accent would arouse suspicion. Travelling pilgrims and traders were always welcome in York as long as they kept moving, but settlers with strange accents were often met with chronic distrust. Bede had disappeared and Robert decided to confront this disturbing spectre alone. However, before he got to the door, it had already opened and in walked the sheriff, John Dobson.

'What is with you lot? Too much trouble to answer the bloody door?! What on earth you up to this time anyway?!' said the sheriff.

'Haha come in. Come in my friend!' Said Robert much relieved. John Dobson looked around and shook his head.

'You're worse than constipation, you are. Wherever there's bloody trouble there's also at least one of you! And what's with that damned mouse! God's teeth! Is he wearing a leather apron?!'

Thankfully, most of this bluster was rhetorical and, whilst he was grumbling, Elspeth had offered him a seat.

'I'll come to the point. A proper mess this murder is. Due to the circumstances of the death of Sir Anthony Bask, I can't see how we'll get the culprit. It won't do!' He looked over to me again and squinted as if he couldn't believe what he was seeing 'no, it just won't do, you have a murder, you hang someone. Proper mess it is. Sure your errand boy didn't do him in Robert?' a whining sound came from the vestry.

'Oh, that's just one of my sick parishioners that I care for. I...err...have to do everything now the monasteries have gone.' Said Father Matthew.

The sheriff looked to Robert for a reply to his question.

'Oh come on John' he said passionately 'you must know that he's harmless. We should be proud and grateful that he tried to save Lord Bask.'

'Mmm. All well and good but Bask has a widow who doesn't know she's a widow!'

'That's awful' said Elspeth 'is there anything we can do?'

'Should we organise a funeral, sheriff? It would be modest but you would be assured that he had been taken care off.' Said Father Matthew.

'Oh no. That wouldn't do. That wouldn't do at all. He has to be taken back.'

'Where?' Said Father Matthew.

'Well to Oxford of course. All I knows about Bask is that he's up to his cap's feather in debt and, he lives in Oxford. That's it.'

'That's some undertaking...' deduced Robert and, almost before he had finished his sentence, the sheriff was at the door and ready to leave.

'Best be getting on with it, mind, he's going off already. He's here, on a cart outside' and then, John Dobson promptly exited.

The impact of this on everyone was significant and, for once, all was quiet. That was until some very intimate noises could be heard coming from the vestry. Elspeth cautiously

opened the vestry door. Whilst he was in the dark, Silas had
sought to embrace Wynnfrith and this embrace gave way to
their very first kiss. However well-intentioned this was, Silas
had been unaware that, during the panic as the sheriff
arrived, Bede had crept into the vestry as well. It was only
when Silas looked down and saw Wynn sitting in a dark
corner on a stool, that he thought it wise to look up again,
only to find that his passion had been shared, solely, with
Brother Bede and, at this point, they were still in a loving
embrace. Everyone turned first to Wynnfrith who was
calmly shaking her head. And then, to Brother Bede who
just looked completely bewildered. The silence soon gave
way to raucous laughter and this had Bede running toward
his room.

'Didn't it occur to you that Wynn can't stand up for long
periods?!' Spluttered Elspeth.

'I....err...I thought we were the only two in there!'

No matter how well-intentioned, anything Silas said
now, it would definitely be stamped permanently on
everyone's memories and used against him, regularly. How I
loved to see everyone laugh and I counted my blessings for
this company and the relationships we had built. Peter was
loving this. He had suffered many miserable months and to
be in good company, and sharing such mirth, was a gift
indeed.

'Oh God! Bede! What must he think!' Said Silas and ran
after him.

'I've got a spare ring if you wish to take it with you'
added Father Matthew and, no matter how much teasing
Silas suffered, his retort was always so much funnier.

'Should I take a ring? Will it make matters better?' And
then, that look on his face when people laughed, Silas
simply not understanding any of it, it was priceless. He soon
returned, informing us that Bede seemed none the worse or
wiser for his encounter. It was then that Wynnfrith first
spoke.

'How on earth could you have thought that to be me?' She asked calmly and innocently. People now stifled their laughter because no matter how serious this may have seemed to Wynn, it was, unquestionably, still very amusing.

'It was dark my dove.' The stifling ceased. This was his defence? Loud guffaws instantly seemed more appropriate.

'It was dark! Is that it?! He has a bloody beard for God's sake!'

Poor Wynnfrith, she was making everyone's day and Silas was now, completely, crumbling. So, what did she do? She stood, hugged him and said,

'It's forgotten about, I wouldn't have you any other way' and she turned to everyone else 'let's just hope that if we ever do kiss, I can easily measure up to Bede!'

He blushed and started rambling. Robert, bless him, put his arm around Silas to reassure and calm him and, at last, Silas laughed too.

'You're never going to let me forget this are you?'

'Not at all' came the chorus.

When everyone stilled themselves they realised, remarkably, that William Fawkes had stealthily entered and was standing there, waiting. No one had any idea how long he had been there. Peter took care to remain discreet.

'Edward get home please' He said, calmly, to his son and Edward dutifully obeyed and moved toward me.

'Leave the mouse here' and, again, he did as he was told.

'Robert, please forgive my intrusion. Your dear wife sought my counsel as she did not know where you were.' Robert was embarrassed.

His wife certainly knew he that was involved in some bizarre intrigue and also, that most days, he would call in on the notorious Mrs Grindem. Fortunately, William Fawkes knew of the regular meeting place of the Agents and offered to "interrupt the Mayor's business in order to pass on her message." As it turned out, William Fawkes had done them a great service, a letter had been delivered to

Barley Hall, but, to put it in Mrs Hall's words, it had a most unusual seal on it. I instantly recognised my own seal, that of the Agents of the Word.

'William, I am so grateful as I suspect this to be of great importance' said Robert. No one else spoke. Wynnfrith, looking on silently, still had William Fawkes perched on a proverbial pedestal as he had, along with Robert, saved her from a serious attack whilst she was still a teenager. Silas also had fond memories of when he had first met the man as a child but that would always be tinged by the presence of Fawkes at his mother's death. Taking all things into account, and the support he had given during the undoing of the Cataclysm, he was, unquestionably, in trusted company but his concerns about Edward's involvement were understandable. No more was said. He had handed over the letter and he left.

Robert hurriedly broke the seal.

'It's from Thomas Farrier!' Father Matthew tried to conceal his delight at the arrival of this correspondence. Robert became silent for a few moments whilst he read it.

'Serous news my friends. Richard Shakespeare's son, John, has been kidnapped. They know not where he is. He is asking for support.' He thought for a few moments 'Silas, tomorrow I want you to make for Nottingham where you will reconnoitre with Eirik and then to Oxford with the body and both of you are to untangle this devilment in Stratford upon Avon.'

'What? You want me riding with Bask through Nottingham? I'll just get arrested!'

Silas, this time had the support of everyone, with Robert himself realising the folly of this plan.

'Yes. Yes. I will get word to Eirik to meet you south of Nottingham. You will go with Bayard. The body will be concealed on his cart and you will also carry a letter from the sheriff.'

'Oh please give Eirik our love'. Said Wynnfrith and, although Silas himself was excited to meet up with his fellow agent, the gnawing issue of Eirik's birth-mark and his claim to be the brother of the girls just wouldn't go away. He's been the best of our Agents, Silas told himself and tried not to think of this ever-present conundrum.

'I will and we'll both be back safely in weeks' He then turned to Father Matthew 'and, who knows, Thomas Farrier may fancy a journey north again?' Clearly, Silas knew and, although it was only a nod, Father Matthew was sure to communicate his gratitude.

Silas picked up my box, walked over to Peter and said,

'You two can stay at my place whilst I'm gone. It's very modest but at least you'll have somewhere to shelter and rest.'

What he didn't say was that he had never made this offer to any other person before which made this a unique kindness. Peter thanked him,

'Oh good Sir, I will take employment and pay you on return. Your goodwill makes my heart glow.'

Silas's heart, now slowing somewhat after the trauma of instigating a new relationship with Brother Bede, was also, surely, glowing. He was truly a very kind and loving person and, it was in this moment that I realised I would be devastated if any harm came to him. I couldn't imagine a world without Silas and this wasn't even my world. He told Peter that he would not have to pay. After all, it would cost him nothing. Following farewells, Silas took us along the most puzzling route through the snickleways that led us into All Saints Pavement churchyard. Having lived there for most of his life, he had fashioned the narrowest path, that was now navigable, to his abode. Even so, it was remarkably well hidden by an immense overgrowth of ivy. Silas had, what could be considered by some, a quite pretty house except, the house couldn't be seen. He turned his head and said,

'I must apologise, this is very humble. So very humble. You must take it as you find it my friends.'

I wanted to reassure him, but this was his moment so, quietly, we followed. Hardly visible was a rusty iron ring-handle and, as he grabbed it an ivy-covered door opened. This was, indeed, a very small space but, to the left, there was clearly an even smaller door and above it a window. When I say window, it was just a small opening in the wall but had a pelmet over it, on the outside that would have helped to keep the rain and snow from entering. There was one chair and one table that didn't match and, upon the table was a candle holder with a single candle. I could clearly see where he would make a fire and, above, a small man-made flu for the smoke. His possessions were few but we hardly had time to look as he took us both immediately to the other door. He held it slightly ajar with a beaming smile and we heard a very loud "neigh!" It was Annie! And, the space he had cleared for her to graze was bigger than his own domicile. He tended to Annie's needs first and then pointed to his bed that, again, had clearly been built by Silas. We worked out that, to get to the road, Annie would have to walk first through the cottage and then navigate the same path we had tip-toed along. How on earth no one had found this place was a small miracle.

'You'll have to sleep over there on the floor tonight, young Peter, but, from tomorrow, you can have my bed here!'

Almost instantly I felt fearful. This was said as if he would never return and, then, it occurred to me that Silas must have felt like this every time he was given a mission. Then, I had the chance to look around properly as Peter had gently placed my box on the table. My heart broke. Before me, I saw two decades of repairs, many bodged. Replacement wattle and daub. Pieces of timbers at all angles that kept the wooden structure together and, there, on one of the whitewashed panels I saw markings. Starting at the bottom, I could see the young Silas's naïve drawings and they were of him and his mother. No more than stick-figures, in them he was a Knight defending his mother from her attacker and, although they only became slightly more elaborate, the same theme was repeated all the way up the panel. A hidden Bayeux tapestry of life as it should have been for Silas and Mary. His father was nowhere to be seen on this storyboard. He saw me looking and darted in front of it. No, I was mistaken, not that panel, the one next to it but it was too late, I had seen his drawings of hearts and angels surrounding his interpretation of Wynnfrith.

God bless him.

'Silas. Please allow me to say what I am thinking. Your love For Wynnfrith, and hers for you, is the best news. It is the most singular joyful thing that has happened since I arrived. Please don't hide it.'

He slid away and leaned over me.

'Oh Micklegate, how rich I am. I could fight dragons with Wynn in my heart!'

'And Bede?' I added. Peter thought this was very funny. Silas put his hands to his head and said,

'Going to be a long time isn't it?' I just nodded.

Not surprisingly, Silas spent the next hour pampering us with humble offerings and I would say that, for all three of us, we then enjoyed the best sleep that we had had in some time.

7: THE EMBALMING

Although almost everyone, especially Silas, wished to completely ignore the cadaver that was previously Anthony Bask, it had to be dealt with. It had been left on a makeshift barrow outside Holy Trinity church but, graciously, Robert and Father Matthew wheeled the body into a secluded area of the interior with the solemn understanding that Silas would have to take charge the following day. The corpse was as messy as when Bask had been pronounced dead but was, thankfully, almost frozen solid and he now appeared as a prostrate tin soldier and, from that moment on, there would be no moving any part of him. He was solid in every respect.

However, Robert was conscious of the onerous task that he had deviously bestowed on Silas and thought to make it as easy as possible. He paid his own servants to have the body delivered to York's finest barber-surgeon and sent word to Silas to attend the following morning.

So, the following day, Silas awoke to a knock on the door which, in itself, may seem like an everyday event but, no one ever went there, ever. This certainly was a shock and stirred all three of us. He drew back the door and there he was. Moonlight. If you wanted any creepy task carried out, apparently you asked Moonlight. Apart from Robert, no one knew who or what he was but, there he stood, motionless and clean as if he had dressed at the door. He said nothing and then handed Silas a note, Silas looked at it and, when he looked up again, Moonlight was gone. I asked him to bring it over to me, as I was the only one there that could read well. The note instructed him to report to the barber-surgeon, who was located close to Walmgate Bar, where Bayard would later meet him.

'Oh Lord! I couldn't think of anything worse. I so hate looking upon a dead body. I have, always, executed all that the Mayor has asked of me but this! Oh, how I wish I didn't have to do it.' Silas was visibly shaken.

This was clearly his worst nightmare and, no doubt was partly rooted in his mother's demise.

'Be calm my friend' I said 'Mayor Robert is trying to help. He is paying a small fortune to have him embalmed so that his body will be preserved perfectly on your journey. If he's covered properly on Bayard's cart, you won't know he's there.'

'As long as I don't have to go into the barber surgeon's place.'

There was a pause, and, to be clear, I wouldn't have hurt Silas any further even if I had been offered the whole world, but I felt duty-bound to read all of the note.

'Silas must stay on-site to ensure that the work is carried out as commissioned' I read.

As I looked up, I saw Peter consoling him. He told him the story of how he had seen Brother Bernard die and how he, and his family, had cared for his body, buried him and gave him a Christian funeral. Peter was so convincing that Silas was persuaded almost instantly that he was doing the right thing for Sir Anthony. Nevertheless, he was sickened and terrified. Silas fed Annie, packed a few, meagre possessions, walked Annie in through one tight entrance and squeezed her out the other. He then wished us a very fond farewell.

He followed the instructions along Petergate and toward Walmgate Bar. He saw the empty barrow outside and decided he would just wait and pretend that the barber-surgeon never turned up. Or, perhaps I could tell Robert I was lost, he thought.

The door was, unexpectedly, thrown open and a man emerged wearing a neck-to-toe leather apron that was covered with designer hues of body parts and fluids. Silas stared at the apron. He stared and stared until he felt sick.

'Well, come on. Get in here lad, the Mayor's paying good money so you'd better observe!'

Silas, now completely divest of any ideas that would get him out of this predicament and with his eyes closed, followed him in. This overzealous butcher didn't give a name but the premises alone told Silas that this man was the real deal. And, he was scary. He had bushy hair that was several shades of brown, red, grey and black or, it could just have been full of bodily shite from his clients, presumed Silas. He spoke like a wild man, enthusing about every aspect of his art. He manically gesticulated as he gave Silas a tour of his tools of the trade and the bizarre premises. Silas lasted for almost five minutes before he asked for a seat and, it was at this point that Silas found a stool and, at the same time, the surgeon whipped the sackcloth off Bask. Silas's eyes came back up from his feet to encounter Bask's current disposition. Now exposed, he was a thawing, pungent and incredibly stiff, dirty corpse. His face was contorted, with his eyes looking upward as if to reference his head wound and a grimace that looked as though he was pleased to see Silas again. His tongue was entirely doing a thing of its own.

'For God's sake, can't you at least close his eyes?!'

'What for?' asked Viscera, for that was the, most unpleasant, nickname given to him by, surprisingly, those who respected him most.

'He can't see' he added calmly, almost as if Silas didn't know.

'I know he can't bloody see!' Added Silas almost at breaking point 'just close his damn eyes'.

'Can't…and stop making such a fuss lad. He'll not hurt you.'

The oddest thing about this man's attitude was that he was joyful. His everyday work, on people that were either on one side of death or the other, was a delight and this, of course, meant that he struggled to understand why others didn't feel the same.

'I'll do his eyes when we've washed him.' Said. Viscera.

'Washed him.! We?!! What do you mean?!'

'You don't expect me to do it all on my own, do you? You are the Mayor's man?'

'Yes yes!' Said Silas 'But I do errands…missions. Not this!'

'Haha! Just jesting lad, I'll get started. You just sit there and watch.'

Watch? He thought. I'd much rather be in battle alongside Eirik and Thomas Farrier.

So, Silas curiously watched with half an eye open but another eye and a half on the door. The door, the door. That beautiful exit beyond which sanity reigned. Throughout, he calculated how long it would take him to bolt to, and beyond, that door. He was now facing almost two hours of terrifying butchery tempered by care and caution.

Viscera started by gently washing the body in warm water whilst constantly stoking a growling fire in the corner which, Silas thought, was the only redeeming feature of this hell-hole. Viscera hummed as he washed away the crusty, slowly melting blood and brain matter and then the congealed blood which seemed to have visited every part of Sir Anthony Bask's torso. He then began to undress him, the outer layers crunching and crackling as they separated from the layers of underclothing, dried sweat and blood beneath. His privy regions, in particular, gave forth an almighty stink as the body had been completely unattended since his final bowel purge, which was, hopefully, post-death. As the final under layer of clothing was ripped away, parts of his flesh came with it and, somewhere around this time, the surgeon started shouting out random words and instructions. It had now become a bizarre ritual and the visitor had had enough so, again, asked to leave but it was as nothing had been said.

'Blade!' He shouted and grabbed the first, small but sharp razor and, as Silas thought to look away, Viscera decided to give Bask a shave and a haircut. After all, this was what Viscera would have done most of the time. Silas began to thank God, presuming that, once cleaned up he would, at last, be put in a box and hidden under something, anything, and, to him, it didn't matter what.

'Knife!' Viscera declared and did a short, but merry dance.

He nodded toward the whereabouts of the knife, and then again until Silas took the hint. Unfortunately, he was glued, if he couldn't get through that door the best option was staying on the chair and looking down.

'Knife!' he repeated so Silas jumped up, stretched his arm out to grab the handle of this curious instrument that combined both a straight and jagged blade. What on earth does he need a knife for? thought Silas as he handed it to Viscera, arm outstretched, without looking at him.

'Sit!'

Silas happily complied, relaxed and then half-stood again as he witnessed this maniac rip Bask's torso in two from neck to waist. This vision, added to the unbearable stench, left Silas wobbling.

'Bucket!'

And Silas, having previously wondered why there was a bucket both on his right and on his left, chose one and emptied his own guts into it. As the room started to spin, his last vision was of the barber-surgeon wielding an instrument that had a short wooden handle and a sharp metal scoop on the end of it. This was zealously plunged into Sir Anthony's innards and Viscera began to disembowel him. Thud! Silas hit the deck and assumed a position incredibly similar to that of the body, and Viscera laughed manically. Silas's tongue hung out, just like that of Bask and his single, but long lock of ginger hair had curled around his crown, much like Sir Anthony's head wound. Apart from the fact that Silas was still intact, the two lay alongside each other, one on the floor and one on the bench, as twins.

Viscera completely removed all of his client's organs, whistling as he completed the task. He continued to randomly shout out orders but, seemingly, these were just for his own amusement. Forty minutes later, Bask was practically an empty vessel, his organs now residing close by in a lead-lined barrel. Viscera then looked at the well in the back of the body. Bask's entire blood supply had rested in one place just above his spine but now looking like red-currant jam. This, along with all other waste, including the encrusted clothing, was thrown onto the fire. Now the real embalming could be carried out. Rose petal water was used liberally to scent the body. Myrrh, musk and a variety of balms were added everywhere. Viscera left these to soak in and so turned to the eyes. A few stitches there, a few more on the lips and Bask was already looking in better nick than Silas. It was hard to reconcile the contrast between the rough handling of the innards and the gentle touch applied to the dressing, scenting and embalming of the corpse but the procedure, from this point forward, was somewhat artistic. Viscera massaged his sweet-smelling applications throughout the body and then, most bizarrely, picked up a round, but weighty, package (clearly not previously part of Sir Anthony's body) that was tied up with string and then covered it with cerecloth (a waxed fabric) and, very carefully, placed it inside the cavity where Bask's organs had earlier resided. He then carefully sewed up the chasm. Next, Viscera wrapped the whole body in cerecloth until Bask was starting to look like a mummy. He stood over his masterpiece, looked at the still unconscious Silas and smiled. The door was opened and he wheeled in a box on a wooden bier, dragged the corpse across, nailed on the lid and wheeled it out again.

The barber-surgeon had completely cleaned his workspace when Silas finally sat up.

'Oh oh…err! Is it over?!...where is?..'

'Haha! All done laddie. Very pleased. Very pleased indeed. Some of my best work.'

Silas felt extremely unwell and seemed to hurt everywhere, but made an effort to stand and brush off some remaining parts of his one-time travelling companion. As they went outdoors, Silas observed the coffin and bier and was taken aback by the overwhelming, sweet smells.

'Now listen lad, he'll only stay this fresh for a week so you should make haste. See that over there?' He pointed to the barrel. 'That's lead-lined and will last forever.'

'Oh very good!' Said Silas with interest, paused and then added 'what is it?'

'All his innards.'

'What? oh no! No. What…what on earth are his innards doing in there…why aren't they in him?!'

'If you drop again lad, I'm leaving you here. My job's done. But, to answer your question, I can't preserve him with that lot in there. However, what I suggest is this. They can be buried here. There'll be a proper Mass for them. Common practice it is, but you must tell his Missus that they've been consecrated. Very important that!'

Silas had been teased so many times in his life that he just stared at this crazy man. Then at the box, then the barrel. No, he can't have made it up, he told himself. The horrors he had learned this day.

'Yes. Yes keep…that…them…him, here in York!! I'll make sure the Mayor and Lady Bask know!'

'Very well' Viscera replied and he pointed at the coffin again 'but he won't last forever, cost too much to lead him completely as well. Mayor has already paid a small fortune for this.'

Thankfully, for a few moments, Silas's attention turned to Mayor Robert. His employer continued to surprise him with his Christian generosity. He was one of the wealthiest merchants in York but, all the same, this was quite magnanimous. It was at this juncture that Silas could hear the familiar sounds of a horse with cart. It was Bayard! Silas told himself, there and then, that there could be no more beautiful sight in the world, apart from Wynnfrith herself, than Bayard and his cart.

'Ho!' Shouted Bayard as he saw his highly stressed fellow Agent before him.

'Bayard! My good man. Oh, thank God! Thank God!'

Although he wouldn't be rid of Bask for some while, Silas would never have to look upon him again and, today, Bayard appeared as a cherub birthed from heaven. Now there's a sentence I never thought I would write. Bayard simply chuckled as Silas, stinking, chose to embrace him.

'Change of clothes here my Lord! Sent from the Mayor himself.'

Silas looked at Bayard, then at Annie, then the horse and cart with its misspelt "Bayad entainer to Kings!" written on the side. He then turned to look at the hell-hole he had been trapped in that morning and decided he would never visit that part of the city again. Within no time, he had wiped himself down, changed and hitched Annie to the cart. Two horses would get them there that much faster. As

Bayard and Viscera had already put the box on the covered cart, they now made their way out of Walmgate Bar and then turned south to head for Oxford.

At first, there was silence but Silas, eventually, decided to share his ordeal with Bayard. Bayard reminded him that the procedure had been necessary and that it made sense that Viscera had been observed, Robert having spent so much.

After that, little was said as they ventured into open countryside until Bayard, seemingly buoyant, decided to break the silence.

'Fine set of fellows the Agents. Eh?'

'Oh yes indeed' said Silas 'the finest of all.'

'Where would we be now without those brave monks?' Continued Bayard.

'Why! Everything would have changed. A disaster!'

'That Brother Bede would make someone a fine husband if he hadn't been a monk' Said Bayard.

As they were both in such an agreeable mood, Silas opened his mouth to, yet again, affirm but then screwed up his face as he quizzed why Bayard would ask such a thing. Eventually, he turned to Bayard who was chuckling and winking at him.

'Oh God, I'm never going to live this down! Does everyone know?!'

Bayard's laughter, having been temporarily oppressed, burst forth. All, then, went quiet. At least for a while.

'Can't have been so bad at the barber-surgeons?'

'Bad?!...'

Silas vented his disgust at the ordeal he had been subjected to.

'But I hear people are dying to get in there.' Silas looked at him as if to say "really?"

'In a good place though, dead centre of the city…' As Bayard's awful jokes and puns continued, Silas resigned himself to what was to come. Is there no peace? He thought.

It then seemed as though York City stood still as the wobbly carriage slowly disappeared below the horizon where the watery winter sun was setting and Bayard's voice, although distant, could still be heard,

'Good man though is that Viscera. He'll take on anybody apparently…'

8: THE UNDERCROFT

February came and the snows continued. Wynnfrith and Elspeth huddled in the doorway of their modest wash house ready to set forth to the Merchant's Hall along Fossgate. Elspeth tempered her sister's haste and pulled her closer to her and the door-post. They both looked along the walls, at the incongruous buildings that drew their eyes toward the ever-present and dominant Minster. For a moment, they chose to admire what God had bestowed on them. In relative terms, the sisters were quite poor but were blessed, in that, Robert would never see them without decent shelter, clothing or food. They were sufficiently swaddled this day as they had drawn around their woollen dresses many other layers in addition to scarves, gloves and an outer gown. Their pretty faces were like children's as they peeped out from their wraps to watch the snowflakes slowly dance upwards and downwards, eventually settling on their random destinations. The sun was only just rising in the east and those welcome, warm, colours complemented the fires that could be seen through the nearby dwelling's windows and the candles being lit in the Minster and it's many offspring churches. Outside, blues and lilacs reflected off the virgin snow. Work? There wasn't any. If the general population was loathe to have their clothes and sheets washed in summer, there was no way anything was coming off in this weather. Their role as washer-women was, for the greater part, a sham. They were, temporarily at least, undercover agents and the pretence was adequate but now that it was cold, it was convenient, to say the least, that they enjoyed an alternative occupation.

'How I love the warmth' said Wynnfrith 'but I wouldn't give away this for anything. Surely this is the most beautiful city in the world?'

'It is something to behold isn't it sister?'

They were both lucky enough to possess pantofles, which were overshoes, or to be more precise, were designed to lift the foot higher than mud, other unpleasant detritus and, on this occasion, snow. They had bandaged these on with leather straps and Elspeth suggested that they enjoy a slow walk to absorb this wintery delight.

The Merchant's Hall was one of York's grandest buildings and was where merchants and guilds met. However, it had from time to time, developed many purposes and it was one of these alternative uses for which the two sisters were, this day, making it their only destination.

They walked as one which meant that they both, naturally, adopted Wynnfrith's wobbly steps as they had done since childhood. They enjoyed the morning and happily chatted.

'You don't say much about Silas' prompted Elspeth after which there was a pause.

A pause so significant that Elspeth eventually peered out of her hood to see what was going on in Wynn's head.

'Oh, I don't know!' Said Wynnfrith exasperated, 'I feel such a fool!'

'Why a fool?' Asked Elspeth sincerely.

'Well…all this nonsense about love and then all the danger and…'

Elspeth stopped her.

'Sister, you know full well I would never, never let any man take advantage or hurt you' she paused 'please do not run away from this friendship. No, no! It's not a friendship, this love, you have for Silas and the love he, unquestionably, has for you. Please don't throw it away.'

Wynnfrith had withdrawn into her shell somewhat, well into her gown, to be accurate. She needed more reassurance still.

'Well, why is it all so slow?! We've barely held hands and then he's in a cupboard with Brother Bede for God's sake!'

Elspeth's role as a serious counsellor was in real jeopardy at this point. I simply mustn't laugh, she told herself biting hard on her bottom lip. Wynn tried to look at her but Elspeth looked away. Following a pause, Elspeth stopped and turned to face her sister.

'He loves you dearly, dear sister and you will be as one, soon, I am sure if it.'

Proud of herself, she could see a welcome settling taking place in Wynnfrith. She added that she believed Silas's mission would soon be satisfactorily completed and all would be well again, knowing full well this was something she could not guarantee. They continued to talk for some time about Silas, particularly why he never talked about his parents or his home but did agree that, although incurably hopeless, he had the biggest of hearts. As the conversation changed to matters relating to Robert and his complicated, but generous, nature, they could not help dwelling also on the death of their parents those many years ago as it was then that their cousin, Robert, intervened and gave Wynnfrith a good home.

'I remember very little. I remember mummy and daddy and our baby, James and then I was told that Robert and his wife would look after me. I'll never forget when they sat me down and said they were dead. The plague they said.'

'You know it wasn't the plague?' asserted Elspeth acknowledging that they had never, before, spoken of this.

'Well, yes' she replied 'but only many years after. There was no plague. So what happened to them?'

Elspeth pondered a little before replying.

'I believe that there was a serious, and very unusual, disease abroad that year that took many people. But, there are no records and, although I was always destined for the convent I do not know what happened to James except that he eventually found himself alone and calling himself Eirik. Perhaps one day Robert might be able to enlighten us more.' Wynnfrith grunted, almost as a submission that the truth would never be known then peeped out of her cowl to observe their destination. Soaked and chilled, but content, they entered the hall and headed below to the undercroft.

Over time, this place had been given to numerous purposes and, it was now generally accepted that the undercroft would continue to be a hospital for those most in need. Social charity was, at times, scarce but since the Reformation, care of the poor had hit rock bottom. Despite any charges levelled at them, by and large, the monks and nuns took care of those who were sick and destitute. The destruction of the monasteries had hit both economy and society hard. Elspeth and Wynnfrith, at least once a week, gave their time to tend to these poor people, many of them in immeasurable pain and most dying.

The undercroft was only slightly warmer but it was dry. As the sisters uncovered their faces they were left in no doubt as to where they were, the smell alone almost driving them back up the stairs. However, it was the noise, the pitiful cries that impacted most on their senses. This was accompanied by outstretched hands, beseeching them to come nearer. The very sight of these two angels solicited instant responses, ranging from those who shouted for them to offer solace, to those that just lay there and forced a smile. They were, indeed, welcome and, although this gave the sisters both heart and a singular sense of purpose, they were, as always, completely torn in trying to work out where to start. A man wearing a woollen jerkin with a long apron and a felt cap hurried over to them.

'Sisters, sisters! What a welcome sight on this cold morning. If I may, there is a couple over here who would benefit most from your immediate attention.'

He too was a welcome sight, for the sisters admired the work this man was doing and the man himself. Marcus seemed always to be there and, surprisingly, they never asked what his role was. He certainly wasn't a physician, for they knew one that visited occasionally, and he was definitely not a barber-surgeon. I suppose it would be fair to say that they knew Marcus for his good works only, which, possibly, is the best way to know anyone. Wynnfrith always stared at Marcus which was swiftly followed by Elspeth digging her in the ribs. He truly was a sight to behold. His skin was dark, very dark, much darker than that of a Spaniard, although, people said, he had come to the Mary Rose via Spain. He was also very handsome. He wasn't, in the least, an oddity to those who spent their last days in the undercroft and, contrary to popular opinion, there were black people to be seen in most cities in England by the sixteenth century. But, to Wynnfrith, and to some degree, Elspeth, he was fascinating. Returning after a similar visit, Wynnfrith spent almost half an hour pondering on her own, sallow, hands only to invite laughter from her sister who enlightened her by saying that this was just the way the English were, particularly in winter! Added to all this, was the simple truth that Marcus was a saint, the sisters wondered how on earth he fed himself or rested as he was always tending the poor. He hurried them over to a corner, where, between two wooden pillars lay a man and wife, both emaciated, barely breathing but lying there as one. It was a pitiful sight. The corner was dark and Elspeth noticed that there had been some repairs to parts of the wooden braces where the damp had, over time, rotted the wood. As she squeezed in, Elspeth leant on one for support.

'I just haven't time for them' said Marcus with a regretful tone 'been together since they were fourteen and insistent that they want to go together and, would you believe, when they arrived, they asked for you two.'

This touched Wynnfrith in particular as the old lady forced out, what was possibly, a final smile, acknowledging the girl's presence.

'Of course' replied Elspeth, decidedly 'we'll spend some time here' and she immediately knelt by the woman.

However awkward this confined space was for Wynnfrith, she was determined to negotiate it and take care of the old man. As she did, she was sure she saw Marcus staring at her sister. Many men looked at Elspeth, she was a beautiful young woman but, even when she noticed, she took no interest whatsoever partly because of her call to faith but mostly because of her incurable stroppy temperament. But, Wynn did notice. This was different. There was admiration in his glance and, possibly, something more. What if? She thought and then corrected herself as the notion of Elspeth allowing herself a relationship with a man was, and would be, out of the question. However, as she did, Wynnfrith caught Elspeth, fleetingly, return his glance before giving her full attention to the old lady. Aware of Wynnfrith's "well, I never!" expression, Elspeth grumbled,

'Oh quiet sister, just tend to the sick!' Wynn, astonished, did just that.

It was clear why these two people were the day's starting point for the two sisters as they were clearly dying. Barely conscious, they recognised their carers which must have given them some courage. Elspeth and Wynnfrith held the hands of the couple. In tandem, the sisters were marvellous, their contrasting styles incredibly efficient. Wynnfrith's pastoral skills alongside Elspeth's pragmatism and hands-on approach meant that they were constantly in demand whenever they visited the undercroft. There was little they could do to help their first patients this cold morning but they did their utmost to ensure that the couple were comfortable. As their breathing laboured, Elspeth started to pray and held the hands of both the man and the woman. It would be hard to over-emphasise the power and importance of prayer. Nothing happened unless God willed it, so, following thanksgiving to the Lord, she prayed for the old couple's comfort, the transport of their souls and speedy death. This was not unusual. This was an age where, quite often, death was seen as an alternative cure. Better to be with God than to suffer. This didn't mean that people didn't care, but death was ever present and offered peace to those who were long-suffering. Technically, Elspeth shouldn't have been giving last rites at all but, those who knew her to have been a nun, asked for her specifically. In any case, if they could have accessed a priest at all, these two would have expired before he had arrived. The old man's breathing almost instantly gave way to a loud gurgle that repeated irregularly. He was now completely unconscious and, within minutes he expired his very last, long breath. Wynnfrith put his arm around his wife's waist and stayed with her whilst Elspeth now applied her skills elsewhere. It was, as always, a busy morning with many of the undercroft's occupants simply seeking the company of these two angels. However, this was not work for the faint-hearted. Dysentery was rife again. This was a painful condition leading to constant, loose stools and, often, blood and it became almost impossible for the victims to eat and, of course, many died of it. Most dysentery patients were moved elsewhere as it was just too difficult to care for them alongside all the others.

It was a credit to the sisters that they never complained, whether they were cleaning up patients, or after them, or assisting with basic procedures. The one thing that did disgust them was the evident lack of care for these people in Tudor society. Typhoid, tuberculosis, measles, malnutrition and 'sweating sickness' were amongst the many complaints that they had to deal with, not to mention many other ailments that remained without a diagnosis. Cures were thin on the ground but bleeding was the default strategy in order to keep a person's "humours" in balance and even the sisters would use leeches now and again as a turn-to cure-all. Patients, presuming that they could eat, were offered bread and, sometimes beer which, generally speaking, was a lot safer to drink than water.

Wynnfrith sat with the old lady until she passed when the bodies were immediately removed. She looked around for Elspeth who was now vigorously cleaning up filth.

'Let me help' insisted Wynnfrith but before she could pitch in, Marcus appeared with two wooden cups of thin beer for them. He was gone within a couple of seconds. They were no longer cold, now grafting continuously, but in vain, to keep the floor clean. Elspeth pointed to a number of rags, sheets and blankets that were in a pile in one corner.

'We'll wash that lot before we return' she said and as they moved aside the straw to scrub the wooden flooring, Wynnfrith realised that her sister was tiring, so insisted that she took over whilst she rested.

'I'm fine…Fine! Don't fuss!' said Elspeth impatiently.

Wynnfrith was a little surprised at her sister's curt reply but stayed silent and carried on. However, within minutes she could see Elspeth start to tremble and as she moved to support her, she could see the colour withdraw from her hands and face. In an instant, she began retching which almost immediately led to her vomiting. Wynnfrith, as best she could, supported Elspeth and lay her down on some, relatively clean, straw. Marcus came over, his first response was to clean up after Elspeth. As he looked over he could see that Elspeth was losing consciousness and soon was unable to speak. She lifted her head to speak to her sister, her breathing laboured, but then collapsed. More vomit and blood oozed from her lips as she fell backwards, completely still.

'Marcus! Marcus!! What's happening? She was fine. What is this?!!'

Marcus told Wynnfrith that her sister may have contracted dysentery knowing full well that this was unlikely, the symptoms being so rapid and severe. In his heart he had an alternative inkling but dreaded the very thought, particularly as this woman was, twice weekly, a candle shining in this dark hole and already meant so much to him.

'Help her!!' Screamed Wynnfrith at Marcus.

She had never screamed at anyone before. Wynnfrith was frightened and felt completely useless and helpless. Marcus shouted for help and, along with a third person, Elspeth, now lifeless, was lifted onto a makeshift cot.

9: LADY BASK

As is the case with all journeys, people either grow close to their travelling companions or, decide unequivocally that they were right in the first place when they felt that they absolutely couldn't stand them. Apart from the astonishingly low standard of Bayard's jokes, Silas's relationship with his driver acquired an admirable high as the miles passed. The one thing you could say with certainty about Bayard was that he told the best tales in all of England. Now, whether or not there was any truth in any of the stories was an entirely different matter, but he managed to keep young Silas spellbound for furlongs at a time with his patter. As Silas was also somewhat gullible, Bayard possibly enjoyed telling the stories better than at any other time previously. Added to this, were the two things that they had in common. Firstly, their part in thwarting the Cataclysm of the previous year and, their understanding of the geography of the land. They hadn't been lost once, so far, and made Boars Hill, that was south-west of Oxford in good time. This astounding timing was, of course, also due in part to them having a rotting corpse in the back of their wagon.

'So there really are dragons in Wales?' Asked Silas, so wanting it to be true.

'Travelled with one throughout a whole summer in '36. Tame little thing it was and knew how to perform when prompted!' Said Bayard.

'Well I never…and three-headed snakes in the east?'

Bayard was about to elaborate on the creative crap he was feeding his young friend when he heard a cry.

'You hear that?' Said Bayard.

They both listened carefully. For a moment there was no more than bird song and an inconsistent breeze that rustled the, now dry, leaves on a nearby holly bush.

'Hulloo!!' Came the cry.

Alerted, Silas and Bayard stepped down from their seats at the front of the cart, Silas still holding tightly onto Annie's reins. Again, the same cry repeated but now they could detect that it was coming from beyond the coppice at the wood's edge.

'Hulloo brethren!!'

And there, walking with a horse, was the athletic silhouette of Eirik, his golden hair being the very first feature to be picked up by the early morning light. Silas, child-like, ran toward his newly-found brother and embraced him. Erik smiled and said little as, true to character, Silas chose to impart the events of the last month in one sentence.

'Haha! Slowly brother, slowly' said Eirik smiling 'we have plenty of time and I have had word in advance regarding the unfortunate Sir Bask.'

This Eirik was almost a different creature from the one that Brother Bernard had first encountered as a prisoner. He was bigger, muscular, now an adult. Wearing the finest of clothes with a casual confidence, he was possibly as far away as you could get from the hopeless Viking mercenary of the previous year.

'Let's have a look at him then' said Eirik nonchalantly, leaving Silas astonished as to why anyone would make examining a corpse their first item of business.

'There's nothing to see!' Said Silas now panicking at the idea of this horror once more being revealed.

'Now Brother, it's only reasonable that we pull him out of his box after such a long journey' insisted Eirik, and Bayard moved to the back of the cart.

Indignantly, Silas intervened,

'I assure you he has been completely waxed…err…erm yes, embalmed, embalmed I say! No need for any further investigation' and placed his wiry frame between the cart and his two companions.

Now older, and of some experience (but none the wiser), Silas chose to study the faces of Eirik and Bayard and, yes, the smiles were already cracking out.

'When will I ever learn?' Said Silas with a heavy tone, realising that he had been sent up once again and knowing full well that they would probably laugh for minutes before things would return to normal.

'You wouldn't be laughing if you'd been locked in a room with that monster. That disfigurer of all that is Holy! I pray I never experience anything like it again. Even when I'm dead!'

Eirik placed his sword hand kindly on Silas's shoulder to comfort him.

'It is nearly over with, we need only take Bask to his widow and then we can speed to Stratford upon Avon to assist our ally, Richard, following his most shocking news. And' he added assertively 'I will deal with Lady Bask so, your job is almost done.'

This was certainly a substantial relief to Silas, he wanted no more to do with Sir Anthony Bask and rued the cold January day that he had rode out of Knapton.

'When did you last eat?' Asked Eirik.

'Best part of a day on just water' answered Bayard almost before the question had been asked. They were all extremely hungry.

'Well, we'll need to do something about it. There…' he pointed behind the coppice into the forest. 'An abundance, my friends. Need not be anything too ambitious. No…no, not a deer but there are white hares a plenty..'

Bayard was completely on board with this idea but Silas, sensibly, reminded them that the suggested act was completely against the law of the land. Silas, in particular, had spent his life travelling the breadth and width of England and was well aware that most land with plentiful game, belonged to someone and often, even as far north as Oxford, it would be definitely and solely the King's territory. Whichever way you looked at it, you could easily hang for as much as a dead bird. He had taken care, all these years, to avoid such complications and had successfully managed for weeks on grains, fruit and berries, sometimes he had some bread but never meat unless it was offered so, he made his stance absolutely clear.

'No, no. I can't be part of that. Just isn't worth the risk brother.'

Astonished at how forthright Silas was in this matter, Bayard and Eirik tried to persuade him otherwise, employing those time-tested techniques that assured him that it was a "one-off" and it would be "impossible to get caught" And, as a group of three, they could post lookouts.

'I won't do this. Never have and I won't now. My mother would be ashamed of me.'

This was an argument against which the other two had no defence, so it was agreed that Silas would take the horses and the cart out of sight, just inside the woods. Bayard would move further in as a lookout and Eirik would hunt with the promise that all would be done within less than a quarter of a full hour.

Half an hour later, Silas was feeling completely lonely and scared. He stretched himself to see if there were any visible signs of his companions but, apart from wildlife skipping through the undergrowth and the branches above, he was now alone. He braced himself against the trunk of a tree and looked down at his shoes, full of holes and moist, as was his hose as far up as his calf. Rustling. He could detect some movement and found himself upright, alert and looking straight ahead. Then, he heard a thin continuous whistle which led swiftly to a very loud Thub! Within seconds, he realised that his nervous and erratic personality had saved his life for there, where his head had been just one second earlier, was an arrow embedded in the oak. He screamed. Actually, he screamed before he knew he had and wished he hadn't as it was now imperative that he became unnoticed. He turned to escape. He grabbed the reigns of Eirik's horse and the two horses attached to the cart and headed for daylight. He could hear footsteps. Running footsteps. These were right behind him and he knew that he had no chance of getting away unless he mounted Eirik's horse. He jumped and fell. He jumped again and found himself lying awkwardly across the saddle of Eirik's tall steed. He was all set to make his getaway, albeit clumsily when he realised that those pursuing him were Bayard and Eirik.

'Brother! What mishap is this? Are you unharmed?!'

Eirik's words were like water dripping from a leaf. They echoed, seemingly meaningless because, amply given credence by his sudden and dark suspicion, Silas was, for the first time, scared of his friend. Accurately, or otherwise, Silas had presumed that the arrow had come from Eirik's quiver. He had, at this present time, no sensible evidence to support this supposition and later, once they had been separated, he had so wished that he had asked to see what Eirik's arrows looked like. This, in itself, would have been of little use as Silas had hardly taken time to examine the one embedded in the tree.

'Silas, friend, are you unharmed?!'

Eirik certainly sounded sincere enough and Bayard had no suspicions at all just standing there open-mouthed. Mind you, Bayard was a renowned blockhead. Silas snapped out of his frenzy and answered,

'Yes, yes, all is well. Just getting a little tired of being in danger!'

There was an edge, a sharpness to his answer that his two companions noticed but did not react to.

'If all is well with you two, I would like to expedite our mission to help Richard Shakespeare.'

Not only were Bayard and Eirik shocked at Silas's use of the word, expedite, but they were also taken aback by his sudden assertiveness.

'What do you suggest?' Asked Bayard calmly.

'I will take Annie and make way straight for Stratford upon the Avon. I have contacts there and I may be able to question them before you two arrive.'

Knowing full well that Silas had had, yet another, almighty shock and, that he had certainly had enough of keeping the company of Anthony Bask, dead or alive, they agreed that they would finalise matters in Oxford and then join him. Of course, Silas knew nothing about the mystery package rolling about inside Bask's perfumed carcass and neither was he meant to. They parted company amicably but with a palpable atmosphere that spoke of something being amiss, this was no longer a small band of happy travellers. Strangely, none of them discussed the arrow further and, it would be fair to say, that they simply presumed it was the gamekeeper or even a bona fide hunter who had caught up with Silas. Oh, and by the way, not even a beetle was caught for lunch. The three of them, their horses, and, presumably Anthony Bask were still left very hungry for the rest of the day.

When they arrived in Oxford, Bayard found himself outside a grand, three-story house that backed onto the university grounds. Word had it that Bask was knee-deep in debt so it was hard for the travelling entertainer to equate these two contradicting pieces of information. The cart had, discretely, been placed inside the east alley of the property. Eirik heartily thanked Bayard and told him that now, he should go and eat whilst he settled matters with Bask's wife.

Now firmly in civilised territory, they could buy food. Delighted, Bayard set off on foot to the nearest hostelry, but his over-inquisitive nature compelled him to wander back a few steps, hide behind the corner wall of the university and eavesdrop. A servant answered the door to young Eirik but, within, seconds, a lady also appeared. Now, if Bayard was expecting a forlorn old widow who hadn't seen her husband for months, he would have been disappointed. Lady Bask was young and beautiful, well dressed and Bayard was sure that she was flirting with the young Viking. She invited Eirik in. This, Bayard deduced, was not the first time they had met. Neither did she seem shocked at a body turning up at her house and she absolutely did not seem poor. Bayard eventually turned away and, although he was now delighted that he would, at last, be fed, his heart became heavy. Something wasn't right but he hadn't got a clue as to what all this meant. The, very infrequently accessed, angel on his right shoulder was telling him that, as an Agent, he must discuss this with Father Matthew, or Mayor Robert? Or perhaps Elspeth? And then it occurred to him that he might just be the odd one out, that he simply wasn't important enough to be privy to all information. However, the, very familiar, devil on his left shoulder told him to sod it, and go get pissed, preferably as soon as possible. Life had always been more fun when he listened to this more playful companion so he wandered over to the hostelry.

Eirik joined him within an hour announcing,

'All done!'

By this time Bayard was in a much better place, not in the least bit arsed about anything. They ate and drank as if imbibing and chewing were an art form and, as Oxford went dark, they collapsed into bunks provided by the landlord, full, pissed, ignorant and stinking.

Now many miles between them, Silas was anything but relaxed.

That weighty thing had happened to Silas's heart yet again. Even after two decades, he felt he had no control over those dark feelings that sometimes happened in an instant. Silas was a champion worrier, his suspicions now well into the league of fables and ridiculous fantasies. It was perfectly understandable that he was suspicious of Eirik but the very thought that this man, recently considered as close as a brother, may now want to finish him off, was unbearable. By the time Silas arrived in Stratford, he had concluded that every one of the Agents was against him.

Decidedly glum, he decided to make straight for the town and, once there, down to the river. He sat on the grassy bank and took time to reflect. Stratford alone raised his spirits somewhat. One of the many swans came to greet him, presumably, but incorrectly, thinking he had some food. As if it were the most sensible thing to do, Silas decided to spend some time chatting to the bird about Eirik, the Cataclysm, Elspeth, Wynnfrith of course, his home and his mother. He turned to his right and marvelled at the church. Can it be a coincidence that this one is called Holy Trinity too? He mused and then contemplated his fate. Life had been hard for Silas, but, he reminded himself that his faith, God and prayer had always seen him through. He noted that Holy Trinity was huge for a church. Nothing on the scale of York Minster but compared to the churches in York this was really big. He then turned to observe the town. It certainly had some grand half-timbered buildings but he concluded that it was unlikely that there was anything in it or about it that would ever make it extraordinary. Unless, he thought, that it was because of one of its extraordinary citizens. Thomas Farrier is extraordinary, he thought, and so is Richard Shakespeare but then instantly found himself laughing at the idea of people travelling to see Stratford just because of Richard Shakespeare or anyone else for that matter.

Breaking out of these meandering philosophies, he started to get up only to feel an overwhelming force from behind him. Before he could even consider what had happened he found himself face down and someone heavy was on top of him but then, strangely, there was laughter and although it was childish by nature, it was a deep giggle, that of a grown man.

'Silas! Friend! Here of all places!'

Silas found himself physically turned upward where he recognised Thomas Farrier. Silas laughed too and embraced Thomas believing immediately that this was God's answer to his black, forlorn thoughts.

'Thomas Farrier! Of all the things? What are you doing here, by the river?!'

'Hinges at the church young Silas. Done now though, heading back to Wolverdington soon.'

Thomas froze, a grim realisation which was evident from his expression, that he was embracing Silas and, so, suddenly let go.

'I do not mean any harm Silas. You do understand? It was just a jest. I was so excited to see a friendly face…no offence friend…' he said slowly backing away from Silas.

Silas ignored every word, gave Thomas a friend's return embrace and said,

'My good friend and most trustworthy ally, whatever this is, and I do think I know what this is, I insist you stop it for good. You never have, and never would do me – or anyone else for that matter - purposeful harm. We are brothers and that's the top and bottom of it.'

Thomas was embarrassed. He had never understood what was wrong with him, for mankind made him think that there was, irrevocably, something very wrong with him. So did the church. Although he never spoke of it, all he did know was that when he was an adolescent, and all the other boys liked girls, he didn't. Girls always liked him but there was no attraction back and so followed that endless torment. The realisation that, not only did he find men attractive and had felt love for them but that this had become a life sentence. Becoming a mercenary had seemed the most logical route mostly because it could well have ended his life. Unwittingly, he often made things worse by apologising profusely even if he accidentally touched another man. This was an awkward moment and Silas could see that Thomas was hurriedly about to change the subject.

'Have you ever considered those contradictions that exist between the world we live in and Christ's teachings?'

Dumbfounded, Thomas didn't know where this was going but took a moment to think about what Silas had said and eventually replied,

'Well, yes, mankind is riddled with violence, hate, covetousness.'

'Absolutely, my friend' announced Silas, newly appointed as the sage of Stratford.

'So' continued Silas quite pompously 'what sort of people did our Lord turn his back on?'

Thomas decided to play along, not having an inkling of what this was about and replied,

'Well…err…no one! He loved all!'

'Exactly. There you have it!'

Admittedly, the next few minutes were uncomfortable, particularly as Thomas Farrier had never been schooled by a village idiot before but, by the time they reached Annie, a little candle flame illuminated in Farrier's noggin. Subtly, privately and internally, he wept. He had never known such kindness before. Although it was almost in code, Silas had told him that he was valued for who he was and, at that moment, he considered that, in any battle of words, he would pit Silas's heart against any intellect, any day.

They settled at the Greyhound inn in the centre of Stratford where Silas refrained from speaking for twenty minutes as he was eating, and very glad of it. Thomas happily downed as much beer as he could in the time that he was there.

'So, Silas, What know you of the kidnapping?'

114

'Just that. I know no more and was hoping for better news when I arrived.'

'Surely you don't think that what happened to that Knight in York could be connected to the child's disappearance. Just wouldn't make sense.' Said Thomas.

'There's even more afoot my friend, the Agents believe that we are all in danger, retribution for our part in thwarting the Cataclysm. Only today someone tried to take my life!'

Thomas's drink spilt as he lunged backwards in surprise, Silas decided to relay the whole story.

'Surely you can't believe that young Eirik was responsible?' Asked Thomas dumbfounded. Silas stopped short of damning his friend completely but it was clear that he was scared, bitter and confused.

'If there's one thing I rely on to get me by, my good Silas, is always making sure that I know as much of the truth as is available before I make conclusions. Try to bury your suspicions for now and concentrate on the mystery at our feet.'

By now, Silas had had enough ale to leave him compliant with almost anything and he was happy to put his entire trust in Thomas Farrier. So much so, there was little mention of the kidnapping until they reached Wolverdington.

Thomas's workshop and house were a welcome sight and brought memories from Silas's adventures, only months earlier, flooding back.

'Come on inside friend, there's a roaring fire' beckoned Thomas. Silas couldn't imagine anyone leaving a fire blazing whilst a house was empty but said nothing, Thomas's proposition was very inviting. The door opened and a soft voice spoke before they even got inside.

'My Silas, how I've missed you'

'Maud! Maud! I never... how are...where?!' Maud put a finger to Silas's lips.

'Hush now child, all in good time.'

Silas was reminded, once again, of how both fortunes and feelings can turn in an instant. He never thought to see this woman again, she being barely alive when he last set eyes on her. How kind she had been to him and how much she reminded him of his blessed mother. Maud explained that following the death of her husband and considering the extent of her injuries, she could no longer keep the inn which would have been forever associated with Wriothesley's men. Thomas had given her shelter asking nothing in return but there was no doubt that he was certainly enjoying her cooking.

'Come with me' she said and took him into the kitchen.

There, sitting at the table were the Shakespeare family with the exception, of course, of Richard and kidnapped child, John. Abigail stood, silently, and embraced Silas. Once the greetings were finalised, Maud suggested that the four adults sit around the table and they complied without comment. She looked each one of them in the eyes in turn and then produced a small letter.

'This came to us via Richard in your absence, Thomas.' Abigail had already read it out to Maud but she was unable to read herself so passed it to Thomas Farrier.

'It asks for a ransom! Bloody cheek!'

'There, Thomas' said Maud 'best not to get upset. We're relying on you for a plan.'

Looking at the blacksmith, you wouldn't think he had any ideas at all, he was completely flabbergasted, shocked that anyone would use a child to settle affairs or whatever it was that was going on.

'And you'll have one. Abigail, we will get your son back, just need to think. No point acting irrationally.'

As Abigail sobbed into Maud's apron, Thomas Farrier's demeanour changed. He now had a look of determination. There was no doubt that his many years of battle experience would, once again, be accessed to put an end to this wicked design.

'It's a trap!' He said, so confidently, that it was some time before he was questioned.

'How so?' Asked Silas.

To each of us here, twenty pounds is a fair sum but realistically it buys you…what? Four horses or so? Who would risk their throat cut if rumbled or a certain hanging if arrested for such a sum? Someone is making a point here. This is someone who knows Richard Shakespeare or holds a grudge!'

'So it could be Wriothesley's men?' Asked Silas.

'That it could, but me and young Abigail are going to sit down and think if it is likely to be someone else.'

As the two of them stayed at the table to hold further conference, Maud explained to Silas that Richard chose to stay behind and mind the farm, keep his obligations as long as he could. Silas then turned to look again upon his muscular friend with admiration. Asking nothing in return, Thomas Farrier had housed the whole Shakespeare family and Maud. Many would say that the house was too big and grand for just the one man but this selfless goodwill, certainly, would have meant the world, particularly, to the Shakespeares.

What followed was a period of calm, the children playing in front of the large wood fire and Thomas left to decide on a course of action. Maud was snoring, the children giggled and, for a short time all was well. Instantly we were all alarmed as Thomas leapt up and screwed up the letter exclaiming,

'I have it! I have a plan.'

10: THE SICK AND THE DYING

It was easy to see why Silas had chosen, and stayed, in his humble home at the end of dead alley. It was his sanctuary and, without doubt, he could be assured of peace and isolation there. Within no time, both Peter and myself found ourselves feeling completely at home, pondering on whether it was best to clean up and make some light improvements or let it be. Peter wisely suggested that Silas would be upset at finding his home changed, he being perfectly familiar with every square inch of his personal, albeit rustic, castle.

We awoke shivering, much as we had done throughout the night. Snow had negotiated its way through every possible aperture, making discerning outside from inside difficult in places. Nevertheless, we were grateful of dear Silas's hospitality and thanked God for his kindness in our prayers.

From my very first day in York, I knew I would not be able to meet my mission obligations without a companion and I had been blessed with the fellowship and friendship of Edward Fawkes during 1541. If Peter, by providence, was a replacement, he was a damn good one. Older and more serious than Edward, he was still acclimatising to the talking rodent and York itself, a place bigger than he could ever have imagined. However, he was civil and put my needs first and, generally, refrained from asking awkward questions.

'What's today Micklegate?'

'We are going to be busy Peter, there is a curious and serious threat to the Agents of the Word and I must devote all my time to making sure we keep everyone safe. Today we meet Father Matthew at Holy Trinity church. Get my box if you will'.

'Yes sir!' He said with sincerity and enthusiasm, then turned and hesitatingly asked 'err…am I…well…could I be…an Agent one day?'

Bless him, he had come such a long way, and for the cause, so he was already in much deeper than he realised himself.

'Of course!' I said unintentionally abrupt.

'What? You mean…?'

'Appointed now on my authority!'

I turned and suddenly realised that he thought I was placating him and, as a consequence he still looked incredibly disappointed.

'Peter, please put me on the table.'

He did as I asked and then rummaged around on the cold floor when I asked him to pick up a piece of straw and hand it to me.

'Bow your head young Peter.'

Nervously he complied and, although he had no clue at all to the contrary, I hurriedly created a, previously non-existent, ceremony in my head.

'Ahem…by the authority…given by…err…oh yes!...The Agents of the Word and, well…erm God himself, I appoint you as a lifelong member of the, aforesaid, Agents of the Word! Notwithstanding…hitherto…blah blah blah…'

That should do it, I thought, slightly ashamed that I had dragged the Almighty into it. He lunged forward, so swiftly in fact, that I shit myself. Yes, literally.

'Put me to action this very day, Sir mouse! I am yours to obey!'

Oh God! Overdone it again I thought. I looked at him ready to give his life to the cause, then down at the pathetic pebble that I had just created and then back at him. Not having any other ideas at all, I said,

'Perhaps start by cleaning that up. Can't do it myself.'

He immediately obeyed and that, I suppose, made us very close, very quickly.

As we pushed aside, and then squeezed through, the roots and overgrowth of the church yard we were left wondering how Silas managed to do this every day and, moreover, with a horse. We left cold, wet and scratched but, once in the open, we were presented with a snow-laden York in all its morning beauty. Church bells were ringing in every corner of the city and people greeted one another as they negotiated the extreme conditions. On our arrival, we were treated to a crackling fire in Father Matthew's privy quarters. Bliss. We talked about the seriousness of our situation, but in comfort and with warmed mead. This was, indeed, a day of firsts for Peter and he was loving it. The life of an Agent was one to be envied, he considered.

'I have, this morning, appointed Peter to the Agents' I said to the priest.

At first Father Matthew gave the impression that he was not particularly happy with my decision but he, like myself, considering the many sacrifices this young man had already made, eventually smiled and congratulated him.

I continued,

'In fact, this very morning, I have......'

I was halted instantly by the main church door being clumsily flung open. Presuming this to be an attacker, Peter and Father Matthew jumped up to confront them. As soon as they were behind the squint, they could see a dark figure whose clothes were practically rags.

'There's nothing of value here!' Shouted Father Matthew frightening the bloody life out of all of us.

Soon, I had caught them up. The figure just stared, agape, he was clearly breathless but now standing completely still. For a few, surreal, moments the three of them just stood doing nothing and, within seconds, I had scrambled around to join them.

'Father, Father! It's me, Scorge!' said the anxious stranger.

'Come into the light man!' Asked Father Matthew.

He took one step forward and, it was at this point that it was clear that the priest knew him. Peter stood, solid as a rock, ready to defend us both. Excellent appointment, I told myself.

'Scorge from the infirmary? What on earth brings you here on such an inclement day?'

'Your nun, mistress Elspeth. She's dying…needs last rights Father.'

As if we all hadn't previously been cold to the bone, Father Matthew and myself now felt completed paralysed, not knowing for a moment what to say or what to do. But then he suddenly became incredibly animated. I could tell he was upset, really upset, but his professionalism had kicked in. He grabbed his priest's stole, holy water and some other religious bits and pieces and was gone. Trembling, I beckoned Peter to put me in my box and then pursue the priest. Uncannily, I was now totally unaware of the extreme weather conditions. I was numb, not able to contemplate a world without the grumpy nun. We had crossed swords so many times but had forged a wholesome respect for one another. My thoughts instantly turned to the Cataclysm. Was this also revenge? Why the hospital? Why Elspeth? I was panicking, so told myself to get a grip. It was the very use of this phrase that had me instantly pondering existentially. I'm not really here. I'm not really a mouse. Elspeth's been dead for hundreds of years. Then the counter arguments. She's my friend. I need to find the perpetrators. By the time we arrived, I was no use to anyone.

The first thing I saw behind the many pathetic figures populating this undercroft was Wynnfrith, now broken and unable to offer anything to her poor sister. She looked up, expressionless, at us. Unsurprisingly, Father Matthew immediately started to administer the last rites. To all those present, this was exactly the right thing to do. Rather than saying all hope was lost (although it clearly was) it was a guarantee of clear passage to Heaven and exactly what Elspeth would have wanted. I could see a man holding her. He was no stranger to Elspeth and I would have guessed that there was something more than tending to her illness in their relationship. A friendship at least, I deduced. I watched on, hopeless and useless, the rites giving the impression that all was at an end. I am still unsure of the reason but I immediately snapped out of my complacency.

'Wynn! Tell me immediately what transpired, her symptoms, how she became so?'

She hesitated, clearly there was a part of her that didn't even understand why I was asking.

'All may not be lost!' I shouted, alarming everyone in the room, although I didn't have a clue where it came from. I then saw an immediate change in Wynnfrith and the man cradling Elspeth.

'Is there anywhere…an ante chamber…a room, somewhere we can separate her from the others?' I asked nervously.

I was suddenly irked by the perpetual need to put all on hold why we had to do the "why does the mouse talk" thing. Today I had no patience with it.

'She needs to be isolated now! Bloody move yourselves!'

Marcus, Scorge and Father Matthew awkwardly manhandled, what they thought was a corpse, into the short corridor which led from the entrance to the undercroft. Of course, I told myself, there are no other rooms, this would have to do. At the same time, Father Matthew was hurriedly explaining about the little bastard in the box.

'Lie her flat on a cloak or blanket!' I rudely demanded 'Wynnfrith, try to get a hold of yourself. What do you think is wrong with your sister?'

'She…she's..'

'She's not dead Wynn.'

I crawled onto Elspeth's face and then put my ear close to her nose and, although, infrequent and only just noticeable, my fur moved slightly. Wynnfrith instantly found renewed energy.

'She has the dysentery, caught it today!'

'No she hasn't. It's impossible for symptoms to appear so quickly.'

I looked at them for speedy answers. Marcus intervened,

'She has emptied herself both ends and…err.. breathing stopped all at once. She was clutching her chest, her stomach!' He offered.

'Peter you will need to run back to the church. In the vestry, on the floor, are rushes and reeds. Bring what you can immediately.'

He was gone as soon as I had said it.

'Marcus go with haste to the Golden Fleece and bring back a gallon of fresh ale.'

Thankfully, he, also, didn't question my method. He just disappeared.

'Wynn, find a small piece of parchment, I don't care how you get it!' and, strangely, she started to rummage around in a rather tired looking leather pouch.

'Elspeth has been poisoned!' I announced.

Not surprisingly there was a gasp from all present.

'How?!' Asked Father Matthew.

123

Wynnfrith, now white-faced, glared at us both and then calmly added,

'The beer. Marcus gave us beer. Oh my good God in Heaven! Why would he do such a thing?!'

Sadly, and much to my chagrin, I found myself again unable to challenge this young woman for whom I held so much affection. Fortunately, the priest did just that on my behalf

'I'm presuming you had beer?'

Instantly realising how poor her explanation had been, she nodded.

'However, that does not mean we can exclude Marcus from our suspicions.'

The discussion seemed a little inappropriate in the circumstances but, if there was any chance of saving Elspeth, I needed to be sure of my assumptions. By now, on my instruction, Elspeth had been turned on her side, vomit still oozing out of her mouth but, although she now moaned quietly but constantly, she was unconscious. I had asked Scorge to warm some water and, thankfully, he returned at the same time as Peter. I warmed one of the larger reeds to soften it and told Wynn to push it down into Elspeth's gut. She reeled back at the suggestion and, whilst reminding her that I couldn't do this myself, I assured her that it would help. I asked Peter to help her to fashion a crude cone out of the parchment and then we used this as an aperture into which Wynn could pour the beer when it arrived. I had to keep telling myself that I was constantly freaking everyone out and that, even a simple procedure like pumping her stomach, probably seemed like witchcraft to them.

The beer arrived and, although this was far from any scientific procedure known to man, Wynn realised why she had to pour the fresh beer into Elspeth's gut, I absolutely could not have risked using contaminated water. We all watched to see what effect this would have. Elspeth

spluttered and violently vomited but was still not fully
conscious. After a few minutes I was satisfied that she was
empty. I tutored her sister in the art of heart massage. It
didn't help that everyone present started arguing about
where the heart was and simply didn't believe me.

'She will need to be kept warm and isolated, at home if
possible, and it is absolutely essential that her hands and
face are scrubbed, wash your own hands afterwards,
Wynnfrith.'

At this point I could see that they were all absolutely
stressed and confused. It was also clear that Elspeth was
still alive, so they were now seeking answers.

'Aconitum napellus!' I announced with confidence.

'What..?' Responded Peter who was, unquestionably,
speaking on everyone's behalf.

'Wolfsbane poison. I believe this to be a purposeful and
diabolical attempt to murder Elspeth and possibly, both of
you, Wynnfrith.'

Marcus seemed genuinely shocked. Could he really have
been part of this? I thought and then reminded myself that
it would be ridiculous to jump to conclusions with
practically no evidence as yet.

'Will she live, mouse?' Asked Wynnfrith still tearful.

'I really don't know, my dear Wynnfrith, but I do believe
there is hope. You absolutely must either clean or destroy
all her clothes and yours.'

Marcus was absolutely dumbfounded and stressed, not
least because of the incredible pressure from the numerous
terminal patients only yards beyond the corridor and the
bewitched rodent bossing him about.

'Dear Wynnfrith, I don't know what to say. She was as
lovely, as healthy as a warrior when she arrived. I know not
what has taken place this morning.' Said Marcus nervously.

I was reasonably assured that he was sincere and
reminded everyone that, for now, the priority was getting
Elspeth well and, now even surprising myself, told them

that I would personally carry out a full investigation. I'm now a bloody detective as well, I told myself. The incredibly diligent and overworked Scorge miraculously had a hand-cart drawn up at the entrance. Everyone present, besides Wynn, removed at least one outer layer and draped it over the patient and Scorge pulled the squeaky cart all the way to Bootham Bar, through the snow, with Wynnfrith walking alongside, cradling her sister. I had told her that we would visit within the hour to monitor Elspeth's progress and turned to question Marcus further about the morning's events.

'So, to be clear, when they arrived, the sisters chose who to tend to?' I asked of Marcus.

'Well, yes I suppose..'

'Forget suppositions for now, you will need to be precise!'

My brusque, inpatient nature was now heightened and he knew I wasn't taking prisoners.

'Thinking back, the old couple asked for them.'

'That's more like it! Can I speak to them please, or if you prefer not to have them frightened out of their skins, you can ask the questions for me.'

'Can't. Dead.' He said.

'What?! Both of them?'

'Yes, sorry' He said ' surprised they made it to this morning.'

'But it wasn't a coincidence that the girls consoled the old couple?'

'No. I suppose not, if you put it like that.'

'Show me where they lay, you may pretend I'm a pet, good luck charm, whatever, if it helps, Peter, you stay here.'

Marcus took me to the nook where the old couple had expired, and, as the corner was now cleared, I asked him to release me from my box then I could peruse the environs.

Within minutes the whole plot against the sisters had unravelled before my eyes. I instantly asked Peter to return me to Holy Trinity Church where I hoped I could make sense of the morning's intrigues.

11: COAL AND CROWNS

As Peter and I arrived at the home of Elspeth and Wynnfrith it was apparent that Wynnfrith had been busy. Often denying themselves the comfort of a fire even in these extreme conditions, the room was now warm and Elspeth was in front of the fire swaddled in cloaks and blankets. Wynnfrith had diligently cleaned or burned absolutely everything. I asked Peter to put down my box and, inadvertently, he placed it on the now, very familiar, barrel that was covering the trap door, the route to many of our previous adventures.

'You saved her life Micklegate' said Wynn calmly.

'All I did was give her a chance, dear Wynnfrith and, I should caution you that she is not out of the woods yet. I have no idea how much Wolfsbane she was exposed to, even whether she has swallowed it or not. Give it time. No water! And if you can access good wine let her have it in small amounts and…when she feels like eating, let her eat.'

'Nevertheless' she added 'we will be forever grateful.'

'Where ever did you get the parchment from so quickly?' I said referring to the makeshift cone that had helped to save Elspeth's life.

'Remember that very first message I had to leave, and pick up, from Holy Trinity last year? Still had it!' She declared cheekily.

Peter kept his own counsel. After all, he didn't really know the sisters and was probably still acclimatising to the events of the last few hours. I looked at Elspeth's truly innocent but pale face. We need her, I thought and, as I stood on my hind legs to see better I could see her straining to speak.

'My go….good….mou…Mouse…' she whispered.

My very good Elspeth, I thought. Many would think us enemies but I hoped that, yet again, we could work together against whatever forces were behind these terrors. I stretched further and then realised that my hind legs had, in fact, left the ground. I looked down only to see the cage floor plummeting downward. Everything was plummeting downward! The trap door had accidentally opened and I tumbled noisily and awkwardly into the cellar banging my head on the floor of my box as I landed. I could hear voices, this was too serious an incident to be funny, I thought. Wynn and Peter must be asking about my welfare. I strained to hear, at first it was as if I was listening to a foreign language. And then, it became clear.

'He's moving. I could swear he was moving' one voice said.

'We're getting him back! All his stats are changing.'

I was clueless. What was this? I asked myself. Who in 1542 says "stats?" And then the penny dropped. At last, I was returning to my former self, to reality. I had given it so little thought that I presumed it would never happen. Nick Douglas. Dr Nick Douglas, my real self, I suppose. But, as I lay there, I was sure I could see upward beyond that cellar door. However, it was clear that I was beginning to become cognisant of the biogel. The gel that had kept me alive throughout this experience was now warm and supportive. Second by second, I gave credence to this notion. Yes, this is where I had been all along. "There is no time travel!" Those words from my lecture. Of course there isn't, I've been here all the time, my adventures nothing more than virtual reality, I told myself. Voices. I could hear more voices. I was alive and well and would soon be restored to my former self, the gel having served all my needs, even exercise, during my mission. I relaxed. Just let them do their jobs, relax, be over soon, I told myself.

And then, for some reason, I felt a tear in my eye. It absolutely couldn't have been a tear as this would have been impossible whilst I was in stasis. Nonetheless, my heart broke for Lizzy, for Elspeth and Brother Bernard. I fought to replace these emotions with logic and, as I did, I could feel myself, yet again, tumbling. It was a most unnerving experience, a little like when you wake suddenly from a dream. Falling, falling, everything seemingly dark and then, unexpectedly, I hit my head again.

'Is this some sort of a bloody joke!' I shouted. I'm the mouse again! I thought. The northern voice, the profanity. What the hell is happening?! I asked myself.

'Get a grip roundmouse! We're all depending on what's in that head of yours!'

I didn't know the voice and couldn't see anyone. Who the hell is roundmouse? Blink! Blink, clear your eyes and ears. And then, noise. Unbelievable and unbearable noise. Shouting, screaming, clashing and clattering. Horses, armour, matchlocks. What? Matchlock muskets?! I'm not in 1542! As soon as my eyes opened I instantly knew where I was. This was the battle of Edgehill, 1642, during the English civil war, I was one hundred years askew from where I should have been and was dressed, ridiculously, as a little Roundhead and just yards in front of me I could see Oliver Cromwell. Bugger, he's even uglier than the paintings, I thought. Facing us was the cavalry of King Charles 1 led by Prince Rupert, looking more like they were in fancy dress than going into battle. I was nearly home!

What had happened? And then, the enemy was on top of us. Having dodged an enormous pike, I tried to calm myself. This had happened before, last year, well not last year, 1541 I mean. This is so confusing! Think. Calm down. Yes, then, I was seeing 1941 instead of 1541, now I'm seeing 1642 instead of 1542. A glitch. Yes, just a glitch in the software. But, I didn't want to be here. The Roundhead that had spoken to me was very familiar, he must know me somehow. He now bowed down so that we were face to face.

'What next roundmouse?'

'The Royalist army will attack your flanks, you will need to deploy your troops accordingly.' I advised.

He rushed off. What on earth was I doing? I couldn't influence the outcome of Edgehill! At least I had rid myself of him.

Although my situation was, to say the least, daunting, I was able to reflect on the last half hour or so and, as I did, for some bizarre reason, I felt the need to be back with the Agents. I needed to sort out why they were under attack. Absolutely dazed by the randomly exploding gunpowder around me, I chose to concentrate on this, my goal.

'Get hold of him!' This, possibly was going to be the end of me as, by now, the enemy must have been in touching distance.

'Turn him over.'

'Is he alright?'

'Yes, yes, Peter he seems fine. Let's get him back up the stairs.'

I was back where I belonged or, at least, everything in the universe was telling me that this is where I belonged. As I, yet again, readjusted, I considered that I had almost wished myself back here. Is that how this works? I perused. Can't be. Completely unscientific. However, these anxious thoughts and suppositions did, at least, give me some temporary confidence that I could think myself back to where I came from.

Wynnfrith cradled me in her warm hands and I saw a smile on her face. How pretty she looked and for a moment, I realised that I had completely forgotten about her disability and that this was how she lived. Cerebral palsy didn't own or characterise her and, apart from struggling with steps and the frequent occurrence of new acquaintances complaining that they can't understand her, life was for her as it was for anyone else and, added to that, she was in love. Courageous and noble Wynn, I thought, how blessed we are to have her as part of our group. I realised that she was starting to shiver, albeit slightly. The once impressive roaring fire was now in its death throes. I hadn't even noticed that they were burning straw, old clothes and essentially anything that they could get their hands on. I even observed the remnants of a barrel that was once part of their furniture. I looked over at Elspeth. It was essential that, at least for today, we kept her stable.

'All we have, Micklegate, the fire will die soon' said Wynnfrith.

I thought and thought, there must be somewhere we could take her that would be warm and I initially, considered Robert's house but then saw how frail Elspeth was after the manhandling and the journey. I looked at Peter who, so far, had said nothing. He started to fidget with his bag. I say bag, it was nothing more than a ragged piece of cloth, tied in a bundle on a stick and, when I say stick, I mean a branch from a tree. It amused me, as in later times this would be often drawn ironically in cartoons when illustrating travellers or hobos. I'm sure it did the job but often wondered what was in there. It had to be considerable as it was clearly quite a burden. I even thought, once, that he may have been carrying coins.

As we watched, the bundle soon became undone. Wynn and I looked on casually as Elspeth dozed. He pulled out a piece of cheese and it wreaked! It was mouldy but only in the places where it wasn't completely black. I had never seen black cheese before. Peter looked at it, clearly considering that it may still come in handy one day. He sniffed at it, pondered and then put it down on the floor. Clueless as to what was going on, and with nothing else to do, we just carried on watching him and, as he dug deeper, we could see that his forearm was now, also, blackened. At least it kept us amused for a few minutes. And then, remarkably, he drew out a huge rock, black as the night.

'Do you know what this is, maid Wynnfrith?' Asked Peter.

'Why yes' she said 'it is coal, but I've never seen a piece so big.'

'Finest there is, mined by myself in Newcastle. This was given to me as a gift when I came away.'

Almost as if I didn't know, I asked him why he was showing it to us.

'This'll burn the rest of the day, keep your sister warm and we can pray that she recovers somewhat on the morrow.'

Of course we went through the routine of feigned "oh no we couldn't" and "oh yes you must" until I insisted that it was put into the meagre flame before it left us all bloody freezing simply due to incurable good manners.

'It will bring good luck too, will coal. It is blessed and will bring good fortune to your home' added Peter.

I, once again, reminded myself that I was in the company of extraordinary people. He was living day to day on trust with relative strangers and, on a whim, gave away half of his worldly possessions, the other half now sitting festering on the floor but within minutes, following further prevarication on the behalf of the young fisherman, the cheese also went in the fire. Half an hour later, the fire was picking up and the silence was broken by Peter's curiosity.

'Micklegate, as you fell into the cellar, you were saying the strangest of things, can you explain?'

Well, I thought to myself, he clearly isn't mincing words today. I decided to fob him off, tell him that, apart from, the comical bump on my head, I was fine. Thankfully, then, there was silence again. But, it wasn't to last.

'Well how come you can speak then? Is that a Yorkshire thing?'

Wynnfrith laughed.

'Oh no Peter, that's a weird-as-you-bloody-like thing. He won't tell us!'

I was being ganged up on. Even Elspeth was now intermittently blinking open one eye and then the other.

'Why don't you just explain?' Asked Wynnfrith in a very lady-like but incisive way.

I thought for a while, and then remembered that I had confided this nonsense in Henry himself and, apart from him wanting details of his own demise, it didn't seem to have caused too much harm.

'Alright, Peter' I said drawing his attention to the, quite, pathetic, window that was adjacent to the entrance.

What do you know of our history. Battles been and gone, Kings?'

He thought for a moment and, quite assertively, said,

'I know of the Vikings, we are of Viking stock.'

I saw Elspeth try to raise her head. Oh God! No! I thought to myself, we're not going to have another bloody long lost family moment are we, still suspicious of Eirik's claim to be Elspeth's brother.

'Any event specifically?'

'Wha…?'

'Think of one thing that happened with the Viking's arrival in Britain.'

'Err…well…I know of some of the villages they raided but mother tells stories of how Vikings settled here and lived alongside the Britons.'

'Yes, yes' I said 'very good. Look out of the window and pretend you can see those people building villages, together, long ago. Do you know what that is?'

'Oh yes! Oh yes I do!'

Thank goodness, I thought

'Witchcraft that is!'

God's teeth! This is going to be hard work I told myself. Like all good teachers I rephrased my question and, eventually, he understood that I was talking about the past, imagining what has been, seeing what has happened in one's mind and, no, it's not flaming witchcraft! I stopped, looked upon Wynnfrith and Peter and realised this wasn't going well. The more I explained the worse it got! I told them that there was no travelling through time and that I could see them "through a window"

'Which window?' They said simultaneously almost as if to annoy me more.

'Well not a real window! Obviously!'

'No need to get so upset!' said Wynn.

I tried again. Virtual reality isn't easy to depict to someone living in the middle of the sixteenth century but I really tried.

'Well…' started Peter. I had no expectations, at all, of anything useful coming forth at his point. 'If you can only just see us, like you would through a window, how can we see you?'

My jaw dropped open. I didn't have an answer. What on earth had developed that would give me the ability to interact with these people? And also, remarkably, to care for them, love them. Understanding that, if I were to be honest with myself, I couldn't comprehend what was happening either. So, I became even more ruffled and blurted out disconnected statements of truth about my time and their future. I felt I shouldn't give all away but was certain this would, at last, persuade them.

There was a pause and then, laughter. Raucous, belly laughter. Wynnfrith was in tears as they revelled in each other's jollity and, then, I definitely detected a smile from Elspeth.

'Ah, Micklegate! You're so funny. Tell us some more stories whilst we tend to my dear sister.' Said Wynn.

I gave up, curled into her lap and nursing the bump on my head. It was probably for the best that they thought it was all nonsense, I told myself. Won't make that mistake again. I slowly fell into a peaceful, warm but dreamless sleep and, as I stirred, felt that I had slept for hours but, of all things, it was my nose that wakened me, and quite abruptly too, I should add. The stink, it was overpowering and my stomach was churning before I had even come round.

'Aaaaghhhh!' that scream. It's me, I thought. 'Aaaagghhh…oh no. God's broken, bloody elbow!! What is that?! Ohhhh…'

But, almost as a harmony, I could hear someone else doing the same thing but with completely different intonation.

'Ohhh!...ahhh..Oooh!..fetch a spoon for God's sake!!'

Fortunately, the latter cacophony drowned mine out for, when I opened my eyes I was alongside Thomas Heneage in the King's privy chamber, the King enjoying his daily drama of purging the royal bowels. What was I doing here? How, ever, did I get from Wynnfrith's lap to Hampton Court? And then, a thought that was much more alarming. Am I back in November 1541? Am I reliving the same experiences over? I was panicking and extremely fidgety. The King was cursing whilst simultaneously easing himself on and off the stool, once again revealing his minuscule and imbalanced prized possessions.

'For God's sake get me out of here!'

It was me. I had, almost inadvertently, protested and then found myself roughly ejected from the chamber being, literally, thrown to the floor. I was breathing heavily, panicking and had, temporarily, lost all reason. Just stop for a minute, I told myself. Look for clues. I looked down. I was dressed as the King was again, but I had never seen this costume before, I'm not in 1541 but where, or to be precise, when, am I? The door, again, flew open and Thomas Heneage appeared.

'What in God's good name are you thinking of? He'll have your head Mouse, no doubt of it!'

I apologised and apologised again, claiming temporary insanity.

'You'll need to rest, difficult times ahead Micklegate. Thankfully, as His Grace was in mid purge, I don't think he heard you. Just wait here until I am out.'

Still kind, I thought, and told myself to relax as Thomas Heneage was my undisputed rock when I was previously in London. Hadn't a clue what the date was though, so I just had to wait until I could make some deductions. My greatest worry was that I now seemed to be jumping about from one place to another. I thought again about home. My real home that is. I was nearly back. What had happened? What was happening and why couldn't I return? For the first time in months I thought about the mix. The brain fog that starts to erase your origins and envelop you completely in the current environment. Think Nick, I told myself, think about what awaits back there and then, almost as a human and not a mouse, I broke down. My heart broke completely because I realised that I was missing my wife but, because, for what seemed like a whole year, I had completely forgotten about her. But there she was, April, back in my mind. I told myself firmly that, firstly, I needed to do what it was I had to do with the Agents and then set myself the task of returning, completely, to my world.

Then my thoughts went back to Elspeth. Yes she's warm. No, was warm! I told myself and, in disciplining my thoughts, I remembered the little things. Yes, that was what was at the centre of my mission, my investigation. People who would never appear in any records but were both influential and significant. Small things? The coal. Did the coal save her life? The young fisherman saved her life with a small gift? Yes. Astonishing. I must remember all these details, I told myself.

A page, without speaking, came to collect me and I was placed in a small chamber that I hadn't seen before. Although it was completely in conflict with my Micklegate Mouse character, I told myself that it was time to simply listen, especially if I were to learn anything.

The page left and someone else came to clean my cage and feed me. Then they left, Thomas Heneage arrived accompanied by the King. Henry really struggled now, his general health and leg ulcer leaving him in almost constant pain, ill-tempered and hampering his mobility. I said nothing, sitting obediently on my little throne. They sat, in silence, clearly waiting for someone else. Within minutes a man appeared. He was handsome with a short ginger beard and the finest of doublets. I knew him instantly. Rarely mentioned in most popular histories, this man was Thomas Wriothesley's equal. Henry had two privy advisors and this man, Sir Ralph Sadler was the other. I didn't know what to think initially. There was something incredibly untrustworthy and creepy about all these people, few got to this level without eating their own grandmother or, at least, a second cousin. He had been a sidekick to Thomas Cromwell for many years and, during that period of Cromwell's demise, also found himself languishing in the Tower. Having been reprieved by Henry, he had been in his favour ever since. Presuming that we were now quorate, I was surprised to hear another set of approaching footsteps and, as I turned to see just who it was, a chill swept through the whole of my furry frame. It was Wriothesley, undoubtedly the chief instigator of the Cataclysm and, astonishingly, now sharing the King's confidence again. The King was still trying to negotiate his frame into a nearby seat but, as he collapsed into it, whipped his head around and reacted quite violently.

'Out you devil's whore!! Beelzebub's filthy, bent cock! Out of my sight!'

Clearly not that much in the King's favour, I thought, and his response even managed to send me reeling. Wriothesley bowed, left and the door was closed behind him.

'Buggerer of sheep!' Henry grumbled to himself.

I didn't take this response too seriously. The outrage could have been a reaction to a momentous failing in state responsibilities on the part of Wriothesley or, most likely, he just turned up at the wrong time. The other two people in the room didn't react at all but I did notice that, within a minute, all eyes were on me. Henry started to speak, although his rhetoric was punctuated by groans. There was no doubt that he was now in, almost constant, pain.

'My strange but reliable mouse! Little King Harry...I told you that I would call on you and your ragged troop of beggars when you were needed.'

My heart stopped. Not only were the strange events that preceded this meeting heavily weighing on my mind, I was now about to be employed by the King at a time when the Agents were already under attack. I then realised that I wasn't listening.

'....We are in the midst of troubling events and constant danger, mouse!'

I instantly considered that he meant a repeat of last year's threats but had to force myself to concentrate. This was clearly of real and immediate importance to the King. Sadler stood and approached me.

'His Grace has become a victim of numerous assassination attempts, all executed in the last few months.'

This did, at least, tell me that I had arrived there sometime in 1542 but also left me astonished.

If not common knowledge, it became an accepted historical truth that, for monarchs, this was a constant concern. There were, after all, many, many reasons why people would want him dead, not least those, like Cranmer, Wriothesley and Seymour who wished to firmly establish the Protestant faith in England.

'You do understand, beast, that this conversation must not travel beyond these walls?'

Sadler was addressing me directly which immediately informed me that the King had told him all. I had no choice but to reply.

'Why of course my Lord.'

'Damn! It really does talk! My Grace are you sure…'

'Get a hold of yourself man, the mouse and I are as allies!' retorted Henry.

'Well, to business…' continued Sadler.

I was distracted and fascinated by the role of Thomas Heneage, reminding myself that this man alone had Henry's absolute trust. He was completely silent throughout the meeting.

'You should know all…' continued Ralph Sadler who sat and unravelled the dark events of the previous few months.

'Our Good Lord and Grace, King Henry the eighth in number is plagued by those who show little gratitude for his love and benevolence for his people…'

Are we talking about the same bloke? I asked myself. I almost said it out loud but this was not the climate for improvisational comedy.

'Even his wives have betrayed him, his most recent treacherous whore being righteously transported to the Tower this very day!'

It's the sixth of February 1542! That's all I could think and that thought repeatedly reverberated around my skull for, what seemed like, minutes. Sixth of February? What happened to the lost few days in between? Is this going to keep happening? I was rambling both mentally and, now, verbally. He stopped mid-speech.

'Forgive me my Lord. I'm Bilious . It's a mouse thing.'

God! How dumb did I sound. Fortunately, he continued as if I had said nothing.

'Since November there have been three attempts on the life of His Grace.'

Sadler then went on to describe three distinct events, one involving an arrow during a hunt, another a poisoning at a banquet and, bizarrely a most cunning and ingenious trap that would have had the King fall many feet into a pit of fire. Truthfully, at first, I just didn't know what to say. I paced about my cage now hamming it up in my extended role as a sleuth.

'Your Grace, is there anything at all that would indicate that these threats were, indeed, part of a plot or could they have been random attempts by numerous enemies?...not that you have numerous enemies!...I'm sure you don't have any real enemies!...may have been accidents!'

I had started so well too.

'Ha ha! You jest again Little King Harry! Of course I have bloody enemies!! I have enemies around every corner. I have Catholic enemies, I have Protestant enemies. I have enemies at home, in Ireland, in Wales and bloody Scotland. Enemies in Spain, in every damn country you can mention!!'

He was on a roll now, and this, in part, was directed at Sadler whose raison d'etre was to keep the Scots at bay.

'God's teeth! I've even got bloody enemies next door! And no doubt some in here!!'

He was now ranting and I was wishing, yet again, that I had kept my counsel. I was left unsure as to what to do. I noticed that he was now half-standing, hobbling and raising his right fist to the skies. Risky as it was, I decided to mimic him. Only Sadler and Heneage could see this at first and it would be fair to say that they looked terrified and frequently glanced away. Eventually, Henry's eye caught me. His face flushed and he held his breath for, what seemed like, half an hour but then, he let it out, spitting confidently over his chief advisor who, straining a smile, simply said,

'Your Majesty…'

'Ha haaaaa! Ha ha ha!! Look! Look Heee he…see how he is the King!'

Sadler feigned laughter whilst Heneage had a, genuine and hearty, good laugh at my silliness.

'Yes, yes' said the King continuing 'Ah, you see, mouse, they are all connected. The bastard that did these evil acts thought it clever to leave little symbols at the scene of the treachery. One stuck on the bloody arrow itself, one on that ridiculous and deadly trap door and one, bare-faced, lay on the bottom of my damned goblet and plates! When we get them….'

You can imagine the rest. We waited patiently whilst Henry reeled off every mutilation, injury and humiliation known to man and, possibly, a few previously unknown. When he had calmed down, I realised that, yet again, I would have to choose my words very carefully as there was so much junk in my head by this time. Almost simultaneously, I was worrying about Queen Catherine, about Elspeth and why I had disappeared from York and reappeared here. I also had images of April in my head that had, so long, been absent. I thought of the diagram that I had seen in Cranmer's study with the spider-like drawings. Could those be the same as the ones Henry was referring to? Added to that, was the bizarre coincidence that these threats were also manifesting themselves in York.

'Your Grace. Be assured that I, and the Agents, will do our immediate utmost to get to the bottom of this diabolical intrigue. May I see the symbols?'

Almost before I had finished speaking, Sadler laid them out in front of me. I couldn't be certain, but these were, at the very least, similar to the ones I had seen in Cranmer's chamber and on the back of Bernard's document but I was incredibly frustrated as I hadn't a clue what they were or what they meant.

'May these be kept with me Your Grace?'

He nodded and then said,

'So…what's the answer then?'

'Erm….well you see…Your most noble Grace'

God no! I'm starting to sound like all his sycophants! I thought. So this is why they stumble over their words. Talk about putting you on the spot.

'I will need to study these. May I suggest that your food and wine taster is more diligent? Perhaps have someone double check, in case there is any suspicion of your staff and, no hunting Your Grace. Not for now. If possible keep to the Palace confines and share this with no one. Absolutely no one.'

I said this looking at Lord Sadler and Heneage. If, for any reason, either of these couldn't be trusted, he was done for. However, the one thing I was confident of, was that this would be kept secret. Except for erratic histories about the general risks to Henry's life, these specific events were seemingly never recorded for posterity.

Astonishingly, Henry was hanging on my every word. He grunted, grumbled, belched and snored in between but he, for whatever reason, thought that I was the sole answer to this problem. If these were random assassination attacks I wouldn't have had a chance in hell of getting to the bottom of it all but I was willing to give it a go, notwithstanding the fact that I was now growing quite weary of the exponential load that was, metaphorically, on my tiny shoulders. I knew I would need help. I pondered on his lack of patience. People had already been dismissed as well as some summary executions for these crimes but, no doubt, they were based on little, or no, evidence.

'Your Grace, you do realise that your initial cull may have got rid of the perpetrator and that I can only succeed in my quest by questioning remaining palace staff?'

He nodded, now only half-interested.

'And' I said quite emphatically 'I do not want to be in a position where I have to reveal my, somewhat unusual, qualities to every member of the Court.'

'Well of course not!!' He shouted, 'that's what your gang of morons is for! Get together your band…Agents…whatever you call yourselves. If you could thwart the Cataclysm, you can find these culprits and then we will watch them suffer!!' and off he went again.

One thing was for sure, Henry was the worst judge, and jury, that the world had ever had and I was still amazed that I was on the right side of him. I realised that Thomas Heneage was mentally taking notes of all that was said but I couldn't put my finger on what was going on with Sir Ralph Sadler. Silent throughout, I was increasingly suspicious of how he seemed to distance himself from the issues at hand.

'Send your damned pigeon today, get word to them and get cracking mouse!' Added Henry.

Faith! She must be here, I thought. I had no idea as to how that could be as, now, I had many days missing from my memory, perhaps even my existence. Not surprisingly, I agreed to everything and anything and promised myself that, at least, I would give this task my very best and work out whether it actually was the one and same threat as in York and, if not, move on to matters there. Confident I had a plan, another voice in my head reminded me that, added to all that, was my passion to get back home again.

That afternoon, I sat comfortably in the quarters of Thomas Heneage where I confided in him, my plan. After all, I had to trust somebody because I could only do a few tasks alone. He took me outside, beyond the stables. We neared an old barn and, gradually, above the sound of his singular leather footsteps crunching the ice, we could hear the collective cooing of pigeons. Faith recognised me and me, her, as she still had a scar from the tear in her leg. Ensuring that, on this occasion, the message was secured properly, I witnessed her speed away to the north leaving me feeling a little less isolated. My hope was that, within a week or two, I would either hear from, or actually receive the Agents of the Word at Court.

Once back inside and with Heneage's help, I compiled and scribed a complete register of Hampton Court staff and all its visitors for the past four months, including their nationality, known religious persuasion and connections to other members of the household. An onerous task indeed, but one in which Heneage happily supported me. I then asked him to put a line through all those that the King had already killed.

Except for just one time, I was not to see the King again for weeks and, on that one occasion he managed to astonish me even further. This time it was just me and the King, almost a uniquely intimate situation.

'I will grant her nought!' He said adamantly. I waited for him to say more.

'Nought I say! They all do it Mouse!! They all seek audience with the King, Lords, anyone who they think will save their bloody neck! Just one last visit My Beloved Grace…'

He said those last three words pathetically, as to emphasise that those who faced death were weak. With those words, he was mimicking Catherine, now desperate. I knew what he was getting at. I had seen copies of the numerous pleas made by those in the Tower and, yes, I think that, truthfully, many of them did simply want to see him one last time. Why on God's earth he was telling me this, I had no clue whatsoever.

'What am I to do?'

This was seemingly rhetoric, or at least I hoped that it was. He continued, 'what can I do?!! When people commit treason they commit a crime against God as well as their King! What good would mercy do? I have no choice.'

This was almost turning into a confessional. He was doing that thing where people say one thing, meaning the opposite. He must have known by now that he had become an uncontrollable and ruthless tyrant but every so often, his conscience gave him a prod. Not often enough unfortunately. However, I said nothing.

'She asks for you.'

I knew instantly what he meant. Queen Catherine must have got wind of my unexplainable visit to London. Momentarily, I couldn't fathom why she would want to see me as I imagined that she would have had enough of mice in the place where she was currently residing.

'It's the one and only concession I will allow her before she dies, mind you, and if she says anything about this current plot you must tell me immediately!'

I had an answer to this already but was certain it would anger him. Nevertheless, I felt it was something he should hear.

'Your Grace, I can assure you that she wasn't involved in any plots against you. Despite her crimes I believe she loved you and still does.'

His fat head whipped around and he stared. For the first time I saw a tear. He knew I was right and, and to be fair to him, seemingly she really had committed adultery. I watched him closely, uncomfortable but digesting what I had said.

'You will be transported today and allowed just one third of an hour. You may say that I acknowledge her affection for her King, nothing more.'

'Absolutely, Your Majesty. Anything else?'

'No. Bugger off and leave me be.'

12: THE CLOCK

You've probably worked out by now that I had previously visited absolutely every location that I write about. When I say previously, I mean in my time, my own timeline. The good news is that almost all of Britain's cherished historical towns and buildings will be preserved and restored. So, yes, I had seen the Tower of London but never, never, like this. Even second-hand descriptions from my friends in York could not communicate the dark foreboding that emanated from this gargantuan structure. What struck me most was the paradox, the change I experienced as I travelled along the river from Hampton Court. The Palace itself was an aesthetic triumph and the journey, where all you could hear were the crows passing overhead and the oars in the water, was welcome and therapeutic after the mental strains that I had found myself so recently suffering from. And, then, as it loomed into view, there was no doubt that the fortification was making an uncomfortable, assertive statement of its very own and, of course, as I, very slowly, got nearer, the bigger and more foreboding it seemed. The smells of the city made it worse and, of course, the trump card in this stack was seeing a head on a pike. Well, several to be honest. I couldn't imagine how anyone finding themselves sentenced to live in this hell-hole coped and couldn't help reflecting on Brother Bede and Brother Bernard's escape.

I reminded myself that I was a visitor but I knew instinctively that, for most, even this could be dangerous. Where were the guarantees that you would be released again? How would you be treated by the guards?

Besides the boatman, I had a companion, a young man called Gabriel who steadied my box and, now and again, exchanged idle chatter with the boatman. I found him pleasant company and I also felt safe next to him. However, I wasn't allowed to talk. From this point on, my ability to speak did have to be contained if I was to get the measure of the immense personnel of Hampton Court that, at this present time exceeded six hundred. We had been advised that, for easy access to Catherine, it would be wise to enter through traitor's gate. Easily said, and could well have been more convenient, but it struck terror through the three of us. I presumed that this was Henry's way of keeping our visit secret although I could only imagine what it must have been like to go beyond this point and never return. Almost instantly, the audible landscape changed. At first, clanking, squeaking and dripping. Metal hitting stone, but where was it coming from? I asked myself. These sounds gradually increased in volume and then they echoed. They echoed and echoed and, if it wasn't simply that this was a matter of science, you would have thought it another device employed to terrify new arrivals. And then, the one thing we didn't want to hear, human sound. Cries, moans, pleas and prayers and, of course, this seemed, too, to reverberate endlessly. It was very easy to imagine that this was really what hell could be like.

Our boat was pulled in and we were almost immediately met by the constable himself. Gabriel bowed respectfully and the constable simply waved us toward a spiral staircase. If I am truthful, he wasn't menacing, clearly having had orders directly from the King to be civil to us. I watched Gabriel carefully as he carried my box up the staircase, totally bewildered as to why the Queen would want a mouse for company and, even if he could work that out, why would she choose this singular mouse? Added to that, I was still dressed in the most ridiculous, if fashionable, garb.

Gabriel's accent was strange, I thought that, at first, this was German but it was very slightly odd and I had heard it before. Having said that, he didn't speak much, and before we knew it we were at the "Queen's apartments" as the constable called them. It was actually, a complete shithole, a shambles but intended to look like a person of privilege should be in there. Objects and furniture were sparse and there was only a little light from one window.

The constable paused outside the cell and this is where I got my first glimpse of Catherine and, as I had expected, it broke my heart. She looked like a lost child and was overtly terrified, pacing the room and trembling. We entered and she paused, a look of hope and desperate expectation of the imminent delivery of good news. I could read her expression, it simply said, "who has come to see me? Has his Grace had a change of heart?" So, not surprisingly, she was devastated when no news came from the constable. Once inside, she started to pace again, unsure of what this visit meant. However, Gabriel knocked on the door and reminded the constable that I was to be left in there alone and, within the minute, they both left. She glared into my box.

'Sir Mouse!' She said with genuine surprise but still trembling.

I didn't know how to address her. If I called her Queen, it was likely that she would read too much into it. "Catherine" was too formal. As it was, I didn't have the chance. She rambled uncontrollably about her fears and repeated denials of her dalliances. I let her talk. This in itself, I thought, may have been therapeutic but once she had finished and relaxed a little, I reluctantly had to tell her that I was not there to offer a reprieve. She wasn't really surprised but the King's message gave her heart. I looked around, the rumours were true. She had asked for a crude piece of timber to be brought into her cell so that she could practice putting her head on a block. This wasn't the party-loving, laughing and cheerful teen I had seen in Lincoln less than a year before. It would be fair to say that she was now almost unrecognisable and I would have done anything to save her.

'Did he die well, Mouse?'

I knew instantly that she was referring to Culpeper and, although I lied, I needed to reassure her.

'He knew nothing Your Majesty and he was excused the quartering'

The last part, at least, was true and I saw some relief on her face. They truly loved one other and, in my world, they would be together soon. In her world, however, they were both damned.

'My visit is, in itself, a sign of His Grace's love for you.'

She sobbed and then collapsed on the floor.

'Take me out of my box' I suggested and shortly afterwards she cradled me in her lap.

I felt entirely inadequate but offered this girl as much affection as I had in the time that we were together. She relaxed somewhat and then managed to talk, almost normally.

'Can you stop the threats to the King?'

She clearly knew, which surprised me.

'I have been given that very assignment Your Majesty.'

'He has so many enemies, Sir Mouse, and I wouldn't like any harm to come to him. He suffers so.' She thought for a moment 'I have so many suspicions. But this is not usual. By that, I mean he is always under threat but these have been quite specific. Did he tell you about the signs that had been drawn?'

'Why…yes'

'I have only one, humble, theory that may help you. When you are back at the Palace, look at the clock' she said.

'The clock?'

'Yes' she insisted, 'just a thought, but it may help.'

I was befuddled completely by this and just as I was to question her about this suggestion, the door opened. I looked up at her with pride and she made no attempt to extend the visit. She was wise enough not to speak directly to me and made every effort to support this deception.

'Thank you young man, for bringing His Grace's favourite pet to see me.'

Gabriel, instinctively, bowed and whilst I was still wrestling with my, ever increasingly complex emotions, I found myself back in the boat and returning to Hampton Court. Shamefully, I was pleased to see the distance growing between myself and the Tower and was delighted that my young companion decided to pray.

'Dear Lord, forgive Queen Catherine her sins and fold her in Your ever Graceful Arms. Remove any fear and make her end a swift and peaceful one so that she may soon see Your Face. Let her know that she is loved.'

Yet again, I was reminded of the power of prayer and also how someone like Catherine touched many lives. It seemed entirely appropriate and I would have thanked him if I was able to.

Soon we were back at Court and, following a night's sleep, I would have to begin my investigation into the threats against the King, confident that, soon, the Agents of the Word would be joining me.

13: HAMPTON COURT

The following day I had a meeting with Thomas Heneage in which we agreed that my unique gift should not be shared with the greater populace of Hampton Court. There was little doubt that this would only have served to complicate matters and would even place blame at the foot of the bedevilled rodent.

He had a suitable and, somewhat devious, plan. Amongst the working staff of the Palace (as opposed to the courtiers themselves) there was only one woman that worked beyond the laundry: the pudding woman. Yes, you heard right. The one person that Henry trusted completely with his puddings and sweets was a woman called Mrs Cornwallis and, so impressed was he, that he gave her a house of her own in Aldgate. As the King got older and bigger, and the Court seemed to grow with him, the demands on Mrs Cornwallis's time also grew exponentially. So, she had, only two months previously, been given a young assistant who was known to all simply as Beth.

Heneage decided that Beth deserved an induction and tour of the inner workings of the Palace and, why not, perhaps the whole damn place. The fact that absolutely no one else had been granted this favour would, hopefully, completely bypass everyone. Perhaps this, also, could be seen as a special favour to Mrs Cornwallis and give her a renewed sense of status. Also, for some bizarre reason, Beth would be looking after the King's favourite mouse whilst this tour took place and, although I knew that not being able to speak would leave me incredibly frustrated, I would be able to get the measure of this crowded community by proxy. After all, within days, the Agents would be with me to assist.

We started immediately. Beth looked so incredibly young and also very scared. Scared to be tending to the King's beast and also scared to be meeting everyone. Heneage was with us constantly, which settled my nerves and I was determined to commit as much as I possibly could to memory. Throughout, besides the odd courtesy or a "hello," Beth said nothing. After the first hour, she had seen so many marvels that she became calmer and openly grateful for this concession. I understood that Thomas Heneage was being thorough but, admittedly, our excursions to the finer parts of the Palace left Beth terrified and courtiers quite shocked.

Even I struggled with the size of this place. We walked through the Wolsey rooms and reception rooms, so-called because this place had been, initially, built by and for Cardinal Wolsey. The paintings and tapestries were breathtaking. And then, the Great Hall which, although often used for grand occasions like masques and balls, was also used as a dining room for the lower ranks. Already, I was dumbfounded at how poor security was. Yes, Henry had always had guards, Knights and Earls around him and, yes, he had food tasters, but access to parts of the Palace was nowhere near as restricted as they could have been. The wooden vaulting was an absolute masterpiece in itself but, yet again, reminded me of where the term "eavesdropping" came from. There were so many spaces amongst the eaves and beyond where people could conceal themselves and, this was one of the few times that Beth spoke. It wasn't what she said, but how she said it, that made me think she may have known something about the threats.

Obviously, we didn't wander into the King's apartments but I was content and convinced that these were secure. Beyond his privy quarters was a watching chamber. Restricted access if you like, constantly monitored by members of the Yeoman of the Guard. However, it was clear that security in Henry's world still meant fortification, strength and the ability to resist attack. Espionage was employed by Kings but was still in its infancy.

I was pleased to move on. I was more interested in the staff, the workers at Hampton Court Palace and what access they may, or may not have had, to the King. Not surprisingly, the engine room of Henry's Palace was the kitchen or, should I say kitchens. We accessed them through the master carpenter's court which was big enough to turn carts around in, having to cope hour by hour with deliveries, the food consumption being almost constant. Before we went in, I nodded to Thomas Heneage as I wished him to detour to the nearby stables. Something had caught my eye. He introduced Beth to everyone, from the Master to the grooms and stable boys. Here, Gabriel was busy brushing a most noble horse, a percheron possibly seventeen hands high and I noticed that Beth caught his eye almost instantly and I would have guessed that there was only a couple of years between them. Heneage mentioned everyone by name and described their responsibilities which was worth its weight in gold to me.

There was an older male, Ramsey, who was startled by our visit. He seemed to be rummaging amongst horse tack that was irregularly placed in the corner of the stable. He jumped up when he saw Heneage, himself suspicious. He told us he was looking for a lost bridle although it was clear from his demeanour alone, that he was not where he should have been.

Already my task was becoming incredibly daunting. So many people, it was like a small town. I told myself that I had to concentrate on those who had access to the King either directly or indirectly. One thing was for sure, the lower quarters represented a huge, well-oiled machine that seldom stopped. There was a range of preparatory rooms. In the centre, a courtyard where fresh and raw foods were stored, including fish and, of course, beyond there were extensive wine cellars. This was a bustling environment, filled with smells and the pulse of diligent energy of all that worked there. It was cold outside but the labour-intensive interior felt much warmer particularly when you neared any of the numerous roaring fires. The last thing anyone would have wanted down there was a mouse but, most, if not all, had heard of the King's new and curious trinket. Beth was introduced to all, many seeming to me as incredibly menial in this maze with little inkling or thought given to what went on beyond their own jobs or their little corner of the Palace. Others, of course, knew the whole process exactly and were even aware of the Kings' particular tastes. Rumour had it, that on special occasions, the King would eat swan, partly because no one else was allowed to. The curiously named, Mr Drake boasted of how he alone prepared swan at the King's request. Even allowing for the fact that Drake just liked talking crap generally and probably also took this opportunity to impress a pretty girl, he was the type of employee I was interested in. Someone, for instance, who had a direct route to the King's palette without affecting anyone else. Although irrelevant, the scruffy eye-patch over his right eye did little to put people at ease. Heneage informed me that, and no pun intended here, Drake was almost always in a foul mood. He had been assisted by a boy, thought to be his son but, one day, he simply didn't turn in. Drake never spoke of it and no one asked about him from that day onward.

As Beth took a few minutes to relieve her bladder, I whispered to Heneage that we needed to see the route that wine took from its delivery, right to the King's mouth. What a nightmare that revelation was. From stories of wine fountains at masques and courtiers having direct access to the cellars, to the various ways in which it was stored, I found it hard to get a handle on any constancy or regular process. Wine had often enjoyed the nickname, sac, as it was often drunk from a leather sack, sometimes even from a bladder and it did, of course, start its life in wood. The King would normally drink from a goblet so, unfortunately, Beth was left completely bewildered whilst introductions turned into questions from Thomas Heneage about how wine found its way to the King's table. In my mind, I calculated at this stage that there were no more than five people who could interfere with the Kings' wine from cask to goblet. Unfortunately, I could times this by three when we were looking at his food, as Henry was not sure whether it was food or wine that had contained poison.

This tour became an incredibly bizarre experience with Beth, just once, asking if she was in trouble, as did almost everyone else we encountered, although Heneage professionally put each one at ease. Beyond the stable, I wanted to meet anyone else who may have taken part in any of the King's hunting excursions. Those who could handle weapons were almost entirely limited to the courtiers but, of course, there were those who looked after and secured them and there were also others who looked after hunting birds and the dogs. How on earth I was meant to detect something suspicious, God knows, but we did have direct access to the Master of the Hounds and his staff who were, in turn, responsible to the Master of the Horse. On this day the dogs were lively and, thinking that we had met all the staff, who else but the Master of the Horse himself, Sir Anthony Browne walked over to greet Heneage, who, in turn, peddled the story of this, most unusual, tour. He personally wandered off into a nearby thicket and dragged back a young man, who, instead of cleaning up after the dogs, was resting by a tree. He was, to say the least, horrified when he saw the bosses-boss yelling at him. All the same, he was also introduced to Beth.

'I could have done with a pretty girl in the thicket!'

He said unashamedly and was immediately awarded with a swipe across his cheek with a white stick. The stick being a sign of authority rewarded to only three officials within the Court.

'This one will have to go soon, Master Heneage. Too much to say and too little to do, only still here because he was first one there when His Grace fell into that trap.'

'Saved his life, did Lyndon' interrupted the boy making his own introduction. 'Mind you the old fool hasn't got long anyway!'

Almost simultaneously, he was reprimanded by Heneage, Browne and Beth although, on this occasion, Browne held back physically. He sighed and said,

'Even I have to be patient with this one. He has an uncanny irreverence for His Grace and I know where it comes from!'

He had said this with a knowing look and, yes, I did know what he meant. For decades, Henry had tolerated the same Court fool, Will Somers. Henry thought that he was hilarious but to most others, he was simply someone who amused the King and it was their place to laugh along. To me he was a complete and utter dick, wobbling about in silly clothes saying whatever he liked. I've seen more wit in a rice pudding. He had this uncanny ability of getting away with saying whatever he liked. Except for once, that is. He, for some strange reason, decided that it would be the world's jolliest jape if he called Princess Elizabeth a bastard in front of the King. Needless to say, this nearly cost him his life and was a true measure of his funniness as far as I was concerned. I knew as well that he continuously got under the skin of almost all at Court, lampooning them but knowing that there could be no retribution. So, having witnessed some of this himself, gullible Lyndon decided it was seemingly fair that he did the same.

'Were you at the trap when the King fell?' Asked Heneage.

'Good thing I was, lucky the fall didn't kill the fat bastard, only just got him out of the fire in time!'

This was more serious than I thought. I also wondered if Lyndon knew how much suspicion he was now putting himself under.

'The King had a fall?!' said Beth, shocked.

'You mustn't speak to anyone of this matter' said Browne 'you never heard it, girl.'

She nodded and never spoke again until we returned. Hundreds of people, a few grumpy and a few stupid, a handful of clues and a massive headache! Why on earth have I been given this to do when there is so much danger in York? I asked myself.

We found ourselves circumnavigating the environs of the Palace and, finally, approaching the central gateway. This building in its entirety was astonishing, a testimony to the relatively new resource that was sandstone brick. The chimneys spoke of limitless wealth and the windows were the finest in the land. Just as we were about to enter the gate Beth said,

'What's that?'

'Why, dear, it's a clock!' Said Heneage almost as if it were his own.

I looked upon it for the very first time, marvelling at its design and detail. It shimmered in the midday milky, winter sun and, as I observed the detail, I was sure that I now had a much better idea of what those wicked designs meant.

God bless Queen Catherine, I thought. She knew that part of the answer lay there.

In an instant, I had also realised that the threat in York and the threat, there, at Hampton Court were not the same. I told myself that, after a good meal and some sleep I would try to straighten out, in my mind, what had gone on and what needed to be done, giving thanks for the good and gracious Sir Thomas Heneage. We parted company with the lovely Beth and she wandered away from the Palace into the woods.

What followed was a macabre and incisive discussion about the dead. Thomas Heneage told me the details of the four men that had been executed because of the attempts on the King's life. None made sense to him, or me, they were just in the wrong place at the wrong time. Ironically, Henry was usually quite happy as long as someone died for a crime. It didn't matter who it was but, in this case, he knew that the threat hadn't gone away so it was up to me to find the real culprits and I was now much more confident that I could do just that.

14: THE PLAN

As I awoke, I ordered in my mind the nonsense that had become like a countless number of threads now inexorably entangled and set this out in short understandable statements.

I had to get home. My home, and be back with my wife April.

I had to protect the King from further danger and find the culprits that had systematically tried to take his life.

I needed to return to York and put an end to the danger so recently prevalent against the Agents.

But, sadly, at this stage, little did I know how things had worsened in my beloved York.

15: THE GREAT WINDOW

Those passing weeks saw many a change in York. Robert had kindly insisted that Elspeth convalesce with him and he and Mrs Hall had even invited Wynnfrith to stay, although Wynnfrith felt a compelling sense of duty and care to their humble home that adjoined the wall adjacent to Bootham Bar. So, Wynn visited daily and there was, albeit slow, some visible improvement in her sister. Having said that, the situation was somewhat awkward especially as Robert seemed to be spending more time at home and much of that time seemed to be spent arguing with his wife. After questioning one of the servants at Barley Hall on this matter, Wynnfrith was told that they were used to it and took no notice. Added to that, was the worry that Robert's well-tested routine of sneaking in the odd grope, would return. This was mostly Wynnfrith's worry as, even though she was recovering from the poison, Elspeth was no match for him.

Now well into February, the weather was still severe but it could not stop Wynnfrith from making her daily visit.

Elspeth was in a room, alone, with almost every comfort she could desire. She constantly asked for less, ever mindful of her vows. But, if there was one thing the sisters had learned about Robert, this last year or so, it was that he was increasingly and more habitually generous.

Elspeth could detect Wynn's irregular footsteps ascending the stairs and then onto the landing and this in itself was a daily tonic.

'Oh, sister it is still so cold!' Said Wynnfrith.

'Come near to the bed, Wynn, it's closer to the warm chimney breast.'

She did more than that, without invitation, she snuggled into the bunk alongside Elspeth and they both giggled as if they were children again.

'I do wish this fuss was over. I am now perfectly fine and very willing to go about my chores!.... I feel like a prisoner!'

Wynnfrith continued to giggle, pleased that her sister's grumpiness was returning, a sure sign that her health was improving.

'Oh? What was that? Was that you complaining sister? Thought the mouse had returned!'

Elspeth gave her sister a glare that would have had the devil fleeing for the hills and then, they laughed again and lay there, keeping each other warm.

'What fun we had when we were little' said Elspeth.

'Yes, what days. We were so poor but how we were happy…but…well…'

'You're not going to ask about mother and father again are you?' Said Elspeth, again with some edge to her voice.

'It's just that, well…Robert is bound to know more than we do and…'

'Can't you just let it go, sister? I understand why it's important but I wouldn't trust anything he told...' interrupted Elspeth.

Elspeth was well into dissuading Wynnfrith when they became aware of a slight murmuring from below. This, very quickly, became loud. Very loud.

'This will never go away I tell you! You've brought an endless curse to this, house. I'm tired of it. Those women of the street are enough to send any wife mad but this! It never EVER! goes away!'

Elspeth and Wynnfrith did what all self-respecting women would do, and eavesdropped.

'Shush, you're making the bed creak' said Wynn.

The noisy culprit downstairs was Robert's wife and she was fuming, publicly reprimanding her husband.

'I am well-rebuked dear…I …err I do have a plan. An end to it…if you could only be patient my dove.' He meekly replied.

'Patient! Patient!! It's been over twenty bloody years. Oh, I give up. I just give up.'

The sisters were relieved that they weren't arguing about them and, to be fair, Mrs Hall had always been kind to them both, but they were heartily disappointed that the fight had fizzled out so quickly or, at least, had gone much quieter and, all their attempts to get closer to the wall, gained them nothing.

'He's had other women for twenty years?!' Said Wynnfrith, quite shocked.

'Probably. But that's not what this was about. Let's wrap up, get warm again!'

This had Wynnfrith wondering if Elspeth knew more about this argument and perhaps even more about Robert's past and, possibly even more about their mother and father. However, almost as if by habit, she knew when to let go. Some clattering and voices, that were changing in both pitch and volume, could be heard for some time and then, to the sister's delight, the door opened and Millie, one of cousin Robert's servants, entered with food.

Snuggled tight in this guest bed, keeping warm by the chimney breast and over-feeding themselves, had the sisters in child-like character for hours to come. Silently watching the snowflakes melt on Robert's grand, brick chimney, they were as happy as they had ever been and no longer paid notice to the events below.

Elspeth insisted that she would return to normal life and normal duties within the week. Robert conceded but insisted that she stay in York. Unusually, Elspeth agreed. However, before that week was out, Elspeth was to witness a most shocking turn of events. It would be fair to say that she had given little thought to her condition, some still thinking that it may have been something she had caught whilst visiting the infirmary undercroft. In any case, she was not of a mind to pursue the matter until I had returned. Abrasive as our relationship was, she knew I would get to the bottom of the mystery.

Robert, a successful and very wealthy glass merchant, was forever having the latest this-and-that added to Barley Hall. He was not alone in this. It was a way of advertising both wealth and success, chimneys, in particular, being a guaranteed sign of superiority. This did, however, somewhat surprise Elspeth. Being, purposefully, a person of meagre means she just couldn't get her head around why anyone would want to, continually, attract attention to themselves. In the weeks that she stayed at Barley Hall, the Mayor had had new fireplaces put in, a kitchen extension, new beams, window frames and windows. It was all, very grand but, particularly in winter, the upheaval seemed, to her, completely unnecessary. Also, for some bizarre reason, he saw fit to oversee the work himself, much to the chagrin of Mrs Hall. This also meant a stream of tradesmen and other visitors tramping in and out of the house in the middle of winter. Perhaps he just can't help himself, thought Elspeth. Some afternoons, she would sit downstairs with Mrs Hall, seemingly never anything less than wonderful and compassionate, but she did pull her face, often, at the incessant human traffic. Thankfully, there were some familiar faces. William Fawkes visited with Edward, his son who, on his days off school and some evenings helped Godwin with the carpentry. Godwin in particular, was grateful for work in a relatively warm environment, in the middle of winter. There was one character whose presence shocked Elspeth. It took many days where she was constantly muttering to herself, who is he? I do recognise him. She asked Robert, his wife and his servants to no avail. As a last resort, she thought she would try her sister who immediately said,

'Oh him. Do you remember sister? The beef thief?'

This was so concise and accurate that Elspeth knew who he was immediately. The previous year, when they first had a cellar meeting with Edward Fawkes and the mouse, the sheriff had barged in, undetected, but had removed a hiding thief from the upstairs room. As they left the sisters caught a glimpse of this criminal but remembered, ironically, that there were no signs of the beef. The mouse, they recalled, was kidnapped shortly afterwards. But, there this man was, seemingly a general labourer for all the crafts and tradesmen helping to tart up Robert's mansion. Added to that motley crew was none other than Hugh, the very man who, twenty years earlier had embezzled from Silas's mother as she struggled to sell her quills.

As far as Elspeth could tell, all was going well. That was, until one day very near to completion, Robert stood alongside the tradesmen, Mrs Hall and some friends (including William Fawkes) to admire his new, coloured glass window erected in the Great Hall. However, it was the most unusual construct, designed by Robert himself. As yet, panes of glass were limited in size so had to be held together by lead and, the size of a complete window was generally restricted as this made the window vulnerable. Usually, even windows that appeared large were actually several windows separated and supported either by wood or stone frames. Not good enough for Robert though, he had been encouraged to install the largest, ever, window in York.

It was magnificent both in its fitting and design and the winter sun dappled rainbow colours on the oak boards and furniture in the Hall. Even the servants peeped around the door to have a look at the finished work. Robert stood right in front of it to bathe in its colour and warmth. It was then, as everyone took a few steps away, that the light in the window seemed to change. The hues began to merge on the window, as they did on the floor. Slightly bemused by this, Robert stepped closer only to deduce that something was creating an illusion of the window moving except, it wasn't an illusion. Crick. Crack. Crick….Crick….Crunch and, whilst everyone was squinting to determine exactly where these troubling noises were coming from (as tradesmen are given to do) several hundred pounds in weight of lead, wood and thick glass toppled downwards and shattered with the Mayor flattened beneath it. He squealed and then shouted for help and everyone, including Elspeth and Mrs Hall, ran to rescue him.

'Stop!' cried Godwin 'every piece of that window is now like a knife. Don't move anything until you have gloves or wrap rags around your hands!'

Meanwhile, Robert lay, injured but completely still, beneath this huge installation. He moaned but, otherwise, was sensible enough not to make things worse by moving. Servants and Mrs Hall ransacked the house for gloves. Any type of gloves. Fortunately, some of the workmen already had some, so began to pull away the hundreds of pieces of glass and shards of lead.

'Oh my! Ooh my goodness!!' Shouted Mrs Hall and, as Elspeth's eyes moved to see what had startled her, she too saw the blood streaming out from beneath the frame.

Instinctively she started to clean it up. Elspeth stopped her, knowing that it served no purpose.

Slowly and steadily, a mound of glass, lead and timber rose on the other side of the Hall whilst, almost uncannily, the amount on top of the Mayor seemed to decrease very little. An hour later he was dragged out, unconscious. A sight which had Mrs Hall and some of the servants in tears. Where his flesh had been exposed, he had scratches and cuts of every shape and size. Within many of his wounds, there were embedded small shards of glass. However, noticeably on his neck, was a significant wound that was still pumping out blood.

'He won't have long now' said William Fawkes in a, very matter of fact, manner.

'No, no' said Elspeth calmly 'see, he bleeds but the flow is slow. Look…' and she pointed at the pool of blood that Mrs Hall had tried to clean up.

'Can't be more than a pint or two!' Said Godwin, now taking a close look at the Mayor's neck. He was right. This was a dangerous and deep wound but well away from his carotid artery. It was likely that his life had been spared simply by the random placement of the broken glass. All the same, he was still in trouble. As Mrs Hall examined the whole of his body for other, serious wounds, Godwin tended to the cut in his neck.

It took four men to haul his carcass upstairs and over an hour for Mrs Hall to change him, clean him and get him in a bed. Ironically, the nearest room was the one Elspeth had been in previously so, they lay him there. The notorious beef thief produced a copper needle and, remarkably, some catgut, removed from sheep's intestines for fine sewing. Nobody thought at any point to ask as to why he had these on his person, perhaps they simply thought that they were accepted trade tools. Millie, the servant, put some stitches in his neck wound and Mrs Hall tended, as best she could, to the uncountable cuts elsewhere on his being.

167

Mrs Hall had felt unhappy earlier in the week but this, now, certainly put things into perspective. Besides a bloody great hole in the wall during a cold February and a pile of rubble on the floor, she now had a half-dead husband upstairs, a poorly nun downstairs and a house full of strangers. The rubble was now no more than that. Rubble and rubbish. It all had to be removed.

Having wandered off, Edward and Godwin returned carrying planks and, within no time, they had managed to temporarily cover the gaping chasm that was, so recently, a beautiful masterpiece. By the evening, the house was habitable thanks to all those people and, by this time, Robert had started to groan slightly. There was no making light of it, it was very unlikely that this was an accident and he was, very poorly.

Elspeth and Wynnfrith offered to nurse Robert not knowing that Mrs Hall had left him lying up there on the bed, naked. Yes, completely naked. The door opened slightly but, on seeing this lardy behemoth stretched out as God intended, they shut it again, quickly. Then they giggled.

'Don't! She'll hear. He'll hear!'

Whispered Elspeth and this resulted in them both giggling more. As devilment got the better of these two overgrown children, Elspeth slowly opened the door again and, very naughtily, they both peeped in.

'God's teeth! There's hair everywhere!' Said Wynn.

'He's almost covered in it!' And then they giggled some more.

'Don't know what all the fuss is about' said Wynn 'it's like he's been bestowed a third little finger!'

Laughter exploded from their supposedly innocent mouths.

'Everything alright up there girls?' Shouted Mrs Hall.

'Yes, no problem. Just seeing to the tiny details now.' Shouted Wynnfrith.

Hands over their mouths but still spluttering, they entered the room and stood, one each side of the bed. The bonnet that Elspeth had kept on the window ledge had fallen onto Robert's face and was slowly rising and falling as he was now sleeping. Wickedly, they looked him up and down and smiled at one another trying hard not to burst into laughter again.

'Mrs Grindem must be a saint grappling with this lot' said Wynn po-faced 'he's just a lump of red hair and fat.'

She threw a sheet over him and they both started to bathe the cuts on his face and arms. Every so often, they would catch each other's eye and they would, yet again, collapse in a heap. Every time they did this, a voice seemed to come from nowhere asking if they were ok and this, of course, made them worse. A few weeks later, they would remark that they had never been happier than when the window fell on top of the Mayor.

Eventually, he started to come around and, truth be told, he was suffering. Mrs Hall looked around the door and, delighted at seeing him gaining consciousness, thought to feed him.

'A little pickle my love?'

He didn't reply which didn't surprise Mrs Hall, but she was bewildered by the reaction of the girls. They stood, stoic, staring at one another, beetroot red, cheeks puffed out and holding their breath. Mrs Hall walked away shaking her head.

Realising that he would soon be fully conscious the sisters did, at last, regain their composure. Elspeth, holding his hand, tried to explain what had happened as best she could.

'So...a fau...fault? Something wrong with...with...the window?' He asked.

'Sadly, I think not cousin. I do believe that the window was meant to hurt or kill you' said Wynn.

He strained to sit up.

'They're….they……they're going aft…after us all dear….send now for Mick….Mickle…'

'Yes yes' said Elspeth 'please do not strain so. I will make arrangements for the mouse to return. I agree, I think we all are in danger.'

16: SISTERS AGAIN

During the period of Robert's confinement, the sisters gave
at least as much kindness and goodwill to him as they had,
in recent times, received from him. They were also to regret
their child-like mocking of his inadequacies, as he soon
became very ill. Many of his cuts were beginning to heal but
the large and more serious one on his neck had become
infected. In the sixteenth century, infected wounds,
generally, meant one thing and that was death. Mrs Hall
feared the worst as he slumped into delirium and an endless
sweating fever. She, along with Elspeth and Wynnfrith
nursed him almost constantly but, within a few days, they
had run out of ideas. Neither had done anything about re
calling the Agents. The sisters knew that, for some bizarre
reason, the mouse had left for London telling no one
except, perhaps young Peter, who had ended up in the
employ of Robert but residing at Silas's cottage.

So, Mrs Hall decided to send for the local barber-
surgeon, Viscera, in the hope he had some remedies. As he
arrived, complaining continuously about the climate, the
bedroom was crowded. After all, this had only ever been
used as a spare bedroom, Robert was put there in a hurry.

Pushed up against the chimney breast were Wynnfrith, Elspeth and Mrs Hall who was saying nothing but was, very loudly, snivelling and blowing her nose into a large flannel. Viscera arrived at the same time as Godwin who, they presumed, was showing deference to the Mayor. Viscera hovered over the patient,

'Mmmm…ohh…mmm…I see' and then nothing, besides constantly repeating the same.

Elspeth was aware that he was looking up and down the length of the Mayor's plentiful body, wondering why on earth he wasn't treating the wound. Within minutes, Godwin was doing more or less the same, leaving the impromptu audience bewildered. Eventually, he muttered,

'Mmm…yes.. a day or two. Maybe more. Big job though, big fella!'

Mrs Hall stalled, thought for a moment until the penny dropped and suddenly lunged forward and shouted so hard that both girls jumped.

'You bloody shit! I want him healed not dead and boxed! Thou ghoul! Thou vulture!! And you…carpenter! You ought to know better!'

She chased them, whipping Viscera about the back of the neck with the cloth but, as he made his desperate escape from this formidable foe, he was blocked by the hulk that was Godwin slowly negotiating the stairs downward. As a last attempt to redeem himself, Viscera turned and said

'Oh…perhaps….ouch! A poultice?... aaagh!!'

'I'll bloody poultice your arse you… grim reaper!' Promised Mrs Hall.

Godwin was now well away and, although it was a stretch, Mrs Hall's last athletic lunge with the cloth gave Viscera one award-winning slap on the cheek as he tumbled downstairs.

Yet again, thinking these were possibly the best days of their lives, Elspeth and Wynnfrith suppressed their amusement as best they could. Mrs Hall returned to the bedroom grumbling and cursing and, later, Elspeth would comment that she had never heard some of those words used by Mrs Hall ever before, anywhere.

'Listen' said Wynnfrith and they all stopped to pick out what Robert was saying. He had previously only groaned, and, to be honest, it was downright irritating at times, but now he was, just about, making some sense.

'Go…..em……go…an'

'Bless him' said Mrs Hall 'he's trying to tell us something.'

It took almost five minutes before these, seemingly unrelated, noises began to make any sense but, even then, they weren't completely coherent.

'Gona…..Gona!' He cried.

This meant nothing until he eventually added to it.

'Grin….grin…Gona'

'Ah bless, I think he wants to smile again. God love him!' said Mrs Hall.

And then, although Robert had no awareness or knowledge of what was coming, he shouted, repeatedly,

'Gona Grindem! Gona Grindem!'

Instantly, Mrs Hall was, yet again, furious. Beyond furious, explosive. She had no idea who or what Gona was but she bloody knew who Mrs Grindem was. Added to her misery was his reluctance to stop shouting out his mistress's name,

'Gona Grindem! Gona Gona Grindem.'

This, particularly in a northern accent, led to some amusement and this was not completely confined to the bedroom. The servant's chuckles were gradually getting louder and there was an audience gathering outside, below.

'Give 'em one for us n'all mate!' Came the first cry.

'Can we come up and join in?!' and on it went as Mrs Hall, yet again, became frenzied.

Mrs Hall, now returning to amply exhibiting her wider knowledge of the English language decided that it was a good time to empty Robert's chamber pot out of the window. The sisters could take no more and had to leave. In time, he calmed and quietened but it was another two hours before Mrs Hall's promises to get the embalmer back had died down. It had done little to help that the, notorious, Mrs Grindem had been christened "Gunnora" a relatively common medieval name.

The evening saw the sisters sitting downstairs by the large fire in, what should have been complete comfort. They did, however, have to sit and look at the impromptu demolition site which was so recently the pride of Barley Hall. Elspeth appeared pensive.

'What's going on up there sister?' Asked Wynnfrith referring to her sister's over-worked mind.

'We must recall the Agents, if we don't, everyone will be dead. I do confess to feeling vulnerable, not just for myself but for all of the Agents.' Said Elspeth.

'Agreed' said Wynnfrith nervously. She started to elaborate but was then interrupted by a rather meek knock on the door.

Wynnfrith leapt up and hobbled toward the door, her limbs aching with the constant climbing of the stairs, an activity few people enjoyed in Tudor England.

As she opened it, she was genuinely shocked, and also blatantly displeased, at seeing Marcus standing there. Marcus, from the undercroft infirmary, had decided to wander in the dark and snow to seek out, she presumed, her sister. Marcus who, very possibly, had something to do with her sister's sudden illness. She was not pleased to see him and this was evident in her constant, dark stare.

'What do you want?!' Came the icy greeting.

'Well, err…Maiden. I was…well…just wondering how your sister was faring?'

He was clearly very uncomfortable and Wynnfrith was doing little to put him at ease.

'Why would you be wondering that?' each word seeming like a separate punch thrown.

'Why Marcus?' Said Elspeth now at the door, behind Wynnfrith.

'Ohh…' he said almost trembling 'I had feared the worst! I haven't slept…' and he continued to mumble about his worst anxieties during which Wynn's gaze never left him.

'Wynn…why so harsh?' Enquired Elspeth genuinely ignorant of the accusations that had been made about him.

'It is so late Marcus. Why it's almost curfew' said Elspeth.

'Absolutely!' Said Wynnfrith very abruptly and slammed the door almost knocking him over.

It would be fair to say that he left reasonably happy, delighted that she was looking so well. Once inside, Elspeth made her disdain clear to her sister and probed her as to why she had been so cruel. They spent some time going over the events of the day that Elspeth took ill although Elspeth herself insisted that they should reserve all judgement until I had returned. Wynnfrith, hardly placated, returned to the subject of recalling the Agents when, yet again, there was a knock on the door. Almost as if an action replay, Wynn jumped up, marched to the door and, before it was even opened grumbled out,

'What on earth do…'

And stopped when she saw a magnificent horse and, in front of it, a man wearing the King's livery. As this was completely unexpected she just stared and looked him up and down, unconsciously admiring his outfit and, possibly, his physique. She was fascinated by the mud that started as dark brown on his boots and slowly graduated into a light dust as it reached his codpiece. As she stared, a little spellbound, a little voice told her that she should not be looking there but a slightly louder one was saying, you might as well as these opportunities don't show themselves that often.

'Mayor Robert Hall? He said, formally.

'Oh no, I'm just a washerwoman' she replied, knowing herself that it sounded bloody stupid and worried that she was catching something off Silas.

'I have a message from the King for the eyes only of either Mayor Robert Hall of York or Father Matthew of Holy Trinity Church of York'.

Blimey, thought Wynnfrith, he looks a lot better than he sounds.

'The Mayor is h'indisposed but you ave my word this will be given toohoo the priest first thing in the h'amorning.'

Said a voice, so posh, that the sisters didn't recognise it, when they turned to look it was Mrs Hall who, all of a sudden, had transformed into a queen.'

The sisters looked at one another in amazement deducing that she was simply trying to impress.

'Very good Lady Mayor. I bid you farewell!'

Why are all the best looking men also nobs, thought Wynnfrith. Elspeth was pondering about how on earth he knew she was the Mayor's wife but in a backward glance saw that she was wearing Robert's chain of office and could barely stand. Wheezing, she threw it to the floor and, very northernly, said

'Should we open it then?'

'No!' Said the girls in chorus. 'We will take it to Father Matthew in the morning'.

When she, reluctantly, passed it over to them, they noticed that it carried both the King's seal and the seal of the Agents of the Word, which gave them heart. The King had been wise enough to invest in his very own messenger, so great was his need at this time. Unbeknownst to Elspeth and Wynnfrith, Faith had returned to their humble wash house at Bootham Bar, was recognised and then purloined.

Against their better judgement, they both went to the church the following day, bundled up and anxiously anticipating the contents of the message. As they arrived, further disappointment awaited them as there was a wedding taking place.

A common wedding at this time was an entirely different creature to what a wedding would become. This was humble, to say the least, and the sole purpose was to ensure a bond between a couple for life, in the sight of God. It was a solemn undertaking and had little to do with extravagant celebrations. That was, of course, unless you were privileged. This morning, the couple's age was no more than 16, if that, and attendees numbered less than ten people. Although they were sporting their best clothes, to most, they looked little more than humble peasants. However, God did not measure anyone by their wealth or self-appointed successes, all, were equal when they took these vows. Although inconvenienced, the sisters stood, shivered and watched with smiles on their faces waiting for the last participant to leave and then hurried in, hoping that it would be warmer inside. Their hope was in vain.

Although surprised, Father Matthew was delighted to see them but his first words were a reprimand. He, like most others, knew that Elspeth was still in danger. As they produced the letter, his attention turned completely to matters imminent. He opened it immediately and read it silently, the sisters shivering and hopping about as well as holding their breath.

'This is not good news ladies and I need to tell you that this information is to be shared only by Agents and absolutely no one else.'

He drew out the word "absolutely" as to leave them in no doubt of the secrecy of this issue. They said nothing, waiting for the rest.

'The King has been under some personal threat for some time and, on the advice of our own Micklegate

Mouse, has commanded us to assist at Hampton Court
Palace. Their initial reaction, of course, was excitement.
Truth be told, God forgive them, they didn't give a shit
about what happened to the King. However, they had made
an oath and were compelled to obey. But then, they realised
that this was impossible.

'What do we do?' Asked Wynnfrith.

'This is so difficult' said Father Matthew, clearly
troubled and he took time to think.

'There is no doubt that we need Agents here in York,
even the mouse. Elspeth can't travel. The Mayor is clinging
on to life so we will have to compromise. If the mouse can
understand this, then I'm sure he can explain to the King. I
have made a decision and will write to Thomas Farrier in
Stratford and if I can get Robert in a half-conscious state,
he has the very man to expedite this mission.'

17: NORTON LINDSEY

Eirik had found his way to the home of Thomas Farrier
after making enquiries in the village of Wolverdington.
Everyone was delighted at his return, Abigail in particular
elated at his healthy and prosperous appearance, bestowing
affectionate hugs and compliments on the young warrior.
Silas wasn't happy to see him at all. He asked himself if he
was jealous. He recognised that, often, his certainty of being
inferior meant that he envied others. He dug deep into that
dark world that had so often been a debilitating burden for
him and, after some thought, he decided that this was not
jealously, it was suspicion and that suspicion made him very
nervous. The questions over whether Eirik really was the
brother of Wynnfrith, added to the shooting in the woods
left Silas unable to enthuse at his companion's return. It was
just as well that, as yet, he didn't know about the over-
familiarity with which Eirik had greeted the supposedly,
grieving Lady Bask. Eirik detected Silas's animosity
immediately but, on this occasion, decided to keep his own
counsel. Generally speaking, everyone was pleased to have
another Agent added to the ranks, that was until Eirik
decided to take a lead. Although it only lasted for a few

moments, Thomas Farrier and Eirik looked upon each other as two dogs would before a fight. Silas gave thanks to the Lord for that intangible, supernatural but ever-present quality known as women's intuition, as Abigail strode forward to settle matters.

'Oh, dear Eirik. How good it is to see you so completely healed. This is your opportunity to thank the man who saved your life!'

Eirik thought for a moment and, struck by Abigail's sincerity and common sense, said,

'My good Master Farrier. I do, indeed, owe you my life for which I will ever be grateful and put myself at your disposal'.

Truthfully, anyone would have been happy to have either of these at their backs. Although years apart, they had both been hardened mercenaries and were experts in self-preservation.

'No argument here, young Eirik. You have arrived at the very moment I was about to announce my plan to rescue young John.' Said Farrier.

'Will we pay the ransom?' Asked Abigail knowing full well that not one of them, besides Farrier had the money.

'The note invites an exchange and gives a time and a place. Did you notice, Silas, that this is the very same building we broke into, to take possession of the counterfeit copies of the Lindisfarne Gospels just months ago?' Asked Thomas Farrier.

Silas looked dumbfounded. Mind you, he often looked dumbfounded. All eyes were on him waiting for a response.

'So!...they…err...it must be…err…those who kidnapped young John must be in league with the Cataclysm conspirators!'

Although everyone was amazed that Silas was now regularly using multi-syllable words, they were sure that there was probably much more to this mystery.

'Or, that's what someone wants us to believe!' replied Thomas Farrier.

'Oh…' said Silas, shrinking back into himself.

'All the same. I just cannot believe that the perpetrators or, at least, an accomplice would not be nearby as we pretend to deliver this ransom. Norton Lindsey is little more than a crossroad with a forest to the west and another small store about a quarter of a mile to the north. I will go to this assigned place at the given time.' Said Thomas Farrier.

'But Thomas' said Abigail 'if it's a trap you may well be captured as well…or you could be killed.'

'If it's a trap, I will take my chances. Meanwhile, Eirik will stealthily approach the forest from the west and secure any potential onlookers. Silas will hide beyond the storehouse in the north, in a thicket. My suggestion is that you hide there, but be prepared to meet the culprit in that very place!'

There was a distinct and very loud, gulp. At this point, there were armies, congregations and crowds all speaking at once in Silas's head. He hated danger but, as one distant but persuasive voice said, he had to save young John. You're an Agent! Cried another. But you could die… and on it went, seemingly endless, whilst his friends awaited a response.

'Aha!...why…err...of course, at your very service my Lords and Ladies!'

Today's gibberish was, at least, a welcome affirmative so they sat and honed the details of the plan. Although he had been aware of the oath that all the Agents had taken, Thomas Farrier insisted that they all be armed for this imminent venture. The crowd noise in Silas's noggin had not yet stilled, with the latest and now loudest voice telling him that this would be, yet another, opportunity for Eirik to bump him off. However, he felt that he couldn't say anything without proof for, if he did, the mission would be in jeopardy and all hope would be lost for young John Shakespeare.

Two days later, they rode toward Norton Lindsey, left their horses a good half-mile south and walked, with arms, to their prospective positions. As the late afternoon slowly disappeared and the winter light went on its way, Thomas Farrier walked slowly, but openly and bravely, toward the hut. Silas crouched just a short distance from the small storeroom, terrified. Far away, in what was left of the light, he could see the huge frame of Farrier nearing his destination. Silas now heard his heart beating so hard that his rib cage began to hurt. He realised that his breathing was also laboured and, although he wasn't aware of it, quite noisy as well. This, in turn, had the bushes that he occupied rustling to the point where he was practically becoming a liability. It now seemed as though no part of him was still. Thomas Farrier was probably only about fifty yards from the hut, he told himself, but this did little to calm his nerves. And, then, something happened that put Silas completely on pause. The storehouse which he was meant to be observing was now making a noise or, to be more precise, noise was coming from inside it. Silas's eyes bulged from their sockets but everything else stopped. He had even decided to stop breathing. You could suppose that this wasn't, altogether, a bad strategy for remaining unnoticed and, you'd be right, except his sudden stillness gave way to an elongated, squeaky fart. Telling himself that his would-be attacker would think this a small animal, his stressed arsehole decided, to deliver an impromptu encore. The rustling in the storehouse become more noticeable and, just as Silas needed him, Thomas Farrier disappeared completely into the other building.

The noises continued but Silas did nothing and, even worse, Thomas Farrier spent forever inside the distant building which left both Silas and Eirik fearing the worse. Silas knew that it was his duty to either inspect the store building nearby or go to Farrier's aid but nothing would move. He just watched. And watched some more. Then, eventually, he saw a figure exiting the forest. He strained to see if it was Eirik or a stranger but told himself that it must have been Eirik. Then, quiet. Again, Silas told himself that he had a duty to go into one of the buildings if there was no sight soon of Farrier emerging. It seemed like hours were passing and he felt so ill. He now had chest pains, stomach pains, wind, headache and his legs were frozen. But then, in this stillness, he could hear the crunching of frozen grass. Someone was behind him. You have to look around! He kept telling himself. Look around Silas! But, as soon as he did, he felt a body lunge at him. Silas was already writing this encounter in his head for future generations. He's huge! Silas told himself. I am as David and he Goliath, he asserted in his cobwebbed brain. There are at least four of them! Silas stood, the weight of his assailant on his back and turned as best he could. The attacker fell back into the bracken and frost making him squeal but as he sat up he stilled, and bewildered, said,

'Silas!' They both strained to see, in what was now an almost completely dark landscape. They cautiously neared one another.

'John! John! Is it really you?!' Silas grabbed him and pulled him close, realising that this gargantuan, was, in fact, a skinny boy. They hugged and talked over each so much that nothing made sense.

'We have come to rescue you' said Silas 'Where is your kidnapper, is he here?'

'Not here' said John. 'I will explain all. Have you any food Silas?' he asked pathetically.

'I am with Master Farrier and Eirik. They will have food but I bid you stay here as I now fear for their safety.'

Silas then explained the plan and his concerns for his companions. Ensuring that the little storehouse was now empty, Silas asked John to remain there temporarily whilst he fathomed what was going on with the other two.

Slowly, quietly and terrified, Silas approached the building which now housed Eirik and Farrier. The holes in daub they had made, as part of their break-in the previous year, were still there and, through one, Silas could just about detect some movement. Ashamed of his recent cowardice and sure that he could still fit through that very same hole, he decided to rush at the building and plummet through the hole dispensing his most ferocious war cry which sounded a little like cats brawling. He tumbled onto the straw floor, dagger drawn and swearing his life to the Agents of the Word.

'What are you doing Silas?' Asked Thomas calmly.

'Oh…Thomas, Eirik…I was about to…well…I'm here to save you.' He said.

They looked at one another. These were his friends and it would just have been too easy to laugh at him yet again, after all, he, potentially, may well have just risked his life but they, respectfully, resisted the temptation. Eirik picked him up.

'We were doing our best to see if there were clues here but there's nothing my friend.'

For once, Silas had the upper hand. Puffed up, he prepared to tell them of his discovery.

'I have found and secured John Shakespeare!'

'What? Are you sure? Think! Have you actually seen him?'

Disappointed at Thomas's lack of faith in him, Silas simply pointed at the other building.

'He is cold and he has lost weight, we need to get him home'.

'But, we must be careful, this could still be a trap' said Eirik.

Silas walked, alone, back toward the store building where he had left John whilst the other two, eight yards apart and armed, flanked him. When they all arrived, John was sitting patiently waiting for them and, as he embraced each one of his saviours individually, they were left in absolutely no doubt that it was him.

'There's no one here. I have been here forever and I am alone, cold and hungry' and he wept.

Bemused, Eirik started to question him but Farrier insisted that they got him home. After all, the simple task of even finding the horses was going to be a challenge in such meagre light.

They quietly arrived back in Wolverdington, stabled the horses and crept into the back of Farrier's house. Abigail sat alone in the kitchen but jumped up when she saw Eirik and Silas, giving them a maternal embrace but greeted Thomas Farrier more formally as she thought that to do the same may well have been inappropriate.

'You're unharmed! What happened? Is there…did…?'

And then a bedraggled child, previously unseen, appeared from behind them… Abigail fell to her knees, broke down in tears and hugged and kissed her child as if she would never have the chance to do it again and, as she did, questions poured from her at a greater rate than her tears. Hearing the commotion, the other Shakespeare children ran down the stairs to greet their brother.

John sat at the table and, whilst he talked incessantly, it was mostly unintelligible as he was cramming bread, cheese and berries into his mouth whilst he did so. Then, he broke down in tears again. Farrier, of all people, put his hand into a purse to retrieve a kerchief for the child and, as he did, coins came tumbling out of it. Abigail picked them up and then, with confidence, stuck her hand in the pouch so she could determine how much money he had all together.

'Thomas Farrier! Twenty pounds! You were willing to pay for my boy after all.' Said Abigail.

'Just a contingency…let the boy tell his tale…' he said as he turned away.

Embarrassed, his kindness and altruistic nature did not go unnoticed by anyone. John did talk, and talk some more and, happily answered questions. This was his tale.

One day, just weeks ago, as the light was failing on the farm, John had been playing near to the pond. He remembered footsteps and then, he thought, two men bundled him into a bag. He was sure that he was then put onto a cart and that, eventually, he ended up in the hut, the one that Farrier had entered that same evening. John had been told that his father, Richard Shakespeare, was solely responsible for his kidnapping and the man kept saying that his father would suffer. Abigail asked how many men kept him prisoner. John said that there was only one. He had told John that when his father came to pay the ransom, he would be released. Thankfully, it had completely escaped young John that this meant that they were going to kill his father.

'So what went wrong?' Asked Eirik.

John told them that this man would come once a day with food, repeat the same threats and would then go but, about three weeks or so ago never returned.

'What does all this mean?' Asked Silas now very content to be safe and in front of a warm fire.

The others, now hanging on every word that came out of John's, overfilled, mouth ignored him completely and Eirik and Farrier began to ask questions about John's captor. The one clue they did have was that John was left, either on purpose or unwittingly, a very good cloak. A gentleman's cloak. Unfortunately, besides this, he could only tell them that the man was tall but that, otherwise, he was a man.

Thomas Farrier had an idea.

'John. You know how Eirik and Silas speak?'

John giggled.

'Mmm...ha ha...yes! Funny voices, but like they're dim? Hehe.'

Although both Silas and Eirik were not entirely flattered by this description of northerners, they could see how it might get them somewhere.

'And the gentleman from Wales who visits your farm?'

'Ah…yes…haha…Ooo boy…glad I am!'

Again, possibly the worst and most offensive impression of a Welshman, ever, but it did help.

'Did he sound like any of those or any other strangers you may have met?' Asked Farrier.

'Oh no, he sounded normal.'

Well, everyone knows what that means. Our own accent always does sound normal to each of us. They all looked at each other and realised that this also ruled out any of those henchmen they had come across that worked for either Cranmer, Wriothesley or Somerset.

'Let's all get some rest' said Abigail 'you're safe here with these gentlemen and we can talk more in the morning.'

Almost before she had completed the last syllable, Eirik had left. He sped out of the door and closed it behind him but within minutes, uncannily, there was a knock on that same door. At a time when Abigail, the children, Silas and Thomas Farrier were ready to get their heads down, they were, yet again, startled and battle-ready. At first, Abigail presumed that it must have been Eirik returning but why would he knock, she asked herself.

'Perhaps it's that man in black again' said young Robert Shakespeare and, although everyone else suggested that this was ridiculous, he thought it made perfect sense. Armed, and cautious, Thomas Farrier opened the door and there, yet again, was the sinister but imposing outline of Moonlight.

'Moonlight! The dark Knight!' Shouted young Robert completely unafraid.

This spoke volumes as, by now, the adults should have accepted this incredibly weird and disruptive stalker as their trusted ally. With no expectation of any returned discourse,

Thomas thanked the stranger and took a letter from his hand.

'Is Eirik also Moonlight?' Asked young Robert innocently.

Not that it hadn't occurred to the other occupants, but it did seem like a stretch of the imagination. Silas, of course, needed no persuasion. Moonlight was obviously Eirik's alter-ego, employed to conceal his many intrigues. All the same, Abigail assured Robert that the two men were just that, two separate men.

Robert continued to mutter on the same subject whilst John told him that he was talking nonsense. Everyone else patiently paused whilst Thomas Farrier read the letter to himself. It was clear that he was purposely omitting something but everyone was so anxious to hear the message that they simply waited until he spoke.

'Our Micklegate Mouse, and…' he paused as his face gave away his incredulity 'and, well the King himself, want the Agents to be present at Hampton Court Palace…he paused again, clearly concealing the detail 'however, this message is from Father Matthew in York who says that it is paramount that we also have Agents in York….'

Again, he paused as he read the shocking revelation regarding Elspeth, which, wisely, he kept to himself.

'Silas, you are to go to the King, I am to stay here to solve the kidnapping of young John…' they all smiled, proud of the evening's achievements 'and to help secure any further threat to the Shakespeares. Erik is to go to York!'

Silas was perplexed by this instruction. Why ever would he, alone, go to aid the mouse? He quizzed. Clearly, Father Matthew wanted to keep, what he saw as a threat to both sisters, secret from Silas and he desperately needed the assistance of someone who could handle themselves in York. Silas being Silas, began to make preparations straight away. Abigail, however, instructed him to get to bed and promised wholesome breakfast at six before he set off.

Within the hour, Eirik returned. He said nothing but put his hand into his purse and pulled out a straw dolly that he gave, initially, to Abigail although it was for John. She broke down crying. Eirik had been to Richard to deliver the good news and, although Eirik would not report it, he had found Richard alone, a broken man. In return for the news, Richard Shakespeare promised him his farm, his horse, his life! Abigail was also very grateful for, in putting Richard's mind at rest, Eirik had also guaranteed her the best night's sleep ever.

Once alone, Thomas Farrier confided the whole of the letter to Eirik. He was visibly upset at the news of his sister and then became very angry.

'You are to report to Father Matthew in haste and, hopefully, once the mouse has done in London, he will put all to rights in York.'

Eirik left immediately without word to anyone hoping that he may find Bayard on the road back to the north. Within days he would be back with his sisters and subject to even worse news.

18: A NEW HOME

17 Years earlier…

On his many errands, Silas the boy would often come across one of York's best-known leather smiths. In fact, he would frequently deliver messages from Robert Hall as daily business changed hands. However, no matter how many ways he tried to engage him in conversation, Silas failed. Normally, Silas knew better than to bother this man but, as the leather smith lived minutes away from dead alley, Silas thought it the right thing to do. Not even as much as a "hello" or a "fine day" were received favourably by Mr McManus. Silas even suspected that the man had children but they were usually kept out of the way, in the back. Despite, this, Silas loved to visit just to acknowledge the massive transformation from butchered animal skin to fine saddles, belts and scabbards. The stink was almost beyond words, mind you, but most of York was infused with a cornucopia of odours daily so, neither did this put him off. Silas, mostly because of his harsh life experiences, didn't judge people, he just realised that he liked some a little more than others so, odd as he was, Silas quite liked MacManus, not least because he knew his name meant "son of Magnus" so in Silas's eyes he was a Viking warrior and, to be fair, he did look like one. He was muscular and sported long curled hair with a beard to match. If Thor was grumpy and generally anti-social, then here he was.

The children Silas never saw were Elspeth, Wynnfrith and a baby, James. For them too, MacManus seemed very distant. They had known nothing different, he had always been like that. In years to come, when they were teenagers, Wynnfrith would cheekily wonder how on earth their parents had ever had children as, not only was there no apparent intimacy, they hardly even spoke to one another! Having said this, the MacManus household was peaceful. Their father and mother were both respected and they never, ever treated Wynn as any different to her sister. They were used to seeing Robert now and again and this was somewhat memorable as, even when he was a young man, he was well-off. They also knew that they were related but, even as adults, they never really knew how distant a cousin he was. Truth be told, the not-yet-born Edward Fawkes would be a much closer relative to Robert than they were.

However, in the autumn of 1525, there was a significant change to all of this. As they lay, huddled together and giggling in their humble cots upstairs one night, the girls were shocked to hear a long and heavy conversation between their parents. Wynn giggled even more as her sister told her to quieten. Apparently, Elspeth thought it important to know what they were saying. Wynnfrith wasn't the least bit interested, happily seizing the opportunity to stay awake and mess about a little longer.

'Shh!' Demanded Elspeth.

Wynnfrith just pulled a silly face, opening her eyes as wide as she could and filling her cheeks with air. Elspeth gave her a shove.

'Stop it!'

'No. You stop!' And then they laughed again. By the time Elspeth had reined in some discipline from her unruly sister, the talk had stopped.

The following evening, the girls didn't have to work so hard to tune in as, for the first time ever, Mater and Pater were shouting. Far from laughing, the girls were scared. They had never heard raised voices in their home before. They were temporarily overcome with anxiety and, although they weren't making any conscious attempt to listen, they picked up that this had something to do with his work, her lack of interest in him, the guild, people of power, the market, and so on. James was with his mother but bawled and screamed throughout. This altercation was no use to the girls whatsoever as it was definitely grown-up stuff and made no sense. All the same, it shook them and neither slept well.

For over two weeks after that, all was well. It never happened again. Both parents were civil and cordial with the girls and life returned to what it was and, it would be fair to say that Wynnfrith completely forgot about it, but it never left Elspeth.

This modest leather trade truly was a family business. Their mother would help with the tanning and the girls could cut, deliver and also promote trade. In the daytime, the girls were often at the other side of the city, sometimes working hard, but mostly skiving, skipping and joking. Except for the rare occasions when they mulled over their future, they were generally content and loved where they lived and worked. The only education they had was at home but there was constant talk of Elspeth going, eventually, to a nunnery. Something, thankfully, she was very happy about.

One Tuesday morning, lost in a pretend medieval sword fight just outside the castle, the girls were approached by Robert completely out of breath and seemingly beside himself.

'Oh thank God!' He puffed out 'I've been everywhere!'

'Why cousin, what is the matter' asked Elspeth.

'You must come with me. Immediately!' He said as kindly as he possibly could in the circumstances.

Meanwhile, the girls became incredibly anxious, asking a hundred questions, all of which he rebuffed with a "not now" or "wait til we are at home." Unfortunately, home was not home. It was his home and his young wife was waiting at the door. She bundled the two girls together, constantly fussing over them but was unwittingly making them increasingly upset. They were left in no doubt that something was very wrong when they saw baby James in the arms of one of the servants. Elspeth immediately asked to hold him but was told by Mrs Hall that it was best that they didn't. They were both completely numb and were now losing any drive they had to ask questions. They stood, trembling and waiting for something that they could, metaphorically, grab hold of.

Robert Hall's house was grand. Although it was autumn, it wasn't too cold but he had a fire roaring and his dog was currently hogging it. However, as Regent (which was the dog's name) heard their sobs in the hallway, he hurried to make a fuss of the children. Ordinarily, this would have completely made their day but today this was unwelcome, they anxiously stared at Robert awaiting answers. Elspeth, in particular, very soon lost any hope of solace or illumination from Robert as he was having problems of his own. One minute he was entirely animated and the next he was frozen, staring out of the window with only his wife's distant voice managing to break through and tap into his responsibilities. In this period of confusion, the door opened. Saying that the door opened would not give justice to what actually happened. It was flung almost off its hinges and, flanked by two bedraggled looking constables, in marched the sheriff. As was the case every year, there were two sheriffs in 1542. This particular idiot was called Hugh

Hulley and, he was, by anyone's account, a quite unremarkable character. His clothes were ill-fitting and dirty and his manners had seemingly been left somewhere near the place in which he was born. Although by some, it could be considered admirable, his lack of sensitivity did little to ease experiences like the current one that the sisters found themselves in.

'Bad business this Robert. Bad business!'

The girls looked at one another, terrified. What on earth could he have meant? What was bad? They thought.

'Yes, yes' mumbled Robert, seemingly with very little else to offer.

Elspeth and Wynnfrith were craning their necks backwards to ensure they caught every grunt and grumble from these men. However, it was to no avail as Mrs Hall bundled them both away from the hallway, into the living quarters and onto two seats by the fire. She purposely sat opposite, facing them. All the same, they looked at the door beyond which, they presumed, this mystery was being unravelled. In years to come, Elspeth would swear to herself that she could hear Robert crying during his discourse with Hugh Hulley. With all hope of receiving any consolation from beyond the door lost, they turned, trembling, toward Mrs Hall who was now the most important person in their lives. The fire crackled, Mrs Hall huffed and puffed and the girls whimpered. The dog decided to join in. Mrs Hall sat upright, leant forward very slightly and said,

'You won't be seeing your mother and father again.' There was an eerie pause, 'no, never again and that's an end to it.'

As well-intentioned as she may have been, Mrs Hall was doing an, almost uniquely, shite job of delivering this news, so badly in fact that, at first, the sisters were relieved thinking that she couldn't possibly be right. When they had

left home that very morning at 6.00 am their parents were
there and they reminded Mrs Hall of this fact.

'Oh, Mrs Hall! Dear Mrs Hall. You had us so worried!
No, no I can assure you that they are fine and working at
home.' Said Elspeth. This was much more to Wynnfrith's
liking and she clung on to it with all her being.

They both presumed that, as Mrs Hall seemed to lean
back and relax a little, that the matter was, more or less, at
an end. However, as she leant forward again she held out
two rings that belonged, respectively, to their father and
mother.

'These are yours now, I've only taken their valuables so
as people who shouldn't have them, won't get their paws on
them.' Mrs Hall said, presuming now that they would be
convinced.

It certainly was an unnerving moment. Why would my
parents give Mrs Hall their rings? thought Elspeth but then,
for the first time asked,

'What has happened to them?'

'Well, you must have known they weren't well?!' She
replied quite indignantly despite this meaning nothing to the
girls.

'Took them this very morning it did! The plague! They
were removed immediately and you mustn't go to the
house. You'll stay here for now so, don't worry we'll look
after you!'

'So...they're...dead?' Asked Wynnfrith rather naively.

'Yes, yes. Dead my dears. Very dead. Need to find a
room for you both!' She added, cheerily as if her favourite
nieces had just come to stay for Christmas. In fact, Mrs Hall
was so wrapped up in her own performance she almost
didn't notice as they completely broke down, sobbing and
clutching each other on the floor. At the very same time,
raised voices could be heard in the hallway and, most of the
time, it was clearly Robert.

As the girls grew up, Wynnfrith's memories of that day would centre around the realisation that their parents had passed. However, Elspeth remembered almost every detail except she couldn't remember exactly when Robert went with the sheriff, or for how long. They both remembered that, in no time, they were living with the Halls, the servants and the dog and that, within two weeks, the baby had "gone to someone who could give him a good home." Wynnfrith practically forgot about baby James, often wondering if she had made him up which was amply aided by Elspeth's desire never to talk about any of it. They were never allowed near the family home or business again but did notice that, in the following year, someone else was living there having taken over the business.

The funeral was respectable. In fact, very respectable. A lot of money had been spent on everything from the coffin to the gifts made to Holy Trinity Church. Bizarrely, the girls were there to watch, but only from a distance (the reason given was that that they could have contracted the plague) but, as Elspeth grew, she learned that plague victims would not have been given such a public burial anyway. Why did she not question it at the time? Well, the one thing that you could lay fairly and squarely at the door of the Halls was that they were diligently devoted to the girls. The baby's adoption story rung true as the Halls were so kind and, as long as Wynn was cared for, Elspeth thought it best not to ruffle any feathers.

Mr and Mrs Hall respected the MacManus's wishes for Elspeth and, by the age of ten, she was seeking Holy Orders. Wynnfrith became like a daughter to the Halls only leaving them after the Reformation.

The next few years flew by and Elspeth had found herself lucky enough to be accepted in York's own Clementhorpe Nunnery, an intimate order hardly ever numbering more than twelve members. She had harboured dreams of a blissful convent in the Yorkshire hills, living with those devoted to the Lord, tending to the sick and ministering to all that came her way but it was not to be. Sadly, there were a dozen common and popular jokes about Clementhorpe, an easy target not just because it housed women but it had been home to some of the most ill-disciplined nuns ever known in the whole of Yorkshire. Its pseudonym of "last whorehouse in York" did little to polish its image. From the unrepentant Cecily who threw off her nun's robes at the gates and ran away with Gregory de Thornton, to Isobel Studley and Alice of Leeds who were punished for sins of the flesh, the nunnery worked hard in the sixteenth century to maintain some respect. Although only a short distance from the Halls' residence, Elspeth never saw her sister and this was entirely through choice. As a local nunnery, visitors were allowed in now and again but Elspeth's commitment was absolute. Everyone who knew her presumed, sensibly, that this was because of her innate and devout nature but it could well have had a lot to do with her loss. However, there was just one occasion when she saw a friendly face. Often, despite regularly being chastised, the young Wynnfrith would negotiate the walls surrounding the nunnery and peep in to catch a glance of her sister. One warm spring day in 1532, she actually managed to catch Elspeth's eye who, instinctively, jumped for joy and waved back at her. She was seen and immediately punished for this indiscipline but ultimately felt that it was a fair exchange.

She enjoyed several peaceful years but was a while before the news of Henry's divorce and the Reformation breached the stone walls of Clementhorpe and, it would be fair to say that it was met with disbelief. Prayer had always been the remedy for all ills and, they believed, it would suffice on this occasion. Thank God that they did have prayer for, in the years to come, they would have little else. There was an uncanny irony that the Reformation should happen to these people of God. If you accept that, for some clerics at least, King Henry was offering pensions and a new life, you would also imagine that this would be the sensible, and most reasonable, thing to do. However, putting aside all those of the cloth that were deemed to be devious and, or, corrupt (and there certainly were enough of them) the ones left were bound to fight for those values that they believed to be right and, largely, Henry underestimated them. The notorious Pilgrimage of Grace was already gaining momentum by the time Elspeth, and her sisters in Christ, had been turned out of Clementhorpe. A fancy name, for sure, for a northern rebellion against Henry's divorce and his arrogance in setting himself up as the Supreme Head of the Church of England. Come the Autumn of 1536, Robert Aske, the instigator of the Pilgrimage of Grace was at York Minster with five thousand horsemen pinning up a note that reinstated all monks and nuns.

Thousands cheered triumphantly swearing allegiance to this cause. Church leaders, Knights, landowners, businessmen and everyday citizens were now united against this southern monster. From his window, Robert grumbled believing that it would all come to no good and possibly thinking more about whether it would affect his income or his standing in society. Wynnfrith looked over his shoulder. There, in the thick of that crowd, animated and exuberant, was a little woman wearing half habit and half rags. If she hadn't have known better, Wynnfrith would have sworn that this was her sister.

It was during this period that Brother Bernard, homeless, had made his way to York, mainly to find his sister who lived there and, in the fray of confusion, excitement and new hope, he met young Elspeth who instantly inspired him and gave him renewed vigour. If this little woman had enough faith to overthrown a King then what may be possible if all those of the cloth unite? He asked himself.

Sadly, their initial quest wasn't to succeed and neither was the Pilgrimage of Grace. After a spell of hiding herself, Elspeth started toward Robert's house one evening, defying curfew.

'About time!' Said Mrs Hall in a matter-of-fact manner 'been expecting you all year…'

Elspeth wasn't quite sure what to make of this but happily accepted the invitation inside. Conflicted instantly, she wanted to reject those comforts that people like Robert took for granted but, truth be told, she had nowhere else to go. Mrs Hall went upstairs to Wynnfrith's room and, before she had finished her sentence, Wynn flew down the stairs and into her stinky sister's arms. Now she was really conflicted. This felt so good. Just to feel the love and warmth of my own kin and yet, she told herself, I'm meant to be secluded from all things of the flesh. So, she chose to stop thinking for a while, got warm, got clean and ate.

Without any fuss, she was given a secret room in the house. Plenty of people would hand over the odd rebel monk or nun for a small price so she lay low for some months. After that point and after much persuasion, she resumed her former life as Elspeth but, before committing to this she prayed.

'Dear Lord in Heaven, our journeys are rarely what we expect and our destination sometimes different from where we intend. I ask forgiveness for my failure to restore our humble order here in York. I pray that the evil that this King has instituted can be stopped and our truth faith restored. Although I wear the clothes, and speak the everyday language of a layperson, I am yours, always, in every other respect. All that I am is devoted to you, Lord. I declare this in the name of our Lord Jesus Christ. Amen.'

And, this was never to change except for when she first encountered Marcus. Previously, she had been lucky. Men were men with all their stupidity and carnal desires and that was that. Why on earth did God have to put Marcus in her head? What was he to her? At times this troubled her so much she would put her head in her hands and pray constantly for it to go away and then, she would consider that this was a challenge that had been sent from above, leaving her even more confused.

Whether it would be regarded as generous or not, Robert set the sisters up in a lean-to shack against the wall at Bootham Bar where, previously, there had been a modest clothes washing enterprise. Both were grateful. In some strange manner, it seemed like a return to the life they had had before their parents had been taken. Wynnfrith often asked questions about them, Elspeth never answered and that's how it was for years. Setting up a washing business was quite easy and, Robert being Robert, meant that they had clients almost immediately. He would call around now and again and, although grateful, there was something they didn't quite trust about him. Having lived in the same house they knew about the other women, although this wasn't at all uncommon with men of wealth. And, to be fair, the whole Mrs Grindem subtext provided the girls with many happy hours. The one thing that had crept in that wasn't acceptable was Robert's tendency to touch Elspeth and, sometimes, make inappropriate comments. Unquestionably, Elspeth was now a woman with a full and rounded figure which she often despised as she felt it conflicted with her calling. She had no need to be attractive and she didn't like the problems it created. She was strong and smart enough to keep Robert at bay but she often pondered on this particularly as, at times, he was almost a father and, in this role, he showed them both complete respect. Wynnfrith and Elspeth only spoke of this once. Wynnfrith, acknowledging that she was now attracting uncomfortable advances from men herself, questioned why Robert would be over-friendly with Elspeth and not her. Elspeth told her that it was because she had lived with him as a daughter for so long and that made a difference. That put the matter to bed, so to speak, but it was the reason why they were still very cautious about seeking his counsel when they first discovered scraps of Brother Bernard's note in 1541.

All in all, they had to concede that they were indebted to the Halls.

As the multiple threats of 1542 loomed, those issues regarding their parents' deaths and the kindness of Robert and his wife seemed, again, to come to the fore and the sisters were in no doubt that they, and the other Agents, were in considerable danger.

19: SHEEP

Whilst Bayard had entered York and was told, essentially, to turn around and transport Agents back to London, Silas was heading toward Hampton Court with a defined purpose. Well, that's what he was telling himself. He daydreamed, pondered, worried, prayed and petitioned, fantasised and even mumbled to himself. Still full of love for Wynnfrith he was also full of troubles, mostly because of the unexpected appearance of Eirik less than a year earlier. Silas obsessively questioned whether Eirik really was the brother of Elspeth and Wynnfrith and whether he had any connection with them at all. Silas was now left in no doubt that Eirik had tried to kill him in the woods and that he was also, secretly, the sinister and beguiling Moonlight. What had started as a few doubts was now concreted into Silas's tiny cranium, often leaving little room for anything else. Over the last ten months, Silas's self-esteem had been like a ride on an unbroken mare. For the first time in his life, he had felt valued, built friendships and been given a real sense of purpose but this was constantly being challenged and now, hundreds of miles away from his beloved, it was dissipating into the ether. The journey was now beginning to tire him. All this is much harder than when I was but a boy, he told himself. He hadn't eaten in twenty-four hours and all he had as provisions were one piece of cheese, an indestructible slice of bread and a pathetic looking, cold sausage. He looked down. His clothes were drenched and he was caked in mud. So was Annie. You damn fool Silas, he muttered to himself. Knight of the realm! of all things, and then sniggered.

Having followed a stream for some miles he found himself in open land with Aylesbury in the distance. He was temporarily heartened by the view knowing that he was nearing his destination. He smiled too, for he was in farmland surrounded by sheep, grazing. The snows had softened and the sheep were also wet and muddy. In an age where there were few enclosures, owned land in the shires tended to start and end wherever was convenient. Around him was open countryside, bare trees, mud, a grey sky and sheep. He paused and spoke to Annie saying that, at the nearest opportunity, they would get clean and give greater care and attention to their appearance. Despite only recently being bestowed new and magnificent clothes, he had managed to outgrow them but not in the usual understanding of that phrase. In fact, Silas would tell you that, for some inexplicable reason, his clothes grew whilst he shrunk. Beyond all human understanding, according to him, his tights became baggy, the front of his doublet would work its way around to his back and his codpiece simply had a mind of its own. Determined to remedy this, he stood up in his stirrups which was when he noticed that Annie had adopted that expression that he had seen so many times on the faces of people whenever he launched into anything physical. He tugged at his doublet and, inch by inch, that which should have been forever at the fore, slowly moved its way around from the back. In doing so, his codpiece and purse slipped down toward his knees with his hose following closely behind. Already losing patience, he grunted, gave a push on the stirrups whilst grabbing the waist of his hose, only to find himself propelled skyward and, as he did, he screamed. Now, I know you're now thinking that, inevitably, he was destined to land face-down in an over-sized woolly pat. However, always thankful for an optimistic viewpoint, he was pleased on looking down that he would land on, what he thought to be, a small huddle of soft and fluffy lambs. The lambs were not soft and neither were they happy as, they too, let out a very loud baaa aaa! On further inspection, the soft fluffy lambs were actually one large and unimpressed sheep.

As he landed, Silas, certain that he was unharmed, let out a sigh of relief but, as he looked around to check that Annie was still there, he then saw, looming over him, a large, discontented farmer.

'Good day' said Silas, almost as if they had just been introduced at a formal gathering.

'Good day?! Good day?!! What are you at, man?' Answered the farmer.

'Just sorting myself out Sir' he said smiling and giving completely the wrong impression, also doing nothing to dismount his new friend. He lay there, pants slipping down with his head turned, engaged in debate with a man who wanted to kill him and leaving the farmer unsure as to whether he should be talking to his head or his arse.

'Might have bloody known. Northerners! It's true what they say then?! Well, you can bugger off and find your own sheep!'

As Silas did his best to explain he, again, made things worse. For some bizarre reason, as he rambled, he slipped off the sheep but then strained to get back on again until he had finished his explanation. It was only as a last resort that he decided to pull his hose up again. All the while his long, thin strand of fire-red hair danced around his face often obscuring his vision. Finally he dismounted, upright and half-decent.

'I am on a quest for the King himself!' he announced proudly and confidently, now full of shite and twigs with the squashed sausage and bread now artistically arranged around his nether regions.

'Well, that bloody well explains a lot. Run out of wives has he?! I hope you two animal lovers have a good life together! Now sod off!'

Everything Silas said after this point just made this man angrier, so his real default mode, that was to run, kicked in. Three attempts to get onboard his horse later, he was away with the farmer running after him and prodding his arse with a stick only to find a soft sausage stuck to the end of it.

'Both a bit tidier now, Annie'

He said confidently as if nothing had ever happened. Annie wondered if there was any hope of Sir Lancelot buying her off Silas one day.

On reaching Aylesbury, Silas was reminded of Wolverdington and his first meeting with his friend Thomas Farrier. Luckily, as in Wolverdington, the first building, on the first street was a blacksmith. Its owner, admittedly, wasn't as accommodating as Farrier but he did suggest a suitable inn where Silas could get him and his clothes washed whilst Annie was cared for. Initiating a much-needed reset, yet again, he found new confidence once smartened up and was excited about the task ahead. He dreamed of the opulence that would await him at the Palace. The food! And, of course, more food! Whether it was just the thought of feasts, there was no doubt that he was inspired anew.

Clean, fed, watered and looking out for farmers, Silas wandered into the market square. Ironically, he now looked the part. Once overhauled, he could pass for a Lord and that affected how he was treated by others. That is if he kept his mouth shut. On this day the market place was bustling and it reminded him of home. In the centre of the carts and stalls, he could see a small crowd gathering and decided to treat himself by indulging in what, seemed to be, some market day entertainment. The crowd was dense, in every sense, and he couldn't see, so decided to ask one of the merchants what was going on.

'It's a story!' said the man 'of Henry Tudor himself. Saw it yesterday I did. Just like being back there! Astonishing!'

Silas was immediately impressed. He understood that "Henry Tudor" was a reference to the late King, Henry the seventh, the current King's father and to suggest that someone was recreating the past, stirred great excitement within him. He politely pushed his way through the throng until he could get some fleeting glimpses. At first, he could hear nothing but managed to catch a glimpse of someone hobbling about a makeshift stage which was on the back of the cart. Oohs and Ahhs were forthcoming and, there was little doubt that an unusual spectacle was taking place. As he got nearer, he could hear the man that was acting. He was stooped, clunking about the stage with a stick and shouting,

'Death to all Plantagenets!' And growled 'victory to the house of York!'

People were agog, some claiming that witchcraft must be involved to recreate history so accurately. Silas thought it was decidedly crap, especially when he realised that just one bloke was playing all the parts. Dim as he may be, Silas did some incredibly speedy detective work. Mmm, he thought to himself, crap show, cheap, dodgy cart…it has to be? and there, as soon as he had thought it, was Bayard, taking money. Truthfully, he was delighted to again see the shittiest showman but decided to wait until the climax, in which effectively, the same actor had to be both Richard the third and his killer. It was a dire performance, to say the least, but the relatively secluded people of Aylesbury soaked it up and happily parted with their hard-earned coins.

The crowd dispersed and Silas, now shiny as a new button, stood there alone. Bayard did a double-take and then ran to greet him. So glad was Silas to see someone he knew that he embraced the chubby showman.

'What do you think?' He asked Silas with great expectation.

'Well…'

'No. Be honest. Just be honest..'

'It was a bit ridiculous Bayard. Well, at least the bit about using just one actor' replied Silas sheepishly and, after his recent encounter, he did sheepishly rather well.

'They loved it!' Announced Bayard defensively.

Not wanting their meeting to result in a dispute, Silas made an effort to massage his friend's ego temporarily but, internally, thinking that there could be no future for performances where people pretended they were people of the past. Bayard proudly introduced his new business companion with glee stating that, at first, he had agreed to work for nothing. He gave his name only as Dramaticus which, Silas felt, was both arrogant and silly at the same time. He bowed as he greeted Silas and then rambled for almost ten minutes, mostly about himself. Bayard smiled throughout as if he had, at last, found his protégé.

'My work has been praised at home and abroad by Kings and Emperors' he casually stated leaving Silas in no doubt that these two in front of him could well have been separated at birth.

'That's just as well then, as we'll be meeting our very own King soon!' prodded Silas. Almost immediately, it was clear that Bayard had not mentioned this and it was also clear that Dramaticus, if that was his name, regretted boasting.

'Really…well…I…err will be pleased to perform for him…again…'

Exposed, he said little more, although Bayard did look a little disappointed that Silas had blurted out their mission plan.

'Well, I suppose we'll need all we can get' offered Bayard not fully grasping what lay ahead of them. 'I have a surprise for you' he said to Silas and took him to the back of a small market stall where a young man was helping secure the awning. It was Peter and, as they saw each other, the young Northumbrian fisherman and Lord Silas, overjoyed, greeted each other as if they were brothers. Although they hadn't had time to get close, they were both extremely pleased to see a known, trustworthy and familiar ally.

'My Lord!' Said Peter breathless 'your home is as it was. The mouse and I have taken care to keep it lived-in without disturbing your precious abode.'

Dramaticus was taken aback at the knowledge that Silas was a Lord but bemused as to how on earth a mouse could keep a house tidy. This initial confusion had him also presuming that the property in question was the Lord's mansion and that Silas was now in charge of everything.

'There is much news from York my friend' said Peter but as he spoke, Silas's attention was drawn away to a shadow behind his young friend. For a moment his desperate imagination, yet again, informed him that there was a Wynnfrith look-alike nearby, his logical sense, which was rarely called upon, calming him and reminding him that this was the fourth time since Stratford upon Avon. But then she moved, turned and he did the same and, after what seemed like an hour of stillness they bolted toward one another. It was Wynnfrith looking even better than he had imagined her to be. Peter, Bayard, the actor and local people, idly shopping, stopped to watch this dramatic meeting of two separated lovebirds. However, as they got within a foot of one another they both stopped and, although they spoke, absolutely nothing was coherent. Even those closest to them reported later that all they heard was "oh…yes…nice….it's you…it's me…nice to see you" and, whereas they both had hoped to bond in a meaningful embrace, they simply, and awkwardly, leant forward at which point their right shoulders touched for a second only for them to bolt backwards again. It is very possible that the origins of the word "awkward" were birthed in this very frustrating relationship. Nevertheless, they were delighted to see one another and within the hour, they found themselves sat by a fire in the inn thinking "well perhaps they just don't like me anymore." If I'd have been there I swear I would have tied them together for the night and locked the bloody door on them!

Silas sensibly asked when the rest of the Agents would be arriving and Wynnfrith explained that there would be no more, expecting in return that Thomas's Farrier and Eirik would have been with Silas. Sensibly, Silas kept his suspicions about Eirik to himself and, it was at this point that he was told about the attempts on Robert and Elspeth's lives. Highly animated, he pacing the wooden boards, clearly distraught. Wynnfrith caught his arm and told him to sit.

'My sister, Robert, Father Matthew and I believe that the mouse will uncover and solve all, just as he did with the Cataclysm. Put your faith in the Lord and trust in Micklegate. Like you, we are all scared, my love, left wondering whether the threat to the King is the same one that we fear. We go to London at the mouse's behest and, I am convinced that, once we have uncovered what is behind the wickedness there, we will put a stop to what goes on at home. Eirik will take care of those in York.'

Although possibly the best speech Wynnfrith had ever made, Silas only heard "my love" and "Eirik" and his internalisation of those two phrases could not have been more at odds with one another. Should I speak of my fears regarding Eirik? He asked himself and pondered on this, shutting out the comments that were being currently returned from Bayard. At this moment Bayard's voice was background noise until one word broke through and, it was the same one.

'Eirik. Yes, Eirik. I know he's meant to be your brother dear, but I'm sure he knows more about the Anthony Bask incident. That's all I'm saying. He's keeping something from us.'

Instead of an ensuing debate on this matter, it had the effect of killing the conversation and nothing more, for the time being at least, was said on the matter.

The arrangements were that, once at Hampton Court, Bayard would take his show (and idiot actor) to the city whilst Wynnfrith, Silas and Peter assisted the mouse. Silas was very happy about this on two counts. He would be rid of the irritating Dramaticus at the same time as enjoying Wynn's company. As they sat on the cart, his head was a maelstrom. What to say? How close can I sit? Should I quote poetry? The latter he abandoned immediately as he didn't know any and he didn't have answers for the other questions either. Perhaps I should tell her the story of the sheep? he thought and then decided it probably wasn't yet a tested wooing strategy.

The kind, smart and sensitive Peter was picking up these signals.

'So how long have you known each other?' Asked Peter, trying to help.

'A year' said Wynnfrith not looking at either of them.

'Six months' said Silas at the same time. And then silence.

'It must be wonderful working together as Agents. You two helped to thwart a wicked event only last year!'

Yes, that's about right, thought Peter. I'll flatter them both.

'Mostly the mouse' muttered Wynnfrith.

'Mostly Thomas Farrier' said Silas into his boots at the very same time.

Peter decided to give up, jumped off the cart and walked alongside the horses. He found Annie much better company and the conversation was also much more enlightening.

Sadly, it was an uneventful journey except for a few minor disagreements. Bayard wanted to perform in every village and hamlet they encountered but the others pressed him on the urgency of their mission. The first time they saw the Palace was at about five miles distance and it took their breath away. Being from York, they had all seen large and imposing buildings before but, a residence so opulent, never. The closer they got, the more astonished they were at how it sprawled, its grandeur and its boldness. Dotted about were other settlements and dwellings, some in the woods and some beyond the clearing. Every so often they would stop for provisions and, when it came to bartering with locals, they were amazed at the wide range of accents and dialects being used. Some were exactly what would be expected so close to London but others were from the regions and a few from abroad.

Scared, in awe, and not knowing what to expect, they braced themselves for what was to come.

20: ELSPETH'S OBSESSION

Elspeth regarded herself blessed in so many ways but, not least, in that she had had one of the best educations available to a young woman of her time. Her father and mother had insisted that beyond sewing and tapestry, beyond making food and gathering fuel and even beyond a tanner and leather smith's skills, they wanted their children to read and write. It was possibly their father's slightly inflated view of his own position in society that led to this but, nevertheless, they were given everything Mr and Mrs MacManus had to offer.

Paradoxically, Robert, who had servants and often treated his wife as only a grade above, also encouraged learning in the girls. Wynnfrith, younger and less interested was grateful but had no natural thirst for it. Elspeth, on the other hand, soaked it up. Before she had even seen the nunnery she knew Latin, Greek and French and, the more she learned of and abhorred the ways of men, the closer she found herself to God. But, it didn't end there. Innately, she had an inquisitive attitude to the Bible itself. She sometimes became aware of its contradictions and was conscious of how mankind had used it to its own ends. By the time she had joined the local convent, she both astounded and impressed her superiors by her knowledge. In addition to this, the Abbess encouraged theological discussion with the caveat that, if nuns ever found themselves outside the wall, their discussions and thoughts would not be shared in the company of others, as a thinking woman in the sixteenth century England was only half a step away from being regarded as a witch. The nunnery was a melting pot of personalities ranging from those who wished to escape the everyday trudge to intellectuals and also those who sincerely wanted to devote their lives to God. Elspeth sought God through each and every breath but ached to know the truth of the faith. In secret, one evening, one of her superiors, known to all as Sister Marian, led the discussion. These could often be exciting congregations, an opportunity for almost free exchange.

She told the story of a woman who had once written her own book and, incredibly, as long ago as the late fourteenth century. This sort of subject matter was the lifeblood of the nunnery. Exciting stories, true, exaggerated or false were always an exciting starting point for any fruitful discussion. In a world where all you did was pray, eat and spend time alone, new and engaging tales completely reinvigorated the nuns.

To begin with, there were no questions, just necks stretching nearer to the whispering nun.

'This book' she said 'also questions some of those values that the church holds as canon law but, nevertheless, she writes about Love, Christ and' she paused for full dramatic impact 'she writes of an encounter with God himself.'

Over the sighs and sharp intake of breath, young Elspeth impatiently questioned her because that's what Elspeth did. Sometimes it seemed as if her curiosity was boundless.

'With respect Sister, how do we know this to be true?'

'Despite all attempts to destroy her work, there is a copy still in existence and, although I haven't seen it, the Abbess has.'

'Please tell us more' said Elspeth now, at least, partly sold on this idea.

'Julian of Norwich…' she continued, creating a buzz around the small cell that left them all feeling that they could, happily, stay within its walls all night.

'…was an educated woman and, in the year 1373, she fell terminally ill. As last rites were administered, the crucifix before her eyes became as real. Christ's face was real and the blood was real. In this point-of-death encounter, she saw God Himself as one single point that connects all things. She miraculously survived this ordeal and maintained, for the rest of her life, that all things of God were good. God, she said, was complete goodness. He does not punish. Love, simply love, is what God is.'

They looked at one another not knowing where to start. They knew already that there were rumblings in Europe that condemned the established church for many reasons and this included its dark and penal nature. These ladies, without any exception, certainly sought peace. Peace for all, and this narrative was as honey to them.

'What happened to her' asked Elspeth.

'She spent her life as an Anchoress. She lived the rest of her days voluntarily in one cell, ministering to those who passed by her window daily. And, during this time she wrote down her thoughts and entitled it "Revelations of Divine Love."

This, to all present, was a Renaissance premier of the biggest blockbuster imaginable. Even the often cynical Elspeth was convinced that there was now, seemingly, some evidence to support this. And, she was right to trust Sister Miriam. Heralded as the first known prose to be written by a woman, this solitary work by a female cleric would become one of the most read of all time.

A nun can do that? And so long ago? Thought Elspeth. What more could I do? This led her to ask questions, more questions and then drifting away, daydreaming. They talked about Julian all night but not before Elspeth had asked where the original copy was.

'It has to be kept hidden. Once destroyed it will be as if it never existed. Her encounter with God himself lost forever.'

Elspeth asked again, sure that this was an evasive strategy by Miriam.

Miriam looked around at the six faces that surrounded her. Could she trust them? She told herself that, if she couldn't trust these people then all was lost. There seemed an, almost endless, silence. In these moments they looked at each other, then at Miriam and then to Elspeth to push the issue.

'It's here.' said Sister Miriam surprisingly casually.

This took their breath away. This story of a woman who lived many miles away and so long ago had come home to them. This exciting piece of work was here, with them. In an, often, mundane lifestyle this was genuine excitement.

'You must not say anything. Ever. Ever!'

They immediately agreed to a vow of secrecy on this subject and this was sufficient for Miriam but the experience was never to leave Elspeth. She had pondered often on how her faith had seemed to have strayed so far from the loving, peaceful and forgiving message of Christ. It would be reasonable to say that it troubled her deeply. Her pact was with Christ and his love for others, one's enemies and, even, possibly one day that would include the irritating mouse. An intellect, a woman. In fact, a nun! had written about personally experiencing the true love of God. There is nothing to fear from God, He is all love. Whether it would be fair to say that, happily, this reinforced her own stance and was just what she wanted to hear, or whether it was an awakening, it simply didn't matter as this was how she would be set from now on and, in the midst of it there was one issue that became her obsession.

She had known Father Matthew for her whole life and he had supported her vocation every step of the way and would also visit her and take gifts to the nunnery. From about the age of twelve onwards, she knew he was different from most men and, she had met other men like him. Apart from suffering from chronic grumpiness now and again, she knew him to be a good and Godly man. Like Brother Bernard, it would have been hard to imagine him ever having a selfish thought that would have sustained itself. As an intellect, she understood that there had always been men that liked men instead of women and the same for women. It was clear that two of her closest friends within Clementhorpe were battling with a love that was more than that which Sisters normally held for each other. She knew Father Matthew was like this. And, there had always, always been people like this. In some ways, she started to regret knowing so much. Learning causes all sorts of problems, she told herself, it makes my head hurt. The more I know the more I find things out and the more I question things. And, by the time Clementhorpe closed and the Bible was being translated into English, she began to question the validity of some of these notions. On this issue, specifically, she unwittingly came to the same view as Silas. Christ was completely inclusive and he never said anything on this subject.

Other contradictions troubled her. The more she became aware of mankind's tampering with the Bible the more circumspect she became. She told herself that she simply had to access Julian's manuscripts and swore that she would, in secret, personally check, recently translated versions of the Bible into English to see if any roguery had taken place. Although this was well-intended and laudable, in the final years of her life this would become an uncontrollable obsession.

21: VISITORS

If you were from the north of England, it would be perfectly acceptable to describe Hampton Court Palace as being in London although, in reality, it was some distance south-east of the city. This afforded it a peaceful and rural setting by the river away from the noise, filth and disease of the capital. It was for this very reason that Bayard had to explain to the others why it seemed like they were starting to approach the Tower of London but then it appeared to get smaller again. Soon to be deep into the Palace environs, they had mixed feelings about this alien world.

I had spent too much time alone and, because of my clandestine role in uncovering the threat to the King, I found myself little more than a mouse in a cage stuffed in a stable. However, I was, of course, looked after. I acknowledged my place as one of the King's favourites and was assured that food and clean straw would be delivered regularly, but I was becoming increasingly concerned that time was slipping away. Although genuinely I wished to serve the King and solve this problem, I was starting to become increasingly anxious for the fate of my friends in York. I consoled myself with the notion that, soon, all the

Agents would converge on the Palace and they would act as my eyes and ears. I had enjoyed one further meeting with Heneage in which I shared some of my initial thoughts and suspicions. Added to that, the only detective work I had been able to do was watch people as they wandered away from the Palace at all times of day leaving me wondering what was of interest behind the woods.

Shamefully, I dozed a lot. I had never considered my physical status as Micklegate. That is if I even had one. Perhaps I was getting old. I had no idea how old I was supposed to be but I decided that I would enjoy my lazy days beyond the limelight.

My mornings were cosy, wrapped in the straw and happy that I wouldn't be bothered whilst all around me was busy. Horses being cleaned out, brushed, dressed and prepared for the hunt, then the dogs would arrive. The hunt was like a well-oiled machine where everyone, including the animals, knew their place and their role. When I first experienced this spectacle I was amazed. It was many things. A quest for food, a display of masculinity, a testimony to horse riding skills and a social occasion but also, surprisingly, a fashion show. At this time of year, the Court would wear matching white furs and doublets, ladies included, with only the King adorning splashes of gold and purple. Truthfully, it was becoming almost impossible for the King to hunt but, with the aid of many a sycophant (who pretended not to notice his obesity and lack of mobility) and some ingenious devices, he still went through the paces. He would remain, whatever anyone thought of him, absolute ruler until the very end, whatever it took. As time passed, this whole ritual became quite normal.

However, one morning when there was no hunt, I awoke, alarmed at the almighty hue and cry and at first, rolled over and hid my head in the straw. After some time, I heard someone shout for the boss himself, Sir Anthony Browne, Master of the Horse. As people ran about and I, reluctantly, peeped one eye out at the hazy rising sun, I saw Browne hurrying to the east entrance flanked by two Yeoman of the Guard, dressed in that, now familiar, red livery boasting a large letter H covering the torso. It was only when they disappeared that I heard one of the last voices exclaim,

'Apparently, peasants trying to trespass, be after food!'

I put my head back down acknowledging that there was no drama. After all, they must have to deal with intruders and thieves daily I told myself. So, you know that feeling when you blissfully drift away again? Not a care in the world? Well, I was there, at peace only to have my cage shaken.

'Micklegate, you are needed.' Whispered Thomas Heneage.

He said no more and I did not reply as, he too, was accompanied by guards. One of them lifted my cage and off we wandered around the courtyard and toward the east entrance. As we turned around the final corner I could hear raised voices, one of the guards was shouting,

'You must not move. On pain of death! You must not move. In the name of the King!'

And there, on the floor and underneath his boot was a rugged, fat man full of mud and horse shit, which may, for all I know, have been from the very ground on which he lay or, alternatively, he had brought it with him.

'What is your business?' He bellowed.

Terrified, the bumpkin beneath his foot kept mumbling the same thing over and over.

'The mouse sent for us. We are here to help the King!'

Every time he said this, all around were shouting "treason!" And "kill him now!"

It was, of course, Bayard and, besides the fact that I was left speechless by what I was witnessing, I hadn't a clue why Bayard was here and then I remembered that he was offering, possibly, the only type of transport available to the

Agents. They must all be in the back of the covered cart, I told myself. I looked up at Heneage and gestured, insistently, that he should take me to one side. As he did, he put his ear close to the cage.

'It's them! Not as I expected, mind you, but it is them. They are the Secret Agents of the Word, appointed by the King!'

He glared at me for what seemed like an eternity. His glare told me that he thought I was joking. How on earth could a fat, dirty peasant, help the King? I assured him that the rest of the Agents, wise and brave, would be inside the cart but he still seemed cautious. Handing my cage to one of the guards he asked Sir Anthony Browne if one of our guards could look inside this moth-eaten covered wagon. He walked around the back, lifted the cloth, let it drop and returned to us both.

'Two idiots, a cripple and a boy, my Lord.'

At first, this made no sense to me. Which one was Thomas Farrier? Richard Shakespeare? Father Matthew an idiot? I thought again. His description of Wynnfrith was both unkind and unfair but I was left in no doubt that it was her. Two idiots? I could be certain of one but who would the other one be? I had to make a decision. There before me, at least, was Bayard. Was he classed as one of the idiots? That would make sense, I supposed.

'It's them' I whispered to Heneage 'definitely them.'

I have to say there's nothing more satisfying than being the best mate of someone with power. Although previously, I wasn't to know, Thomas Heneage, being so close to the King now had the trump card.

'Release them immediately on the King's orders. This man speaks the truth.'

They instantly backed off without question and even helped to pick up the bedraggled, and smelly, travelling entertainer. Bayard stood, shocked, looking at the man who had given the order not sure whether or not he was in the clear yet.

I now found myself back in the hands of Heneage.

'I think it's best to get them all first to the stables where we can talk if that is alright with you Sir Thomas' I said, now in awe of this man.

Within minutes, everything uncannily went back to normal and Thomas Heneage, myself, two horses, a covered cart and Bayard were in an enclosed stable where we were all alone.

Thomas stared at the unsightly Bayard.

'You sure he belongs to you?' He asked me.

'Yes, sorry.' I said, not being able to find anything else to say.

'Shall we see what's going on in the back then?' He asked.

'Yes please, let's get on with this' I said.

I was expecting that my personal army of Agents would be mightily relieved to get out of the crammed cart, still pondering over the guard's description of its manifest. Thomas Heneage carried me around the back and, authoritatively, drew back the cloth.

'Micklegate!' Shouted Peter, pleased to see me.

On reflection, I was sure that I was pleased to see him but, in that moment, I was dumbfounded at this meagre showing of support. Realising that, for months, I had tried to suppress this nauseating new personality of mine, I let go and, somewhat regrettably, said what I thought.

'Are you kidding?!' I blurted 'is this is it? Really? Is this it after I have waited so long?!'

Thomas Heneage stood by, startled at my outburst.

'Have you any idea what I face here. In York as well! And this is the best Robert could do. Wait until I see the fat, idle, womanising fraud…'

Wynnfrith let out the biggest of sighs leaving me, temporarily speechless.

'He may be dying' said Wynn exhausted and deeply hurt by my assault.

'Wha…?' I meekly replied.

'He's been attacked too so, you may as well know that, while you've been living in this lap of luxury we've had a really hard time…and the journey has been awful too..!' And then she started to sob. For the first time, Silas protectively placed his arm around her and he looked at me in disgust.

'You know' said Peter calmly 'it might be an idea if we started afresh?'

By this time that thing had happened where, even I, realised that I'd been an arsehole so apologised. Not surprisingly, there was an atmosphere that wasn't going to go away immediately. I had no clue who the stranger was and sympathised with the guard wholeheartedly as he was, indeed an idiot, making faces and grand gestures that made no sense at all. Bayard made a modest attempt to introduce him but, however harsh it seemed, I had no use for either of them. As it was, Bayard was bursting to perform in the city so, once Heneage had ordered a servant to bundle them up some provisions and Annie was untied from the cart and taken in, off they went. Heneage sensibly gave them an address near the river where he could check in every few days for news as, once we were done, he was our transport back to York.

I thanked God for Heneage who was so very authoritative and reasonable. In particular, I was worried about his response to Wynnfrith's disability but, following a brief but awkward moment, he took her as she was, although I'm convinced he must have been dumbfounded at what he saw overall. These were not the Secret Agents of his imagination. He guided us all to the very rear of the stable where there was a small commissioner's office. It was cold but private and, in this small place, we were left in no doubt, both by his clothes and his demeanour, that Thomas

Heneage was in charge. The visitors sat in awe as he introduced himself and then explained briefly about the King's dilemma. In the middle of his, most able, presentation, a page entered with food and drink and some of it was warm. Warm beef and bread! My friends had not seen food like this for so long and it did help to get me off the ropes somewhat. Silence, apart from groans of satisfaction, followed for almost twenty minutes after which, we resumed our conversation. I asked Thomas Heneage to take me out and place me on a table. Before anything else, I wanted to know about Robert and, besides resetting the atmosphere, the details left me feeling that there may now, at least, be some hope for him. I was shocked at the story regarding the dodgy window and there was no doubt that, temporarily, my mind was in a spin trying to handle all the pressure that was being brought to bear on my tiny brain, not least, how Elspeth was faring and my quest to return home and sort out the unholy mess in York. However, in no time at all, we were all much more relaxed. This was, without doubt, totally due to the warm spiced wine ordered by Heneage. Peter was snoring, Wynnfrith startled to giggle and Silas did short and pathetic farts that made Wynnfrith giggle even more. She then decided she would tell us those stories of when she and her sister had found Robert naked and when he became delirious, shouting out for his mistress. This, in particular, had everyone in pieces. Our emergency whodunnit meeting had turned into a party with only Thomas Heneage having the presence to reel us all back in. I giggled too as he addressed me directly.

'You'll need to brief your Agents' said Heneage.

This, combined with the chill that was seeping into our bones, brought us somewhere near to reality again and we, slowly, sobered.

I needed first, to have their assurance that they were in the right frame of mind to handle the complex and serious information I was about to impart. Whether it was pretence or not, they made the effort to, at least, look serious and interested.

'There have been a number of attempts on His Grace's life. One by arrow shot whilst hunting, another was an attempt to poison him at a meal and the third was a trap, set so that he would fall into a fire whilst walking. One food and wine taster died from poison and the King, at random, had three others executed.'

Silas, unsurprisingly, wanted to ask why the people had been put to death without any investigation but I raised my paw to stop him.

'The King suffers from ill health but you are not to mention this, he believes his suffering is a complete secret apart from a few trusted advisors including Sir Thomas and myself. At this very moment, I do have some thoughts and suspicions but I am far from identifying the culprits if, indeed, there are more than one. However, I now believe that the purge we are suffering in York is different from the one that the King fears.'

Again they were hasty, wanting to know why, but I had so much more to impart and I was struggling to get it into some order so that Silas could understand. I looked at Thomas Heneage for approval to go further.

'The needs of his Grace are now urgent, good mouse, please continue.' Said Thomas.

'When you see the Palace in all its glory, particularly its massive population, you will be overwhelmed. You must adapt quickly as I need you to interact with the Palace staff.'

By now the three of the world's most unlikely Agents had sobered completely and were hanging on to every word.

'We have done our best to investigate who may have had access to the King during the assassination attempts and we have examined the processes: where food and drink begins, how the hunt is organised and so on....and I have, possibly incorrectly, decided to hone our inspection to a handful of people. I will tell you who these are now and, once Thomas has returned to the King, I will rehearse you in your roles and test you on your knowledge of those people.'

Silas looked horrified. He had never turned away from any adventure, he had always been up for a mission, but speaking to people, especially for the first time, was a nightmare to him. Perhaps Wynnfrith will be with me, he thought.

'You will be split up and, when you do meet one another, you will make out that it is the first time.'

Silas dramatically flopped his head into his hands.

'Look, you must forgive me for my outburst as you arrived' I said 'I am under tremendous pressure and I had worked out, to the finest detail, a plan involving almost all of the Agents. Trust me, my friends, I do have complete faith in every one of you and, one thing is for certain, I will not be able to do this without you. There are only a handful of people who know that I can speak, so I'm not able to ask questions in public. Peter, I will accompany you on your mission.'

Before I continued, I emphasised that the people they were shadowing were not all necessarily suspects rather, that they would, hopefully, lead us to the truth.

Archbishop Cranmer wasn't a surprise to them. I then talked about the highly favoured, Mrs Cornwallis, the King's cherished pudding maker and her assistant, the newly appointed Beth who had helped me to tour the Palace. Then Drake the, possibly too proud, keeper and carver of Swans. A delicacy that only the King enjoyed. Gabriel, the most affable and able, stable boy and Ramsey, his colleague whose behaviour gave some concern. Sir Anthony Browne the Master of the Horses and, of course, Lyndon, possibly the most disaffected member of the household, difficult to handle and overcritical of the King. I then, trying as hard as I possibly could to remain objective, discussed Will Somers, the King's fool. This man had almost unrestricted access to Henry and, his constant quest for prominence at Court, was definitely out of place. I looked at them.

'I know, I know, it is so much to take in. Be assured that I have some thoughts so, at first, you'll just be getting to know people. All other staff will be told that you are new and that you reside off-site. If asked, don't answer any questions on that subject.'

I asked Peter to open the office door and I pointed beyond the stable.

'There. Directly ahead, and beyond the door, are three doors next to each other, horse bays converted into your accommodation. You will eat with other staff but we will all congregate secretly in Silas's cell every evening at seven of the clock unless you are commanded to do otherwise. Beyond all that, I want you to enjoy this experience. Unless you behave suspiciously, you won't be in any danger. Ask only those questions I have briefed you with! And, be confident about your position. Peter, I will go with you as we retire. We sleep now and tomorrow you will be taken to your stations: Wynn, you will be an added assistant to Mrs Cornwallis and Beth. Peter, you will be with me and, I hope, we will have opportunities to cross paths with the, absolutely bloody irritating, Will Somers. Silas, you will assist the hunt organiser and, as such, I will have you spend time with Gabriel, Lyndon, Ramsey and the Master of the Horses.'

I could see that he started to panic.

'Silas, I have every faith in you. Please, please! Be yourself and, if that means making an arse of yourself every so often, then so be it!'

Wynnfrith and Peter laughed and, eventually, Silas joined in. Wynnfrith gave him the sweetest smile, not having any idea how much strength this gave Silas.

'Let's sleep my friends I will tell you more in the morning.'

22: THE HUNT

Surprisingly, even in the sixteenth century, hunting had its critics. Humanists like Erasmus and even Henry's minister, Thomas More objected on the grounds that it was barbaric. Not that anyone was lobbying for the end of eating meat. Most men of medicine, by this time, thought that humans could not survive without it, it was the systematic and barbaric chasing down of live animals that they were opposed to. Practically every household would have at least one member who was familiar with how to kill fowl or beast humanely so, it is likely, that most ordinary and everyday citizens struggled to understand this elaborate, cruel and expensive pastime.

It was, of course, chiefly the sport of Princes, also often described as the obligation of Knights but did have a very important purpose. The whole operation was, not by coincidence, similar to battle and it has been regularly reported that it was regarded as a particularly healthy exercise in an age where it was all too easy, especially in winter, for the rich to sit around warm fires, imbibing. At the Palace, it was rare that the King would hunt simply to put food on the table, he had plenty of staff who could do that. Rather, it was a statement of his masculinity, his fitness and his superiority. There is no doubt that, as a young man, he was an able athlete and excelled at hunting and the joust. By 1542, his role in the hunt was largely a pretence with his involvement being little more than turning up and appearing as if he had hunted down and killed a beast single-handedly.

The beast was, almost always, the hart, or stag as it was more commonly known and, rather than the kill being the complete focus of the event, it was the exhilaration of the chase that got the ailing King out of bed on a winter's day. One can only imagine the thrill of being surrounded by nobles, perfectly bred horses and beautiful greyhounds. By the 1540s, the greyhound had become the preferred dog of the elite and many an hour would be spent discussing the attributes of individual dogs over ale or wine. White and speckled greyhounds were preferred for the hunt and these would be bred within the Palace walls. Often, the King could claim activities solely for himself and this, the Royal hunt, would look like nothing else in the land. You could point at any one of Henry's greyhounds and it would have been worth more than any of the young men that worked in the stables and, any one horse would be worth more than all the stable staff put together. Imagine, if you will, Knights, horse and dog masters, men at arms and, yes, ladies dressed in fineries worn just for the hunt. Long white winter, ermine gowns covering highly decorated, puffed sleeve, doublets. The noise as they prepared, their icy breath greeting the dawn, the bustle of staff supporting their superiors set against the sound of ravens overhead. No wonder servants of all ranks pushed their faces up to the windows to marvel at this spectacle. By the end of the sixteenth century, the English landscape was changing in every sense of the word and hunting on this scale would almost die out with the Tudors although, as a questionable tradition, it would be exercised by the privileged always.

The King never travelled light and this was as true on the hunt as anywhere else. A range of weapons could be used but, at a time when guns were in their infancy, there is no record of them being employed and this was, presumably, because it was considered ungentlemanly. Surprisingly, sometimes a type of spear was utilised alongside bows and arrows. Evidence suggests that, although they were no longer used in battle, crossbows were deemed to be effective whilst hunting. Unbeknownst to anyone but Henry and those who witnessed the event, he was nearly killed by a crossbow quarrel, not an arrow.

Once a hart was cornered, and deemed dead, the huntsman would offer the hunting knife to the King who would then plunge it into the animal to claim the kill. Cheers and celebrations would follow. Although it is unlikely that Henry ever did so, the carcass was often offered as a gift, being particularly useful as a diplomatic gesture and Thomas Cranmer himself valued this strategy when making allies.

Henry would vow his hunting team to silence in case he ever made a fool of himself now he was older and infirm. The pretence of being God's representative on earth was paramount and presumed weakness would potentially damage any stability that the nation enjoyed. In truth, the word was out. Most of the population was expecting him to die soon and this was, in part, the drive behind the Cataclysm of 1541. No one was expected to speak of the crossbow bolt that missed him by inches. On the hunt, accidents happened and in this macho world, they could often be overlooked but, this was the first time, that no claim was made to a shot. He had with him that day two crossbowmen but the bolt came from a third shooter that was never identified. No one else was discovered in the woods so, presumably, it must have been fired by someone who had ridden out with the King on that cold morning. For some reason known only to Henry, the nearest crossbowman, someone who had been loyal for a decade, received an immediate death sentence which was carried out within the week. The King, fat, disabled, neurotic and completely out of control had no other way of dealing with it and, although the fire pit incident was yet to come, he thought of the Agents in York as he returned to the Palace on that unpleasant morning. Taking his natural propensity to be dictatorial into account, he did have a broader view regarding these incidents. Again, he presumed it part of a movement for religious security. For all he knew that could have been either Protestant or Catholic but he also feared for the succession. Only a few knew how frail his son, Edward was and, even if the boy did succeed him, the Prince would easily fall into the role of puppet to whoever held the strings. Therefore, the commissioning of the Agents had so much more to do with the future of England than it did his own safety. It is even possible that, by 1542, Henry had lost all regard for his own mortality and, it was with this in mind that I, and my ever-deteriorating number of Agents, had to meet his demands

23: MOLLY

It was the 13th day of February and everyone, perhaps except for its newest members of staff, knew what this meant. On this day my dear, sweet Catherine Howard would be put to death. For those she had met, popular opinion would already have been split between two camps. The first baying for her death, revelling in denouncing her as a whore, even a witch, and in contrast, those who had become close to her for which the day would be a traumatic tragedy. Of course, no one was allowed to comment or pass judgement, they were simply expected to get on with their duties. True to type, Henry would find a way of either celebrating this day or taking his mind off it, so a grand hunt was organised.

To say that Silas was unprepared for this event would be a gross understatement, the previous two days were a time of settling in but, no matter how carefully the Master of the Horse briefed the other stable boys, Silas was still seen and treated as an oddity. They were told that the King himself had approved his employment and he wasn't to be

lampooned or bullied but, once the gaffer was away, this
instruction made no difference. He was now out of his
expensive, Lordly, clothes that had been bestowed on him
by Mayor Robert, looking every bit a serf. He was mocked
for his physique, his ill-fitting clothes and his northern
accent. This was particularly hard-hitting as Silas's fortunes
had changed since becoming one of the Agents and he had
almost forgotten how cruel people could be.
Unquestionably, he had experienced all this, many times
before but had wisely chosen a life where he was mostly
alone, running errands and then upgrading to one silly
mission after another. The worst of it was that he suddenly
felt like that child again. The child that was picked on in
dead alley as he tried to innocently play, his mother only
yards away. Added to his misery was the fact that he was
also missing Wynnfrith. Every time she came back into his
life he felt a much stronger desire never to leave her again.
Now, he would only be in her company at the seven o clock
briefings. However, he decided eventually that this, in itself,
was a great blessing and so counted the minutes until that
took place. Out of them all, Gabriel was the kindest
colleague choosing to teach Silas a few useful skills. He told
him to take no notice of the other stable boys and dog-
handlers and, helpfully reminded Silas that, in his current
employment, there was no room for error as mistakes on
hunt day could lead to death. This, of course, terrified him
but, at the same time ensured that he was diligent in his
duties. Although he felt trapped, there was an unexpected
turn of events that, although not unpleasant, played on
Silas's mind even more. At the core of these events was
Molly.

Molly wasn't an employee at the Palace but was allowed
to sell berries to the lower staff as long as the kitchen got
some for free. When the stables gaffer was around she was
treated with respect and often, the stable boys, in particular,
would buy a few seasonal berries. When he wasn't, this

could deteriorate into the most offensive language and, on occasion, she would even been groped by the stable lads. Fortunately, the first time Silas encountered Molly, the gaffer was around. At first, he didn't notice her at all as he was up to his neck in horse shit wondering why everyone else had almost downed tools. As he stood upright and turned, he encountered her for the first time and new and conflicting thoughts rushed through his tiny noggin. He reprimanded himself immediately for he had had a thought that he didn't put there. It was a thought that made him uncomfortable and, he had decided, that the rational Silas, wouldn't have thought. However, once thought, it was there for good and he hated it. This is what Silas's thought said:

"Oh, a girl. She's very pretty. She is so much like Wynnfrith…but she doesn't have Wynn's illness."

He didn't know what to make of this as he wouldn't, even on pain of death, change one thing about Wynn, so why was this girl here playing with his head? He told himself without hesitation that this was the devil himself and blatantly shook his head to rid himself of it. This latter thought was probably one of the wisest that Silas had ever had.

'Hullo stranger, you new here?'

Oh God, she speaks as well, he said to himself and decided that, if he said nothing, she would go away.

'Shy are we, my Lord?'

She was, of course being quite silly. Referring to him as a Lord simply because he wasn't taking her on but, of course, Silas being Silas presumed she knew his secret identity so spun around, dropped his spade and staggered backwards until he fell. With no intention of being offensive, she curtsied and smiled at him. He knew that the words, "get behind me Satan!" were almost about to vent forth from his daft gob but, for once, curtailed it. He introduced himself as Silas but said no more.

'Well, if you're ever about and a bit cleaner when I visit! I might sell you some of my berries. I'm Molly and very pleased to meet your acquaintance.'

She then make another comedic curtesy and she left. Soon after, the gaffer left.

This was another, fortuitous moment in which the other workers would deride Silas. Calls of "he's a quick worker" "your luck's in there, peasant" and much worse was bandied about. If he had been used to this sort of banter he probably would have laughed along but he took it all to heart spending the rest of the day apologising in his heart to Wynnfrith although he had done nothing wrong. Out of all the workers, Lyndon bothered him most. Lyndon who had run away when I first encountered him and who had wished for the King's death. He was determined to get anyone possible to join his cause. When he wasn't canvassing Silas, he was abusing him and, on one occasion, even kicked him. Silas was better than this. As long as Annie was treated well, he didn't care. He adhered to his new identity and put the King's matter at the fore of his thoughts. Ramsey, the young man I had described as suspicious, hardly bothered Silas but Silas was sure that he was up to something as he was forever going missing. Gabriel he really liked. His soft Germanic accent was often the first thing to greet Silas each morning and there was no doubt that he was trying to look after him. Silas also believed that some of the other lower staff were apprehensive of crossing Gabriel as he seemed so self-assured. Just as the light was being lost each day, Gabriel was the first to leave. Silas didn't understand why he was given this concession so asked. Gabriel simply said that he lived beyond the Palace, in the woods, a journey which he needed to negotiate in the light although, Silas noticed, he always carried a torch that the gaffer lit himself.

Fortunately, on the 13th February, the hunt day, Silas's tasks were easy. In fact, most of it was cleaning up everyone else's shite including the horses and dogs, and he was left wondering what use he was in the midst of all this. However, providence was to put an end to his frustration as he took the time to watch how the hunt was organised and, eventually, take flight. The horse and dogs were taken by their handlers to the beginning of the run and Silas could see, in the distance, all the Lords and Ladies mounting their steeds and, he told himself, that he could also glimpse the King although this may just have been fanciful. Then, two of the older horses were being prepared almost as an afterthought and, from behind him, walked Gabriel and Lyndon dressed so much more smartly and carrying saddles, bridles, harnesses and all manner of horse tack. Bundles were brought out and he would later learn that these were holding equipment, provisions and even spare clothes. All of a sudden this made sense to Silas. Of course, he thought, they need to cover a range of eventualities, particularly in these extreme conditions. Gabriel and Lyndon would bring up the rear as insurance. If anyone of note was dismounted and, or, hurt, they could take one of their horses whilst they walked back. Silas, therefore, immediately presumed that it must have been one of these two that had tried to shoot the King but then remembered his brief and that was simply to report back anything he had discovered rather than deliver his opinion. This spectacle was an oasis in Silas's dry and humdrum day, he had never seen anything quite like it but before he knew it, they were all gone leaving him to shovel even more muck.

'All alone?'

His head whipped around.

It was Molly.

'Why yes' he said "err…everyone on the hunt…or…err...busy'

Molly was being so nice to him and he was finding it very hard to be rude just for the sake of it but he desperately wanted her to go. What would Wynnfrith think if she saw us together? He thought flattering himself.

Actually, Wynnfrith would have thought nothing, meaning that the guilt complex was entirely his own.

'Berries?'

'No…err…thank you. I stink.'

Why did I say that? He asked himself. She giggled.

'You're funny Silas. You make me laugh!' She then placed her hand gently upon his arm and said 'I'll see you soon then…bye!' And left.

Don't know why she's being so nice. Make her laugh? Who am I to make a pretty girl laugh? Not pretty no…strange girl, I mean. Such nonsense. Wonder what time she comes tomorrow? And on it went. Silas hadn't had much attention from the opposite sex and so hadn't a clue as to what to make of this. He decided to busy himself acknowledging that shovelling shit was now the best job in the world.

Besides creating a lot of work and an unholy mess, the hunt returned without incident and, before they all knew it, the day was over. The high points of Silas's day were to come, that was meeting with the other Agents at seven and then bedtime. He slept in his small, converted stall knowing that his love was resting next door, he would lie awake thinking of her soft, raven hair lying on a pillow and would strain to hear her soft breath as she slept. As he drifted off, the demons crept in, entering a world where Molly and Wynn were one and the same and now grilling him on his fickle fidelity.

24: A GRAND APPETITE

My greatest anxiety about the task bestowed on me by
Henry was in negotiating the scale of Hampton Court
Palace. To talk simply in terms of a Palace hardly does it
justice. Most towns and villages in England were nowhere
near the size of this place. Unless you had come this close
to royalty, you would simply not be able to comprehend
what this was. It was a world of its own, boasting of the
wealth, power and success of the monarch.
It is true that, even in 1542, Henry had advisors and, yes,
even a parliament but, to all intents and purposes, King
Henry V111 was an absolute ruler. Hampton Court was a
castle, a leisure centre, an art gallery, a theatre, a place of
worship, a power base and, overall, a testimony to what
mankind could achieve in the sixteenth century. It had
tennis courts, mazes, extensive lands and ponds in which to
breed animal, fowl and fish. A tiltyard, designer gardens, an,
almost arrogant, number of kitchens, stables and
accommodation for staff. Slightly to the north-west was an
area called the wilderness, where Lyndon would often

disappear and it was often used as a route for those who lived beyond the Palace environs although, what was beyond that, was the real wilderness. People were constantly coming and going. During Henry's divorce from Catherine of Aragon, the traffic was non-stop. Ministers, cardinals, ambassadors, lawyers, spies, you name it and, to meet the needs of these people, the staff would have to deliver food, wine, clean rooms, bedding almost around the clock. The clatter of horses' hooves were almost constant, the horse population larger than the number of Princes, Lords and Ladies.

It was, therefore, with some trepidation, that I set my Agents to work. Peter and Wynnfrith would surely struggle with the enormity of this place, I told myself. It was for this reason that I urged Heneage himself to introduce Wynnfrith to Mrs Cornwallis. The astute, and overbearingly confident, Mrs Cornwallis would struggle with the idea of two new staff within a few months and, unsurprisingly, would think that there may be some threat to her unique status.

This Palace had over five hundred rooms, a tenth of those allocated to the preparation and delivery of food with over two hundred people employed to keep the cogs turning and to keep hundreds of people happy. Added to that, it was nigh on self-sufficient with boar, pheasant, duck, pigs, oxen, wild boar and fish accessible within the limitations of the Palace grounds. Fruit and vegetables were also grown with the latter reserved for the lowly, being deemed unfit for their superiors. You could spend months in the Palace and never even bump into someone of note. It would be fair to say that there was a powerful sense of every person knowing what their place was, but little had been done to protect the King from any subversive activity from staff, he presuming that all threats would be old-school, that being, a full-on physical attack. Having Stonehenge-shaped guards in every doorway looked good but was of little use if someone was trying to poison you or bring you down on the hunt. And, the very subject of poisoning was a very touchy one as far as Henry was concerned. He hated the very idea of poison which he, not only thought cowardly, but was constantly aware of how easily it could be administered. In 1531, there was an incident that would stay with Henry for the rest of his days partly because his response had been so extreme. A lowly cook, Richard Roose, had been charged with attempting to poison Bishop Fisher who, on refraining to imbibe the soup, did survive. Two guests of his, however, died. Because he was able to do so, Henry condemned Roose without a trial, committing him to be boiled in oil. Yes, oil. And, yes, boiled. What a bastard. However, suspicions around the incident just wouldn't go away with many thinking that Henry had commissioned Roose to kill the Bishop, hence his knee-jerk reaction to the whole affair.

During this more recent poisoning incident, Henry also issued an immediate sentence but the man was hanged and, yet again, the man was almost certainly innocent.

So, you can now put into perspective exactly what I was asking dear Wynnfrith, and the others, to do. This was dangerous territory and, although I am loathe to say it, there were few people worth trusting.

Heneage, give him his due, did his best to protect Wynnfrith. He told Mrs Cornwallis that the King, in his great mercy for all the members of his realm, whether they be fit and able or otherwise, chose to have this girl, Wynnfrith work in the kitchen. He also added that her disability wasn't to be mentioned. This, of course, was complete bollocks but did, at least, save her from a lot of questioning. Truth be known, Wynnfrith was quite able to discuss her disability quite confidently and was certain of her personal adaptability and ability to perform.

'But what I don't understand, Sir' bellowed the very London-centric Mrs Cornwallis 'is why I need to be teaching someone else. Am I out of favour with His Majesty?

'Why no, of course not madam. You are heralded as the greatest pudding maker in the realm, His Grace says…..' and on he went, bestowing a fountain of flattery on this gobby Cockney woman.

'She looks like Molly!' Interjected Beth. This, at first, attracted no response at all. However, in the great book of rules of life written circa 800, it says that women, generally, didn't like being compared with other women. They like to be told they are special and look beautiful. It was, bearing this in mind, that Wynn didn't know what to say. And, yes, I did make all that up about the book.

''S'pose she does a bit.' Grumbled Mrs Cornwallis 'well let's get working, there's no time for any idle chatter' and, with this, Heneage legged it, reminding himself that looking at the King's arse was a much safer job than working with this old nag.

Mrs Cornwallis, truth be told, welcomed the labour. This now meant she didn't have to do everything herself but she wanted nothing to do with companionship. It will come as little surprise then that this woman had her own kitchen and it was, to say the least, spacious. She put Wynnfrith to work with Beth on a bench that put thirty yards between her and the two girls. Wynnfrith had already deduced that Mrs Cornwallis had too much power and independence. There was seemingly no one to check what she did or how she did it and that included what ingredients were used. Wynnfrith saw this as a curiously dangerous, autonomous position. Beth chatted and gossiped. In fact, she chatted and gossiped a lot. Mostly, it was everyday stuff but, every so often, she would give something away about her boss and other staff and, sometimes, she would even try to discuss politics which amused Wynn. Wynnfrith told Beth that she was very happy to be an assistant to her which, besides being a clever and efficient idea, also smoothed the girl's ego.

Henry and his entourage ate copious amounts of meat. All sorts of meat in large quantities and that included almost all the innards of any beast. All was valuable and little was thrown away. But, Henry also had a sweet tooth. He was one of the few people that could afford sugar but honey was used in considerable portions as well. One common misconception, however, was that there was an endless variety of sweets and puddings. Many dishes, like their Christmas pudding, was more like a sausage and, like most other items on the menu, contained meat. Spiced fruit, marzipan, gingerbread and sometimes, artistic, jellies were consumed and he was particularly fond of "maids of honour" which were similar to custard tarts. Rumours that it was Anne Boleyn who had introduced him to these resulted in them being absent from Court for a while but they had now returned. The ability to combine these, somewhat limited, ingredients with anything from egg to imported spices meant that there was plenty of room for Mrs Cornwallis to be creative. However, there were few dessert dishes that resembled what was to come centuries later. But, the Tudors did have the pie. Anything could go in a pie, even live birds that would fly out at the table when cut, so, as long as there was some honey or ginger or marzipan around, practically anything could become a dessert. Today, Beth and Wynnfrith were making sugared almonds. Hundreds of them. Wynnfrith quickly decided that she liked Beth and knew, that eventually, Beth would spill about the recent attempts on the King's life.

'Does it hurt?' Asked Beth.

'What?...Oh…I see. Not in the way you think. I get tired and I have some limitations. My cousin has a house with stairs and that can be hard..'

Wynnfrith surprised herself for, within minutes, she was explaining that she was born that way, knowing that Beth was simply being inquisitive.

'Well his high and mighty must think a lot of you to personally recommend..' continued Beth.

'Oh, no…it's just…' Wynnfrith almost gave herself away as she had no answer, so reverted to the default story about Henry's diverse nature which, frankly, was bloody ridiculous.

Just as they had settled into a routine and chattered incessantly, they found themselves interrupted by the almighty boom of Mrs Cornwallis's voice.

'Be gone girl!' She shouted 'how many times. If you don't leave the kitchens now I'll send for a guard! You know I'll do it! Bloody peasant!'

Wynnfrith looked over to see a girl carrying a small sack who froze and now looked like a stag at the wrong end of the hunt. She stopped in her tracks, fearful and then turned to leave hurriedly.

'You two go after that witch and take this with you!' Said Mrs Cornwallis.

She presented Beth and Wynnfrith with a similar sack but it was smelly. When they peeped inside they saw blueberries that were rotten.

'Don't want your poor pickings here!' Added Mrs Cornwallis.

Beth and Wynn chased her into a corridor and asked her to stop. Wynnfrith and Molly looked at each other.

'See!' Said Beth 'twins!'

Neither of the girls appreciated this comparison and neither did they understand it.

'Why do you keep risking it, Molly?' Asked Beth 'it's one thing to go around the stables but you simply cannot come into the kitchens.'

'I know, I know. But she hates me. Simply hates me. Those berries were fine when I brought them and I gave them to her for free.'

For an instant, Wynnfrith felt sorry for the girl who was, presumably, just trying to get by, but that sympathy was soon to dissipate.

'Best get back to my Silas then...' she said in a very matter of fact manner and she turned to walk away.

A cacophony of ill-tuned cathedral bells started to ring inside Wynnfrith's skull. Silas? My Silas? Can't be the same. Must be loads of workers with that name....she mulled.

'He'll be ready for a bit of warmth after shovelling shit in the cold all day, I expect.'

'What's he look like?' Wynn unwisely asked as the gap between them widened.

'Oh, you wouldn't miss him. Skinny, long strand of fire-red hair...'

As Wynnfrith continued to pursue this girl, Beth took her arm.

'You know this Silas don't you?'

'Yes' mumbled Wynnfrith, wondering what had just happened.

'She knows' said Beth.

'Knows What?'

'She knows that you know him. She's toying with you so don't take it to heart.'

'But why....' Wynnfrith stopped herself. Already a gossamer thread of evil was winding its way around her pure spirit and she did not want it to become between her and her mission. However, a little voice in her head spent the afternoon saying 'wait til I bloody see him...'

When she had calmed, it did give her the chance to discreetly ask about the flow of food and ingredients throughout the Palace and was astonished at how much Beth knew. Beth told her that there were commissioned and trusted suppliers of things they didn't normally have within the boundaries of Hampton Court. These were evidently very few and guards would usually check wagons, bags and baskets when suppliers arrived. Everyone else, from fishermen to huntsmen and from butchers to cooks were employees and, as such, enjoyed an existence much greater than folk in general. Throughout most of this, Wynnfrith did little more than nod. By adopting this stance, Beth talked even more. It was almost when they were finished that Beth's conversation became intriguing, almost bizarre.

'I'm sure things will settle down when we are all of the Protestant persuasion' she said without any filter whatsoever. Having a sister who was a Catholic nun, and being from York where change had been courageously resisted, Wynn didn't know what to make of this except she did presume that she was possibly right and that it would be that way in years to come whether she liked it or not.

'Be much better when he's gone don't you think?'

This shocked Wynnfrith. Not so much what was said but the fact that she was so open about it and Wynnfrith already knew that other workers, like Lyndon in the stables, were of the same persuasion. It made no sense to her at all until she considered that this was a world apart from York, the very hub of state affairs and intrigues. Perhaps it's just too hard to ignore the politics and personal events that consume the monarchy, she thought. Pleased that the working day was coming to an end Wynnfrith enjoyed supper and looked forward to meeting with her fellow Agents.

25: INFIDELITY

As I swayed back and forth with Peter carrying me toward the stables, and our lodgings, I mused over the complications of this place. It seemed that, out of hundreds, only a few were minding their own business leaving us, as Agents, illogically suspicious. However, even within the first few days, I could begin to see a trend. I believed that the solution may be in sight as every little piece of information seemed to fit a theory I was gestating. From the very first words that Beth had said to me, to the revelation of the Court clock by Queen Catherine Howard, this ball of string was, excruciatingly slowly, unravelling. However, the perpetrator I had in mind seemed to be a ridiculous notion. Why, if I'm honest, I thought it impossible and had good reason to think so.

I could smell Silas a furlong away which had Peter giggling. There was, almost, only one pong where Peter came from and that was fish. This was a completely different world and he revelled in it. Quite rightly, he knew he would never have such an experience again so was my perfect and obedient companion throughout. Outside of our three stalls in which we slept was a huge pile of straw

and Silas was fast asleep on top of it, exhausted from
constant physical labour. We sat and just looked at his sorry
state, bewildered as to how anyone could get so much shit
on them.

'If he comes home with any more shite they'll start
charging him for it!' I whispered to Peter who giggled,
almost waking our dear Lord Silas. We let him be and so sat
and rested on a nearby stack of straw and it was then that
we could hear little pads in the mud. It was Wynnfrith's tiny
shoes spattering the ground as she ran toward us. She
looked beautiful in the way a child does. Carefree, not the
least interested in the filth, or even the fact that the light
was fading, she smiled as she neared us. Her cap fell off and
strands of her hair decorated her face almost as if it had
been artistically placed there and, as she turned to pick it up,
I was reminded of how much I would miss these people
and how dear they had become to me. When she reached
us, she gave Peter a friendly smile, it was clear that she felt
like she had been away from us for days and was incredibly
happy to see us. I pointed toward Silas and she raised her
eyes to the sky.

'How long has he been like this?' She asked, quietly.

'Could be all day for all we know, just found him so.'
Said Peter.

'Mmm' was her reply and she walked toward him, which
was no mean feat considering the pervading and now ever-
present stench. She then picked up a long pointy branch
from the floor and moved even nearer. She drew it back
and forcibly stuck it in his ribs.

'Who the bloody hell is Molly, then?!' she shouted.

He stirred, only slightly at first, but then opened his eyes
and saw the stick, then Wynnfrith and he heard that word,
"Molly." Had he said it in his sleep? He thought. This is
when panic really set in and, as Wynnfrith repeated the
question, he leapt up, wobbling and falling back onto his
boney posterior. He then struggled for over a minute to get

upright deciding that it would be wise to deliver his explanation simultaneously.

'Oooo…oh my! No!...not at all…who?...I don't think…'

As much as a mouse could laugh, I was and Peter howled at this impromptu, but marvellous, sunset performance.

'My dear…you see…there I was…my shovel!...you see…' and on he rambled but yet still not upright.

'Moll?...no…erm…have I? Why err…..'

I looked at Wynnfrith. She was loving this. Poor bugger had done nothing wrong but she reserved the right to make him feel guilty if the situation arose. Part of a girl's prerogative and a recipe for a perfect relationship, too I supposed.

'For God's sake stop rambling man. You'll talk yourself straight into a noose one day! Let's just say I've got my eye on Molly and that's an end to it for now.'

At last, he was standing. There was nothing in or on, his face. Well, apart from horse shit that is. No colour, no expression and I was sure that, momentarily, he had stopped breathing. Poor Silas. So sensitive, and always on the receiving end of, well, everything I suppose. He so wanted to ask what had transpired but naturally, and quite stupidly, presumed that Wynnfrith had seen them together which is, exactly, what she wanted him to think. He watched her every word and movement throughout our meeting and, truth be told, I couldn't help feeling sorry for him.

One of the incredible things about us now being employed within the Palace walls was that we were fed well and, here we were, still snacking in the evening. We listened intently as Wynnfrith told us what she thought of Beth, Mrs Cornwallis and, yes, even Molly. Molly with the blueberry stained hands, intent on upsetting whoever she came across. I had no idea that my Agents would be so useful. Everything she said had value and, to some degree, fit my theory. However, Wynnfrith didn't give away one word of what Molly said about Silas, so he was still left stewing for another forty minutes into the meeting. I told them I would deliver any information uncovered by Peter and myself during the following evening which meant that, whether he liked it or not, Silas would have to contribute there and then. Enthusiastically, he told us about the roles everyone played in the preparation for the hunt and how many of the stable and dog handling staff he believed to be suspicious. I told everyone to rule out any suspicion based solely on wishing the King dead, or on political statements as I was sure that most people at Hampton Court had their own opinions and thoughts and that it was, most probably, only to be expected. Things were stacking up nicely and, more or less, slowly coming together. However, it was far too early for me to speculate and I must repeat that, although I had a powerful notion of what was going on, in some ways I also felt that it just couldn't be. So, although I was conflicted, I did at least, feel some sense of progress.

Poor Silas was still beside himself as we parted company for the night and returned to our cells. Peter and I were already outside the stable but I could see him, eyes fixed on Wynnfrith as an obedient dog would waiting for a familiar and positive word from its master. She stood and made to leave and, without turning back said,

'Got my eye on you now my man!' Which almost broke him.

In his lonely, dreary and, often unbearable, existence his recent missions and his inclusion as one of the Agents of the Word had changed everything. He was cared for, even respected and had friends. Added to this was the hope that the love he felt so deeply, day and night, would one day be returned. Full of crap, in every sense of the word, he had hit rock bottom again. However, just as she disappeared and he had let out the heaviest sigh, her smiling face peeked back around and said.

'Just teasing my love, sweet dreams' and she blew a kiss.

His legs gave way and he folded back into the earth. There can never, ever, have been a man so happy rolling around in muck and the, now famous, Silas inner barometer was almost bursting its glass. Needless to say, with some meagre attempt to clean himself up, he never slept for one moment that night and neither did he wish to. He was also in good company, as neither could I. Everything raced through my mind and, unquestionably disturbed, I decided to stay awake and try to put everything into some order that I could deal with. I still suffered from the mix but had learned to cope with it, so that was my starting point.

I reminded myself that I worked in historical analytics and that this wasn't my time. Supposedly, my body and brain were suspended in a biogel that met my every need whilst on a mission. My mission was to verify the increasing evidence of a Cataclysm in 1541. What I am seeing and experiencing was no more than advanced virtual reality. Already I was troubled, there were holes in this idea. How I have I built relationships? Have I influenced events? I asked myself. How is that possible. I began to become extremely anxious so paused and reset my thoughts. April, yes my wife April. That is now my goal. I was almost home once and, for whatever reason, it just didn't happen. And then the anomalies. I seem to have experienced 1642 and 1941 and even, once, disappeared from York and appeared here at Hampton Court. How was that possible? I checked myself again. Back to April. That's my goal. How to get to April? Seemingly I am compelled to finish my work here. I was sure that my ability to return home was commensurate with the completion of these missions. I decided that, ambitiously, I would attempt to wrap up matters at Hampton Court within a week and turn to the intrigues in York. Panic set in once again. No matter how much we chose to lampoon him, Robert had been and still was, in perilous danger. I did not know how Elspeth fared and

there were dozens of questions over the reliability of Eirik
and what he had been telling us. I had had no word, so also
had no idea whether the danger had increased there. Calm, I
must be calm, I told myself as these thoughts ran away with
themselves. Again, I had a reasonable theory about what
had taken place in York and also believed that there was no
connection to the events at the Court. But what if I was
wrong? If I'm wrong this could go on all year! I'll never get
back! My head started to hurt.

'You ok Micklegate?' Asked Peter.

'You awake Peter?'

'Yes, can't sleep. Too many thoughts!'

'Same here" I said.'

'Listen Micklegate' He said with some air of authority
'you take on all the responsibility. Well, for everything I
suppose! Why not talk about it. You do trust me, don't
you?'

I assured him that anyone who would seek to help a
dead monk based on the smallest scrap of parchment and
then travel from Bamburgh to York and York to London
for the cause, was someone I would trust unequivocally. He
listened, without judgement, to all my thoughts and, I have
to say, it was a relief just to get rid of it. I was sure, still, that
he would struggle with all the virtual reality stuff (as was I)
but I definitely needed someone to lean on. When I had
finished he simply leaned forward and said.

'Well here's the thing….I know you will work out who is
trying to kill the King here and who is trying to kill the
Agents in York. No doubt about it. Do this first, then make
haste to York, deploy Agents to support you there, hang the
bugger responsible and then you can go home. Not
complicated is it?'

I stared at him for, what must have been a couple of
minutes and then said

'Well, yes. When you put it like that, of course. Thank
you, my friend'.

I'm sure he had no idea what he had just done for me and it left me in no doubt that, from time to time, I needed advice and counsel too. I made myself comfortable and for the next three hours, I slept like a mouse.

26: THE FOUNTAIN

If the general populace of the Palace found the sudden introduction of Silas and Wynnfrith bizarre, they were to get their routines turned upside down by the notion that a boy carrying a mouse was allowed to question them. No less than a new, and singular, edict had been issued on this very subject stating the following:

"At the most recent pleasure of His Grace, King Henry V111, generous and most noble ruler and Supreme Head of the Church of England, a young man has been commissioned to consider costs and efficiencies of the Court, having been successful in major Manor Houses and Palaces in the far north of the land. At his pleasure, Peter (as he shall be called) will be accompanied by the King's favourite beast. Their business is not to be interrupted and all souls will cooperate on pain of punishment."

Sometimes, such edicts would be announced in a most formal manner, shouted from one end of the campus to another but, on this occasion, it was posted as a written document throughout. Where there was no one that could read, an officer would be sent to make the proclamation.

You would think that there would be considerable uproar and consternation at this sudden, ridiculous proclamation but there were new rules established almost every day and, most were a lot more stupid and threatening than this one. A few household members were worried that their livelihoods were at stake but most were more anxious about a beast wandering around the Palace. However, news travelled very fast at Hampton Court. Many had already seen the mouse dressed in all sorts of fineries and some had been most amused by this. By now, I had no feelings whatsoever about being dressed, not being dressed or, even what I was given to wear. Peter was kitted out with his first-ever leather doublet and hose and a cap with a feather in, and, no surprise, I wore the same. Perhaps the King should have had more children I told myself. I was so proud of Peter. There was no doubt that he loved his new look but at no point did he become distracted by his rocketing status and remained focussed on what was before us. He even tried to moderate his accent somewhat. People huddled and whispered as we approached them but I, certainly, was past bothering. We needed, desperately, to get to the core of this matter.

I suggested that, first, we took a walk. In doing so we saw Silas maintaining his guise and continuing to labour in the stables. We headed toward the pond where fish were bred and then took a direct line to the maze. This wasn't the maze that was famous many years hence but a more simple affair, the hedges having been honed from hornbeam. It was used both as an amusement, for walks and also for courting. The path was, in parts, insecure but this was mostly due to lack of use and it becoming waterlogged in early winter. There was a clear exit if needed but, otherwise, provided an interesting conundrum for anyone who wished to while away some time here. We found the area where the pit had been. The pit that had been set as a trap for the King. It had been poorly corrected and I also noticed that the whole maze hadn't been used since the event. Peter alluded to the uneven gravel around the area, I inspected it and then we made our way out. We deduced that, whoever laid the trap, also knew their way around this maze. It also left us wondering why Lyndon had been there at the same time as the King, as he had claimed that he saw the accident and had helped Henry.

Now out of the maze, I could see that Peter was cold so we ventured inside. Out of view of anyone, I briefed him.

'I have every faith in you lad. Try to remember that, when you speak, you speak with my authority and the authority of the King.'

I think this may have made him worse so I reassured him that he was to keep me on his shoulder and I would prompt him with pertinent questions. I wanted to start with the crabby, unsociable one-eyed Drake, the swan man.

'I'm not to be bothered whilst on the King's business' he grunted as we approached.

This startled Peter so, as rehearsed, I told him what to say.

'You will cooperate, my man, or this will get to the King's ear this very morning.'

Again, he grunted.

'Is your only job to prepare swan?'

Drake looked up, then back at his knife and he then answered without facing us.

'Why, of course not! Expert in all fowl I am. As soon as they arrive I care for them, look after the dears…' his eyes slowly raised and penetrated Peter's 'the bird-man I am!'

Already this was sounding a little strange, I indicated to Peter that we should just let him talk in the hope that he would give more away.

'They're like my children you see. When I've finished preparing them, they are perfect. My little dears…'

'So' said Peter now appealing to this madman's ego 'where do they go when they are so perfectly ready?'

'Why straight to that kitchen there…through the arch see…' and he nodded in the direction of one of the kitchens. I prompted Peter again.

'Is that all of the birds? Even the swan?'

It was at this point that he became animated, quite crazed in fact.

'Ohhh! The swan. Beautiful swan. No… special, she is. Just for the King…Drake unveils her as if a work of art!….Drake and his masterpiece!'

One of his assistants crept up behind us,

'Mister Drake is a master of his art. He's not an everyday butcher you know' he said, quite indignantly.

'There is no offence intended' said Peter 'just my ignorance, there is so much to learn. I congratulate you on your fine work Mister Drake and I will bid you farewell.' Said Peter at my behest and we left.

'You are doing so well' I said to him 'do not let these people terrorise you if you can help it.'

Nearby, was one of the servants' quarters and, almost everyone there was responsible for serving food. By the time Peter had finished questioning them I had now worked out that many, even maybe thirty to forty people were, to some degree, given access to Henry as they delivered food and wine and, of course, many others if you add messages, documents and clothes. I was convinced that, for most, there would be absolutely no motive to harm the King considering the potential and horrendous punishment awaiting them and, also, quite simply they were protective of their livelihood. Nevertheless, we asked everyone about their specific duties and, also, how long they had been at the Palace.

Although I had an inkling of what had transpired, I was still overwhelmed by the number of people who had, some sort of, access to the King, no matter how limited. It did little to help affairs and, I promised myself that it would be the first thing I would mention to Sir Ralph Sadler when I reported back. The next stop was Sir Anthony Browne, Master of the Horse, who, at first, was quite indignant that he would not speak to a boy whose English was barely understandable. Peter had often been confused with a Scot because of his thick Northumberland accent and that, at this time, was worse than being French. I whispered to Peter to politely request a private audience with Sir Anthony who, only slightly conceding, took us to one side. It was at this point where he gave the lad a dressing down, threatening him and then deciding to walk away.

I had had enough.

'How about you bloody well speak to me then, smartarse?!'

He leapt back and grabbed his dagger.'

'Hello! Aren't you meant to be wise? Why the bloody hell do you think the most powerful man in the land keeps a mouse. You arrogant bastard! Poncing about like you own the place, you are not to speak to the boy in that manner, he is on His Majesty's business.'

I'd lost it. This hadn't happened in a while, not this bad since the pin in the arse affair and, to be truthful, I'm not sure, as yet, that it was having the right effect. His breathing became heavy, still clutching his knife but then whimpered something unintelligible.

'For God's sake man, never seen a talking mouse before?' I blurted, now completely out of patience. 'So, will you cooperate or should me and the lad go find His Grace?'

'Ohhh…oh dear…I err suppose well, yes' and then he stopped agitating, turned to Peter and whispered,

'How are you doing that?'

'Not me, my Lord. And, it's not witchcraft and it's not a trick, he's just smart that's all.' Replied Peter, politely.

I realised that the poor sod just needed to calm down so I suggested that we walked out of sight of everyone else. As always, there was a settling down period where he acclimatised to the shock but eventually we did get somewhere.

'I need detail about the hunt' I said 'specifically about the day that the King was shot at.'

'Yes. Yes,' he said now coming to his senses 'what do you need?'

'Take me, and my lad here, to the run please.'

'Now?'

'Yes immediately' I said 'this very morning.'

I warned Peter that we would be in for a long ramble on a very cold day but he didn't seem to mind. We stood at the point where the hunt would have set off but, before going further, I decided to ask Sir Anthony Browne a few more questions.

'Do you have it?' I asked.

'The quarrel?'

'Yes, I need to see the bolt that was shot please.'

He was gone no more than fifteen minutes and, when he returned, he handed it to me.

'Just as I thought' I said.

'Yes, I know' added Browne 'small isn't it?'

'Certainly is. Did no one think to investigate this anomaly further?' I said, now impatient again.

'Well… no. His Grace told us that he was bringing down some superior investigator from the north but he never came.'

'It's me, you nob!'

Then, even I thought this was going a little too far, so apologised. How was he to know that that the Kingdom's greatest sleuth was a mouse?

'So what does this tell you, Browne?'

'Well, for certain' he said 'it's a crossbow or weapon like no other. Certainly wouldn't work on any we have here or at the Tower.'

'Absolutely. So where is it?'

He shrugged his shoulders but like me, must have known that it had been hidden somewhere.

'I would now like you to take me on the exact route of the hunt, more precisely, to where the King was shot.'

As we were not on horseback, it took fifty minutes to get to the spot where the attempted assassination took place. It was an unpleasant and, considerably risky, journey on foot. We were now well into wild territory and I was almost black and blue having been rocked about for so long. Having taken stock of where the incident had taken place I turned to Peter.

'Now we need to go back.' I said

'What?!' Said Peter, who was, by this point, ready for some warmth and food.

'Not all the way back, just to what would have been the rear of the hunt.'

'Wasting your time' said Browne, all puffed up 'nobody but those flanking the King carried weapons.'

'Please humour me' I said.

Once there, I asked Peter and Sir Anthony Browne to walk backwards and this, quite ridiculous exercise, went on for some time.

'There!' I shouted

'What?' Said Browne who now had had enough of taking orders from a mouse 'just another tree trunk, we've passed dozens.'

'Look at the size of that hole in the trunk, an elongated oval shape, undisturbed by wildlife. But, more to the point, it has been stuffed with decaying autumn leaves.'

Browne and Peter took a closer look.

'You're right!' Said Peter '

'If you look closely it is now no more than mulch. But, see....the leaves have been compressed by hand to fill this hole. Wildlife can no longer get in or out. We should be grateful that it is still undisturbed.'

Browne stuck his gloved hand into the mulch.

'Yes, of course, this isn't solid it is a covering, a deception.' He said.

'And that is exactly where you will find your weapon.' I told him.

Already bent over, he peered back over his shoulder almost as a way of asking permission and I nodded indicating that I wished him to proceed. It wasn't long before he started to pull out sticks, leaves and, eventually a dead mouse which, incidentally, made him quite smug, and then a piece of bark. He almost discarded it because it looked like piece of, what was referred to, as a 2 x 2, meaning a lump of timber of indeterminable length but, otherwise, two inches by two inches. As he held it, I could tell that he was initially pondering why on earth a piece of cut timber would be down there.

'I think you will need to clean it somewhat.' I suggested.

There was little else available besides icy puddle water but it did help to remove the surface detritus from the object. Browne brought it close and continued to wipe it with his glove and then, although, in just one spot at first, it was glinting in the winter sun. This was unquestionably a metal object.

Eventually, we returned to a private stable at Hampton Court where he was able to clean it properly. Still looking like a block, it was bronze with copper inlays boasting the most intricate design.

'Not English' I suggested.

'Absolutely' said Browne 'never seen the like before. And it's so small.'

For a few moments, he handled it carefully as if it were precious although I was content that he had never set eyes on it before. He then put it down, left momentarily and summoned a guard to bring cleaning materials that were left at the door. As this metal moth gradually became a butterfly we were absorbed in its unveiling and the intricacy of its design. In addition to the fine copper inlays, there were jewels. This had once belonged to someone of note.

'But What is it?' Asked Peter, unable to correlate what he was seeing with any known weapon.

'There' I said to Browne almost ignoring Peter. 'One of the jewels is more pronounced. In fact, it is the only one that is false.'

Browne cleaned the misfit jewel and then pushed and tapped it without success until he tried to pull it away from the shaft completely. Then, incredibly slowly like a bird waking and stretching its wings, it whistled and screeched until eventually, it did, indeed, resemble a miniature crossbow, all manner of detritus falling from in. Browne noticed that a stirrup was also trying to birth itself from the front of the object and so he assisted its journey.

'Try it!' I said and Browne, understanding what I meant, took out the bolt that he had had in his possession for weeks and put it to rest in front of the latch. As he did so, it was clear that it was a perfect fit and, bizarrely, a trigger then emerged from underneath. It was a most beautiful, and expensive object and not something that would be thrown away lightly.

'Well' started Browne, quite sure of himself 'we can be sure that none of the estate or lower gentry were culpable.'

'Not so' I said 'I agree that someone of worth once owned this but it remains to be seen who shot the bolt. My Lord, I will need you to take care of this and, at some point onward, I will wish you to recall what we have seen and discovered this day and I will ask you to bring it to a designated location beyond the Palace when I am ready for you.'

'Beyond the Palace. Whatever for?!' He replied quite indignantly.

'I promise that you will understand soon, but I must ask for now that you remain completely silent on this matter and also in what you have witnessed concerning my ability to speak. I have a powerful gut feeling that, yet again, I do not think it will be long before it is necessary to reveal my secret to a wider audience.'

He paused, but I had pre-empted what he was about to say. Today, however, I was in no mood for explaining my unique, and irritating, gifts. Until now, I'm not sure that the penny had dropped with Peter that we were in a real, attempted murder investigation and the sight of the crossbow certainly worried him. It had all, suddenly, become very real. I reassured him that we were getting nearer to the end of our task each day and asked him, too, to trust me.

I decided that this was investigating enough for the day and, as we headed back toward our stable, I caught a glimpse of Silas and Molly together.

'I imagine a fine young Lord like you will have women at his feet.' She said very softly and within touching distance of our smelly friend.

'Oh…err…well, not really Maiden. You see, I'm just Silas.'

Although he couldn't see us, we could see and hear both of them and this already had us stifling laughter at Silas's compromised situation. What in God's name did that mean? I'm just Silas. He is terrible at this, I thought. God bless him, you could see how he was still feeling guilty so it was very hard to work out whether he was enjoying Molly's advances or not. I put this to Peter quietly who, by now, had fostered a healthy fondness for Silas, as all do who know him.

'Think he'd rather be in battle! And, I think we should rescue him.'

I agreed so decided to sketch out a quick plan, remembering that we couldn't expose any connection between him and Wynnfrith or even ourselves.

'Stable boy!' Shouted Peter with some authority. You are needed by Lord Browne.'

The gormless bastard just stared. I mean, give him his due, he didn't blurt out either of our names, but it must have been over a minute before he either moved or spoke. I could even feel myself holding my breath waiting for the impasse to break. Molly had already moved towards us and then, spoke to Peter.

'Oh. You new here then? I'm Molly.'

Doesn't waste much bloody time, I thought, what the hell is in those berries she's picking?

'Maiden, we must all depart on urgent business so we will bid you farewell.'

Peter, I could see, was almost falling into the same trap. He walked away but she just didn't give up. She was swaying and sauntering, alongside us, at the same time as doing small, seductive waves and pouting. It was at this point that I had to prompt Peter to stop staring at her. When I looked, Silas was following as well.

Hoping I was out of her earshot I attempted my loudest whisper in his direction.

'Right Silas. Bugger off...we have work to do, we'll see you later.'

I then hurried Peter on our way as I now had urgent business and I directed him to a much more interesting part of the Palace where anything from horseshoes to crossbows and armour was made and repaired. The sense of industry there was breath-taking and the quality of the work as good as it possibly could have been anywhere in Europe. I caught a glimpse of one of Henry's old jousting breastplates hanging on the wall, clearly too small for him now. The intricate decoration spoke volumes about the standard of craftsmanship within the Palace and also the pressures that must have, at times, been brought to bear on these craftsmen. All manner of weapons were to be seen either hung in rows or about the workshop, the latter presumably needing some work. I knew that if I used the right names and the right words, we would leave with exactly what I needed but I was relying on young Peter to both remember and deliver those words. It was perfectly clear who the gaffer was and, once Peter had delivered his lines, he marched back over to the bench where I was. He looked me up and down, particularly at the ridiculous clothes I was wearing, marched back to Peter and said

'Very well! Be half an hour. Wait over there.'

He was as good as his word and we left happy. As we walked away Peter acknowledged, as I did, that these people were set apart from so many of the Palace staff not just geographically, but how they behaved. Sure of their indispensable skills, they weren't the least bit interested in Court tickle tackle.

That evening we compared notes again and Silas and Wynnfrith became completely absorbed in the crossbow affair. Once I had summed up on this evening, I asked Wynnfrith and Peter if they would retire early as there was something I had to discuss with Silas. Being as he was, I knew that explaining any plan to him would be hard work but, to be fair, he listened and I believed that everything was understood and in place. I then sent him, along with a guard, straight to Thames Heneage and, around midnight, he returned clean and in his best doublet, hose and hat. He looked marvellous and, I know he felt good too although he was unquestionably nervous, so we worked for hours on his dithering and his delivery.

Just beyond our stable was an ornamental fountain that was used by almost everyone and, it was here, as the sun came up, that Silas could be seen wringing his hands, intermittently adjusting his codpiece, scratching his head and bending at the knees as if he needed a pee.

Peter and I stood outside Wynnfrith's cell and, as she opened her door, she was bemused to see Peter, with the mouse, waiting for her.

'Good morni….What's going on?' she said.

'Why, What makes you think there's something going on?' I said sounding distinctively shifty.

'You do…look very suspicious, both of you!'

Her eyes were flickering back and forth between the two of us, she looked behind her and then beyond us to the rear of the stable.

'Let's just say you are required by the fountain, my dear.'

Only her head turned. The sunrise was beautiful and, at first, she could only see the fountain until, eventually, there was also this hobbling, wobbling, apprehensive creature that kept moving back and forth in front of it.

'What?' She asked again.

'Please Wynnfrith…' I said and I believe from the tone in my little voice that she could tell that this was important to all of us. So, off She went. I swear, at first, that Silas considered legging it but then, he sort of froze, as did she.

For a few moments, nothing whatsoever happened though, God and all the Saints know we were willing it to with every fibre of our being. Silas then knelt, genuflected and then stood up straight again and took her hand. I noticed that she trembled a little, bless her. He huffed puffed and grunted for a few seconds and then spoke. It was, undoubtedly, the greatest speech he had ever made and, possibly the most number of words said by him that had made sense to any other human being.

'Wynnfrith….my dear Wynnfrith. Please be patient as I am not as other men… and I am so sorry for that. So sorry for how inadequate I am. I am clumsy, both with my body and my words but…but…I promise I will speak from my heart this day…'

And then the longest pause, she was completely still, surely wishing for more but nothing, he just became more and red in the face. And then, a huge intake of breath and, as he breathed out again,

'There was never….there has never been one moment…since falling off that stool in your wash house…that my mind has been free of any thoughts of you. I know…I think…I am not worthy and I know that you must have many suitors…but…well….this love that resides in my heart and soul could not be felt by anyone else. I would like to have…I would like to take your hand in marriage if that is suitable to you?'

I was so very proud of him. This was so much more than I could have expected but, as he finished, the colour drained from his cheeks and his jaw, unflatteringly, dropped open. Having run the gauntlet, it was obvious that he had no confidence whatsoever in receiving the answer he desired. Poor Silas. Never, ever, feeling worthy.

She wasn't coping much better either. Of course, he loved her, of course, she loved him but she never expected this. She presumed that the coy, embarrassed thing would just go on endlessly. Why would anyone want to be shackled to me? She thought. And then, he produced the ring, and what a fine job the armourer had done of it. It was way too big but that didn't matter, it could be made to fit anytime. She looked down at this tiny, beautiful object in his shaking hand and tears just poured down her face. This, in turn, shook Silas and he started to back away.

It was during this moment that I was, yet again, reminded of how ridiculously awkward this relationship had been and, no matter how much it wound me up, I had to tell myself it was an indicator of how low their self-esteem was. Yes, both of them. Growing up in a world where anything beyond "acceptable" or "normal" was, to be frank, totally unacceptable, abnormal and not to be considered worthy, and that included relationships and marriage. So it was, during that pause, that I was sure I had made the right choice for this, supposed courtship would probably have lasted a lifetime without a little encouragement. Then Wynnfrith took the initiative.

'No' she said 'come nearer again please' and, as he did, she placed her right hand on his left cheek as a parent might do with a child.

'I know how hard this is for you. I know you feel like an outsider. It is why I always liked you and that has grown into love, the love a woman has for a man.'

She pushed herself up on tiptoes, wobbled and kissed him on the cheek. Then she kissed the hand that offered the ring and then, just briefly, his lips. Now, with the fear ebbing out of him, his wiry arm folded around her waist to support her. They separated and as the engagement ring was placed on her finger, she whispered, 'yes.'

There was a beam across young Peter's face and as I turned to absorb this poignant and serene event, there came an instantaneous uproar taking us all by surprise. I looked beyond the fountain where a sizeable group of muscular and sweaty blacksmiths were cheering, leaving Wynn and Silas, yet again, dumbfounded. So much for it being a secret, I thought. I told Peter to usher the daft couple inside, giving the blacksmiths and armourers a thankful wave. As Silas and Wynnfrith came into the stable I noticed that she was still examining that wonderful ring, not entirely sure about what had just happened. Silas was, once more, trembling but had now adopted a strange, affected giggle which made me just want to slap him. We all sat, they held hands and I explained about the ring. In perfect circumstances, her father would have had to approve this bond in advance and, of course, the nearest thing we had was Robert so I was hoping he was still alive and well and okay with all this.

This was a moment of real joy amidst this desert of intrigue, suspicion and secrecy and I implored them to enjoy what they had. In truth these two would be, for many months to come, still uncomfortable with one another. Wynnfrith wasn't used to physical affection and poor Silas simply wasn't used to any affection. However, my heart sang. I loved them both and I thought them a perfect match.

Of course, I had also created more problems than I had solved and, possibly could have made a considerable error. It was with this in mind that we had to, immediately, return to the forge in the hope of securing the secrecy of all who worked there. They were all proud of the ring and the story that went with it and I was certain they wanted nothing to do with anyone else in the Palace or, indeed, their intrigues. For now, it was essential that no one else was aware of any connection between Wynnfrith and Silas.

I was insistent, too, that we all returned to our default guises after an unusual day and, I hoped that at seven o clock that evening, we would be able to start making some assumptions about the threats on Henry.

27: THE MASQUE AND THE FOOL

Truth be told, the day was rather unfruitful although I still believed that I now had a theory that was worth pursuing. Almost at the very moment that we were to have our evening meet, we were disturbed by distant sounds. Wynnfrith leapt up, clapped her hands together excitedly and said

'Music!'

'Ah yes,' I said 'I had forgotten. Yet another of the King's ridiculous indulgences, no doubt spending enough in one evening to keep a hundred people fed for a year.'

As I looked for a response I could see what they were all thinking, "miserable bastard" was what they were thinking, looking down at me as if I were vermin.

'Well, look' I said 'I have no doubt that this will be an incredible spectacle but we are, after all, secret agents. Secret?'

Again they glared.

'I have just got engaged and I want to see it!' said Wynnfrith.

'Me too' added Silas, already under the thumb in my opinion.

'And me.'

Peter's postscript had me in no doubt that I had been ganged up on. I reminded them of the dangers but they, more or less, persuaded me that due care would be taken so off to see the silly masquerade we went. It was no trouble to walk, unseen, following the walls of the Palace in the dark although we were risking much. Eventually, we were right next to the Great Hall but underneath a huge red brick window sill. I had instructed them to take turns to put their eyes just above the sill and peep, that being dangerous enough.

'You first Wynnfrith, please try not to overreact, if we are seen, all is lost.'

She was silent at first but then started to whisper.

'Ooh. It is so beautiful, they are all dancing but wearing masks, the King watches from his throne. Ha ha…he is clapping along! Oh my, they are so athletic leaping up and down, people enter dressed as eastern characters, it is so exotic.'

All this did for me was to bring back the most unpleasant memories of when I had had to dance for Culpeper and the Queen in Lincoln. Bloody ridiculous pastime, I thought. She continued,

'The colours and…oh! I can see the Prince, what a sweet little boy. Ah…he is being taken to his bed…ohh…ha haha! The fool! He is so funny! He has bells and mocks the dancers!'

Yeah, bloody hilarious! I thought to myself. About as funny as an enema. What a dick, forever in the King's favour getting paid a fortune and, seemingly untouchable. He could say and do practically nothing and people would laugh. Fortunately, I kept all of this to myself and grudgingly watched as Silas took a turn. He didn't say as much as Wynnfrith but, as his head kept still so as not to be noticed, his hips swayed back and forth and then his knees would bend and straighten and then, astonishingly he did a little leap and fell on top of Wynnfrith and subsequently into a bush, hastily grabbing his hose which seemed to be forever wanting to be around his ankles. I still had difficulty understanding why Silas was forever challenged by gravity.

'Silas!' I said in my very loudest whisper 'what do you think are you doing?!'

He looked at me and then at Wynnfrith and Peter who were laughing and apologised as he struggled to get back up again.

'I have never seen such costumes' said Peter 'and the food! Why! there is everything you can think of and it is being delivered constantly. Haha! The fool! His dance is so silly!'

As you may have gathered, I had no love for Will Somers. I was suspicious of him and I believed he had too much power although, if I was completely objective in the matter, I had no evidence that he had done any wrong.

'Look, Micklegate!' Whispered Peter 'He is so close'.

Having previously had no interest whatsoever in this selfish exhibition and extravagance, I agreed to sit on his shoulder a while and watch. Uncannily, Will Somers, the fool, jester, King's confidante, nobhead, call him what you want, did seem to be nearing the window.

'Don't worry, there are so many candles indoors, all he will see is a reflection, we won't be noticed' I reassured them.

However, he was still dancing, gesticulating, ringing his bloody bell and dancing ever nearer to us. He was singing his own words to the music but repeating them over and over. At first, this was indistinct but, eventually, we could all make sense of it. Repeatedly and annoyingly he would recite the same words, hopping and dancing closer and closer until his face was up to the window.

'Buried a saint
Buried his kin
Angel at heart
Devilish a sin
The future secure
Where snows fall
Falls the crown
Falls the pall'

He then tilted his head to one side and sang louder, looking straight at us. I had been wrong. He could see us! Eerily, on and on his ditty went, round and round as I quickly issued orders.

'Get to your beds all three of you, now!'

Astonished, they backed away from the window and I could see that Wynnfrith in particular, wanted to challenge me but I was insistent. I told Peter to tear off the silly clothes that I had been wearing and put me down onto the earth below.

'Are you mad?! You won't survive!' He protested.

'I'm sorry my friends, I have no time to argue. I'm having that daft bastard here and now, let me get at the pretentious bugger!'

Unreasonable as a drunk in a fight and driven by this newly acquired curmudgeonly, crude and unreasonable personality, I was having no resistance so, assuring them that I would not be stopped, I sped away from them, following the muddy contour of the building. Within minutes, I had found my way inside. I wasn't entirely unnoticed but, particularly between the stables and the kitchens, there were rodents of all shapes and sizes that were normally only expelled or killed when people had time so, for the moment, I was safe. I realised as I had left the kitchens and entered the corridor leading to the Great Hall that I was more exposed, so hid in a nook in one of the decorative oak panels. However, I was not alone. I was face to face with the first mouse I had seen in some time and I was severely compromised. However, this was the first female that I had encountered in months and she was gorgeous. No seriously, she was hot stuff. Temptation with a tail, presumably sent by the devil himself to tempt me. Moreover, she took a liking to me. My ever-responsible conscience knew I had to get to the overpaid jester before he left although other parts of my anatomy were shouting an entirely different narrative.

Anyway, ten minutes later, I resumed my journey but, as I could hear the music getting louder and laughter emanating from the hall, I also saw guards coming in my direction. I thought it wise to freeze and wait for them to pass until it became clear that one of them thought that it might be fun to give me an even more distinct split personality by trying to cleave me with his halberd. I darted into a nearby chamber and they merrily walked past laughing at the ridiculousness of his improvised attempt at pest control. For a moment or two, I felt I could breathe and think. That was until I turned around. This was the very same chamber in which I had, not long ago, encountered Thomas Cranmer and, not surprisingly, there he was again and next to him was the fool. He danced, gurned, fell about and recited his rhyme over and over whilst the Archbishop just stared at me. And then he stopped. They both glared in my direction almost as if they had been expecting me. Will Somers then inclined his head, pulled a daft face and wobbled out again. I was now left alone with Cranmer, well aware that during our last encounter, he tried to fry me in his fireplace.

'Ah, the beast' he said calmly 'come, be comfortable Micklegate Mouse.'

And he picked me up, gently, and placed me on a cushion even though I was plastered with mud.

'I might have known you would be behind all this.' I said firmly and pretending I wasn't in the least bit scared, but he laughed. It would be fair to say he guffawed and when he finished, he smiled, benignly.

'Oh Mouse, you are so wrong. I'll give it to you, your work on the Cataclysm was spectacular and I must concede, you beat me to it.'

'What do you mean, beat you to it?' Absolutely confused by what was going on.

'Unbeknownst to you, I was a plant, a spy. My presumed alliance with Thomas Seymour and Thomas Wriothesley even fooled you. I was commissioned with the singular task of unravelling their deceit, by his Grace himself.' He said.

'Mmm. Sounds good, Archbishop but it doesn't make sense. You were overheard by Brother Bernard and Brother Bede in the Tower of London swearing an oath to the new covenant that was the Cataclysm or, as you called it, the Clarification.'

'Part of the deception' my friend 'and you should know that the King still has his eye on them both.'

'And your attempt to burn me alive? Was that a deception?!'

'Think, Mouse, think. Did I really try to burn you? All I did was grab you by the tail. As I didn't know who was approaching, it was my intent to hide you. Rather than being your enemy, the King himself has appointed me to watch your back, why do you think you are here?'

The more I thought about, the more it made sense. This was pre-arranged and I was daft enough to fall into it. The fool had goaded me into leaving my friends. He started to talk again.

'Well, can I presume that you have worked everything out?'

I said nothing, reluctant to give anything away.

'Well. How about this' he continued 'the fool's rhyme made sense didn't it?'

He had me. Yes, that was what had riled me. The fool knew as much as I did.

'I will give you a short phrase and, when I do, you will know that we are both on the same page.' I listened intently to see if any of this would make any sense and then, calmly he just said,

'the woodcutter's lodge.'

I let out the biggest sigh. He did know or, at least, he knew enough.

'So why the secrecy? What does the King need me for?' I asked somewhat deflated.

'Because His Grace knows that you will get the job done. I've just got your back, that's all.'

'So where does Will Somers fit in with this. I have to be honest, I can't bloody stand him!'

'He knows all, Mouse. He sees all and knows all, even more than Thomas Heneage does. Almost like a priest though, he's not allowed to talk about either state affairs or intrigue so, it often comes out in other ways, if you get my drift.' Said Crammer.

'Therefore the rhyme' I said.

'Therefore the rhyme' he confirmed.

'And the diagram, you still have it?' I asked.

'Here' and there it still was on his table and beside it was a more ragged, amateur version.

'You understand it now, Mouse?'

'If I'm honest' I replied 'I struggled with this more than anything, my knowledge of alchemical symbols and astrology not what it should be. Astonishingly, it was the Queen herself that pointed me in the direction of the grand Palace clock, boasting some of the same markings.' I said.

'Ah, the Queen. If not for her indiscretions what an ally she would have made for his Grace. A great loss, but you never heard me say so' said the Archbishop.

'A great loss' I concurred.

'I presume you can deliver soon Mouse?' He asked.

'Tomorrow. I will reveal all tomorrow.'

'Then I will ensure that you have all the support you need. I will have a guard take you back to your cell.'

Having shared with me a few more incredibly illuminating details before I left, I was then thinking that this was possibly the strangest encounter that I had had during the whole of my mission to date. I had to believe him and kicked myself for getting this part wrong. I lay awake thinking about my arrogance and then doubted my abilities overall. I then pondered on the nameless lady mouse and wondered if our liaison counted as being unfaithful to my wife and then, finally, thought about my bias regarding the fool. If nothing else, he had given me some certainty that I had solved this puzzle. Get tomorrow over with, I told myself, and then to York and resolve things there too. And then home. What a wonderful thought and then I slipped into a long dreamless sleep.

28: THE WOODCUTTER'S LODGE

As I woke, I realised that I wasn't alone. I found myself warm, comfortable, relaxed and, beside me was my new friend, the female mouse. I realised that the warmth of a fellow-creature was possibly what I had needed for some time. Silly as it sounds, and to be fair, it probably looked bloody silly too, we lay together as the sun rose, giving each other some solace and, yes, even affection. Then, just as I thought I would have to leave her and conclude my business in London, she moved to leave my tiny cell. She scurried away using a small hole left by rotting wood in the door and then turned back.

'You have less than two weeks Nick, and then you won't survive.'

And then disappeared.

Stunned and speechless I chased after her but she had disappeared. Was I imagining this? Surely not. I concluded that this must have been some cunning way to connect with me. One thing was for sure, I heeded the warning and became incredibly anxious at the thought of the possible consequences if I could not return home. It sharpened my senses and my resolve and, within no time, I had everyone up and ready for business. I told Wynnfrith, Silas and Peter to find their finest clothes as our work was now at an end.

'Whatever do you mean?' Asked Silas.

'I mean, my good friend, that we will expose the perpetrator this very day and be on our way!'

They were dumbstruck but also relieved, they desperately wanted to get back to York.

I sent word to Thomas Heneage with details of my plan and my, somewhat irregular, demands. We would meet Heneage and Sir Ralph Sadler in the woods at midday and, shortly after, would be met by Palace guards and a number of the staff. Also, I asked that both Sadler and Heneage inspected the pit into which the King had fallen to confirm a final suspicion of mine. Having explained, Heneage agreed but told me that he would, first, have to seek the King's permission. We were assured of his authority at around 11.35 so set off behind the so-called wilderness and into the forest. Eventually, we came across an abandoned woodcutter's hut being positioned almost exactly where I expected it to be.

'All the wood is supplied by a family now. They were appointed by the Queen herself. Much more efficient.' Said Sadler 'so this cottage is now abandoned.'

I asked Sadler, Heneage and my companions to be patient whilst we walked around the property. Once, then twice and then continuously until I was satisfied, all the while knowing that I was irritating my companions. Silas incessantly asked questions and I firmly had to insist that he stop or there would never have been an end to it.

The door opened without being forced and I wasn't surprised to see a small fire lit within. Heneage and Sadler were expecting an abandoned cottage but this was clearly a home. Soon, we heard footsteps. Upstairs, someone was moving. Heneage shouted up and demanded that they expose themselves.

'Molly!' Said Silas as she appeared, at which point, Wynnfrith gave them both a deathly stare.

As rehearsed, Heneage and Sadler ignored Silas and sat Molly down facing us.

She sat without saying a word. Ten minutes later, the guards arrived along with Gabriel, Lyndon and Ramsey, the stable and dog boys. Drake the obsessive bird-man, Mrs Cornwallis, Beth, and Sir Anthony Browne, the Master of the horse. I would have happily added Will Somers, the fool, but there was no way that the King would release him. They were all silent except for Drake.

'How dare you! Wait until the King gets wind of this. Why, this very day…'

'Shut it' said Sadler, his hand on his dagger 'you won't speak unless spoken to! That goes for all of you!'

I looked around. Apart from Drake and Sir Anthony Browne, everyone looked terrified. I had to remind myself that this wasn't the same as simply looking guilty. Of course, they were terrified, they had been hauled up in front of Palace officials who would have needed no excuse to have them all executed, guilty or not. Although it wasn't meant to be, by any stretch of the imagination, Sadler's next statement was amusing and the looks on everyone's faces reflected this. It was probably mostly to do with the way he said it, rather than the words themselves.

'I want you all to regard the small rodent now perched atop yonder table.' He said formally.

Scared to upset him, all eyes moved toward where I crouched. He continued,

'This Mouse is a personal favourite of His Grace and has been transported from the north as he is also his most reliable investigator.'

Gabriel spluttered and then looked at everyone else who didn't know whether to laugh or not. However, Sadler's glare made it clear that this was not meant to cause amusement.

'And, ahem…err…he talks. He has the strangest accent, but talks. He will talk and you will listen.'

They now, collectively, appeared completely freaked out wondering what on earth was expected of them.
Tentatively, I spoke, knowing that this was now my cue and that there was no getting out of it.

'For some time…'

I waited for the shrieks to die down.

'For some time I, alongside my colleagues' I gestured to Silas, Peter and Wynnfrith 'have been investigating the numerous attempts on the life of King Henry. These include an attempt to poison him, an attempt to shoot him with a crossbow and a wicked plan to have him fall into a pit of flames. There were, many more plans that either failed or never saw the light of day!'

By now they were listening to the mouse. Hanging on to every word, in fact.

'Mrs Cornwallis…' She said nothing as I addressed her 'you are, quite rightly, favoured for the magnificent sweet inventions made solely for His Grace but, you already know that it was one of your fruit jellies that was consumed on the day that the attempted poison took place'

She began to weep.

'However, you did not know that the blueberries that were atop the jelly were replaced nimbly by your assistant, Beth. And you, Beth, were supplied those blueberries in a devious and clandestine manner by your sister Molly.'

Heads were now spinning in all directions but, as yet, no one was denying anything.

'And, of course' I continued 'those weren't blueberries but hand-picked deadly nightshade. Even you, Mrs Cornwallis, gave way to personal pride as you placed the over-sized blueberry on top of the dessert without due inspection.

As a prelude to the jelly, the King was given pheasant prepared, of course, by Mr Drake who added a little lead. In fact, for almost a month you were adding trace amounts of lead to the King's fowl in the hope of a long, undetected demise.'

He arrogantly looked away.

'And!' I said angrily 'Do you not think that I would uncover who you were Mr Drake? Thankfully, Wynnfrith here, recently recounted one of her brother, Eirik's, stories that had been told, in turn, to him by Brother Bernard, I realised immediately that you were Samuel, the ex-Benedictine living in Bury St Edmunds. A monk who had given up all resistance to the Reformation and just wanted to be left alone, apparently! But not so!' I shouted 'your embitterment caused by the Reformation and your eviction as a monk drove you to find personal retribution!'

It was at this point that he protested. Out of all of them, I knew he would be the one to wriggle.

'You want evidence? Firstly we now have within the Palace walls a copy of that diabolical diagram that was uncovered in your cottage last year by Brother Bernard. In addition, Wynnfrith was told that you bore a resemblance to Brother Bernard, which clearly you do, and, the missing eye, in particular, you couldn't hide. I will now have to insist that you are silent whilst I continue.'

One of the guards stood directly behind Drake.

'And, for this cause, you gave up your very own great-nephew. I can't imagine how anyone could stoop to lower depths than this…' It was now his turn to weep.

'Sergeant, please tell all here what you found in the pit where the King was to meet his end?'

The sergeant took two steps forward.

'This very morning I have removed the scorched body of a boy from the crudely dug pit, I would say aged about ten years old.'

'Thank you, Sergeant. Yes, you had him wait for, goodness knows how long, tasked with using gunpowder to start a fire. Your very own kin for God's sake! The King stumbled awkwardly but was helped out by young Lyndon here. Yes, Lyndon, the King's greatest critic who followed him as he had seen someone tampering with the maze in the dark. He described a man whose head was twisted to one side throughout. Perhaps a man with only one good eye? Lord Sadler' I said turning to him 'this young man, Lyndon is not only innocent but should be rewarded for the care he gave to the King's safety. He has been, throughout, the perfect decoy and was also in the employ of Archbishop Cranmer.'

Sir Anthony Browne, who had repeatedly reprimanded and punished Lyndon for his lack of diligence, wildly inappropriate comments and behaviour now looked both embarrassed and angry. Understandably, he felt that he should have been party to this deception.

As the innocent, Mrs Cornwallis and Lyndon had joined our ranks, I turned again to Drake.

'Your own family, Drake? Whilst struggling to light the gunpowder in the pit, the draft naturally came from above creating a fireball that engulfed him completely whilst he hid in a tunnel dug at ninety degrees to the pit but, remained almost unseen from above as His Grace's mass threw melting ice and slurry ahead of him. You sacrificed him for this cause. What possible influence could have possibly been put upon you to make you do such a thing?'

He said nothing but still wept.

'So are you are all connected to each other? That was what alluded me at first but, before I go any further I have to confess that you, Beth, confused me the most. That accent, I just couldn't make it out. Gabriel did nothing to hide his strong Germanic tones but you, you were trying to hide it for, you, Gabriel and Molly are all family aren't you?'

She nodded compliantly.

'So, to be precise, you three are, in fact, Austrian?'

They nodded again.

'And kin?'

Again they nodded and, at this juncture, their heads went down in shame.

'Do you know, that was what really confused me. How could any one person carry out all these wicked acts? I thought to myself, but then it occurred to me that, if at least two of you could get employment at the Palace it would be much easier. You, Molly, you are trouble. Too much trouble. You enjoy getting between people too much and that gave you away. I am guessing that you have been in England the longest, mastering the language and the accent? No one was going to give you a job so you devised your own methods of infiltrating the stables, the kitchens, anywhere you willed, in fact. And, it was so easy for you to smuggle in the poisoned nightshade, particularly with Beth's help. Shame on you for implicating poor Mrs Cornwallis and, even worse standing by as others were mercilessly killed.'

Molly sobbed, her head now in her apron.

'So, Gabriel. Now to your beautiful, and expensive, Austrian crossbow, neatly concealed amongst all the other necessities that were taken on the hunt in case of an accident or other emergencies. I have no doubt that you were an experienced huntsman yourself in Austria and had plenty of practice with this weapon, but you missed your target that day and, I have deduced that you couldn't hide it without someone else covering your tracks at the very moment that the alarm went up. As you hid this within the tree trunk, Ramsey here, acted as a watchman for an act that took no more than thirty seconds. See, the Sergeant has it here.'

The Sergeant dutifully showed everyone the miniature crossbow.

'I swear I am not part of this greater plot Sirs…err….Lord Mouse he just paid me to keep watch while he hid the weapon!' Protested Ramsey.

'Oh yes. This I know' I said ' all the same, you saw Gabriel shoot the crossbow intending to kill the King of this land so you are, unquestionably, guilty too.'

'So, what a motley crew!' I continued 'Drake, I can probably work out your motive. Your pretence at giving no care at all to the Reformation was just that. In reality, you despised this King beyond measure. You just needed a flag to follow and the flag bearer will be revealed very soon. But what about you three? What in Heaven's name could you have in common that would have you take such risks, besides being siblings, that is?'

Even Heneage and Sadler looked confused. Enough for Thomas Heneage to comment.

'Well, it looks like we have our culprits, mouse, not sure there's much more to be said.'

'Oh there is more, much more Sir Thomas' I said sounding every bit a smartarse 'it is what binds these four miscreants and their unassuming ally that will put an end to this matter for good. For your benefit, my Lords, I will offer some clues. The real perpetrator of these schemes had devised so many alternative plots and yet, these plans were hidden in plain sight. Drake, or Samuel if you wish, had a copy himself and by espionage, the Archbishop himself managed to purloin his copy. I had seen it long ago but it made no sense to me at the time. It is a complex diagram cross-referencing astrological signs with alchemical symbols, each indicating a time period and a method of assassination. Sir Thomas, would you oblige please?'

Heneage unfurled the document, having removed it from a cylindrical leather satchel, then placed it for all to see on the floor. I looked at the perpetrators, not the diagram, seemingly, it was not the first time they had seen it either.

'May I point out those most obvious?'

Sadler, Heneage and Anthony Browne nodded, now fascinated.

'Firstly, Sagittarius reflecting November 28th when the shooting took place. The sign of the archer surrounded by two symbols, copper and silver.'

'Like the crossbow!' said Sir Anthony Browne.'

'Yes. And, if I'm honest there are others that I haven't worked out yet. Over here, Capricorn, December 26th, an earth sign depicting the pit and these symbols around it: phosphorous, fire and sulphur!'

'This is indeed diabolical' said Sir Ralph Sadler, now furious as the degree of premeditation was revealed.

'And this' I said 'the January poisoning. Aquarius the water bearer. So many symbols here'

I looked at those responsible.

'endless permutations of how you could succeed, nightshade, alcohol, lead and quicksilver and, yet, you still failed!'

'So what about the rest?' asked Browne.

'Quite simply, my Lord, these represent at least a dozen other opportunities indicating date and method. Unquestionably a diagram of pure evil. I have to add that, as yet, no one has deciphered all of them.'

'Right Sergeant! Let's get this lot to the Tower this very morning!' Demanded Lord Sadler now absolutely furious.

'Ah' I said, calmly, 'I have still not done. Apologies my Lords. Would anyone of you care to tell of the missing link?'

Apart from the incurably arrogant Drake, everyone's heads went down again.

'You mean there's more?!' Said Browne.

'Yes, my Lord, I said 'why do you think we spent so much time circumnavigating the cottage before we entered?'

He thought for some time and, I really did need someone else to contribute at this juncture as I was exhausted.

'Yes!' He said 'I think I understand. It is no more than a square wooden building although, on inspection, it is asymmetrical. The northeast corner is larger than the others!'

'Just so my Lord!' I said with some relief. 'And where would that be from where we now stand?'

'There, where that panel is Mouse. Behind the girls.'

'Thank you. If there is one thing that a mouse is extremely familiar with, it is a panel. You may notice…' heads turned 'you will notice that the moulding on the panel directly behind Molly doesn't line up with the one adjacent to it.'

I needn't have gone any further, the Sergeant at arms was already there pulling at it.

'Thank you, Sergeant, but perhaps, Molly, you could make things easier? After all, the game is up now.'

Weeping, she pushed her blue-stained fingers underneath the moulding and it creaked open as a door would and exactly like the one in Samuel's home in Bury St Edmunds. There, sitting, looking pathetic and as guilty as any man ever had, was the perpetrator and engineer of all this grief.

'You!' Said Sadler 'you were thought surely dead!'

'That is the one thing that threw me, I discounted this scoundrel time and time again because I was assured that he had been executed last year. The very man that performed the deception known as The Cataclysm, Paracelsus himself!'

The Lords and guards became very animated, almost uncontrollably angry. It was almost as if they felt personally responsible that this man still walked the earth. Neither did I have any answers. History records that he died in Austria in September 1541 but the King himself had told us that he had been executed in summer.

'So this is revenge for the failure of the Cataclysm?!' Said Sadler.

'Yes, in part my Lord but it is much more than that' I said 'Would you like to explain?'

I was hoping Paracelsus, now uncovered, would confess all but he sat, crouched in his hiding hole saying nothing.

'Well, perhaps I can shed light on this. I am sure that, once this reptile had returned to his beloved home he would have had no trouble recruiting followers but what better deception that to use your own nephews and nieces? Then, create an ingenious method that communicates almost limitless methods of assassination, practically indecipherable to anyone else. But, it is that very document that speaks volumes. This creature here Gentlemen! is obsessed by prophecy. His life's reputation hinges on the authenticity of his prophecies. The Cataclysm, the change in faith, the King's death! So, what do you do if your prophecies don't quite work out?!'

Heneage turned to me and quietly said,

'You make them come true.'

'Exactly my Lord, you…MAKE…them…come…true!!...This man is not only a total fraud but riddled with wickedness and an ambition to make his constant nonsense worthwhile. In addition to that, he put his own kin at risk even during the Cataclysm plot. Look! Look at the girl's hands!'

Molly, almost, inadvertently, held out her blue-black fingers 'not, as many supposed, caused by berries but by ink. Labouring night and day to forge copies of the Lindisfarne Gospels!'

At last, I had managed to break him, as he spewed forth his hatred.

'He will die soon and all of you along with him! You will see that I was right about everything. All will come true! All will happen!'

He stood and, as he did, it was clear that Molly, Gabriel and Beth were terrified of him although Gabriel did make some effort to silence him.

'Uncle…please, you will make things worse.'

'Couldn't be worse' I said 'and, I confess that even I have some pity for you younger ones but the game is now, completely, up. Sergeant, you may take them all away now. Sir Ralph, I suggest your guards collect up everything in this cottage as I am sure there will be much more evidence here.'

Unexpectedly, Silas lunged forward and confronted Paracelus,

'You will tell is right now what else you have planned for our friends in York!'

Paracelus screwed up his face, genuinely puzzled.

'Ah Silas' I said 'alas, he is not responsible for our troubles up north…'

'But…but Bask…present from Somerset? What does it all mean?'

He was very upset, but I informed him that this man had nothing whatsoever to do with the events in York and that this was my very next assignment.

Wynnfrith asked about the rhyme, the riddle that the fool had repeated right in front of our faces.

'I have to give Will Somers much credit' I said 'he verified so many of my suppositions:

"Buried a saint" refers to Bury St Edmunds where Samuel, also known as Drake, was in hiding, "Buried his kin" meaning the death of Drake's nephew, burned in the pit. "Angel at heart" clearly young Gabriel here, "Devilish a sin" I fear, speaks for itself and "The future secure" alluding to Paracelus's attempts to make his feeble prophecies come true. "Where snows fall" their homeland, Austria and "Falls the crown" the King's Demise. Finally, "Falls the pall" the cloth to cover his coffin and herald a new regime.'

'Absolutely astonishing' said Sir Ralph Sadler 'now I understand why His Grace put so much faith in you. You have my utmost respect, dear mouse.'

I was worn out and I felt like shit. How on earth did I get in the middle of all this? Excitedly I had taken a job in historical analytics to study past anomalies in a new and exciting way but I seemed to have taken on the problems of everyone who lived in this foreboding century. I could tell that they all thought me a genius but it didn't make me feel any better. Truth be told, there had been a few lucky guesses here but, as is always the case, the guilty parties couldn't help giving themselves away. I would go as far as saying that if Molly wasn't such a nuisance it would have probably taken me a lot longer to get to the bottom of it all. I was still clueless as to why Paracelus was still alive and couldn't help thinking that it had something to do with the King. However, before the day was out, I was informed that Henry had watched Paracelsus's execution so I could only presume that there was a deception on the part of the sell-appointed prophet himself.

As we returned to the Palace, There was an almighty fuss and then none. Within hours it wasn't spoken about and it wasn't to be spoken about, ever. I didn't ask what happened to the perpetrators but, I suppose, I knew. Mrs Cornwallis was given a severe reprimand, Lyndon got a promotion and the endless admiration of his boss, Sir Anthony Browne.

I was led to a chamber where I had a sort of, debriefing with Heneage and Sadler. I told them that I wasn't interested in gratitude but did implore them to listen to my recommendations about security. I had certainly deduced that it was no longer enough for the King to post chubby constables every few yards around the Palace or simply to employ food tasters, everyone Henry employed had to be accountable. I suggested streamlined systems for employing and maintaining staff and regulation of everything that came in and out of the Palace, including during the hunt. I did go on a bit but they listened and a scribe committed it all to paper.

Shortly afterwards, we learned from Sadler that the King was in a fit of anger. Grateful that we had found a resolution, but beside himself at the knowledge that any of his subjects would treat their King with such contempt. To be accurate, by and large, they weren't his subjects but, apparently, he was swearing, thrashing and threatening like a spoiled child. As we concluded our conversation, I had noticed that Silas was missing. I thought nothing of it until I heard, in the distance, raised voices and Sir Ralph Sadler running toward two guards to placate them. At that point, I left them to it but I was later to learn of Silas's intent. He had nonchalantly marched all the way to the Great Hall, only to be stopped by guards. Sadler asked him what he was about and Silas, calmly said it was essential that he spoke to the King before he left and also that he had a gift for him. The gift was wrapped in a thin cloth and was about fourteen inches long and a few inches wide. Sadler, once assured that this wasn't a weapon, politely told Silas to be on his way. Whilst this took place, the King could be heard, within the Great Hall, bellowing and threatening still. Silas, unwilling to give up this quest stood and waited for calm. Calm never came but there was, eventually, a lull where his fat head appeared, curious as to what was taking place in the corridor.

'God's breath! Can't I have a bloody tantrum in peace?!'

'So sorry Your Grace' said Sadler 'he will be on his way now' and he grabbed Silas's arm.

''You! You're the idiot from York!'

'Yes, Your Grace' answered Silas surprisingly confidently.

'Get in here you piece of string!' Silas moved himself into the Hall 'and you, you've done your duty so bugger off!' He said to Sadler.

Henry then turned to the guards and told them to leave as well.

'Well, well. So you helped to find these demons who would have me dead?!'

'I did very little, your Grace but happy it is at an end' said Silas.

This was a confident Silas. He was there for a reason and was quite sure of himself. He had prepared himself for the King's behaviour and he wasn't disappointed. Henry raged, roared and self-pitied without any thought that there was another human in there with him. He bewailed and bemoaned the fact that he had never been truly loved, that his subjects were ungrateful and that his aides could not be trusted. He whipped around swinging his fist and then stopped.

'You still here?'

'Yes, Your Grace.'

'Well, get on with it then. What do you want?'

'I have a gift, Your Grace but also have a message.'

Bewildered and knackered, Henry slumped into his throne and listened or, at least he pretended to.

'You have, in your time got the better of the Scots and the French and fortified our coastline.' Henry screwed up his round face bemused as to where this was going 'Also, England and Wales have become as one under your rule. Particularly as a young King, you were a master of many languages, music, jousting and theology and some of the greatest minds of our time such as More and Erasmus, whatever their views, felt you were more than an adequate match for them. You have undoubtedly been loved, not least by the saintly Jane Seymour…'

Although he had rehearsed this for some time, as he paused, even Silas himself was wondering if he had swallowed a library. However, things had now returned to normal as he hadn't got a clue what came next. Henry drew in an enormous breath as, he, wasn't sure whether to carry on complaining or to respond. Silas thought for a few moments taking advantage of the icy silence.

'The girl….the cripple.' Said Henry 'Yes, she's here. When I was in York she ministered to me.' He almost smiled 'ha! A washerwoman ministering to her King! Who would have thought it but…it was…sincere. You lot drinking bloody kindness water up there or what?' He blustered, perhaps thinking it was funny.

'Northerners speak the truth, Your Grace. You have friends there…remember that…that's why I came, to tell you that you're not alone.'

An uncanny hush fell upon the room. A becalmed King looked the village idiot in the eye and fought back a tear.

'I brought you a gift.'

It was rare that Henry found anything touching. Sincerity had become completely alien to him but, here, right now with this commoner, his heart was moved. King Henry the eighth had had gold, jewels, furs, horses, buildings and yes, even women, as gifts. What could he possibly want from a skinny errand boy?

'My mother was killed when I was but a boy. She made quills…marvellous quills and the ones I have here are all I have of her.' He stretched out his arms holding the small bundle and, inside, were those four quills that he had kept dear, and close, to him always. 'You are King. You may discard them if you wish but they are yours, Your Grace.'

Henry wanted to weep. He wept often in private as, by now, he was convinced that he had offended God himself and that he would never again see any good fortune. Following a Kingly gulp, he spoke softly.

'Well, bold northerner these, indeed, are riches and I do appreciate your kindness. Return to York City with my thanks and my blessings.'

Silas himself waved for a guard to show him out. This was the end of their discourse and Silas would never see the King or Hampton Court ever again. As the Great doors closed, Henry Tudor sobbed like a child wondering what had just happened. Within days, Henry decided to try out one of the dated quills and, as they were to his liking, he raised a statute proclaiming that the Royal crest be carved into each one and that they should only ever be brought out when signing an Act that would benefit the common people. Needless to say, they didn't appear that often but, not only did his daughter, Elizabeth, like the tale behind the quills but ensured that they were to be used as promised. A Mary Smith quill, crafted in a hovel within the York snickleways, was used to sign the Act of Uniformity that made some effort to ease religious tensions in England. Another signed a docket that released payment to Richard Shakespeare's grandson, William and a third dutifully employed to record Elizabeth's famous speech at Tilbury, as the Spanish Armada was defeated.

Silas left the Great Hall none the wiser, his fluffy head assured that he had done his Christian duty. This man that feared his own shadow, and to be fair everyone else's, talked to the King of the land as if it was his best mate at the pub. Silas returned to the stables and told us nothing of his adventure.

I made a point of thanking Thomas Heneage. We had truly made a friend in this man and he had even sent for Bayard and his cart whilst we were in congress. I wished him many a happy day looking up the King's anus but, for whatever reason, he ignored me. I was given the impression that the whole affair of the talking mouse was to be forgotten about, although the Tower guards, apparently shared some interesting anecdotes about prisoners who swore that they were thwarted by a possessed mouse.

Back in our stable, we made sure that we were clean and fed before our journey and went into our cells for the last time. Unexpectedly, a page approached my cell but then walked past and seemed to go to the door of Wynnfrith's room. He closed the door behind him so, being curious, Silas, Peter and myself stood outside the door waiting for them to emerge. It became completely silent, we could hear

absolutely nothing and then, what followed, was the most
excruciating and soul-destroying wail that I had ever heard,
followed by a series of howls. It was Wynnfrith. Silas
forcibly pushed the door open to find Wynnfrith on her
knees sobbing, the page standing over her holding a letter.
Silas snatched it from him and showed it to me, it was
signed by Robert and simply said,

"regret to inform you, Elspeth has died…"

29: MARCUS

One week earlier…

The weather in York had changed little. When it wasn't snowing, it was below zero, imposing an eerie stillness on the city as if all was well. The sun shone and, as children happily played on what was so recently a river, adults took advantage of the ice to clumsily cross wherever they chose. It did, however, create several inconveniences, not least that the common privies at the water's edge had frozen over. Even worse, the already elevated, infant mortality was heightened and old people were dropping like flies.

Thankfully, once I had notice of Eirik's whereabouts, I wrote to him, in York, trusting him with extending the investigation there whilst I was otherwise employed in London. From the staff in the undercroft to all of those who had worked on the window, and from Edward and Godwin to the sheriff, Eirik was tasked with meaningful questioning. So, that covered almost everyone except for his employer, Robert, the Mayor of York. I was determined to speak to him personally on my return. This decision did, of course presume that I entirely trusted Eirik which was not absolutely the case.

Surprisingly, all was relatively well in the Mayor's household. There were almost constant fires and good food and Robert had broken his fever and overcome his infection, now insisting that he was completely well. He stood, looking out of the very same window that Wynnfrith had daydreamed about Silas less than a year before, wondering how his Agents were faring in that moral cesspit, London. He had mixed feelings about the great window, the attack and his subsequent illness. He knew that, soon, the mouse would return and there would have to be a conclusion to the bizarre events, not only of the last few months but, he believed, much longer. It would be fair to say that, taking all these occurrences into account, Robert probably knew more than any other individual aforementioned, and also that he would have to reveal the knowledge that he had kept to himself so long. He pondered as he stared, barely focussed on the frost that had taken his expensive bedroom window captive. He thought about secrecy. Moreover, he challenged the notion that all secrets were bad. Usually, they were bad, he thought, but sometimes, just sometimes, secrets were there to help. Secrets are kept to protect people and sometimes they are kept because you had made an oath to someone else who may either be very dear to you or no longer of this world, he told himself. He realised that, internally, he was trying to justify the predicament he found himself in. So, then, his thoughts went back to his recent illness and injuries and, with very little of that thought, he decided that he wished he had died. He decided that absolutely everyone he knew would manage just fine without him. Now, whether it was providence, he would never know, but, at that very moment, he was awakened from his depression by his wife's voice. She was calling from downstairs.

'Be right there!' He replied.

As he entered the hallway he looked upon Elspeth, all swaddled and ready to combat the morning chill. She was in an embrace with Mrs Hall.

'I cannot thank you both enough for how you have cared for me. God bless you. It's time I returned home and made it habitable for my sister's return. I have lived in luxury far too long!' She said smiling.

'Nonsense!' Said Robert 'for it is Wynnfrith's, and your, good care that brought me back to life.'

'We will never forget what you have done, Elspeth dear.' said Mrs Hall, now openly emotional.

'For me?!' Elspeth said 'I would be dead if not for you two and my sister' and, uncommonly, she hugged them both.

'I expect there is much to do in our abandoned little wash house so I will make haste!'

Elspeth really did need to make haste for there was a secret that she was, very successfully, hiding from them both.

After all that had passed, from her illness to the trauma around the new window and, of course, Robert's near-death experience, the house felt unbearably vacuous for the next day or so. Robert was clueless as to the details of what had transpired in Stratford upon Avon and had heard nothing from any of the Agents in London. Not only was he dreading the investigation on their return but was increasingly saddened by their absence. At 3 o clock that very afternoon he threw open the door to the living quarters and said,

'Perhaps we should visit to see if she is ok?'

Mrs Hall laughed.

She was warmed by his compassion but reminded him that it would not have been received well. Elspeth's path in life was a solitary one and kindness could often be misconstrued as interfering. This only led to an increase in the Mayor's introversion. He chastised himself for treating

Elspeth differently from her sister. As, yet another, court case took place inside his rotund head, the defence reminded him that Wynnfrith had been as a daughter, that they had brought her up so he could be excused for looking upon Elspeth as a man does a woman, rather than as how a father looks at a daughter. The defence also referred to her natural endowments, what man would not find her attractive? It enquired. However, the prosecution won hands down. How could he have said and thought such embarrassing things? Silly sod, he said to himself. Not that Elspeth dwelled on any of this, she was adept at taking care of herself, and others for that matter, and, more often than not, just took this as the way her cousin was made and, truth be told, she was very fond of him. Snapping out of this mental duel, Robert thought to turn to administrative business in the hope of taking his mind off things.

Meanwhile, Elspeth had returned to her home, no more than a lean-to alongside Bootham Bar, but she was no longer smiling. She slumped onto a stool, barely able to get her breath and acknowledging that all was not well with her health. Following the poisoning, it had taken her weeks to recover but only she knew that there had been long-term and permanent damage. You may ask why she would hide such a thing and the answer lies simply in who Elspeth was. First and foremost, she had dedicated her life to Christ and that, in itself, entailed complete selflessness. She, almost by nature, cared little for herself but was intent on playing her part in thwarting the Cataclysm and unravelling the mystery of the attempted murders in York. Added to that, was her obsession with Julian of Norwich and her supernatural experiences, as those around her thought her to be dying. It would be fair to say that this was something that, daily, she craved. Did she have a death wish? Probably not, but it would be reasonable to say that she cared little for life. Realising that she may become a burden to those around her, this day was the ideal time to retreat to her home. She relaxed and dozed not knowing that Robert, despite advice to the contrary, was almost in her street desperate to enquire after her health. However, as he turned the corner, he saw that someone else was at the door, knocking. She broke out of her shadowy thoughts and answered. It was Marcus. By now, she knew that she was being pursued and didn't let it worry her. After all, he meant no harm. Robert, now diligently keeping a watch of the closed-door wondered whether to go further but, as yet, felt no ill will toward Marcus so returned home.

Struggling to her feet, she let him in and as Marcus fumbled and stumbled over his words asking after her welfare, Elspeth interrupted him.

'I don't mind you calling, Marcus. Tell me, how are things at the undercroft? It's been an unforgiving winter.'

'Oh, you can imagine, Maiden. So many deaths but we manage to keep them comfortable and some do recover. About that day when...'

Again she interrupted him.

'Oh, that's long gone. Let's talk of brighter things.'

This certainly put him at ease and they chatted for a while about, well, very little but they were both comfortable and content. However, Elspeth felt the need to conclude their conference with a degree of disclosure.

'Marcus, you are a good man. And, I implore you to carry on your good works as long as the Good Lord wishes it.' He thought to reply but she stopped him.

'No. No, you must listen. I haven't said this to anyone else, but I am not long for this world... No, hush...I am sicker than anyone imagines and, more than once my heart has failed so much that I have collapsed, left wondering what had happened. Truth be told, I have never properly recovered from the poison. I thank God every day that he has given me this time to conclude my business here. Marcus...I know that you have had, very proper designs on me...'

Again he tried to intervene, explain, but she would have none of it.

'You already know, don't you? I am married to Christ and if I lived until a hundred that wouldn't change. Give me your hand…'

He complied without question.

'My predicament means that I am in a position to be very straight with you! It is true that I am, also very fond of you. You are good through and through, your life given to others and you are so handsome!' she laughed 'I have never before beheld skin as beautiful as yours and, I have given up on the notion that the devil himself sent you to tempt me!'

She laughed again but, this time started to splutter and cough.

'I want you to take what I say to you now, and keep it in your heart always...' she now engaged with him completely, looking intensely into his eyes 'If I were, ever, to marry a man it would be you.' She heard him gulp 'be assured, it would be no one else but you. I'm sorry I cannot give you more but I won't have you arguing with me about my health. I know I am soon at an end and good intentions are worthless to me.'

At last, she let him speak.

'My dear Maiden Elspeth, I acknowledge all you say and accept it for, in part, it is that supernatural strength that you have that feeds my love for you. If you are to die, dear Elspeth, then what you have just given me is more than I could ever have hoped for.'

For moments they stared at each other as storms were brewing inside them both. He grasped her hand lovingly and tightly and, as he did, her body became close to his and she kissed him. This wasn't the affectionate and fleeting meeting of lips that may have been employed by relations, this was a passionate, romantic kiss. Elspeth gave this to Marcus freely and wholeheartedly. Having so recently acknowledged that, inwardly, her body was failing she was now discovering parts of her humanity that had been, until now, practically dormant. This confused her. This felt so wonderful, meaningful, exciting and fulfilling and yet, something still told her that neither could it have been a sin. In worldly terms, this was the first time she had ever been as one with another person and pondered, momentarily, on what it meant. Her chest and arms hurt, due to her fatigued heart and yet, somewhere, way south of her heart, uncannily, there was a festival taking place. She tried hard not to intellectualise this or to chastise herself. Surely I am allowed this? she told herself.

It was Marcus who sensitively broke away, genuinely content in the concession that this, once distant, nun was now giving. They held hands, looked at one another and said nothing. That was until, suddenly, he jumped up.

'My dear. Your hands! They are so very cold. I will make up a fire for you…no, no. I have a better idea, here…' he covered her with blankets 'wait for me here, I will return in minutes.'

It took Marcus a swift minute and a half to run to Barley Hall where the Mayor was just returning home.

'My Lord Mayor' He shouted.

Robert turned, astonished to find the man he was thinking about was there, behind him. It wasn't really that Robert had any serious suspicions about Marcus, he was just uncomfortable, or perhaps it was just plain old possessiveness, a sense of losing someone close. He decided to say nothing until Marcus spoke to him. In a frenzy, he explained that he thought Elspeth to be still very poorly and begged the Mayor to take her in again. Benevolently and benignly, he grasped Marcus by his upper arms to still him and said,

'My good man. If what you say is true then we must have her return in haste, I will have the indomitable Mrs Hall prepare the room, fire n'all.'

Seemingly, Elspeth had thought it wise to die alone in her depressing and cold wash house but, strong as her will still was, she was going back to Barley Hall whether she liked it or not. Within the hour she was wrapped up in that familiar bed with a roaring fire nearby.

'Has he explained?' Said Elspeth to Robert and his wife.

'Yes, yes dear' said Mrs Hall 'Perhaps if...'

'No perhaps, dear Mrs Hall. I am content in what you are doing, I ask for nothing more, I accept my journey from this life to a better one, in fact I welcome it. I now have the added comfort of making those steps here. I am so grateful.'

They both fought back tears but Mrs Hall, in particular, was beside herself, so much, that she could say or do nothing practical.

'Perhaps we could pray?' Suggested Mrs Hall.

'You may pray all you want, where you want and how you want!' Said Elspeth, affording herself a giggle. 'Prayer is good!' Remember that cousin Robert!'

And he chuckled too.

So they did, and a peace that absolutely did pass all their understanding descended on their grand home. Then she slept but, was now, almost constantly, rubbing her chest which was becoming increasingly painful.

Two days passed when there was little change but on the third, she asked for Father Matthew so Robert obliged. Troubled by the news, he trudged through the snow from Holy Trinity church to Barley Hall and, with very little formality, raced up the stairs.

'Oh my dear' he said tearful and exasperated 'is this true?'

'I fear so Father but it is so important to me that you help me to communicate to everyone that I have no fear, and I know where I'm going.'

Elspeth handed him a bundle of letters.

'I now doubt that I will see my beloved sister again in this world, please could you distribute these when I am gone?'

Father Matthew, like everyone else, wanted to take his turn at that human routine that everyone, quite passionately, feels they have to perform at a time like this. Perhaps there's a cure. Miracles do happen. Perhaps it's not that bad. However, he looked at her and knew, and he also acknowledged that, her faith being so much stronger than his, she was on a happy pathway and had accepted her fate.

'It is very important to me that you administer last rites, no one else mind, has to be you.'

'I will stay here day and night if necessary my dear.' He said, meaning every word.

'Now, this is why I asked you here.'

Father Matthew was surprised as he could think of nothing more that he could offer.

'God loves you, dear Father..'

'Why....'

'No interruptions please, Father....He loves your very soul and sees your goodness.'

He hung his head in humility.

'He loves Thomas Farrier, a kinder man you couldn't find.'

Father Matthew found this a very curious turn of conversation but presumed she was of a mood to bestow blessings on every one of the Agents.

'God sees inside you and he sees inside the blacksmith, and all is well.'

He looked directly into her eyes looking for some confirmation of what this meant, but he knew. This left him feeling embarrassed, exposed but, eventually, blessed with the feeling that a great weight had been lifted from his being.'

'It is possible to love someone from afar, Father. I have given my pledge of love to a man, knowing that I never could and never will be married. Love from afar and be content Father. God is good.'

Astonished, he said nothing and Elspeth moved another few degrees closer to sainthood.

What followed for well over an hour was prayer. Prayer led mostly by Elspeth but with intercession by the priest. Mr and Mrs Hall were invited into the room as were the servants. By his own choice, Marcus stayed downstairs. Elspeth blessed and issued kind wishes to everyone. Even the current tanner, that worked along Bootham Bar, got a blessing.

Robert wept, cursed his memories and hated himself inwardly, begging in his prayers for a reprise for her. In the midst of all this Elspeth slept and, a short while later having been fed by the Halls, Father Matthew made his way back to church.

Robert had got word to Eirik. As he ran into the bedroom, Elspeth managed to raise her head very slightly to behold this now, extraordinarily handsome, young man. He was wearing some of the finest clothes that could be seen around York and his athletic physique spoke of confidence and adventure.

'Come sit on the bed, brother.'

She held his hand.

'What a blessing it has been to have you back in our lives this…past year, dearest brother. Thank you…for all you have done for our fight against tyranny. Wynnfrith…will need your love and support when she returns. I wholly…bless her union with Silas and I want you to do the same. Please tell them that it is my wish…that, one day, they marry.'

Unlike her other visitors he was well behaved, resisting the temptation to interrupt but, when he saw her take a rest, tentatively he muttered,

'Dearest Elspeth, there is something you must know. I believe that the security of my very own soul depends on my confession, here and now.'

She forced a smile.

'I know. No need…I know and, you have nothing…nothing…to be ashamed of. You know that?'

Of course, he knew. Strong as an ox and wise as an owl to the end. He kissed her. Robert walked into the room.

'She needs rest now' he said and Eirik went downstairs and cried with the very man he had been interrogating only a day earlier, Marcus.

That night, as Mrs Hall kept vigil, Elspeth had a most aggressive heart attack and, during her throes, Mrs Hall prayed for a speedy passing. It did not come and Elspeth was left barely alive, her breathing strained.

Eirik was sent immediately to Holy Trinity church where he awakened Father Matthew.

'So soon?!' he declared nervously and awkwardly grabbed his vestments, stole, bread, communion cup and wine, cross and then he dithered.

'Let me help you, Father.' Said Eirik and offered an on-the-spot checklist for which the priest was thankful. Off they ran, his stole trailing in the snow and wine spilling so frequently from the chalice that it was a wonder that there was any left for Elspeth's dry, blue lips.

Robert sat downstairs trembling, he had tried to help her but to no avail and the spectacle had shaken him to the core. As the priest entered, she was calm but her breathing shallow and she now was barely conscious. He started with her confession, satisfied with a few mumbles and then gave communion. Rushed as it was, he was intent that this was to be done correctly to the last detail. If anyone's final journey was important, it belonged to Elspeth. Having prayed for her passage into Heaven, he knelt and prayed.

In desperation she gestured, desiring his ear to be close to her lips.

'Oh, Father…it is magnificent, the music!...Can you hear?'

Father Matthew's faith, still strong, informed him that the angels she heard were real.

'They are all here, my mother and father too…I can see him in all his glory. My Lord, arms outstretched…oh, it is so wonderful. Sister Julian was right…everything is good. God is good, he is pure good. The light! I am bathing in it Father. Do you feel it? Good….God is good…goo……'

It was at an end and Elspeth was at peace.

Father Matthew wept as he had never wept before. He had seen many deaths, performed this ritual countless times but this moved him more than anything he could remember.

Downstairs, Eirik and the Halls kindly told Marcus that he would be welcome at the funeral.

Only weeks ago this woman had been playing practical jokes on Robert as if she and her sister were little girls again, but there she lay motionless and discoloured.

In the early hours of the morning, Robert found himself alone, wondering how he could let Wynnfrith know. His heart was heavy, so recently they had been reunited as sisters and he, himself, had envisioned a future where all the threats and murders were over with and they all lived as an extended family, reminding himself also that William Fawkes was his brother-in-law and that young Edward was his nephew. Truth be told, by now, Robert even thought of Silas as a distant, dysfunctional and embarrassing son but wondered whether he would ever verbalise this. All this focus on happy families was probably, in part, due to his guilt which he now wore like an extra layer of fur and this sudden and tragic event had reminded him that all was not well and may never be.

The following morning he invited Marcus around to make him party to a decision that he and Mrs Hall had made as it was done with some reticence. Marcus thanked them, agreed that it was the best course of action and went to tend to the sick and dying in the undercroft. Within the hour, the Halls had another visitor who was given very precise and strict instructions as severe as if a judge was passing sentence. With some reservation, they had invited Viscera, the barber-surgeon into their home.

'This girl is very dear to many people' announced Robert, authoritatively 'when your work is done I want her looking like she did a week ago. As if she were asleep and well.'

Viscera knew better than to interrupt.

'This is a woman of God. Completely pure! Untouched and unseen by any man! Mrs Hall will oversee your work from start to finish which must be executed with dignity. And, you know me, surgeon, I will pay you handsomely for this task!'

Wisely, they had decided that, if Elspeth, could be sensitively and professionally embalmed it would give Wynnfrith a chance to see her one last time.

Viscera was in no doubt of the gravity of this commission, so happily agreed to the terms as did Mrs Hall. Later that day Godwin called in offering to create a decorative coffin for Elspeth but he was told, with thanks, that this would not be appropriate for someone who had chosen a life of poverty.

As the sun went down, Robert looked at the dozens of scraps of parchment on which he had tried to communicate this tragedy to Wynnfrith. Exasperated, he kept it as simple as he could, acknowledging that nothing would soften this blow no matter how well-intended. He then took to his knees and prayed. Robert never prayed unless he was prompted but, today, he felt at the end of his tether.

'Dear Lord, I humbly beg and beseech you to put an end to these horrors and deliver us from all evil. I ask forgiveness for past and present sins and put myself wholly at your service. I pray that we can all, this year find happiness and peace somehow.'

He wasn't to know it but his prayers were to be answered, although there would be something of a bumpy ride on the way to his desired destination.

30: THE JOURNEY HOME

Reflecting on that journey home from London, it seemed as
if no-one spoke. Of course, they did, but there was such a
pall over our return that conversation was strained at times.
We were pleased to see Bayard, not least because he was
our ticket home but also because he reminded us of York.
After the first hundred miles, Wynnfrith cried a little less
and started to talk about her sister, telling funny stories as
we all tend to do when someone dear has left us. Silas fell
into his role as fiancé admirably and I would go as far as to
say that I don't know how Wynnfrith would have managed
without his support. At last, they spent more time in each
other's arms, a sight that pleased the, now angelic, Elspeth.
For a change, I said very little. In this guise, I seemed to
have had little in the way of a bedside manner but felt the
loss as much as anyone. As we approached Sheffield,
Bayard spoke for the first time. Gladly, he had deposited
his, very eccentric, actor friend outside of Cambridge
having told him that he would, one day, need his services
again. At first, he seemed to struggle to converse. He knew
what to say but we were all confused as to where he was

going. Soon, it became clear that he wanted to talk about Elspeth.

'Dear Bayard' said Wynnfrith 'feel free to share your stories with us. Talk of my sister helps me to stay close to her.'

Tentatively, he started to tell us about her reaction when she first learned that she would be travelling to Lincoln in his cart. He told it as it was, Elspeth belligerently refusing to get on board, expecting a royal carriage. Already we were laughing. Peter kindly said that, in the time he had known Elspeth, he had held the greatest regard for her.

'Bayard!' I said 'Wynn has not heard of her sister's encounter with Culpeper!'

'Oh, yes. Please tell me' said Wynnfrith sounding bright 'we never got around to discussing it!'

Culpeper certainly had taken the nun by surprise, she had never experienced such flattery before and, truth be told, she couldn't hide the fact that she quite liked it. Bayard elegantly embellished this tale and we laughed for the next mile. I then told of some of my greatest battles with this formidable lady, particularly during our encounters in Lincoln.

Bizarrely, this seemed to help and it was now our intention to get home as soon as possible in the hope that we wouldn't miss the funeral. As, eventually, we saw in the distance, the great walls of York the silence was broken once again.

'Micklegate' said Wynnfrith softly 'you will get to the bottom of this purge in York swiftly, as you did in London, won't you?'

I gave her my pledge, there and then, that as soon as we had put her blessed sister to rest, I would see an end to those nightmares and that, following that, I would be on my way. As I said it, we all looked at one another knowing that we were coming to the end of a journey in more ways than one.

31: THE GREAT HALL

Wynnfrith was delighted that she could see and kiss her sister one last time and, as well as thanking Mr and Mrs Hall, went out of her way to find Viscera and praise him for what he had done, at last he had redeemed himself. There was some, muted, celebration at the news of their engagement but even Wynn and Silas thought that it was out of place. Elspeth's funeral came and went. She was interred with her mother and father and close to Godwin's daughter, Lizzy who had died the year before. I promised Silas, Wynnfrith, Peter and Bayard a few days rest before we tackled, what had become a murder case, in earnest.

I spent much of that time with Eirik who, quite expertly, had documented his conversations and investigations that I had asked him to carry out.

'I can't thank you enough, Eirik. The situation at Hampton Court became something of a nightmare so I am glad to be back.' I said.

'But what does it all mean, Mouse?' He asked, genuinely confused.

'Oh believe me Eirik, all these puzzle pieces fit together very nicely, have no doubt. Two days hence, I will put you, and everyone else, out of their misery!'

He looked down, still trying to make sense of what he had heard and seen but, still, seemed bewildered.

'Worry not.' I said, reassuringly and then told him how I was now running out of time if I were ever to get home again. Stupidly, I confided in him about the lady mouse and he laughed as I had never seen him laugh before.

'I tell you it is the truth!' And then I laughed too, realising how bloody silly it sounded.

The following day, I had Peter take me to Barley Hall. Robert was expecting me but, even so, he seemed incredibly nervous. I took the time to thank him and his wife for all they had done for Elspeth and told him I was happy that he was now well. He then took me, in my box, into the living room where there was a warm fire.

'Mayor' I said 'we are almost at an end but practically all hinges on the conversation we have, now, this morning.'

He nodded.

'Robert, I have many facts and a few theories and suspicions. You can help with the latter but, unless you give me a full and honest confession I can take this no further and I will need to leave in a few days. You do want an end to this, don't you?'

'Yes, yes. And be sure, good mouse, I am of a mind to help you but it does mean talking about things that I have locked away for so long.'

'Then it may be good for your soul as well as your family Robert.'

The conversation remained awkward for some time but then he talked. At first, there were gaps and, when he stopped speaking, I was anxious that he might not pick up again but, eventually, he told me everything I needed to know, confirming what I had previously presumed. When it was at an end I thanked him.

'You do know I cannot keep this secret now?' I told him.

'If only…no, no you're right. How will I be exposed?' He asked.

I would like everyone to meet here. I will give you an extensive list of who is to attend. Some of those names may surprise you but it is essential that everyone is there. I will also require the sheriff and two constables and you must give me your word that you will not abscond in the meantime. Looking almost like a man who had been beaten about the head, he stood up and reached to the mantelpiece where there was a Bible and he swore an oath upon it and I had no cause to doubt him. At the other side of the hallway, there was a larger room, the Great Hall from which Barley Hall got its name and I pointed to it to indicate that we would all meet there in two days. I could see that the window had been replaced with something more modest and sensible. Reluctantly, I then went to speak to Silas and Wynnfrith. They knew a reckoning was coming but, besides their individual and particular suspicions (and for Silas, it was, increasingly, Eirik), they said little. However, I felt it a personal duty to prepare them for what was to come.

'It will be very difficult…' I started.

'Oh I think we know, Micklegate, I expect a shocking revelation' said Wynnfrith quite innocently.

'No. You need to understand. For you two, tomorrow will be very hard. So much so, I thought to keep you out of it but, my friends, you will have to brave this storm.'

They looked at one another, bemused, presuming that I was referring to them as a couple, whereas, essentially, I was saying to each of them that the revelations would be tough.

'I will say no more except that I have given the sheriff orders to sit you both together then you can support one another.'

I had done a really bad job already, I had, unintentionally, scared them. But being the Agents that I expected them to be, they forced a smile and asked if there was anything they could do.

I now only needed to spend some time with the sheriff and a number of his predecessors praying that this would be the very last time that I would have to reveal my annoying abilities.

As I entered the Barley Hall, the following morning, I saw for the first time the longest of tables and, sitting around it, was everyone that the sheriff had told to be there. Notwithstanding the grandeur of this space, it still seemed, somewhat crowded. There was an elaborate plinth at the end of the table on which I was to stand. The room was full of familiar faces but there wasn't a smile amongst them for they all knew why they were gathered there and the whole set-up spoke of serious business. I would even go as far as saying it looked like a courtroom but it did have a warm fire and comfortable seats. Everyone was seated except the constables who took the door once I had entered. Some greeted me, others looked at their feet. Clearly, we would all be glad when this was over with. It wasn't like London at all. Almost everyone in the woodcutter's cottage was guilty. I knew it and they knew it. This was a very different situation and I had regarded many of those present on this day as friends. A good number were very surprised to be invited if that was the word, but all were told the purpose of this meeting. To my immediate left were Silas, Eirik and Wynnfrith and to my right, Father Matthew, Robert and Mrs Hall. Next to her, consecutively were Bayard, Hugh, Viscera, Scorge and, finally, young Peter. Glancing back to my left I saw, sitting next to Wynnfrith, Godwin and his wife who was next to Marcus. After that, William Fawkes and his son, Edward and Scorge and the dubious beef thief were right at the end. Bede had no place in this so stayed in his humble domicile at Holy Trinity church.

'May as well start!' Instructed the sheriff wondering if the talking mouse thing was actually a trick.

'Just a moment, please good sheriff, we are not yet quorate.'

And, right on cue, was a tap on the door. As it opened half the room jumped up in delight. They had made it and how gratifying it was to set eyes on Richard Shakespeare and Thomas Farrier. They sat right at the end of the table, facing me. I settled everyone, reminding them that, generally speaking, there would be time for socialising later.

'I beg your patience all of you, this will take some time. I have made sure that there will be some refreshments but, beyond that, I require your complete attention.

Why are we here? We gather here today because of the wicked and tragic events of the past few months. Since the Agents, now hardly a secret, put an end to the Cataclysm last year, there has been an assumed attempt on Silas's life, the death of Sir Anthony Bask, a scheme to kill the Mayor, Robert Hall, the kidnapping of Shakespeare's son and the murder of our beloved Elspeth. I have been given permission to inform you all, that also during this period there have been several attempts on the King's life!

After some considerable investigation, I can also say with certainty that the latter had nothing to do with events here, in York.'

Following a few moments of genuine awe, the questions started although I had no choice but to disregard them.

'Those who know me, know that I can only do this with your full attention. Please only speak when I ask you a question, I guarantee I will reveal all this morning. Without any attempt to patronise anyone present I will deliver my findings as a series of stories in the hope it makes easier listening.

I start with…the story of the monster…

This tale takes place more than twenty years ago. Apart from Edward, Peter and, I'm guessing one of the constables, this would be within all your lifetimes. During this period there stalked a man, if he can be called so, who preyed upon and killed women. His killings were sporadic and there were, possibly, months and years between his crimes. Hard as this is to hear I have to tell you that this man's motive was sexual pleasure. He likely kept reoffending almost certainly because he was never caught. Silas..' I said turning to him 'one of his early victims was your mother, Mary Smith.'

Silas jumped up.

'Oh no! Who was this man? Why…why on earth would you say such a thing in front of everyone?' He exclaimed.

As Wynnfrith tried to console him and he sat down, I resumed.

'Please forgive me, my friend. You will understand all as these tales unravel. Be assured that your mother was not interfered with in that way but was killed instantly by one blow.'

'But, you said!..'

'Please. Be patient if you can. People around the snickleways were well aware of this devil's activities and women were terrified when his crimes became more intense.'

I could see some heads nodding, this apparently wasn't new to most of those present.

'It is likely that he moved in and out of York City, he may even have been abroad but, a few years later he returned, deviously stalking his victims to find out when they would be alone. So brazen was he, that one murder took place years later in broad daylight.

One Tuesday morning whilst a well-respected, local leather smith went to his guild, as he did at the very same time every week and his daughters having been sent on errands….'

Wynnfrith was already shedding quiet tears but I chose to continue.

'He took advantage of a woman who was alone and beat her to death. As you have probably deduced, this woman was Mrs MacManus, the mother of Wynnfrith, Elspeth and James, now known as Eirik.'

Wynnfrith broke down completely at this point but made little fuss or noise. It was an indication that she was allowing me to carry on.

'What this beast never accounted for was Mr MacManus making an early return but, unfortunately, the brave Mr MacManus, despite his obvious brute strength, could not get the better of the murderer who was wielding an axe, already enraged and, at this point, irreversibly violent. And, I know this because I spoke only yesterday to Hugh Hulley, who was sheriff at the time.'

A deathly hush now fell on the room. Many present were surprised that I was going so far back in time and that I had dug so deep but those events were to affect many other incidents to follow and I needed them all to be with me on this trail every step of the way.

'So, yes, my dear Wynnfrith, this is how your parents died. There was no plague that year, but please be assured that the plague story was contrived in good faith to keep you as far from the horror as was possible. You were so very young at the time.'

Wynnfrith thought about the many times she had broached this subject with her sister to no avail. Of course, she was protecting me, she told herself.

'So? What next?' I said somewhat provocatively 'Ah yes…There was another man abroad that morning and, that man witnessed the death of Mr MacManus. He subsequently tackled the murderer and got the better of him. In fact, he killed him there and then.'

'So, why weren't we told any of this, especially if this monster got his punishment?' Asked Wynnfrith puzzled.

'That, dear Wynnfrith, is because the hero of the day went to great lengths to keep his intervention quiet and, unfortunately, this wasn't due to modesty.'

'So, are you going to tell us who the murderer of the MacManus's was?' Asked Thomas Farrier, trying to keep up with events.'

'It is with great reluctance that I have to inform you that the killer was Mary Smith's husband, Clifford Smith.'

There were all sorts of reactions to this. One or two people seemed to know this already but, for others, it meant nothing. Silas sat with his head in his hands. I started to offer some consolation but a number of those present were already reassuring him that this could not, and would never reflect on him. Silas had barely known his father. I waited a moment or two before continuing.

'Having told his wife and child that he was in France with the King, Clifford Smith got drunk one night and returned home choosing to take her life and that of the boy, Silas, but he wasn't there. Silas' I said turning to him 'the sheriff assures me it was swift, unlike his other victims.'

I could see that he wished to speak.

'Truth be told, I always thought it was him' he addressed everyone present. 'He had no redeeming features and, I had, long thought him dead. I'd like to shake the hand of the man who killed him!'

'That may very well be possible, my friend' I said.

So, for my second tale.

The tale of two secrets!'

In my attempt to be somewhat Chauceresque, they remained bemused but were also hanging on my every word.

'The hero of the hour was a young, handsome and successful local businessman and, if he hadn't been around that morning, there may well have been many more murders. He sits here to my right.'

I gestured to Robert Hall which was greeted with some astonishment. 'Is that a fair description Mrs Hall?'

'I have no quarrel with that' she said without giving me, or anyone else, any eye contact 'He was a very good looking young man.'

'It is important that, as this tale unfolds, you disregard this overfed, wealthy and ageing man here and think of him as we have described. Thank God he was, coincidentally, walking by the leather work shop that morning.'

I looked at Robert hoping he would assist but he could not face me.

'Was it a coincidence Mayor?'

He still couldn't answer.

'Well, what if I told you that he, coincidentally, was in the vicinity of the leather shop every Tuesday morning. Perhaps you would think that it was on his way to some regular business? And, in a sense, you would be right.'

Wynnfrith leapt up now angry.

'You were seeing my mother! You were, weren't you? This is why so many of my questions to Elspeth were unanswered!'

Robert gently began to weep as his head went further down, he could not face anyone in the room.

'Wynnfrith, dear, I will be as fair as I can in my delivery. Please be patient if you can' I said.

'My discussions with Mrs Hall, the sheriff of the time and, yes, dear Elspeth have left me in no doubt that the young Mayor, although already married, and Mrs McManus were very much in love. Wrong as it was, you have to accept Wynnfrith that sometimes this happens. Finding herself in a loveless, lonely marriage, her relationship with Robert Hall started as a friendship. He was genuinely kind and generous to the whole family when there were difficult times. Before she knew it, she was looking forward to his visits and even her husband made him welcome. They fell completely in love and for some considerable time, they fought this and even had a spell of almost a year when they didn't see one another. I excuse nothing, I just offer a narrative for you to follow.'

Compete silence.

'I said there were two secrets. The first was his part in the killing of Clifford Smith. Mrs Hall was no fool. She knew what was going on but, even so, he wished for the incident to be covered up. I will return to this secret and the uncanny consequences that followed but I will turn now to the second secret…'

'I think I can guess!' Said Wynnfrith, now angry and accusative.

Already this was too much for her to bear and my feeble attempt at asking people to be objective and even-minded was already failing. Who could blame her? She glared intensely at Mr and Mrs Hall, then the priest. Yes, he knew. Women in particular harbour this uncanny ability to see lies and secrets as if they are worn. She may well have done a better job than I. She then turned her glare to Eirik.

'Of course, you know as well' she said calming somewhat.

A hush came over the room, seemingly, too many people knew, but Silas's head was spinning, still clueless.

'So' continued Wynnfrith 'you are still, sort of, my brother but Robert, the Mayor, is your father?'

Whilst Eirik did little more than nod, Mrs Hall sobbed. This had been a burden for decades. Had she forgiven her husband? Yes. Had she forgiven Eirik? Yes. But, it still hurt deeply.

'That's why, when you took Elspeth and me in, as little girls, you had the baby sent away. He was never mentioned so, eventually, I thought I had made up his very existence' said Wynnfrith.

'That's right Wynnfrith' I said 'the Halls took you in as their own but Mrs Hall drew the line at having James, or Eirik, as he became known, being part of that new family.'

Eirik stood.

'I'd like to offer…I'd like to say…Mrs Hall has been as a mother to me since my return. No fault should be found in her choices at all.'

She then wept uncontrollably.

'I agree' said Wynnfrith 'you have been an angel to us all Mrs Hall. Bless you.'

She wept even louder.

'So…' started Silas still not quite grasping it all.

'So!' I said 'Eirik's tale has been all true. Yes, he has a different father to the girls but all was true, including the oak leaf birthmark.' I chose not to elaborate on this ridiculous story as I did not wish to mention that bizarre morning when Thomas Farrier thought it wise to brand a new oak leaf brand on Eirik's chest.

'Of course, the baby had to be kept a secret. After all, Mr McManus thought himself to be the father. However, the problem with all secrets is that they fester over time and, with the best will in the world, they never go away' I said.

Robert was sat with his head hanging low but I absolutely needed him to engage with me now.

'My next tale I call the tale of the adventurer.

This story takes us some eight years further on from the killing of Clifford Smith. Business was booming for Robert Hall and he made many connections in York and beyond but it was, during this period, that he met someone who would change his life…'

Mrs Hall growled.

'He was to become your very best friend wasn't he Robert?'

Robert did little more than nod.

'Not surprisingly, as this man had fought on Henry's ships against the French, developed his own glass company and had properties all over England, Robert admired him immensely. They became so close that, one evening after a few drinks, Robert felt he had found someone at last onto whom he could unload his emotional burden. Anthony Bask seemed understanding and even reminded Robert that similar predicaments were shared by many men, particularly of wealth.'

I then paused, not for dramatic effect but, again, to gauge how this was being received. None of this was news to Mrs Hall, Father Matthew or Eirik but some of the others didn't seem to have any clue as to why they were there anyway. I drew in an impatient breath and continued.

'It was the best of friendships and, it would be fair to say that you, Robert, lost many a night's sleep when you discovered that Bask was rapidly losing money. Unlike you, he had specialised in Christian iconic glass and, demand had dropped as the Reformation approached. Elaborate Christian stained glass windows were gradually falling out of favour. Bask even sold his house in York, settling in Oxford with a handsome gift from yourself.'

I looked at Silas. He, of all people, was now starting to make sense of this and understood the motive of why Robert, in particular, would want Bask dead.

'Rooted in jealousy, Bask had the idea that he could blackmail you, test how important this secret was. It took twelve months for you both to reach a compromise: You would pay him a sum monthly to be picked up locally by an employee of his.'

'Aelfraed and the five sovereigns!' Said Silas.

'Would you like to elaborate?' I said to Silas.

'Yes, yes!' He said excitedly 'I have only been tasked with this once but there is a man. A one-legged man in Knapton. The Mayor sent me with five pounds!'

Expressing their collective shock, particularly at the size of the sum, people began talking amongst themselves.

'Please!' I said raising my voice 'there is more to come….yes, Aelfraed a man who Bask thought he could trust was near enough to York to collect this black fee but far enough away for anyone to notice. Bask was Aelfraed's officer aboard the Mary Rose and a reasonable trust had developed between them. For years, Robert had a system of getting the monthly five pounds to Aelfraed but that, only recently, broke down, hence your little mission Silas.

Truth be told, the whole agreement broke down, didn't it Robert?'

For the first time, he chose to contribute looking already like a man who had nothing else to lose.

'During our work on the Cataclysm, I found out...well, Micklegate found out, that Bask was supporting Wriothesley himself' said Robert 'This I could not tolerate so wrote to Bask telling him that he would be exposed. In return, he, yet again, threatened to tell all about my so...Eirik so we came to an agreement. I would never mention to anyone his involvement with the Cataclysm and he would keep my secret but for a final sum of £500.'

Everyone gasped. This was a huge sum. To put this into some sort of context, Godwin had earned £10 in the whole of the previous year so even the five-pound sum seemed extortionate to him.

'Carry on' I said.

'I agreed. I wanted to put this at an end for good but I'm sure he didn't trust me. He became even more difficult to deal with. He was to come to York and I would give it him, in person, but only when we had both signed a contract and sworn an oath, I wanted this buried for good. As you know, he didn't get here.'

'Thank you Mayor' I said, genuinely grateful that he was now helping out.

'So, you may wonder what transpired between Oxford and York. Here I can reveal the one and only link between the wickedness in London and that here in York. Bask had been put in charge of the Lindisfarne Gospel copy house last year. On his way from Oxford, he stole one of Richard Shakespeare's children from under his nose whilst he played in the field. Bask now deranged, took the boy to the abandoned copy house and immediately issued a ransom from the Shakespeares. Manically, he intended to keep the boy hostage until he had Robert's gold in his hands but saw an opportunity to rob the Shakespeares as well!'

Richard had gone white and Thomas Farrier had put his huge hand on his shoulder to console him. There were to be many feelings of guilt, remorse and shame in Barley Hall this day.

'So, the boy was left there alone. If there was one redeeming feature for Bask, it was that he did at least, make sure the boy had warmth and food but he told him that if he left of his own accord, his father would be killed. So, patiently, the boy waited.'

I looked around, fascinated by human nature and psychology. So many of those present had, not so long ago, mourned the merciless killing of Sir Anthony Bask but now revelled in his demise.

'Silas, as you met Aelfraed in Knapton on that cold day, Bask was there, listening, hiding and, as soon as you left he took his share. Four pounds, nineteen shillings and ten pence. This left poor Aelfraed just tuppence for his monthly troubles. However, on this occasion, he was told it was at an end. They argued. Aelfraed wanted compensation if he wasn't to get his monthly payment of tuppence any more. It was then that Bask made his greatest error. He laughed. He laughed in the face of this proud veteran and he did it publicly. As you ambled back to York, Bask caught you up. He knew exactly who you were, Silas and thought to make conversation. As you stopped to relieve yourself, Aelfraed, with head and body completely covered, took his revenge on this completely selfish bastard, Sir Anthony Bask.'

'And good riddance!' Said Mrs Hall, now animated. No one disagreed.

'But, he said…' said Silas ' he said "a present from Somerset?"

'The thing you didn't talk about my friend' I said to Silas ' was his accent?'

Robert intervened 'it was where Aelfraed came from. There is a proud heritage of soldiers-at-sea from Somerset.'

'Shouldn't someone be apprehending this Aelfraed character. After all he is still a murderer!' Offered William Fawkes.

'Dead!' Exclaimed the sheriff 'hung yesterday and what a bloody performance that was! I even asked him if he wanted the damn leg still attached or not when he dangled but kept changing his damn mind! We left it on in the end and the silly bugger ended up spinning around and then up and down. Died eventually but gave a good show I should add. Decent crowd too.'

Not one person in the room had anything to offer in response to this including me. I did, however, notice how uncomfortable Marcus was. He did, of course, from his days at sea know of Aelfraed and Bask but I knew no connection between this sinister intrigue and Marcus.

There was a moment's silence and then,

'How on earth is that connected to Elspeth?' Asked Wynnfrith, becoming impatient.

'I'm sorry dear, I'm some ways it isn't and in some ways it is.'

The crowd didn't like this at all. I wasn't trying to be cryptic, it was the truth.

'However, I am not at an end, what you have heard is half of the story, the other half will completely explain your sister's death.'

'Robert' I said, addressing him directly 'not only were you terrified that people would think you to be Bask's killer, but your nightmare still wasn't at an end was it?'

'Not at all!' He answered 'I knew that she would start where he left off.'

'She' I said 'being Lady Bask?'

'Yes,' he answered 'I knew that she would still want that money, they were losing the last of their properties. As the Cataclysm was thwarted, they got no payment from the perpetrators and she was now desperate and as wicked as her husband.'

'Are you able to tell all here what you did next?'

'No' he said 'I am ashamed of this too.'

'Then I shall tell. Silas, you may remember that terrifying ordeal of Bask's embalming at the hands of the barber-surgeon, Viscera?'

'Possibly the worst day ever!' He replied.

'Both Robert and Viscera knew that you wouldn't stay the course so as you...' I looked at him, he was signalling that he didn't want to be shamed in front of Wynnfrith 'as you...err...looked away for a few moments, Viscera, on Robert's instructions, placed the five hundred pounds inside the corpse now bound for Mrs Bask. Eirik was tasked with ensuring that this was reviewed and signed for on arrival at the home of Lady Bask.'

Bayard spoke for the first time.

'You were in there a long time just to get a signature!'

I realised that Bayard was trying to lighten then situation and there were a few raised eyebrows. Shakespeare and Farrier suppressed laughter as it was clear what Eirik had been up to. Robert glared at his son, Eirik who was sitting there like a peacock.

'Did you get want you wanted?' Said Wynnfrith quite innocently but creating a few more stifled giggles.

'Yes. Absolutely!' Said Eirik. She was undoubtedly pleased with such a large sum of money and I believed, that she would be silent.' Said Eirik.

'Silas, I have fathomed all' I said 'but, as yet, I have no answer as to why an arrow almost hit you in the woods. We may have to accept that it was, indeed, a gamekeeper. There is no reasoning in all of this why you should suspect Eirik.'

I noticed Bayard grunt. I asked him if he wanted to say something but then mumbled,

'No…err…no.'

'Bayard!' I said raising my voice somewhat.

'Well, you see…' he paused 'it was me.'

Silas's mouth opened so wide it was a wonder that he managed to shut it again.

'We were so desperate for food I asked young Eirik here if I could have a go.'

'I'm guessing that you haven't shot a bow before?' I asked him, calmly, at which he became agitated.

'Oh, dearest Silas! My friend. I swear it was an accident and…and…I was so worried that you would think it was intentional! I'm so ashamed!'

Eirik, thinking this was quite funny, completely backed up Bayard's story and apologised as well. Silas said nothing and was, presumably, pleased that this mystery was also solved.

'So' said Father Matthew 'am I to presume that the attempt on the Mayor's life and the death of Elspeth are unrelated?'

'Not at all, Father' I said 'and absolutely all events are tied to that singular morning, long ago, when Wynnfrith and Elspeth lost their parents. We will pause now. This has been exhausting for all. There is no way out of the building, all is secure. We will start again in fifteen minutes.

32: AN END TO IT ALL

I had pre-arranged with the sheriff to be kept apart from everyone during this break. I simply wouldn't have been able to answer the countless, personal enquiries from each person there.

'They are mostly shaken to the core, rodent. Perhaps too many revelations at once?' Said the sheriff.

'Perhaps' I said 'but there needs to be an end to it all today sheriff, too many mysteries for far too long. Soon be over. Thank you for your support, I understand how strange this is, how weird I am but, perhaps, I am here in this guise for some reason.'

He stared, absolutely astonished at the King's talking beast, but keeping it all together for the sake of law and order.

Throughout, there had already been questions about Moonlight but I had no answers. As far as I knew he was, if anything, an ally and Robert refused to comment so I had to tell everyone that he simply wasn't relevant and that we would deal with that particular issue at another time.

I watched them all skulk back in. There was no conversation. Heads, mostly, were contemplating the floor, although one or two were subtly checking for exits.

'We are nearing a conclusion so I ask you to bear with me a little longer. My next story I call, The Great Error.

Why? Because it illustrates how one mistake, one presumption, one judgement, may change lives for good.

I return to that Tuesday morning when the MacManus' and Clifford Smith died. It was broad daylight for goodness sake! People were milling about and so, in agreement with the sheriff, the incident was hushed up as soon as was possible. However, the best lawmen in the world cannot account for gossip. One woman was near enough to the end of that very snickleway to see the sheriff, a body, blood seeping forth from the property and, who else but Robert Hall carrying an axe. This woman put two and two together and has been making six ever since. You will appreciate that, once that human gift for persuading one's self of a revised truth embeds itself, nothing on earth will change it. So, you would not blame Godwin's good wife here, for running home to tell her husband that the snickleways killer was Robert Hall himself and that it was being hurriedly covered up by officials, including the sheriff. As this tale spread, few took any notice but she was intent that it would stick. With this in mind, I ask you to put yourself in the place of Mrs Hall, the Mayor's wife.'

I deliberately looked at Godwin's wife. She was at the core of this issue and I could tell by the shake of her head that she thought that I, too, was assisting in covering up Robert's "crime." Given that this truth of hers had had decades to settle itself in, there would be no way of convincing her that she had made a mistake so long ago.

'I say again, put yourself in the place of the Mayor's wife faced constantly with these false rumours. Robert had, and still has, a habit of dealing with such things in a particular way, he says nothing. He hides, in the hope that all would go away. However, to be fair to Mrs Hall, it was not going away, ever, so she decided to brow-beat her husband until something was done. Now, York is proud of its excellent and historical guilds, not least the carpenter's guild.'

For the first time Godwin bristled, but I noticed it was his attempt to hide his discomfort as I moved onto this subject. Robert remained looking downward at the table as if now disengaged from my constant drone.'

'That was how you would quieten these rumours wasn't it Mrs Hall?'

'Well, what was I….' she interrupted.

'I'll take that as, yes' I answered 'can you imagine what it was like for this highly skilled and inoffensive man to attend the guild meeting to find that no one would speak to him? And, it took only two weeks before it was confirmed that he was barred from the guild only hearing, eventually, from a stranger that this was due to malicious rumours spread by his wife.'

At last, there were signs of a little humility from Mrs Hall as she knew where I was going next.

'This became a life sentence, didn't it? Exiled and destined to work long hours in a pathetic lean-to along the walls at Micklegate, never again receiving any recognition of his masterful skills. Who in this room ever heard Godwin complain about this imposition?!'

I realised that I had raised my voice and so deliberately waited for an answer but it would never come.

Demoted, demoralised and humble, thanks to the conflict between those two women, Godwin had accepted his lot. Everyone else happily took advantage of his low prices. So, despite the animosity between these two families, he was still called upon when money was tight.

The mood had darkened in the room and it was now up to each individual to make their own judgements about who was at fault. Edward was saddened. He knew, as his father did, that there was no love lost between Godwin and the

Mayor but the feud between these two women was complete news to him. Godwin had proven to be a good Master during Edward's apprenticeship and he also maintained a healthy respect for his uncle, the Mayor. Others now seemed as spectators at an event, learning all of this for the first time so I continued,

'Apart from this constant unpleasantness between the two families, little happened beyond tickle-tackle and gossip, until last year, that was...'

I looked toward Godwin hoping he would make this easy for me. And then, he quietly spoke.

'All was fine. I was happy, especially when young Edward worked with me. I saw it as a compliment from the good Mr Fawkes, over there, that I was considered worthy of an apprentice. But then...then that cursed Cataclysm. Couldn't keep a low profile could he?'

His head was now raised and he was looking directly at Robert who returned his gaze. He continued,

'Not content with grovelling to the King on his arrival, he is taken in by the King himself in a ridiculous charade! Even so, I would have said nothing, even as his arrogance grew day by day and then....and...well...'

'And then you lost Lizzy, didn't you Godwin?' I said.

He started to tremble and weep.

'She was everything to me, everything! I prayed and prayed and I believed she was better. I trusted God, I trusted everyone! When she went, my life was over.'

His wife consoled him as he completely broke down in front of everyone.

'I didn't mean for anyone to die. You have to believe me! I didn't want anyone to die...' he said.

All eyes were on him now as this was as good as a confession. To say the least, almost all present were shocked. And then, the questions. It was almost as if everyone wanted to speak at once.

'Please, please' I said 'we are almost at an end. Marcus can you now make a connection between the old couple in the undercroft that died and this man sitting here?'

'Yes, yes!' He replied enthusiastically 'The beams down there…they get damp and rot so we have them repaired almost…well…patchwork style when we can afford. Godwin, the very day before, had completed an excellent repair.'

'And did he speak to anyone?' I said.

'He actually brought the old couple with him, begging for a place for them to die in the warm.'

'Is that what he said, Marcus? To die?'

'Yes, yes…it was part of the agreement.'

'And were they dying?' I asked.

'Oh…no doubt. I was surprised they had made it that far.'

'Thank you. Thank you, Marcus. The old people were a plant. They agreed to Godwin's plan in exchange for a decent Christian funeral with good coffins. Once they were settled, very conveniently near the repaired beam, he took time to amateurly smear Wolfsbane along the beams and the beds and it was even on their hands. It wasn't going to make any difference to the old couple, and they had been briefed to ask specifically for Elspeth and Wynnfrith when they arrived.'

I turned to Wynnfrith.

'The poison was meant for you too dear, you just got lucky.'

Expressionless, she said nothing. Godwin cried, trembled and then repeated,

'I didn't mean for anyone to die…I didn't know what I was doing…'

'Nevertheless' I said 'this was murder and it cannot be undone!'

Robert turned to me,

'So the window was never safe?' He said.

'Never. Although the craftsmanship would be the envy of any property owner in York, the casing was barely fixed to the structure of this building. It is hard to know what his intent was but it could easily have killed you, Robert, or any of your household.' I turned to Eirik 'please show everyone.'

He held up a piece of, what appeared to be, half inch oak dowelling, one that was used to key the window frame to the oak structure of the building. He tore it in two easily.

'Nothing more than wood shaving, perhaps enough to support the window for a minute or so.'

'So' said Robert quite calmly 'all these imaginings about grand plots, Wriothesley, Seymour and so forth. All of that was just nonsense? This scruffy bastard was responsible for it all?'

'Just so' I said 'and, erratic and amateur as his efforts to murder were, he had us all in a panic. His daughter's death was the straw that broke the camel's back. He cared little for anything after that point, even purloining Faith on her return, and sought to hurt you and those close to you, ultimately leading to the death of someone dear to us all.'

Already the sheriff had moved toward Godwin. His wife's demeanour spoke volumes. None of this was news to her and she stood, too, to go with him. Now, there was a deathly silence apart from Edward who, despite his father's reprimands cried openly.

Once past the length of the, seemingly endless, table, he stopped, now facing the door and hanging his head low. Unexpectedly, Wynnfrith jumped to her feet, stumbling slightly as she did, wielding a letter.

'Wait!' She shouted after Godwin and started to read almost as a proclamation to everyone.

"Please say to Godwin that I forgive him with all my heart…"

It was from the collection of letters left by Elspeth. She knew! I thought. Of course she knew, I told myself. She was Elspeth.

Godwin turned.

'God bless her!' He said ' God bless all of you! I swear I never intended anyone dead. I repent wholeheartedly.'

Edward stood.

'I forgive you Master…' he said.

Then silence again. An uncanny stillness where one by one people stood. As they stood they weren't so much saying that they forgave him but that they acknowledged the chain of events that had led to this tragedy. Secrets and selfishness brewing over decades. Father Matthew then joined him, publicly, but silently offering to minister to this condemned man and, as he did, he brushed by the still seated Thomas Farrier and placed his hand, momentarily, on his shoulder. And then, uncannily, almost as Godwin had disappeared through the front door of Barley Hall, Robert uncomfortably bustled through everyone and grabbed Godwin's tattered and ancient doublet.

'If it is dear Elspeth's wish, I forgive you true and proper right here now in the sight of a God and pray for a good hanging and peaceful passing carpenter. An end to this nightmare, here and now.'

Godwin held out his hand and Robert shook it.

As he left, the atmosphere that remained was thick as December fog. No one in this room had been left untouched by these events. Most were somewhere between denial and self-judgement. Silas felt, unreasonably, guilty about his father and Eirik was wishing that he hadn't had to keep up his father's charade for so long. Marcus and Scorge were kicking themselves because they hadn't seen through Godwin's deception when he brought the old couple to the infirmary. For a while, Mrs Hall felt quite indignant in the face of everyone forgiving this dirty and unkempt murderer but, on her husband's return, regrets started to settle in and a twenty-year feud seemed ridiculous and certainly un-Christian. Robert had been named and shamed throughout the afternoon but, the weight that had been lifted from his rotund frame made him feel like a man renewed. William Fawkes had obviously been a party to this lengthy dispute and asked himself why he hadn't intervened sooner. Added to that, he wondered if he could have done more to save Mary Smith all those years ago. Richard Shakespeare was publicly embarrassed as he had allowed a stranger to steal his son from under his nose. Viscera told himself that he only did what he was commissioned to do but, internally knew that what he had done to Sir Anthony Bask's body brought his profession, and his faith, into the worst repute. Although he had been at Barley Hall when the window fell and, he had had dealings with Mary Smith, Hugh simply wondered why he was there but was satisfied that it was the best afternoon's entertainment he had ever seen. For the greater part of the meeting, Bayard lamented the loss of Elspeth for whom he had grown increasingly fond. He had also regarded the Agents as heroes but this unravelling intrigue had dented his faith somewhat.

Others were more or less spectators. Peter and Edward were still young enough to put their elders on pedestals. This session had left them in no doubt that the world that they had entrusted to adults was possibly in great peril. Hearts certainly went out to Wynnfrith and Silas who had suffered so much because of the selfishness and self-righteousness of others. Thomas Farrier sat there simply wondering how he could best help them. Wynnfrith herself was stoic as ever, proud that her sister was several steps ahead of everyone and that she had reminded her of the power of forgiveness. She stood and looked around at the fallout from the tirade of dire news that had been foisted upon these people on this day.

'Take heart. From this moment we move on to better and kinder times. Please pray with me'.

In the absence of the nun and the priest, Wynnfrith took it upon herself to petition God on behalf of all.

'Dear Lord we beseech your love and forgiveness amidst this horror and wickedness. We pray that you can, on our behalf, seek out the very best in each of us so that we may meet the futures as Agents, Agents of the Word. No, Agents of Your Word! Show us the path that leads toward you and far from selfishness, earthly desires and deviousness.'

As she continued, only I could see how uncomfortable this made those present, particularly Robert. Heads low, they hung onto every syllable.

'Continue to teach us to find the best in ourselves and the best in others. We openly and gladly confess our misdemeanours and ask for redemption for those present and for Godwin who faces his end in this world today. We wait in hope for renewed purpose and better times. In the name of The Father, The Son and The Holy Ghost. Amen.'

33: REFLECTIONS

Days after Godwin's hanging, it came to light that Father
Matthew had administered last rights and, by arrangement
with the sheriff and the Mayor, Godwin was given a
Christian burial alongside little Lizzy in Holy Trinity
churchyard.

Lots of forgiveness? Well, yes. That was at the very core
of what the Agents had come to be. The Reformation itself
had forged their deep beliefs. Not because of what it taught
but in spite of it. They had decided that, in an age where
doctrine was changing by the minute, their devotion would
be to Christ alone. His central message of inclusion, loving
and forgiving your enemies, served the world better and
there was no doubt that Elspeth was prompting them from
beyond.

There was, to say the least, a degree of awkwardness
following the meeting and my priority was to get home.
Some people thanked me, others avoided me but it was all
the same to me. I had completed, fully, my mission. Of
course I had feelings for these people and, yes, that

included Godwin but this wasn't the time for hugs and nostalgia, I was in a hurry.

Almost as if providence, Edward and his father walked up to where I had been perched all afternoon. I asked him to place me in my box and, in doing so, I was reminded of the various classes of accommodation and transport I had enjoyed whilst in this place.

'I have things of mine that I have to remove from Godwin's workshop. I've no doubt it will be repossessed very soon.' Said Edward.

'Of course' I said 'I will come along and then to my designated place for return.'

He giggled and I knew why.

'I am more confident this time Ed' I said 'when I last tried, I hadn't finished my work here.'

I could tell that he still didn't believe me and probably had no idea where I had come from and why I had been able to talk. He wasn't alone, I remained a curiosity but, despite my indiscretions, I had managed to restrict my unique talents to the ears of a few dozen people only. Six months hence it would be unlikely that anyone would have believed such a ridiculous story.

Those remaining hardly noticed as William Fawkes, Edward and I slipped out of Barley Hall and headed toward the river. There, still, as forever, stood the magnificent Minster thrusting skyward and dominating all for miles and miles. Suddenly, my heart became heavy as each landmark became a page in this most unusual story. I understood there and then that every visitor to this great city for hundreds of years would be walking the same steps as Robert, Silas, Eirik, Elspeth, Wynnfrith, Father Matthew, Edward and the others. The adventure is there written in the cobbles and the cream magnesium limestone of the Minster, the walls and the churches. The half-timbered buildings like Barley Hall and the snickleways and abandoned monasteries and convents. Perhaps this is why

York is frozen in time, I asked myself. Those more sensitive wouldn't be able to avoid connecting with the past. I chuckled unintentionally as I mused. Hardly a notion for a scientific historian, but all the same I believed it. In my former guise, I had visited York many times and there simply is something quite electric about the place, as if our ancestors wish to inform us and teach us about mistakes that we make over and over again. It was at this juncture that I realised I didn't want to leave. My heart was breaking and I was deeply confused. I understood now that I had two homes and did not want to be in a position to choose. I thought about the female mouse I had encountered at Hampton Court and realised the extent that many people had gone to, to get that message to me. I will get home, I told myself with the caveat that I would return. It didn't matter how ridiculous that sentiment seemed, I convinced myself that coming back would be easy.

We arrived at Godwin's workshop and it looked, unsurprisingly, as it always did. Tools put down where he had left them before he had made the walk to Barley Hall that morning. Edward passionately wanted to tidy up but his father forbade him. I told them both of my intention to get just outside the city wall where I would disappear.

One last time I looked at my very first home in York. A hole in the wall inside Godwin's workshop where I would work and be concealed from the world, a secret until my mission was complete. Didn't quite work out as planned, I told myself. Again I felt sad. As I turned to hurry William Fawkes and Edward, I felt uneasy and then quite nauseous. I developed the worst headache and then my vision became seriously impaired and subsequently lost consciousness.

After that, I remembered nothing until I heard chatter again. Only slightly regaining my senses, I could hear a voice. It was Wynnfrith although what she was saying made no sense. In particular, she was describing a walk amongst forests and waterfalls. It meant nothing to me at all but I was aware that I was recovering albeit slightly. My headache was still there except it was everywhere. All of me felt so heavy. So much so I couldn't move at all, seemingly paralysed. Beyond that, I was comfortable. I was warm and I knew that I was lying on my back. I tried to speak but nothing would move. I was thinking a sentence but it could not be heard and then, I felt my lips, heavy as they were, move a little.

'Wynn….what…..'

And that was it.

I heard her gasp and grab hold of me. I was determined to make contact with her. I will made sense of this and then get home, I told myself. I knew that time was slipping away and I started to panic. It was, I do confess, a very strange panic as all the anxiety was in my head, nothing else seemed to move but I willed it with every fibre of my being and was rewarded with a little light seeping in. I had managed the smallest aperture in my left eye. Blurred at first, I thought I was looking straight into the sun until I realised that this was artificial light. I strained further to see a silhouette. I was so wanting to see Wynnfrith that it almost became a reality but, there above me was my dear wife, April. At this point, I knew it. I could smell her and I started to recognise her voice as she repeatedly uttered 'Nick. Nick!'

It took another ten minutes before I could see and hear her properly. I was back. In my home and in my own bed which told me that I had been unconscious for some weeks, I was no longer at the institute or in the biogel. April embraced me and showered me with kisses. In no time at all, medical professionals were attending me as well.

Within a day I was sitting up and could speak, see and hear. My voice was incredibly strange. I had become so used to that ancient and lively Yorkshire dialect that I now sounded monotone and wondered constantly about how I must have sounded to others. I did take some time to acclimatise. Yes, I nearly did die in there and April gave me a brief account of how hard they had to work to get me back. I'm not sure that I was helping from the other side, I so much wanted to be there. Wisely, it was over a week before the historical analytics team were allowed to speak to me and, even then, it was brief as my recovery, thankfully, was paramount. Apart from April teasing me about Wynnfrith, I didn't want to talk of any of it. I was truly bereft and was missing some of my friends with all my being. God bless them, I thought, and then realised that, in this form, I had rarely referenced God at all. Few people did anymore.

The tale of my struggle for life was protracted and, if I'm truthful, I wasn't interested in it although I was grateful that I had been so well looked after. What did astonish me was April's willingness to be subjected to the biogel and I had no idea how on earth they managed to project her into exactly the same frame as me but, I would, one day find out. What we do for those we love? I thought. I almost became obsessed with that philosophy. All that was good about my adventure was rooted in love and, yes, forgiveness. A resolution to move on positively, whatever the situation. Love has been a constant throughout history although still, scientifically, it is difficult to say exactly what it is. I was, of course, disappointed that I had left so suddenly. Part of me now desired those fond farewells and I doubted, at this point, whether I would ever be in service again.

Eventually, I would have to publish a report and I knew that, in time, I would enjoy delivering it but, in the early days of my return, it was not possible. I spent weeks in bed and, although I avoided talking specifically about my experiences, I could laugh at some of the fallout. Kindly, one morning, April brought in a cup of tea. It spilt slightly onto my hand and, without thinking, I reacted,

'Bloody hell woman! What you thinking off!'

From nowhere came this, ill-tempered, curmudgeonly northern reprimand. We both laughed wondering where on earth it had come from. Sometimes, I would lapse so deeply into sixteenth-century English that neither of us understood what was said.

After some time, just two members of the team were allowed to properly visit. They were genuinely pleased to see me and didn't push the feedback too much. However, they informed me that, still, there was no concrete evidence of a plot naming Prince Edward as the second coming of Christ and that, beyond major figures like the King, the Lords and the Mayor of York, they could find no trace of some of the people I had been rambling about on my return. Of course there's not, I told myself, the important people are always forgotten in written histories. I realised that I felt quite indignant. The real heroes of my story were everyday folk. Then, I had the worst feeling. I went cold. What if my adventure was a protracted psychotic episode. I wasn't sure how I would cope with this. After all, those experiences and feelings were so real. Mind you, so is a dream, I told myself. You may remember that I began my story by saying that not only was there no such thing as time travel but also that our work was in its infancy. What if I saw nothing? I discussed this with my colleagues who, of course, like me didn't want to even contemplate the idea, although I could see they were concerned that our missions were very hard to explain and prove to others. Thankfully, one of my visitors was someone who had been a colleague of mine for many years, Constance, who besides being the most qualified in the group also, thankfully, had an imagination.

'We still have much to do Nick! No rush for the report, we're still researching.' She said.

'You can imagine how I feel though' I said 'I'm now questioning my own sensibilities!'

They looked at one another, I knew they had something.

'No, no' said Constance 'I think that it could make some sense.' She turned to me 'we have something, Nick, but it hinges on just one word you uttered. We are very concerned that we don't dash any of your hopes too soon.'

'Please...let me see.'

She carried a portfolio that, amongst other items, housed a scruffy piece of parchment. It was damaged around the edges and the ink had faded but there was, unquestionably, a decipherable letter in front of me.

'It was written in York by the Mayor, Robert Hall, in May 1542...'

I interrupted,

'That's just a few months after I left!'

'Yes. Yes' she said 'but that in itself means very little. Are you certain you are up to doing this so soon?'

'Yes! Give it here!'

And we all laughed as I had, yet again, accessed my alter ego.

'So sorry Constance. Yes, yes, please. I would like to examine it.'

She handed it over and, at first, I wished that I had said nothing as I could see so little and it was very, very faded. April passed me some lens correctors. Glasses. Yes, glasses, spectacles they used to call them. I had forgotten that, temporarily, I was using this quaint piece of apparatus to correct my vision.

To begin with, I stared. I stared and stared, realising that I was claiming this scrap because it connected me, emotionally, to my other home. I must have looked ridiculous as I started to weep which, of course, did little to help my sight. Eventually, I calmed and attempted to read it through. What I read was to change my life and my career completely.

34: THE LETTER

I instinctively looked at the assignation and the signature first. It was written by Robert and was sent to William Fawkes.

"It is my personal regret that your grave duties at the Minster have dominated your obligations so soon after receiving my invitation. Firstly, I must tell you of the burden that has now been removed having handed over the Mayorship to my dear friend, John Shadlock. Shamefully, I am dealing with my past indiscretions and, in making amends, hope to build relationships anew with my family and those good friends in York and Stratford on the Avon that have helped me to get through the last two years.

My good friend and brother, be assured you were missed as this was as fine a wedding as I ever saw and yet vows were sworn in that most humble of God's houses, Holy Trinity Church along Goodramgate in our beloved city. It was but a small hole in my purse to fully adorn the wedding party and family which included a fine horse and carriage to take the couple, to and from the church. The groom was fashioned in ruby leather from his boots to his cap and the bride had a white gown fit for a Queen."

I stopped reading now exhausted, and somewhat disappointed. He seemed to ramble endlessly about what everyone wore and then listed dignitaries. I had so desired to find a familiar name in there that would normally be beyond official records. I told my colleagues and April that I would rest as I was sure that searching for hope that may not have been there would set me back. My psychological state was frail, to say the least.

Constance, in particular, was insistent that I persevered although, at first, I could not see why. I asked April to help sit me up and I agreed to try again. Whether it was force of habit or simple professionalism, I'm not sure, but I started at the beginning again.

"It is my personal regret...."

Then, at last, I saw a glimpse of what I was looking for.

"Young Wynnfrith looked every bit the lady, beautiful and innocent as the day she was born and Silas very much a gentleman."

'There! There!! I said 'that's it. That's what I've been looking for. Silas and Wynnfrith! I knew them. I saw them as I see you now!'

'We appreciate how excited you are, Nick' said Constance 'but we have to account for every possibility including that you may have seen this letter before you went.'

'Nonsense! I said indignantly 'I know them. Why, I probably know everyone there!' So I insisted, there and then, on finishing the letter.

"Eirik and Silas stood together as brothers at last, my son proud to be his man with no fear of the bride escaping."

I understood this reference. Historically, groomsmen and what became known as the best man had their origins in ensuring the bride didn't get away. I chuckled and resumed.

"This wedding represented so much more than the union between Silas Smith and Wynnfrith MacManus. It was a celebration of the part we played in thwarting the Cataclysm and the resolution of the purge in York and at Hampton Court. Our friends from Stratford on the Avon travelled once again to be with us. You were very much missed as was our friend, Micklegate, without whom we would not have succeeded. Wynnfrith herself asked for prayer for his soul."

I got this far and looked up. They knew why.

'So, is that you?' Asked Constance.

'Yes. Absolutely. I was given so many names but, yes. Micklegate Mouse. That is what they called me.'

They laughed.

'May as well finish it' She said.

"But what follows is why I make haste to write to you, dear William. The wedding over, the whole party paused as we heard a horse draw up at the church door. I took to my sword, suspecting danger but, as we all turned, an officer wearing the King's insignia marched toward the altar. An equerry of the King no less. As Father Matthew stood aside he read out a proclamation that said: by proxy of our great King and Lord, Henry the eighth, God's good servant and supreme head of the church I call upon Silas Smith.

Dearest William, we all feared for Silas but not near as much as he did himself. He looked terrified, so used to falling from favour he surely thought his wedding day to be ruined. The equerry continued: You are this day, from the very moment of this proclamation appointed as Knight of the realm and although, not of noble birth, you are to be known, henceforth as Lord Silas.

William, I am sure I heard his mother shout with joy from the heavens themselves as did we. Silas, would you believe, is a Lord. The equerry handed to Silas the document, and the quill that had written it, to keep. After all that has passed, Mary Smith had ensured her son's Knighthood from above!

We had celebrations that will not be surpassed for many a year and the happy couple, quite rightly, now reside with me until they have means of their own. I do hope this letter of mine brings you that joy too and I look forward to seeing you soon, in the summer.

Yours...."

'Happy?' Asked Constance.

'Yes, and eager to complete my report.'

'Just one more thing' she said 'whilst you were away from us, on your mission, we have, of course, been researching in York itself as well as in the archives.'

'Any luck?' I asked presuming that they would have already said if they had found something significant.

'Well...yes and no' she said.

I looked at her curiously.

'One of our zealous junior researchers took it upon herself to physically scale Micklegate Bar in York and, besides getting arrested, came up with this.'

She passed me a hard copy of a photograph, something you hardly encountered outside the archives. It was of a four-inch sculpture that sat high atop Micklegate bar, out of sight of passers-by except, of course, our over-enthusiastic researcher. It was a mouse wearing an apron and wielding a small hammer and, underneath it had a date, 1542.

'That's it!' I said now incredibly animated 'that's me, exactly how I looked! Bless her soul for finding this. How I would love to thank her.'

'Well' said Constance 'she's in the hallway trembling and hoping for a chance to meet the hero of the hour'

'Oh yes,' I said 'please show her in, I'd love to meet her.

'Very well' said Constance and raised her voice 'come in, he's happy to see you' and, around the door peeped a face that was so familiar that I was left completely at peace and sure that everything I had experienced had its basis in fact.

This young girl assured me that she would make my story her life's work and that she was incredibly excited to see my report when it was complete. I told her I still had reservations, it all now seeming like a dream.

Unexpectedly she held my hand and said 'not to worry now professor, everything will work out for the best and you will see service again.

All will be well.

God is good.'

THE END

About the Author

Rob holds a degree in both History and Art & Design and for his postgraduate studies, concentrated on British History. He has taught both subjects for many years and his students have ranged from early teens to undergraduates. Later in his career, he specialised in the application of new technologies in special and alternative education.

Rob started writing when he ran his own business, Jester Productions, in which he wrote scripts for plays and musicals that were used eclectically, but most often in theatre groups internationally and for major tour operators. He has completed commissions that have ranged from magazine work and book covers to church interiors.

More information can be found at:
www.rwjauthor.co.uk
Instagram: robjones4043

Other books by Robert William Jones

1542 the Purge is part of a trilogy, the other two books are:
1541 The Cataclysm
1543 The Disfiguration

One of his musicals *'A week in Space'* is also available on Amazon for just 99p and backing tracks and lyrics are available free through the website.

'Be a Teacher!' is a collection of anecdotes and stories from Rob's 40 years at all levels as an educational professional, will be available January 2021.

1542 The Purge